The Dream

Other books by Christopher Priest

NOVELS

The Separation
The Extremes
The Prestige
The Quiet Woman
The Glamour
The Affirmation
A Dream of Wessex
The Space Machine
Inverted World
Fugue for a Darkening Island
Indoctrinaire

SHORT STORY COLLECTIONS

Real-Time World
An Infinite Summer

The
Dream Archipelago

·

Christopher Priest

This edition published in Great Britain in 2009 by
Gollancz
An imprint of the Orion Publishing Group
Orion House, 5 Upper St Martin's Lane, London WC2H 9EA
An Hachette UK Company

1 3 5 7 9 10 8 6 4 2

A CIP catalogue record for this book is
available from the British Library

ISBN 978 0 575 09106 1

Typeset by Deltatype Ltd, Birkenhead, Merseyside

Printed in Great Britain by CPI Mackays, Chatham ME5 8TD

www.christopher-priest.co.uk

www.orionbooks.co.uk

The Orion Publishing Group's policy is to use papers that
are natural, renewable and recyclable products and made
from wood grown in sustainable forests. The logging and
manufacturing processes are expected to conform to the
environmental regulations of the country of origin.

Like all dreamers,
I mistook disillusionment for truth

Jean-Paul Sartre

CONTENTS

•

The Equatorial Moment   1

The Negation   6

Whores   45

The Trace of Him   66

The Miraculous Cairn   74

The Cremation   141

The Watched   182

The Discharge   256

The

The
Equatorial
Moment

•

Up there in the sky, high above the sea and the islands, while the aircraft cruised through air barely dense enough to support it and too thin for you to breathe unaided, you sometimes thought that you might at last understand how time worked.

You never could; it was an illusion. The sudden sense of intuition was familiar to many aircrew, a realization, as it seemed, that they alone had been granted a privileged insight into the nature of the vortex. The feeling was a false one. The vortex was beyond comprehension. All you could do was enter it, make use of it, leave it.

Sitting in the pressurized rear turret of the jet transport, supposedly on watch for incoming missiles or enemy fighters, with the length and weight of the aircraft unseen behind your back, and the thrust of the engines so steady that the plane seemed hardly to move, and the sound of the jet exhausts so swept away by the air-speed that they were almost inaudible, then you felt as if the world below you extended for ever, an unfolding panorama without limits. Land and coastline, seas and islands and clouds, picked out in brilliant contrasting colours by the noontime sun, sliding slowly by beneath. The height lent a sense of aloofness. You felt that you had become a part of the sky itself, not a temporary intruder into it. The world lay below you, and you sensed that anywhere on it could become part of your domain simply by choosing to set down upon it.

From this height, though, it was obvious there was not much

land. Most of the world at the equator was the sea and the sky, with only intermittent darker patches where the equatorial islands lay, their brilliant white margins of sea meeting shore. You were supposed to be able to land on some of the larger ones if you needed to, but one of the properties of the vortex was that it seemed to protect you from emergencies. No one had ever heard any stories about planes that crashed out of time. Accidents happened elsewhere: on take-off or landing, or when an incoming missile found its target before or after you were inside the vortex. You were safe from attack when inside: missiles also flew through time, they too never went anywhere in real time.

The dots that were the islands had other temptations, though, principally the lure of neutrality. Most of the men actually involved in the fighting wanted to be out of it; war was ever thus. The knowledge that most of the surface area of the world constituted a neutral zone was endlessly confounding to the young and usually frightened men who fought the battles. While you flew above the islands you could look down at them and dream of war's end, of not having an enemy, of wandering from one island to the next, of lying in the sun and trying exotic foods and making love with the sound of waves around you for the remainder of your life. But you also knew that in reality wherever you were flying to was not into neutrality. On the further side of the Midway Sea, when you reached the southern continental mass, you and your plane would become combatants again, because there all neutrality ended. Treaties and alliances began.

When you returned to your base you again crossed above the neutral islands, dreaming in the sun, and you landed in your own belligerent nation in the cooler north.

The plane swept you on, the pilot in the distant cockpit at the front imperceptibly correcting the drift, the momentary losses of altitude, the alignment of the flying surfaces. It was tempting to dream while you flew above the Archipelago, or while you were flown above it, while you were held in the thrall of the timeless noon.

Glancing above or below you would be able to see the other

aircraft soaring with you in the vortex of time. Their condensation trails lay like chalked lines across the deep blue of the heavens, meeting at the centre, multi-layered. All time met at this vortical point, midday at the equator, or more rarely midnight, marked by the converging trails and the vertical stack of jet aircraft that produced them. If you were at the top of the stack you could sometimes glimpse the sheer scale of the vortex effect. Although the planes flew straight tracks, the twin actions of coriolis and the sweep of time made each white condensation trail curve to the golden mean. The lines across the sky spiralled into the central point, the eye of time, so that seen from above the vortex looked like a swirling of white ribbons, a spinning nebula, or the wispy outer clouds of a hurricane.

If you were in the stack itself, or close to the bottom of it, you could not enjoy the coriolis effect in full, but if you glanced up through your tinted, impact-proof canopy you would see the craft nearest to you, directly above, pointing at an angle away from your own flight path, churning through the sky, apparently motionless in the air, blocking the light of the zenithal sun. Above it would be another plane, heading in its own direction, flying along, going somewhere. Above that one several more, higher and higher, up through the stack to the altitude where the air was so rarefied that even a charging jet transport could not gain enough lift beneath its wings.

If you could look down you would see many more aircraft, some of them skimming along just above the sea.

And beneath them was the place on the earth's surface – usually a point in the sea, but several islands also straddled the equator – which for an instant twice a day, solar noon and midnight, was the exact focus of the temporal vortex.

So here in the sky you believed that you had glimpsed the insight: the mystery of the vortex appeared to be laid bare before you. It made time cease, you reasoned. All flying aircraft that entered it were held by it so long as they maintained a steady course, only to be released when they made their crucial change of direction. So it seemed. In fact, all you had gained was a

3

different view of the vortex. You could see up into its effects, or down upon them, but the mystery remained.

Because of the vortex every point on the surface of the earth existed in the same subjective moment of time, the same apparent day, the same season. The vortex spread with invisible gradients across the surface of the world to alter perception of time.

No matter where you stood to view the going down of the sun, the same sunset could be seen by anyone else in the world – north or south of your position, east or west of it – who cared to look. When it was mid-morning on one side of the world, it was perceived to be mid-morning on the other. There were no time zones, no date lines, no hours gained or lost by travelling to east or west, no interruption to diurnal rhythms should you travel by jet across the world. Seventeen minutes past the hour here, or anywhere, was perceived as seventeen minutes past the same hour everywhere else and anywhere else.

Night followed day, summer followed spring, no matter where you were. The fact that the same night, the same summer, was occurring everywhere else in the world, was not in itself interesting. Why should anyone know, who could not compare a clock on the other side of the world? Why should anyone care?

For centuries no one did. Then came the modern age and modern travel, and when man began to fly his fast jets at great heights his eager wings first grazed the edge of the vortex. Looking down he saw where he was but flew further before looking down again, only to find that he had not travelled as far as he had intended. Then, dipping down to the land, confused by this, frightened by the way his sense of time and space had been distorted, he found the time apparently sweeping past him, the ground racing by at a greater speed than anything his engines could produce. When he at last set down again upon the ground he was nowhere near where he thought he would be, and in the two or three subjective hours of travel he had traversed half the world.

Many men died and many aircraft were lost while the struggle to solve the puzzle went on. In the end, with the puzzle unsolved, it became possible to measure the vortex, work mathematically with it, plan routes from one part of the world to another with the use of it. You left your starting place, and climbed towards the equatorial noon. You joined the stack of other aircraft at the altitude you had calculated, you flew steadily on, trailing your thin white spoor of condensation behind you. You watched the ground, read your instruments, waited for the moment which you had computed was the one that would take you close to where you wanted to be, then you throttled back the engines, lowered the nose of the aircraft, and began your descent through the gradients of time.

If you had calculated correctly you arrived within a short flying distance of your destination, a twelve-hour flight accomplished in thirty minutes, a twenty-hour flight in two hours, a six-hour flight in twenty minutes. Flying became routine, a necessary ingredient of the world's economy, but for it to continue uninter-rupted it was essential that the equatorial zone remained neutral. That dark shape above you, with those swept-back wings, its long barrels of engines, the huge fuselage throwing down its shadow on you, was as likely to belong to the other side as it might be one of yours.

So you flew, undisturbed by others, with the only apparent movement being the keeping in step with the slow progress of the sun, at its daytime zenith, over the equator. You grew to recog-nize the shapes of the equatorial islands, the changing colours of the sea where the currents flowed more slowly or deeply, where the surface was broken by rocks. You grew to know the islands without ever visiting them. You yearned to travel among them, to discover what neutrality meant, where it would lead you.

One day the war would have to end. But for now it had not.

The
Negation

•

The sound of the trains was a melancholy reminder of home. Dik would listen for their arrival whenever he was not on patrol in the evenings. Sometimes, when the mountain winds had temporarily stilled, he could hear the rhythmic drumming of the wheels while the train was still a long way from the depot, but he always heard the blast of steam as it arrived, and the shriek of its whistle when it left. He invariably thought of his parents, the house in Jethra where he had grown up, his school, his friends, the ordinary accomplishments of childhood, less than a year in his past, but now unreachably remote from him. The railway line was the only contact with that vanished childhood. When his time was up, and he could leave this desolate, snow-bound frontier, it would be by the same means as he had arrived, on one of those nightly trains.

He had recently written a few lines of verse about the train, in the pretence that conscription and military training had not managed to change him at all, but the writing was unsatisfactory and he destroyed the poem soon afterwards. It was the only writing he had tried since being inducted into the Border Police. The failure of the verse made him feel it would be unlikely he would try any more, at least until he was moved to a less harsh posting.

For the last two weeks he had been listening for the train with extra attentiveness because he knew that Moylita Kaine, the novelist, should be arriving soon. He clung to the irrational notion that the train would sound different merely by having her aboard it, but he was not entirely sure what the difference would be. In the event her arrival in the isolated village was revealed in another way.

As he left the canteen one evening, half an hour before the train was due, he noticed that several of the burghers' limousines were parked in the centre of the village. They were lined up outside the Civic Hall, their engines idling and the drivers sitting inside. Dik walked by slowly on the other side of the street, smelling the gasoline fumes and listening to the soft rhythmic concussions of the muffled exhausts. Clouds of white condensation rose around the cars, infused with colour by the ornamental lights nailed to the eaves of the hall.

The large double doors of the hall opened and a broad beam of orange light fell across the polished cars and the trodden snow. Dik hunched his shoulders and trudged on towards the constabulary barracks. He heard the burghers leaving the Civic Hall, the car doors slamming. After a few moments the vehicles passed him in a slow convoy, turning from the village street into the narrow track that led to the station further down the steep valley. It was only then that Dik guessed at the reason for the burghers' expedition. When he reached the entrance to the barracks he paused to listen for the train. It was still too early for its scheduled arrival and with the wind in this particular quarter it would be impossible to hear the wheels in the distance.

Inside the overheated building he walked down the corridor past his room and went out on the outside balcony. No fresh snow had fallen that day. His frozen footprints from the night before led to the corner of the balcony and lost themselves in a confusion of stamping and shuffling. He went to the same corner, thrusting his hands deep into the pockets of his greatcoat. Soon he was stamping to keep his feet warm.

From this position he could see up the narrow street that led back to the centre, but apart from the coloured lights festooning the exteriors of the larger buildings most of the windows seemed dark and the village had the appearance of emptiness. From the bar in the barracks cellar there came the sound of an accordion and men were talking and laughing drunkenly.

When he looked in the other direction, across the sharply angled roofs of the houses on the edge of the village, he could glimpse against the starlit sky the dark outline of the mountains that loomed above the village from the other side of the broad glacial valley. There was a thin moon and Dik could discern the dark smudge of the pine forest clinging to the frozen scarps. On the northern ridge, several thousand feet higher than the village, was the frontier wall that protected the valley and the routes to the sea. It was impossible to see anything of the wall from here, particularly at night, but when patrolling it you were afforded magnificent vistas of the valley and the surrounding mountains.

Dik waited, stamping his feet and shivering, until at last he heard a jetting of released steam, echoing up through the chill, blustery air of the valley and he felt again the now familiar pang of homesickness.

He went back into the building at once and found some of the squad in one of the common rooms next to the bar. Most of the young men, like Dik, were too hard up to be able to buy drinks. They usually spent the evenings joshing each other and bragging, adding to the noise from the bar, distracting themselves from thinking about what they had to do up there on the border. Tonight, one of the lads had brought out a bottle of home-distilled schnapps, and this was being passed around, eked out in a succession of small sips and extravagant backhand wipes of the mouth. Dik was soon shouting and laughing with the rest of them.

Some time later one of the lads by the window let out a yell and beckoned to the others. They moved over to cluster around him. Peering with them through the hand-wiped gap in the heavy film of condensation, Dik saw the convoy of burghers' cars returning from the depot, the powerful engines making hardly any noise at all, and the fat tyres crunching softly across the compacted snow.

*

Dik had been about to enter college when his draft notice arrived. Because of this his conscription was a marginal case, and after a few anxious days he had been relieved to learn that his course qualified him for three years' deferment of service. Like all youths in his position, he felt that the delay had to be good enough for the time being and that by the end of his course the political situation might have improved. It was unlucky for Dik that the draft papers arrived more or less coincidentally with the first of a series of air and missile attacks on the industrial sections of the capital, Jethra, and a few weeks after that there was an unsuccessful invasion in the east of the country. All around him, lads of his age were joining up, even many of those who had also been given deferment. Dik held out as long as his conscience would allow him to but then at last signed on as a volunteer.

Before all this he had been intending to read modern literature at Jethra University, and it was the writing of Moylita Kaine that had directly prompted the decision. Although he had been reading fiction and poetry for as long as he could remember, and had written many poems of his own, one book – a long novel entitled *The Affirmation*, more than a thousand pages in extent – had so impressed him that he counted the reading of it as the single most important and influential experience of his life. In many ways a deep and difficult work, the book was little known or discussed. During his one interview for the course at the university he had expressed his interest in the book, but none of the academics on the panel appeared even to have heard of it. For Dik, the book's apparent obscurities were among its greatest pleasures. The novel spoke to him in an intensely clear, wise and passionate voice, its story an elemental conflict between deceit and romantic truth, its resolution profoundly emotional and its understanding of human nature so perceptive that he could still recall, three years later, the shock of recognition when he read the book for the first time. In the months since he had re-read the book more times than he could remember, he had urged it on his few close friends (though had never once allowed his precious copy out of his possession) and tried, as far as was humanly possible, to live his own life

9

within the philosophy and moral precepts of Orfé, the novel's protagonist.

He had, of course, searched for other books by the same author but had found nothing. He instinctively assumed the author dead – because of the common misconception that most books found in second-hand shops were by dead authors – and because two of the preliminary pages of his copy had been torn out he hadn't been able to find the publication date. A letter to the publisher had eventually elicited the deeply gratifying information that not only was Moylita Kaine still alive, but that she (for no good reason, Dik had until then tended to assume that the author was male) was presently working on her second novel.

All this had been happening at the forefront of his life as the political dispute with neighbouring countries developed into hostilities, but before the actual fighting along one of the common frontiers broke out. As a growing boy, bookish and isolated, instinctively peace-loving, physically clumsy, unaggressive to a fault, Dik had been painfully aware of the encroaching war, terrified of what it might mean for him, and alarmed by the changes it had already brought to everyday life. As he absorbed himself in Moylita Kaine's enthralling novel he tried to wish the war away, to retreat into the satisfying and complex imaginary world she had created.

Many changes had taken place while he lost himself in this intriguing inner world, not only in the society around him but also in his own circumstances. Three years had slipped by, and now he was in one of the bleakest and potentially most dangerous theatres of the war. So far, the actual fighting had been confined to a large area of the coastal plain in the south, and the mountain sector had maintained grey alert status ever since his arrival. Nonetheless he was in the front line. All his private hopes and plans had to be suspended until the war ended, but he took his much read copy of *The Affirmation* with him wherever he went. It was, like the unseen nightly arrival of the train from Jethra, a tenuous link with his old life and his past, and in another sense a hoped-for link with his future.

10

A day or two after the night of the burghers, a printed sign appeared on the noticeboard in the main hall of the barracks. It said that a government-funded war writer was on duty in the village, and available for consultation.

Dik applied at once for a pass to consult the writer. Rather to his surprise, the pass was issued almost without hesitation.

'What do you want to see the writer for?' his platoon lieutenant said.

'To improve my mind, sir.'

'You get no relief from duties.'

'It's in my own time, sir.'

That night, Dik slipped the pass between the pages of the novel, choosing as its place the passage describing the momentous first meeting between Orfé and Hilde, the captivating wife of Orfé's rival, Coschtie. It was one of his favourite scenes in the long book, rich with ambiguity, intellectual challenge and a throbbing undercurrent of sexuality.

Before he could make use of the pass Dik returned to duty. The next day he was sent up the mountain and began a three-week tour of patrol missions along the walled border. His squad arrived as a series of nuisance raids were taking place, and mortars and grenades were being exchanged across the wall. On part of the wall on the other side of the same mountain six constables from another platoon were killed and several more were injured. While reinforcements were being brought up from the village the weather closed in and all military action temporarily ceased. Dik was sent back to the village.

The blizzard continued for another two days, blocking the streets with immense drifts. Dik was confined to barracks with the others, boredly watching the grey-black sky and the driven snow. He had grown used to the weather in the mountains and no longer saw it as an expression of his own moods. Dark days did not dispirit him, clear days did not cheer him, as they frequently had while he was still at school. It was rather to the contrary, in fact, because he had been out on enough patrols to know that enemy attacks were fewer when the sky was heavy with snow, that a day that began bright with winter sunshine often finished bright with spilled blood. It was curiously exciting to know that Moylita Kaine was somewhere in the village but also depressing that he still could not use his pass to visit her.

The blizzard ceased on the third day and Dik was detailed to a snow squad, working alongside the tractors to clear the streets once more. Digging with the others, his arms and back straining with the heavy work, Dik spent most of the long hours obsessively wondering why the burghers had not laid electric warmways through the village as they had done along the approaches to the frontier, and on the banquettes behind the parapet of the wall itself. But beneath the snow and ice were the ancient cobbles of the village streets, grating against the metal edge of the spade as Dik laboured at the task.

Repetitive work induced repetitive thoughts, but it relieved him of some of his bottled-up resentment against the burghers. He knew little of what life must have been like in the village before the frontier was closed, although some of the lads who came from the region talked knowingly about gun-runners, drug dealers and shady businessmen buying up many of the local businesses, moving into the outlying farmhouses and taking over the burgher responsibilities, while the local folk who remained worked in the timber industry or as subsistence farmers. Now the village's importance was its strategic position beneath the wall along the mountainous frontier.

Dik slept deeply that night but in the morning, as he huddled in the back of the lurching truck while it followed the steep warmway up towards the frontier, his over-used muscles were in agony. The pack on his back, his rifle and grenade-thrower, his steel helmet, and his snow boots and ropes, felt as if they carried the same dead weight as all the snow he had shifted.

The chance to see Moylita Kaine had come and gone and his hopes for a meeting would have to be put on hold until the next spell of stand-down. Dik was resigned to it with the weary stoicism of the part of him that had become a foot soldier. He accepted that if he survived the next tour of operations, or wasn't injured or captured, she might well have completed her work in the village by the time he came back from the wall.

The frontier had fallen quiet again and a few days later Dik returned unharmed to the village. He had two days of stand-down to look forward to and the time which normally was spent uselessly hanging around the barracks suddenly had a meaning and purpose.

The pass the lieutenant had given him allowed him unsuper-vised access, during daylight hours, to the disused sawmill on the edge of the village. Dik knew the sawmill as a landmark but had never been close to it. During the long hours of the patrol he had rehearsed the walk to it in his mind a score of times. This aside, he did not know what to expect, either of himself or of Moylita Kaine. The prospect of meeting the writer was such an immense, unimaginable one, that he had not thought through beyond the first moments. He had nothing that he had prepared to say to her. It would be sufficient simply to see her, or with luck shake hands with her.

However, as he left the barracks Dik slipped his copy of *The Affirmation* inside the front of his greatcoat. He most definitely did want her autograph.

At the edge of the village, where the street narrowed to a path, Dik was surprised to discover that a warmway had been laid on the ground, cutting a black swathe through the snow. White vapour rose from it in the frosty air. He stepped on to it, his feet slipping slightly as the crusted snow and ice he had picked up on his boots melted beneath him.

The old mill soon came into sight. As Dik climbed up the slope towards it he saw someone standing by a window high up in the front wall. It was a woman. When she saw him climbing the warmway she opened the window and leaned out. She was wear-ing a large fur hat with flaps that fell untied over her ears.

'What do you want?' she called, looking down at him.

'I've come to see Moylita Kaine. Is she here?'

'What do you want her for?'

'I've got a pass,' he said.

'There's a door – round there.' The woman withdrew her head and firmly closed the window.

Dik walked obediently towards the corner she had indicated, leaving the warmway and stepping along a narrow strip where the snow had been trodden down into a hard and uneven path. It was only as he rounded the corner and saw a door set into the side of the building that he realized he must have spoken to Miss Kaine herself.

While he had not built up a mental picture of the author, and had imagined her neither young nor old, he realized that he had not expected her to look quite the way she did. The glimpse he had been afforded of her had been of a woman in her early middle age, plump and fierce-looking, totally unwriterlike.

The author of *The Affirmation* had been, in Dik's indefinite imaginings, more ethereal, more a romantic notion than an actual person.

He opened the door and walked into the sawmill. The old building was unlit and freezing cold but he could see the angular shapes of the benches and saws, the immense storage racks and conveyor belts. A huge engine, dark and covered in rust, squatted in a corner beneath an arrangement of overhead wheels, belt drives and shafts. Daylight glinted through dozens of cracks in the thin planks of the walls. The smell of wood and sawdust was in the air: dry and distant, sweet and stale.

He heard the sound of feet moving above and the woman appeared at the top of a flight of wooden steps built against the wall.

'Are you Miss Kaine?' Dik said, still hardly believing that it could be her.

'I left a message at the Civic Hall,' she said, coming down towards him. 'I don't want to be disturbed today.'

'Message ...? I'm sorry. I can come again another time.'

Dik backed away, groping behind him for the door handle.

'And tell Clerk Tradayn I'm engaged tonight as well.'

She was almost at the bottom of the steps and waiting as Dik fumbled with the handle. It seemed to have jammed, so he took his other hand from his pocket to get a better grip. As he did so, his copy of *The Affirmation* slipped down inside his greatcoat and fell to the ground. The pass, until then still wedged between Orfé and Hilde, slipped from the pages and fluttered away. Dik stooped to pick them up.

'I'm sorry,' he said again, flustered by the closeness of her, her immense height, her brusque manner. 'I didn't know ...'

Moylita Kaine came quickly to his side, and took the book from his hand.

'You've got a copy of my novel,' she said. 'Why?'

'I was hoping ... I might talk to you about it.'

Holding the book, looking at him thoughtfully, she said, 'Have you read this?'

'Of course I have. It's—'

'But the burghers' office sent you?'

'No ... I came because, well, I thought anyone could visit you.'

'So they told me,' she said. 'Why don't you come upstairs for a while? It's warmer.'

'But you aren't to be disturbed.'

'I thought you were from the burghers. Come up to where I'm working. I'll sign your copy for you.'

She turned and went up the stairs. After a moment, gazing disbelievingly at the backs of her trousered legs, Dik followed.

The room had once been the sawmill's office. The window looked down the hill towards the village, and across to the distant mountains beyond. The room was bare and grubby, furnished with a desk and a chair and a tiny one-bar electric radiant heater. It was not appreciably warmer here than it had been downstairs and Dik understood why Miss Kaine wore her furs as she worked.

She went to the desk, moved some papers aside and found a black fountain pen. As she opened his book Dik saw that her hands were clad in gloves, with the ends of the woollen fingers cut away.

15

'Would you like me to dedicate it?'

'Yes, please,' Dik said. 'Whatever you think is best.'

In spite of the moment, Dik's attention was not on the signing of his book because as she started taking the cap off her pen he had noticed that in the centre of the desk was a large pad of lined paper, with handwritten words covering about a quarter of the page he could see. He had found her actually in the process of writing something!

'Then what should I say?' Moylita Kaine said.

'Just sign it, please.'

'You wanted me to dedicate it. What's your name?'

'Oh ... Dik.'

'With a C?'

'No, the other way.'

She wrote quickly, then passed the book back to him. The ink was still wet. Her handwriting was loose and wild and it looked as if she had written, *To Duk ... will evey beet wisl, Moylilo Kine*. He stared at it in joyous incomprehension.

'Thank you,' he said. 'I mean ... er, thank you.'

'I would have signed the title page, but you seem to have torn it out.'

'That wasn't me,' Dik said, anxious to correct a wrong impression. 'It was like that when I found it.'

'Maybe whoever had it before didn't like the book.'

'Oh no! That couldn't be true.'

'Don't you bet on it. You didn't see the reviews.' She went behind the desk and sat down, stretching out her hands towards the fire. Dik glanced at the pages in front of her.

'Is that your new novel?'

'A novel? I should think not. Not at the moment.'

'But your publishers said you were writing one.'

'My publishers told you that? What—?'

'I wrote to them,' Dik said. 'I thought *The Affirmation* was the best novel I had ever read and I wanted to find out what else you had written.'

She was peering at him closely, and Dik felt himself beginning to redden. 'You really have read it, haven't you?'

'Yes, I told you.'

'Did you read it all the way through?'

'I've read it several times. It's the most important book in the world.'

Smiling, but not patronizingly, she said, 'How old are you, Dik?'

'Eighteen.'

'And how old were you when you read the book?'

'The first time? Fifteen, I think.'

'Did you find some of it rather, well, bizarre?'

'The love scenes?' Dik said. 'I found them exciting.'

'I didn't mean those especially, but ... good. Some of the reviewers—'

'I looked up the reviews. They were stupid.'

'So you did see them.'

'Yes.'

'I wish there were more readers like you.'

'I wish there were more *books* like yours!' Dik said, then instantly regretted it. He had vowed to himself that he would be dignified and polite. Miss Kaine was smiling at him again and this time Dik felt his enthusiasm had made him deserve it.

'If that isn't your next novel,' he said, pointing at the pages on her desk, 'do you mind telling me what it is?'

'Nothing much. It's what I'm being paid to write while I'm here. It's a play about the village. But I thought everyone knew what I was doing here.'

'Yes,' Dik said, trying not to reveal his disappointment. He had seen the leaflet setting out the war writer scheme and knew that sponsored writers were commissioned to produce drama about the communities they visited. He had clung, though, to an irrational hope that Moylita Kaine would somehow be able to rise above that sort of thing. A play about the village lacked some of the appeal of another novel like *The Affirmation*. 'Are you writing a novel, though?'

17

'I did start one but I've shelved it for the moment. It wouldn't be published ... not until the war is over. There's no paper for books at present. A lot of sawmills have closed.'

He knew he was staring at her, unable to look away. It was difficult to believe that she was truly Moylita Kaine, someone who had been in his thoughts for three years. Of course she did not *look* like Moylita Kaine, but she didn't even talk like her either. He remembered the long philosophical dialogues in the novel, the subtleties of debate and persuasion, the wit and the compassion, the sheer storytelling verve. Was it the same person?

His first impression of her appearance had been hasty. It was her bulky winter clothes that had made her seem plump, because her hands and face were slender and delicate. He found guessing her age to be impossible: she was obviously several years older than he was, but that was all he could be sure of. He wished she would take off her fur cap so he could see her face properly. A wisp of dark brown hair fell across her forehead.

'Is the play what you want to write?' he said, still staring fixedly at her.

'No, but I have to make a living.'

'I hope you're paid well!' Again, he flinched inside at his own forthrightness.

'Not as well as your burghers are being paid for having me here. But because of the war – well, I didn't want to give up writing altogether.' She had turned away from him, pretending to hold her hands closer to the fire. 'Many writers are in the same position. You do what you can. Provided the war doesn't go on too long, maybe a fallow period will be good for us all.'

'Do you think the war will be over soon?'

'Both sides are at a stalemate, so it could go on for ever. What's that uniform you're wearing? You're in the army, aren't you?'

'The Border Police. Same thing, I suppose.'

'Why don't you come and stand over here? You'll be warmer.'

'I think I should be going back. You said you were busy.'

'No, I want to talk to you.'

She turned the electric fire, indicating that he should go nearer,

18

so he went to her side of the desk and leaned awkwardly on the corner, letting the heat play on his legs. From his position he could read some of the words she had been writing on her pad of paper.

As soon as she saw him looking, Moylita Kaine turned the top page and laid it face down on the others.

Taking it as a rebuke, Dik said, 'I didn't mean to pry.'

'It isn't finished yet.'

'It'll be marvellous,' he said sincerely.

'Maybe it will and maybe it won't. But I don't want anyone to read it. Do you understand?'

'Of course.'

'But you might be able to help me with it,' she said. 'Would you?'

Dik felt an impulse to laugh, so ridiculous and thrilling was the notion that he could offer her anything.

'I don't know,' he managed to say. 'What do you want?'

'You could tell me something about the village. The burghers aren't interested in me now they've received the bursary for having me here and I'm not allowed to see anyone else. I have to write some kind of play but all I can write about is what I see.' She gestured towards the window, with its view of the frozen valley. 'Trees and mountains!'

'Couldn't you invent something?' Dik said.

'You sound like Clerk Tradayn!' When she saw his instant reaction she added quickly, 'I want to write about things as they really are. Who lives in the village, for instance? Is it only the burghers and the soldiers? There are no women here.'

Dik thought.

'The burghers are here with their families,' he said. 'They must have their wives with them. I've never seen them.'

'Who else is here?'

'There are farmers in the valley. And there are people at the railway depot.'

'I might as well write about trees and mountains.'

'But you seem to have been writing something,' Dik said.

19

'It's drifting along,' Moylita Kaine said, explaining nothing. 'What about the frontier wall. Do you ever go up there?'

'On patrol. That's why we're here.'

'Can you describe it to me?'

'Why?' Dik said.

'Because I haven't seen it and the burghers won't let me go up there.'

'You couldn't put it in your play.'

'Why not? Surely it's at the heart of the community?'

'Oh no,' Dik said seriously. 'It runs along the tops of the mountains.' As Moylita Kaine laughed he squirmed with embarrassment, then laughed too.

'The wall goes right round Faiandland, Dik. But how many of our people, ordinary people, have ever seen it? It's part of what the war is about, and so for anyone writing today it's an important symbol. It's even more crucial here. To understand this community I have to know about the wall.'

'It's just a high wall,' Dik said, helplessly.

'What's it made of?'

'Concrete, I think. There are some sections of it, the older parts, made out of brick. And there are earthworks behind it. The main wall is high, several times the height of a man, but there are levels behind it called banquettes, where we patrol. The steep sections have steps. Parts of the wall are hollow and there are ammunition trolleys that run along rails inside. There's razor wire along most of the parapet and machine gun posts and towers. The enemy have put up floodlights on the other side, and we have a few as well.'

'And it follows the old frontier?'

'Right over the peaks of the mountains,' Dik said. 'That's where the old frontier is supposed to be. The wall is ... symbolic,' he added, using her word.

'Walls always are. What do you get up to, during patrols?'

'We're there to make sure no one comes across from the other side. Most of the time nothing happens. Every now and then someone on the other side throws grenades or gas capsules at us, and if they do we throw some back. Sometimes it quietens down straight away. At other times it goes on like that for days. Mostly, though, it snows and the wind blows.'

'Is it frightening?'

'Boring, mostly. I've learned not to think while I'm on duty.'

'You must think about something.'

'I think about the cold, and going home. I think about your book, and the other books I've read, and the books I want to read in the future.' She made no response, so Dik went on. 'I sometimes wonder who's on the other side of the wall and why they're there. They must be the same sort of age as us. They don't have burghers in their country, you know. I think not, anyway.' Her silence was disconcerting him. 'I don't like burghers, you see,' he said, trying to explain.

She had been idly fingering her pages as she listened to him. 'Do you know who built the wall, Dik?'

'They did. The Federated States.'

'Do you know that's what they say?' she said. 'That we built the wall?'

'That's ridiculous. Why should we?'

'They believe we built the wall to prevent people from fleeing the country. They say we live under a dictatorship, and that the tithe laws restrict our freedoms.'

'Then why are they trying to invade? Why do they bomb our cities?'

'They say they are defending themselves because the government of Faiandland is trying to impose our system on them.'

'Then why do they accuse us of building the wall?'

'Don't you see that it doesn't matter who did? It's a symbol, as we agree, but a symbol of stupidity. Didn't you find any of this in *The Affirmation*?'

Dik was taken aback by her unexpected mention of the novel. While she was talking about the war she was on the subject that easily overshadowed most of his waking hours. But suddenly to relate her book to it brought him back with a jolt.

Trying to think what she meant, he said, 'I don't remember.'

'I thought I'd made it clear. The duplicity of Hilde, and the lies she tells Orfé about Coschtie. When Orfé—'

'I know,' Dik said, seeing at once what she meant. 'The first time he makes love to her. Hilde wants him to be treacherous, to excite her, and Orfé claims she will be the first to betray them.'

'Yes.'

'And she leaves the room and comes back with a large sheet of blank paper, and challenges him to write down what he has said. And he says that the sheet of paper will inevitably come between them and blames her for holding it up, that it puts her on the other side, but Hilde claims that the paper was his, he kept it in his house—'

He would have gone on, letting his detailed memory of the book's plot carry him forward, but Moylita Kaine interrupted, 'You really did read it closely. You see what I mean, then?'

'About the wall?'

'Yes. The blank sheet.'

He shook his head. 'I know what it means in the book, but you wrote that before the war started.'

'There have always been walls, Dik. Two sides to everything.'

Then she began to talk about the novel, leaning over to dangle her fingers before the electric fire. She was guarded at first, apparently watching for Dik's response, but as she saw the eager interest he displayed, as he made a point of revealing that his reading of the novel had been close and intelligent, she talked more freely. She spoke quickly, made deprecating jokes about herself and her story, explained what she meant even when she must have known that he understood, and all the while her eyes sparkled in the snowy light from the window. Dik was more excited than he could ever remember. For him it was like reading the book for the first time again.

She said there was a wall in the novel, a figurative barrier that lay between Orfé and Hilde. It was the dominant image in the book, although only ever described indirectly. 'Walls everywhere!' Moylita Kaine said. Walls lay between them from the outset, because of Hilde's marriage to Coschtie, but after his death the walls remained in place because of the betrayals. As first Orfé then Hilde tried to draw the other one closer, both finding sexual infidelity arousing, the wall became higher and more impregnable. The labyrinthine involvements of the lesser characters – fulfilling Coschtie's demands on them while he was still alive, revenging themselves on his memory after he died – formed a pattern of moral attitudes. Their influence was divided: some controlled Orfé, some Hilde. Every conspiratorial action further fortified the wall between the two lovers, and made the final tragedy more inevitable. Yet the book was still the affirmation of the title: Moylita Kaine said she intended the novel to make a positive statement. Orfé's final decision was a declaration of freedom – the wall fell as the book ended. It was too late for Orfé and Hilde, but the wall had nevertheless fallen.

'Do you see what I was trying to do?' she said.

Dik shook his head vaguely, still lost in his new insight into the book he thought he had known so well, but when he realized what he was doing he nodded emphatically.

She regarded him kindly, and sat back in her chair.

'I'm sorry,' she said. 'You shouldn't let me talk so much.'

'No, please ... tell me more!'

'I thought I'd said it all,' she said, and laughed.

It was Dik's opportunity to ask the questions he had been saving up since his first reading of the book. How she had come up with the original idea, whether any of the characters were based on real people, whether anything in the novel had ever happened to her personally, how long the book had taken to write, whether she had ever visited the Dream Archipelago where the story was set ...

Moylita Kaine, obviously flattered by his interest, gave replies to them all, but Dik was unable to judge how literally she was answering. She made more self-effacing comments, and sometimes was deliberately vague, raising more questions than he could ever ask.

It was after one more such deprecating remark that Dik took stock of himself, realizing that his barrage of questions must be sounding like an interrogation. He lapsed into awkward silence, staring down at the uneven and none too clean surface of the desk she was using.

'Am I talking too much?' she said to his surprise.

'No, it's me. I'm asking too many questions.'

'Then let me ask you some.'

Dik had no high regard for himself and did not have much to say. He told her about the degree course he had been offered and how he had intended to make use of it to study her book, but he wasn't sure what might have come of that. He nurtured secret ambitions to become a writer – and given half a chance he wanted to try to write a book like *The Affirmation* – but that was a secret he would never reveal to Moylita Kaine. It blocked his mind and he gradually became monosyllabic in his replies. Moylita Kaine didn't press him.

Finally Dik said, 'May I come and see you again tomorrow?'

'If you are able to.'

'I have another day before I go back on duty. If you're not too busy.'

'Dik, the idea of the scheme is to encourage people like you to meet writers like me. Why don't you bring some of the others with you?'

'No!' Dik said. 'Well, not unless they ask.'

'They have been told I'm here, haven't they?'

'I think so.'

'You seem to have found out without much difficulty.' She glanced at his copy of *The Affirmation*, which he had tucked under his arm. 'As a matter of interest, how *did* you know I was here?'

'I saw the scheme announced in the police magazine,' he said. 'Your name was there, and I wanted to meet you.'

He confessed all. The scheme was open to any community on or near the front line, and the intention was to encourage the arts during the emergency. Many leading, and not so leading, painters, sculptors, writers, musicians, had agreed to take part. Dik, hungering for contact with the world he had left when he was conscripted, had been astonished to see Moylita Kaine listed

24

as one of the participants. With extreme nervousness he had put in a request through his platoon serjeant. A few weeks later a printed notice had appeared on the board, describing the scheme and asking for nominations. Dik, who sometimes felt he was the only constable who ever looked at the noticeboard, had written Moylita Kaine's name on the form, and then, for good measure, had written it in three more times in different hands and using different pens.

He did not know at the time but a bursary was paid to the administrators of the community – in this case the Council of Burghers – and the unexpected bounty had probably had the desired effect.

She listened to his account in silence.

'So is it you I have to thank?' she said.

'I'm sure I had little to do with it,' Dik lied, his face burning.

'Good,' Moylita Kaine said. 'I shouldn't like to think I'm having to put up with this because of you.' She waved her gloved hand to take in the grimy room, the one-bar heater, the wintry view. 'So, will you come again tomorrow?'

'Yes, Miss Kaine.'

'Um ... don't call me that. I'm technically married.'

'I'm sorry. I didn't know.'

'Neither did I. Well, never mind. It's all in the past. You can call me Moylita.'

She didn't explain, but it gave Dik something to think about that night. He could hardly sleep for thinking about her, and loving her with a tremendous passion.

A time for reflection followed, unwelcomely. Dik had intended to return to the sawmill directly after breakfast the next day, but he was detailed to cookhouse duties by a sharp-featured caporal who waylaid him outside the canteen. Given a morning of tedious chores Dik retreated into his usual survival state of inner contemplation. In the clattering, steamy cookhouse he saw his remembered conversation with Moylita Kaine in a new light. The heady euphoria of his thoughts in the night had faded. Now he

25

began to think more analytically about what she had said.

While he had been getting ready to go to college Dik began reading literary criticism in the hope of gaining new insights into the literature he enjoyed. One book in particular had made an impression on him. In it, the author made out the case that the act of reading a text was as important and creative an act as writing one. In some respects, the reader's reaction was the only completely reliable measure of a book. What the reader made of the text became the definitive assessment, irrespective of the intentions of the author.

To Dik, who was largely untutored in literature, such an approach to reading was an insight of great value. In the case of *The Affirmation* – a novel that mysteriously to Dik was not mentioned in any of the criticism he read – it gave further weight to his belief that it was a truly great novel. It was great because he considered it to be great.

Putting his conversation with Moylita Kaine into this context, not only were her intentions irrelevant to his enjoyment of the book, but it was arrogant of her to impose them on him.

The instant Dik thought that he regretted it because he knew her motives were kindly. Even to think it was to presume himself her equal, when it was abundantly clear she was superior to him in every way. Chastened by his own arrogance, Dik resolved to make amends in some way, without revealing why.

But as he worked in the kitchen, waiting for his duties to finish with the serving of the midday meal, the thought would not go away.

In explaining her novel to him, had Moylita Kaine been trying to tell him something?

Walking up the warmway to the sawmill, Dik passed one of the burghers. Automatically, he stepped into the snow at the side and stood with his gaze humbly averted as the man swept past.

Then, 'Where are you going, boy?'

'To see the writer, sir.'

'By whose authority?'

'I have a pass, sir.'

Dik fumbled in the pocket of his greatcoat, thanking the stars that he had remembered to bring the pass with him. The burgher examined it closely, turning it over to read both sides, as if trying to find the least irregularity. Then he gave it back.

'Do you know who I am, Constable?'

'Clerk Tradayn, sir.'

'Why did you not salute me?'

'I didn't see you approaching, sir. Until it was too late. I was watching where I placed my feet.'

There was a long silence while Dik continued to stare at the snow-covered ground. The burgher was breathing stiffly, an irritated sound, made by a man of authority who could find no application for it at that moment. At last he turned curtly away and walked on down towards the village. He held his head at a lofty angle, disdaining the dangers of the steep and slippery descent.

After what Dik deemed a respectful few seconds, during which he mentally thumbed his nose and waggled his fingers at the burgher's retreating back, he regained the warmway and hurried up to the sawmill. He let himself in, ducked under the rusting racks and sawing machinery, and went up the stairs. Moylita Kaine was sitting at her desk, and as he opened the door she glanced at him with an expression of such anger that he almost fled.

But she said at once, 'Oh, it's you, Dik! Come in quickly, close the door.'

She went to stand by the window, craning her neck as she looked down in the direction of the village. Dik saw that her fist was clenched tightly, the knuckles white.

'Did you pass Seignior Tradayn on your way here?' she said.

'Yes. He wanted to know where I was going and what I was doing.'

'I hope you told him.'

'I had to.'

'Good.'

'Is there something wrong?' Dik said.

'Not really. Not now.' She went back to her desk and sat down, but almost at once she stood up again and paced about the room. In spite of her welcoming manner she continued to be upset. At last she returned to the desk.

'Was Seignior Tradayn ordering you about?' Dik said.

'No, not that sort of thing.' She sat forward. 'Yesterday you said the burghers were married. Do you happen to know that, or was it only a guess?'

'No, a guess really. A feeling I had. When my troop arrived there was a function at the Civic Hall for the officers. I saw a lot of women going in that night, accompanied by the men I knew were the village burghers.'

'Clerk Tradayn ... was he one of them? Is he married?'

'I've no idea.' Suddenly suspecting what might have happened, Dik wanted to hear no more about it. He reached into the front of his greatcoat and brought out the object he had been carrying.

'Moylita,' he said with some hesitation, it being the first time he had dared to use her first name, 'I've brought you a present.'

She looked up, took it from him.

'Dik, it's beautiful! Did you carve it yourself?'

'Yes.' As she turned it in her hand he went and leaned against the side of her desk, as he had done before. 'It's a special soft-wood. Some of the trees here are like that. I found this piece in the forest. It was easy to carve.'

'A hand holding a pen,' she said. 'I've never seen anything like it.'

'It was the way the wood had grown. It looked a bit like that before I started. I'm sorry it's crude. All I did really was smooth it down.'

'But it's exactly right! May I keep it?' When he nodded she stood up and leaned across the desk. She kissed him on the cheek before he could turn away. 'Dik, thank you!'

He started to mumble about the inadequacy of the gift, delighted with her reaction but also remembering his repentant motives. Moylita moved her papers aside and set the carving on the desk in front of her.

'I'll treasure your gift,' she said. 'Well, I was going to give it to you later. But you can have a present too.'

'You're giving me a present?' Dik said stupidly.

'I wrote something for you last night. Just for you.'

'What is it?' Dik said, but at the same moment Moylita produced some sheets of white paper, clipped together in one corner.

'I came up with a story yesterday, after you had left. It all happened rather suddenly so I don't suppose it's much good as a story, but it came about because of what we were discussing.'

'May I see?'

She shook her head. 'Not yet. I want you to promise me something first – that you won't read it until I've left the village.'

'Why not?' Dik said. He added with a flash of insight, 'Is it about me?'

'There's someone in it who's a bit like you. You might recognize one or two things he says.'

'I don't mind that!' Dik said. 'I'll read it now.'

He held out his hand.

'No. I want to tell you about it first, so you know the score. If anyone found you with the manuscript you could get into trouble. You see, I've made the central character someone who is on the other side. Beyond the wall. If the burghers found the story, or one of your officers, they'd wonder what you were doing with it and where you got it from. Are you sure you still want it?'

'Of course I do! I can easily hide it – our kit is never searched.'

'All right. But there's something else. The story isn't set here, up in the mountains. It's not even in Faiandland. I've set it in the south. Do you know where I mean?'

'Jethra,' Dik said, guessing.

'No, on the southern continent. On the other side of the Midway Sea.'

'You mean beyond the Dream Archipelago!' Dik said, remembering the fantastic scenes she had written in the novel, the endless island-hopping of the restless characters, the sultry heat, the exotic colours, the displaced main players of the story forever

29

seeking a sense of identity. In reality few could escape to the neutral islands except in their minds.

'Well, yes. I have to warn you because although to you and me it's simply a story, not everyone understands how fiction works. If some of the burghers saw this they might assume you were a spy.'

Dik said, not understanding what she meant, in spite of his pretence that he did, 'Moylita, how can—?'

'Listen, Dik. Before I came to the village there were rumours in Jethra. I've got several friends who ... well, they don't completely agree with the government. They've maintained contacts with like-minded people in other countries, including in the Federation. They believe there are secret negotiations going on with our side. It's complicated. I don't know how much of it to believe, or where to begin telling you. But there's an economic dimension to the war. There always is, but in this case everything is being concealed by a cloud of ideology. Some people in industry are making fortunes out of it. Not only here, but in the Federation too. It's a real war, and those air-raids did a lot of damage and killed hundreds of people. I don't think that was expected. What they've been negotiating since is in effect an attempt to find ways of keeping the war going without actually destroying each other's country. My friends think the war will be relocated, down to the south, so it can be fought out where there are no cities.'

'But the Dream Archipelago is neutral.'

'They want to go to the land beyond. The southern polar continent.'

'There have been a lot of stories set there,' Dik said.

'Yes, but not about the war, about *this* war. My story's about someone like you but I can't say as much, can't spell it out literally.'

Moylita fell silent and peered intently at Dik's face, seeming to study it for his reaction.

'Would you still like to have the story?' she said.

'Oh yes,' he said, because although he hadn't fully understood what she had told him, it was enough that she had written it for him.

'Very well. Look after it, and don't read it for another couple of days. Is that a promise?'

He nodded emphatically, so after another thoughtful look Moylita placed the thin sheaf of papers on the desk and smoothed them with her hand. The words were typed or printed, Dik noticed with some surprise. From what he had seen yesterday he had assumed that she did her writing by hand. She scrawled her signature on the top sheet, then folded them all in half and passed them over.

Dik took the story. As if the paper was the skin taken from a living animal it seemed that every fibre was alive and throbbing with organic chemistry. He could feel the words indented on the paper and he ran his fingertips across the reverse side of the bottom sheet, like a blind man feeling for meaning.

'Moylita ... will you tell me about the symbolism in the story?'

She did not answer straight away. Then, 'Why do you ask?'

He was thinking about the way she had interpreted the novel the day before. She had made him understand it when before he had only loved it. He wanted her to explain the story, fearing he might never see her again.

'Because I might not understand it unless you do,' he said.

'It's simple. I didn't have time to mess around with it and complicate it. It's about a soldier who reads a novel and he later becomes a poet. Nothing symbolic at all.'

'What I meant—'

'Because yesterday we were talking about how symbolic walls could be?'

'Yes. The wall in this story. Is it the one on the frontier?'

'It's a wall,' Moylita said. 'It's built of bricks and concrete and it's just a wall.'

'And the soldier, this ... poet, he climbs it?'

'Dik, I think you should wait until you've read the story. I don't want you to think it has meanings that aren't there.'

31

'But he does climb the wall, doesn't he?'

'How did you know?'

'Because—'

The door opened without warning, and Clerk Tradayn came quickly into the room. He slammed the door behind him.

Because of what you said, Dik thought, his intuition fading away.

The burgher said, 'Mrs Kaine, would you—?' He saw Dik, who had moved back against the wall and turned at once towards him. 'What are you doing here, Constable?'

'I told you, sir ... I have a pass.'

Dik reached into his pocket, groping for it.

'I've seen the pass. What are you doing here, in this room?'

Moylita said, 'He has every right to be here, Seignior Tradayn. While I'm writer in residence, the troops—'

'The Border Police are under the command of the Council, Mrs Kaine. Passes issued by non-commissioned officers have to be approved by me.'

'Then you can approve it now. Have you got it there, Dik?'

While they spoke Dik had found the slip of paper, and he held it out towards the burgher. He had never heard anyone ever speak back to a burgher and it was awe-inspiring to see the confidence with which Moylita did it.

Clerk Tradayn took no notice of him or his pass but went to Moylita's desk and leaned across it, resting his plump, liver-spotted hands on the edge.

'I want to see what you've been writing,' he said.

'You've seen the play. I haven't written any more of it since yesterday.'

'Your computer printer was heard being used late into the night.'

'So what? I'm a writer. I was revising what I've done.'

'Let me see it.'

'Why are you spying on me, Seignior?'

32

'Mrs Kaine, so long as you are at the frontier you are subject to military law. Let me see what you have been writing.'

She scooped up all the loose papers on her desk and thrust them at him. Meanwhile, Dik, still standing with his back pressed against the wall, could feel her typescript hanging conspicuously in his hand. He moved his arm slowly, trying to get the papers under his greatcoat.

'Not that, Mrs Kaine. I want to see what you were printing. What are you holding, Constable?'

'The pass, sir.' Dik held out his other hand.

'Give it to me.'

Dik glanced helplessly at Moylita but she was staring impassively at the burgher. Reluctantly, Dik held out the pass, but Clerk Tradayn reached behind him and snatched the typescript from his other hand. He moved to the window, and with a shake of his hand unfolded it.

'*The Negation*,' he said. 'Is that your title, Mrs Kaine?'

Moylita's gaze did not waver.

'Why did you call it that, Mrs Kaine? It seems like a strange title for a story, if I may say so.'

'You may say what you like, since you clearly have no sympathy with literature. It's a counterpoint to a novel I wrote and published before the war. The novel was called *The Aff*—'

'Yes, we know all about your novel, thank you very much. I am more concerned with this.'

He scanned the first page then began to read aloud from the top, adopting a scornful, mocking voice.

'"It no longer mattered which side had first breached the treaty that prohibited the use of sense gases. They had been illegally available and in use for so long that they were no longer questioned. Nor did it matter who it was who manufactured and sold the gases. To the ordinary soldier, nothing mattered. Nothing he saw, felt, heard could be trusted. His sense of vision, touch and sound had been permanently" ...'

The burgher stopped reading, then leafed quickly through the remainder of the pages, scanning the words.

'Have you been reading this, Constable?'

'No, sir—'

'The boy knows nothing about it. I was lending it to him. I wrote it several years ago.'

'Or several hours ago.' Seignior Tradayn squinted again at the first page, his small, deep-set eyes moving quickly from side to side. He held out the typescript for Moylita to see. 'Is this your signature?'

'Yes.'

'Good.' Tradayn stuffed the typescript into an inner pocket. 'Constable, return to your quarters at once.'

'Sir, I—'

'Quarters, Constable!'

'Yes, sir.'

Dik shuffled hesitantly towards the door, looking back at Moylita. He knew that if there was any hope of retrieving the situation it must lie with her. In spite of the burgher's imperious manner he was obviously somewhat overawed by her. But Moylita said and did nothing, returning Dik's desperate gaze with eyes that were steady and calm. He wondered if it was some kind of message for him but if it was it was so subtle that it was lost on him.

When he reached the cold air outside he started to walk down the warmway, but halted when he had gone only a few paces. He listened, but could hear nothing coming from inside the sawmill. He hesitated a few seconds longer then left the slippery warmway and ran across the snowfield towards the nearest trees. Here the snow had drifted deeply and he jumped down and hid behind the broad trunk of a fir. He had only a few minutes to wait. Moylita and the burgher soon appeared, walking together down the warmway towards the village. Moylita was in front of the man, walking with her head bowed, but other than that there was nothing submissive in her manner. She could as easily have been watching where she stepped on the smooth metal surface of the warmway. She was carrying under her arm the carving Dik had given her.

Dik hid in his barracks room for the remainder of the day, waiting for what he assumed would be the inevitable summons to Clerk Tradayn's office in the Civic Hall. It seemed nothing in life was inevitable, though, for the summons never arrived. By nightfall, Dik was more in terror of the uncertainty than he would have been of punishment. At least punishment would signal an end of some kind.

The story he had not been able to read – his story, the one she had written for him – seemed, for reasons he still did not fully comprehend, as potentially explosive as one of the enemy's flat-cake mines. Moylita had warned him herself, and the burgher's reaction to it had confirmed it. She would be charged with spying and treason, and later imprisoned or exiled or shot.

The fact that something of the same might also happen to him was of less importance.

The constant nagging fears and worries sent him into the village streets as soon as evening mess was complete. He had eaten virtually nothing, sitting in morbid silence as the other lads had shouted and laughed.

The night was clear but a strong wind was up, whipping the powdery snow from the roofs and sills and sending it stinging into his face. Dik walked the length of the main street, hoping for a glimpse of Moylita or even some clue as to where she might be, but the street was empty and dark and the only lights showing came from windows high under the ornate carved gables. He returned slowly, halting when he came to the entrance to the Civic Hall. Here the tall windows showed light, gleaming in horizontal slits through the slats of the wooden louvred shutters. Hardly thinking what the consequences might be Dik went up to the main doors and walked inside. There was a long hallway, brightly lit by three gigantic chandeliers. The broad passage was wavering with heat from large hot-water radiators on all sides. At the far end of the hall, opposite him, were two more doors, made of wood and thick glass, ground or engraved with ornate curlicues and leaf designs. A ginger-haired Border Patrol caporal he had never seen before was standing before them.

'What's your business, Constable?'

'I'm looking for Moylita Kaine, Caporal,' Dik said, with simple truth.

'Who's that, then? What troop are you in?'

'K Squad, Cap.'

'Never seen you before. There's no one in here you're allowed to see. Just the burghers. Back to the barracks, or I'll put you on a charge.'

'Then I'll see the burghers,' Dik said. 'Clerk Tradayn summoned me.'

'The burghers are in Council session. They summoned no one. What's your name and number, Constable?'

Dik stared back silently, fearing the caporal's petty authority over him: in normal patrol circumstances there would be practically none, but the caporal was wearing the ribbon with the diplomatic flash, giving him unknown exercise of power. Even so, Dik was still compelled by his anxieties about Moylita and he backed away, not wanting to be detained or diverted by this man who probably knew nothing of what had been going on.

He returned to the breathtaking icy blast of the street, closing his ears and mind to the caporal's commands, shouted behind him. Dik expected he would be followed, but once the main doors had swung closed behind him he could hear the shouts no more. He ran away, sliding on the frozen ground as he reached the corner of the building.

Dik came into the tiny square which lay beyond. This was where the local farmers could come down from the hills to petition the burghers during the daytime, and where, before the war started, there had been weekly livestock and produce markets. The square was divided up into a number of pens where the tithe livestock would be kept while the petitions were heard. Dik vaulted over two of the metal fences, then paused to listen. There was no sound of pursuit.

He looked up at the shuttered windows of the Civic Hall, behind which he knew was the council chamber. Dik climbed on one of the metal barriers forming the pens and shuffled forward until his hands were resting on the ice-crusted brick of the building. He raised himself as high as possible and tried to peer through the shutter into the chamber. Although the outer shutters were made of flat planks of wood, with several carved apertures through which he could see, the inner shutters were again louvred and all Dik could see was a small part of the ceiling, richly ornamented with plaster mouldings, and delicate, pastel-coloured renderings of religious tableaux.

He could hear the indistinct sound of voices from within. After several unsuccessful attempts to see what was going on Dik discovered he could swing the outer shutter to one side. He pressed his ear against the cold glass.

At once he heard the sound of a woman's voice, Moylita's voice. She was speaking loudly and rapidly, and her voice was pitched high with anger, or fear. A man said something Dik could not catch, then Moylita shouted, 'You know the sense gases are in use! Why don't you admit it?' Several voices were raised against her and she was shouting again. A man said, '... we've found out who your friends are!' Then Dik heard Moylita shout back, 'The young men out there have a right to know!' And, '... drive most of them mad! It's illegal, and you know it! Most of them are boys! Hardly out of school!' The chamber was in uproar. Dik heard a series of loud thuds and the hollow sound of wood falling heavily against wood. Moylita started to scream.

Then Dik was found by the caporal.

He was dragged down from his precarious place against the sill of the window and he fell kicking and struggling into the drift of windswept snow at the bottom of the wall. The caporal cuffed him about the head until he quit struggling, then hauled him away. He was taken to an unheated guardroom by the entrance to the Civic Hall, where he was given another beating by the caporal. This one, out of the sight of anyone who might have passed the building, was efficient and painful. Two platoon serjeants later arrived, and they too gave him a thorough kicking.

The sky had clouded over and the rising wind was carrying a full blizzard with it. By the time Dik was dragged through the streets back to the barracks, the gale was bearing thick, suffocating snowflakes, settling in for a night-long storm, piling up new drifts against the walls and posts of the village.

Bruised and disconsolate, aching in head, stomach, groin, legs, chest, Dik lay locked inside his room for the remainder of the night and for all the following day. He was given water, but no food. The heating in his room was turned off, and when he tried to read one of the many books that littered his room the overhead light was abruptly turned off.

He had much on which to ponder and nearly all of it was concerned with Moylita and the possible fates that he imagined had befallen her. They were all awful, and he could barely countenance them. For the rest, he wondered again and again about the little story he had held, unread, for those few moments. All Moylita had told him was that it concerned a soldier who became a poet. From the burgher's reaction after skimming through it Dik could easily imagine there was rather more to the story than that. There were those few sentences the burgher had read aloud: sense gases, distortion of perception, nothing that might be trusted. Later, the fragments of the shouted argument he had overhead through the closed window of the council chamber: the right to be told, the illegality of the gases, the madness.

Moylita had written the story exclusively for him. She had not discussed the background with him; she only mentioned the poet. This was for her the true statement of the story and so the same should be true for him.

He had not told her about his own literary aspirations, of the bundles of unpublished verse that lay neglected in the cupboard in his room at home, of the numerous incomplete drafts of stories. Had she somehow guessed about these?

She had interpreted the novel for him, perhaps divining correctly that he related his own life to it. Had she been intending him to do the same with the story?

Dik did not know. Whatever part of him had once been a poet had been beaten out of him by the military basic training: those long brutalizing weeks in the camp had had their effect and he could not easily forget the failure of the verse he had attempted when he arrived in the village. The studious, sensitive boy who had never made many friends was a long way behind him now, beyond the wall thrown up when he reluctantly volunteered.

His precious copy of *The Affirmation* was safe in his room. He had half-expected someone would take it away from him, but clearly none of his superiors was able to appreciate how important it was to him. When daylight came and he was sure no one was checking what he was doing, Dik squatted down on the floor, leaning his back against the door. He read a long section of it. He chose the passage he had always found the most intriguing: the last five chapters.

This was the part of the story where Orfé had finally escaped from the conspiratorial machinations of Emerden and the other minor characters and was free to go in search of Hilde. What followed was a journey not simply through the exotic landscape of the Dream Archipelago, but also a voyage of self-exploration. In a moving irony, the more Orfé understood himself and the events that had led up to his escape, the more remote from him Hilde herself became.

Reading the book for the first time since Moylita had talked about it, Dik was suddenly aware of the wall symbolism that ran throughout it, and he cursed his lack of percipience in not having seen it for himself. As Orfé sailed from one island to the next, following the obscure trail of clues left behind by the fleeing Hilde, he encountered a series of barriers. The images chosen by the author, the dialogue she wrote for Orfé, her actual choice of words, all reflected the fact that Hilde had retreated behind a wall of Orfé's own making. Even Moylita Kaine's locale for the end of the quest – the island of Prachous, which in Archipelagian patois meant 'the fenced island' – was appropriate to her theme.

The last irony, that the wall behind which Hilde retreated was the one he had earlier built to keep others away from her, now took on a resonance that made Dik silently shed a few tears. His younger self reached out from the past, briefly touched him, reminded him of his earlier sensibilities, his old ways of feeling and of being.

Behind him, in the bare corridor of the barracks beyond his locked door, booted feet constantly moved heavily to and fro.

The book left him with a sense of artistic satisfaction, but soon enough his thoughts returned to the lost short story. Moylita had been trying to tell him something with it. Did he know enough about it that he could try to imagine what that could be?

Affirmation/negation: opposites. A wall lay between them?

Orfé failed to climb his wall when he had the chance, and thereafter it was too late. In the story the soldier climbed a wall and became a poet. Orfé started the novel as a romantic idler, a dilettante and a sybarite, but because of his failures he became a haunted ascetic, obsessed with purpose and guided by moral principle. In the story, what?

Dik, still not fully understanding, but trying hard, began to sense what Moylita Kaine might have wanted of him.

On the mountain frontier, high on the ridges, there was no greater penalty for disciplinary offences than to be sent back on wall patrol. Dik was therefore not surprised when he was restored to normal duties. He never saw the ginger-haired caporal again, and nothing was said about the events of the past two days. By the middle of the afternoon of the following day he was pacing an allotted sector of the wall, high above the countryside he was supposedly protecting. It was bitterly cold: at intervals he had to remove his goggles. Narrowing his eyes against the glaring sun he chipped away the encrusting ice from the dark filtered lenses. It was also necessary to work the breech mechanism of his rifle to prevent it jamming.

While climbing up to the frontier in the morning, Dik had for a time been able to see the sawmill from the slopes above the village. There had been no lights on that he could see and the unbroken snowfield around it revealed that the warmway had not been switched on, or had possibly even been removed.

While he had been down in the village certain changes had been made to the physical defences along the wall. New flood-lights had been installed close to many of the guard posts, and enormous drums of electric cable had been dumped on the slopes immediately below the wall. In addition, several immense and bulbous metal shapes had appeared, half buried in the snow beside the warmway. Complicated arrangements of pipes and nozzles led from these across the warmway and up to the parapet of the wall. Although there were many warning signs, and strict enjoiners that only trained technicians were to approach, Dik had tripped over the bulky pipes several times until he learned to watch out for them.

He was allowed a short break at dusk, when he sipped a hot and spicy soup in one of the guard posts, but after the early nightfall he was back in his sector, pacing to and fro in numb misery, trying to count the minutes that remained until the end of his watch.

Night patrols were especially nerve-racking, because for most of the time he and the other constables were effectively alone against the hostile alliance of dark and cold and unexplained noises. Reinforcements waited in the forward quarters a short dis-tance below the wall, but if an attack came it was the patrols who had to bear the brunt of it for the first minutes. On this night the Federation side had not turned on their floodlights, so Dik could hardly see even the bulk of the wall looming beside him. All that was distinguishable was the dark strip of the warmway against the white snow, and the sinister, half-buried cisterns.

Whenever he passed the guard post he checked the current state of alert. He was reassured to be told each time that little enemy activity had been detected.

He wondered, as he had often wondered, where the enemy were and what they were doing or planning on the other side. Was there someone like himself, a few feet away on the other side of the parapet, stamping to and fro, thinking only about how long it would be until the end of the watch?

Here, at the place where the two countries met, where two political and economic ideologies clashed, he was physically closer to the enemy than almost anyone else. If there was a sudden invasion across the wall, or even a skirmish, he would be the first to have to fight or die. And yet the frontier united him with the enemy: the men on the other side obeyed the same sort of orders, suffered the same fears, endured the same physical hardships, and they, presumably, defended their country to support a system that was as remote from them as the burghers and their tithes were remote from himself.

Dik again worked the breech mechanism to free it. There was a pause in the whining of the wind and in the brief lull Dik heard, from the other side of the wall, someone there working a breech mechanism. It was something the patrols often heard when they were on the wall: it was at once alarming and perversely comforting.

Dik could feel the weight of Moylita Kaine's novel in his pocket. He had brought it with him, in defiance of standing orders. He knew that his return to patrols did not of itself prove he was in the clear. He knew or suspected that his kit would be searched, and the thought of losing the precious copy was too awful to bear. Anyway, he felt after the events of the last two days that the act of carrying it was the least he could do for her. He had no idea what had happened to her, although it was almost certainly unpleasant. Carrying her book was the only way he knew of enacting her ideas. She talked to him in symbols, and in return Dik was prepared to enact symbols.

He could not act in reality, because he had realized at last what she had been urging him to do.

He glanced up the immense bulk of the wall beside him. It looked bleak and unsymbolic, and almost certainly unclimbable. It was booby-trapped: certainly on this side, and almost certainly on the other. Flatcake mines had been laid by both sides. The tripwires and scramble fence were touch-triggered and electrified. A man had only to show his hand above the top of the wall and a fusillade of radar-directed shots would come from automatic

42

trap-rifles set by the other side. In the period of less than two years that the war had been in progress there were already scores of stories about grenade duels brought on by little more than the sudden sound of sliding snow.

Dik walked on, remembering the momentary resentment he had felt about the way Moylita had interpreted her novel for him. This was the same. It was all very well to create symbols in the pages of fiction. It was an entirely different matter to be out here, exposed on the wall, in the grip of a winter gale, coping with the grim reality of war. In Moylita's negation of ideals, a man could climb a wall and find his destiny as poet. Dik's own sense of destiny was well formed, but it didn't include making a suicidal leap into the unknown. He too could make his own negation.

Then he remembered the sound of her voice coming from within the council chamber. She had taken a risk in writing the story and she had apparently paid a price for it. Conscience and a sense of moral responsibility returned, and Dik thought again about climbing the wall.

It was high along here, but there were firing steps further along. Sometimes they were used.

He became aware that somewhere around him was a hissing noise and he halted at once. He crouched down, holding his rifle ready, looking about him in the gloom. Then, from a long way away, from the depths of the valley, a shrill thin sound reached him, distorted by a combination of the wind, the distance and the snow-covered walls of the mountains: the train was in the depot, letting its whistle be heard.

Dik stood up again, relieved by the familiarity of the sound.

He walked on, rattling the bolt of his rifle. On the other side of the wall, someone else did the same.

The hissing continued.

Another hour passed and the end of his watch had almost arrived, when he saw the figure of one of the constables walking along the warmway towards him. Dik was frozen through, so he stood and waited gratefully for the other to reach him. But as the figure came nearer Dik saw that he was raising his arms and holding his rifle above his head.

He halted a short distance from Dik and shouted in a foreign accent, 'Please, not shoot! I give up, wish surrender!'

It was a young man of about his own age, the sleeves and legs of his protective clothing ripped and shredded by the razor wire. Dik stared at him in silent astonishment.

They were near one of the cisterns, and the hissing of gas was loud above the wind.

Dik himself could feel the bite of the freezing wind through the gashes in his tunic and trousers and as a floodlight switched on high above the wall he saw a huge stain of blood below his knee. He looked at the young soldier standing amazed before him, and said again, much louder this time, 'Please don't shoot. I'm surrendering.'

They were near one of the cisterns and the hissing of gas was loud above the wind.

The enemy soldier said, 'Here ... my rifle.'

Dik said, 'Take my rifle.'

As Dik passed him his, the young man handed over his own and raised his arms again.

'Cold,' the enemy soldier said. His goggles had iced over, and even in the brilliant wash of the floodlight Dik could not see his face. 'That way,' said Dik, pointing towards the distant guard post, and waving the muzzle of the captured rifle. 'This way,' said the young soldier, pointing to the guard post.

They walked on slowly in the wind and snow, Dik staring at the back of his enemy's caped head in admiration and envy.

44

Whores

•

At last I was granted the leave for which I had been waiting since the beginning of the year. I left the war behind me and travelled to a seaport on the temperate northern coast of the continent. Fifty days' sick leave lay ahead. My trouser pocket was heavy on my buttock with the wad of high-denomination back-pay notes. It should have been a time for convalescence after the long and agonizing spell of treatment in the military hospital, but even after so many weeks I had still been discharged too early and my mind continued to be affected by the enemy's synaesthetic gases. My perception was profoundly disturbed.

As the train clattered through the devastated terrain of the bleak, unnamed southern continent, I seemed to taste the music of pain, feel the gay dancing colours of sound. Amid these pre-occupations I knew only that I craved to be among the islands.

As I waited in the port for the ferry across to Luice, the closest island in the Dream Archipelago, I tried to understand and rationalize my delusions in the way the medical staff had trained me.

The brick-built terraced houses, which between perceptual lapses I knew were antique and beautiful, and which I saw glowed with the mellow pale brown of the local sandstone, became in my delusions synaesthetic monstrosities. They gave off a cynical laughter that tormented my thinking, they somehow emitted a deep throbbing sound that shook my chest cavity and weakened my knees, and their well-built walls were so cold to the touch that they chilled my heart like a shaft of tempered steel. The fishing boats in the harbour were less unpleasant to perceive: they were a gentle humming sound, barely audible. The army hostel, where I stayed overnight, was a warren of associative flavours and smells. The corridors tasted to me of coal dust, the walls were papered with hyacinth, the bedclothes enfolded me like a rancid mouth.

I slept poorly, waking many times from vivid, lucid dreams. One in particular had become a familiar nightmarish companion. I had experienced it every night since leaving the front line: I dreamt I was still with my unit in the trenches, advancing through the minefields, setting up a monitoring complex of some kind, a fantastically detailed and demanding technical task, then immediately dismantling it and retreating, again somehow finding a safe way through the mines, then returning to the same place, reconstructing the electronic equipment, dismantling it, repeatedly, endlessly.

In the morning my synaesthesia had receded once more, a sign I took to be encouraging. My periods of remission were becoming longer and closer together. During my last week in the military hospital I had suffered only one minor attack. For this reason they said they had cured me, which made the new outbreak doubly alarming. I wanted to be completely free of the effects, but no one knew if that would be possible. Thousands of other men were similarly afflicted.

I left the hostel and walked down to the harbour, soon finding the quay where the Luice ferry berthed. There was more than an hour and a half to wait, so I strolled pleasurably through the narrow streets around the harbour, noting that the town must be a major centre for the importation of war matériel. No one seemed to be concerned about who I was, and security was lax. I walked into one warehouse where I saw several stacks of crates containing hallucinogenic grenades and neural dissociation gases.

The day was hot and sultry, a tantalizing foretaste of the tropical climate of the islands I was about to surrender myself to. Everyone around me said the weather was unseasonal, that an unexpected area of high pressure had settled inland, pulling down the soft warm airs from the tropical sea to the north. The townspeople were obviously relishing the novelty: windows and doors were wide open, and the harbourside cafés had placed tables and chairs outside for their customers and were enjoying a healthy trade.

I stood with a large crowd on the quay, waiting to board the ferry. It was an old, diesel-stinking boat, apparently top heavy, riding high in the water. As I stepped across to the deck I experienced a wholly normal kind of synaesthetic response: the smell of the hot oil, salt-stiff ropes and sun-dried deck planking summoned a strong and nostalgic memory of a childhood voyage along the coast of my own country. The experience of being gassed by the enemy had taught me how to recognize the response from my sensations and within moments I was able to recall in great detail my thoughts, actions, hopes and intentions of that time, so long ago.

There was a delay and an argument when I came to pay for my ticket. The army money was acceptable but the banknotes were too high in value. Smaller tender had to be found for change, and the disgruntled ferryman made me wait for it. By the time I was free to explore the ancient boat it had long since embarked, and we were a great distance out to sea. The coast of the war-torn continent I had left was a black, undulating outline across the southern horizon. Sea-birds wheeled in our wake. The decks throbbed with the vibration from the engine. Ahead were the islands.

I was returning at last to the Dream Archipelago, landscape of my childhood imaginings. In the days of mental torment in the hospital, when food had seemed to shout abuse at me, and light sang discordant melodies for my eyes, and my mouth would only utter pain and hurt, a consolation lay in my remembered dreams of the islands. In reality I had been through the Archipelago only once, aboard the troop carrier on my way to war, and had then only glimpsed from afar the verdant islands in their sapphire sea. Their remoteness had been like a taunt. I urged to return to them, as others around me also urged.

'You must go to Salay,' a rehabilitation orderly said to me

47

while I lay recovering, over and over. 'I was on Salay once, and have never forgotten what happened to me there.'

'Tell me about it! What happened to you there?'

'No ... I cannot describe it. You have to go yourself. Or try Muriseay, the biggest island. I know someone who was posted there, guarding the neutrality of the Dream Archipelago, or that's what they told him. That wasn't what happened at all. Or Paneron. Have you heard about the women on Paneron, and what they do to you?'

'Why are you tantalizing me?'

'You're going to the islands when you leave here, aren't you?'

'Yes.'

'Then you should know.'

But I knew nothing then. On the ferry heading towards Luice, I did think about the women on Paneron. I knew we were passing nowhere near Paneron. It was somewhere beyond the equator in the northern part of the Archipelago. I studied the chart of the Midway Sea on the wall in the main saloon, trying to locate the other islands I had been told about. There was Salay, there were the Serques, there was the Ferredy Atoll, Paneron far away by the Aubrac Chain, the Ganntens, the great chain of reefs and skerries known as the Swirl. And there was Winho, where a nurse called Slenje had once told me she was from. Because of Slenje, I had many times thought about travelling to Winho. How far could I go in the Archipelago, how many islands could I visit, in the mere forty-nine days that remained? Paneron or Winho, the Aubracs or Muriseay?

I found a seat on the bow deck and mused about women, a subject that now I was away from hospital was never far from my mind. There were dozens of women travelling on the boat with me, and I could see many from where I was sitting. A part of me longed to have them all. There was one sitting opposite me, leaning against the white-painted side of the boat and stretching out her bare legs in the sunshine. I had been idly appraising her, wondering if she really was as pretty as I thought or if I only thought that because it was so long since I had been amongst civilians. She noticed I was looking at her and she returned my stare, forthrightly looking at me with invitation hinted at in her eyes. It was so long, so long ago. She was the first woman I had really looked at, the first I had singled out from the crowd. I turned away from her, wanting to choose, not to rush at the first woman I saw, nor to accept the first who stared back at me.

She made me think again of Slenje. I decided to try to find Slenje.

Slenje had nursed me for a time in the hospital. It was then that she had told me about Winho, her home island. While I lay in my hospital bed, the bewildering images chasing through my mind, Slenje sat beside me for several nights and spoke about her life. She described the sea, the reefs, the shallow lagoons, the towering range of thickly forested mountains, the little towns built on the fertile plains between the mountains and the lagoons. In my torments, the fevered attacks of synaesthesia, Slenje's presence had been balm to my agony: she spoke like musk, laughed with the texture of spring water and made me love with feelings of deep vermilion. She talked endlessly to me, knowing that I could not reply and perhaps thinking that I might not even hear. In fact I heard everything she said. She told me of her life at home, of her mother dying when she was little, her beleaguered father moving to find work on another island, leaving her and her sisters to stay with a neighbour, other children in the strange house, other girls, the endless grind of poverty. Then the Faiandland troops passing through and the poverty deepening. The realization came to Slenje, but reluctantly, that there was always one infallible way for young women to make quick and easy money from an army. We became whores, she said, laughing with a sound of glass shattering and falling around me. All the girls she knew. I ducked away, clenching my eyes tightly closed, waiting for her to tell me that the troops had moved on. They did leave Winho at last, moving on south and away from the Archipelago, and most of the whores ceased to be whores. Slenje grew up, she said, milk flowing from her lips. She wanted something better for herself so she moved to another island where she could train to become

49

a nurse. She travelled south and there she was at last beside my bed, talking into the nights. But one night Slenje was there beside me no more and another nurse took her place. Later I found out that there had been some kind of trouble on Winho, and Slenje had returned home suddenly.

I looked again on the chart for Winho, noticing only now and for the first time that it was within the area of the Archipelago marked as still under military occupation. Luice too, which was only three islands away from Winho. How could that be, since the Dream Archipelago was widely thought to have been demilitarized? The chart was dated two years earlier. I knew that in the constantly changing fortunes of war nothing remained the same for long. I had to go there to find out.

Three days later I was on Winho and I heard the news I least wanted to hear. Slenje was dead.

Winho had already been occupied once by the Faiandlanders, but our troops had fought their way in and liberated the island. Under the terms of the Covenant of Neutrality we had withdrawn afterwards, but Faiandland had moved in a second time, illegally. Now we were back in control yet again but this time we had placed small town garrisons across the island, intending to maintain the peace. It was during the second round of fighting that Slenje had left the hospital where I was, but soon after she arrived home, and along with many other civilians, she became a casualty of the fighting.

Even so I became obsessed with finding her, needing to be convinced that she had really died. For two more days I paced about the streets of the town, searching for her and enquiring about her. She was well known and well remembered, but the answer was the same: Slenje the nurse was dead, was dead.

On the second day I suffered yet another attack of synaesthesia. The pastel-coloured cottages, the lush vegetation and the streets of dried mud became a nightmare of beguiling smells and flavours, terrifying sounds and bizarre textures. I stood for an hour in the main street of the town, convinced that Slenje had been swallowed: the houses ached like decaying teeth, the road was yielding and hairy like the surface of a tongue, the tropical flowers and trees were like half-chewed food and the warm wind that came in from the sea was like foetid breath.

When the attack had run its course I drank two large glasses of iced beer in a local bar, then went to the garrison and found a junior officer of my own rank.

'You'll suffer from it all your life,' the lieutenant said.

'The synaesthesia?'

'You ought to be invalided out of the army. Once you lose your judgment ...'

'Don't you think I've tried?' I said. 'All they would let me have is sick leave.'

'You're more of a danger to your own company than to the enemy.'

'I know it,' I said, with bitterness.

We were walking through the enclosed inner ward of the castle where the company of soldiers was garrisoned. It was suffocatingly hot in the sun, for no breath of wind could reach down into the deep yard. The castle battlements were being patrolled by young soldiers in dark blue uniforms, who paced slowly to and fro, ever alert for a return of the enemy. These guards wore full battledress, including the recently introduced gas-proof hoods that covered their heads, faces and shoulders.

'I'm looking for a woman,' I said.

'There are plenty in the town. You want any woman, or someone in particular?'

'A particular woman,' I said. 'She was a nurse, but before that she worked as a whore. The local people say she was killed.'

'They're probably right.'

'I wondered if there was anywhere that kept the records of casualties.'

'Not us. Maybe the civil authorities. You could ask.' We had strolled up to one of the battlements, and now were staring out across the roofs of the town, towards the silver, sun-dazzling

51

sea. 'If you want a woman it's not difficult to find another. You know how to look. Or use one of the ones we have here. We keep twenty whores in the garrison. Medically certificated, nice-looking women. Keep away from the local women.'

'Because of disease?' I said.

'In a sense. They're all off-limits. No loss.'

'Tell me about it.'

The lieutenant said, 'We're fighting a war. The town is full of enemy infiltrators.'

I glanced at him and noted his bland, non-committal expression as he said this.

'That sounds like official policy from section HQ,' I said. 'What's the truth?'

'No different.'

We continued our walk around the fort and I decided not to leave until I heard a fuller explanation. The lieutenant spoke about the part he had played in the Dream Archipelago campaign and how he had twice been involved in liberating this island. It became obvious that he hated the place. He warned me about the ease with which you could pick up tropical infections, be bitten by large insects, undergo abuse or threats from the populace, suffer through the endless heat of the days and the humidity of the tropical nights. I listened with simulated interest. He told me about some of the atrocities carried out by the Faiandlanders while they occupied the island and I listened with real interest.

'They performed experiments here,' the lieutenant said. 'Not with the synaesthetics. Something else. We never found out what. Their laboratories have been dismantled.'

'By the army?'

'No, civilian scientists appointed by staff officers. It was almost the first thing they did after we landed. The town was closed to all troops, then afterwards we found out there had been some kind of scare.'

'And what did happen to the women?'

'The local people have been infiltrated,' the lieutenant said, and although we paced together about the sun-hot ward for another hour I learned no more. As I left the castle one of the black-hooded guards on the battlements fainted from the heat, and collapsed against the high rampart.

Night was falling as I went back into the centre of Winho Town. Many of the townspeople were walking slowly through the streets. Now that I had abandoned my search for Slenje, finally accepting that she was dead, I was able to see with a new clarity and I observed the town more objectively than before. The tropical evening was still and humid, with no trace of a breeze, but the oppressive heat could not by itself explain the way people were moving about. Everyone I saw walked slowly and painfully, shuffling along as if lamed. The hot darkness seemed to amplify sounds: there was the sound of cranes and ships from the harbour, distant engines, a strain of melancholy music from an open window, insects rasping high in the trees, but the only sound made by the huge crowd was the painful shuffling of their feet.

While I waited in the street I reflected that in this stage of my recovery I had ceased to be frightened of the hallucinations brought on by the synaesthesia. It no longer seemed odd to me that certain kinds of music should be visualized as strands of coloured lights, that I should be capable of imagining the circuitry of the army monitoring equipment in terms of geometric shapes, that words should have palpable textures, such as furry or metallic, that strangers should exude emotional colouring or hostility without even glancing in my direction.

A small boy ran across the street and darted behind a tree. He stared towards me from behind it. A tiny stranger: he emanated none of the nervousness his manner indicated, but playfulness and curiosity.

At last he came out and walked across to me, staring frankly at me.

'Are you the man who was asking about Slenje?' he said, scratching his groin.

'Yes,' I said, and instantly the child ran away. He was the only quick movement in the street.

A few minutes passed and I continued to stand in my place. I saw the boy again, running back across the street, zigzagging through the shuffling people. He ran towards a house, then vanished inside. A little while later two young women came slowly down the street, their arms linked. They walked directly to me. Neither of them was Slenje, but then I had not hoped.

One of them said, 'It will cost you fifty.'

'That's all right.'

As she spoke I caught a glimpse of her teeth. Several appeared to be broken, giving her a sinister, demoniac appearance. She had long dark hair which looked unwashed, and she was plump. I looked at the other woman, who was short, with pale brown hair.

'I'll take you,' I said to her.

'It's still fifty,' said the first one.

'I know.'

The young woman with the broken teeth kissed the other on both cheeks, then shuffled away. I followed the second woman as she headed down the street in the direction of the harbour.

I said, 'What's your name?'

'Does it matter?' It was the first time she had spoken to me.

'No, it doesn't matter,' I said. 'Did you know Slenje?'

'Of course. She was my sister.'

'Literally your sister?'

'She was a whore. All whores are sisters.'

We passed along the quay, then turned into another more steeply sloping side street leading away from the harbour. No wheeled vehicles would ever come along this road because at intervals the gradient was so steep the surface had been fashioned into steps. The street stank of dog droppings. The young woman climbed slowly, pausing at each of the steps. She was breathing heavily in the warm air. I offered to take her arm but she snatched it away from my hand. She was not hostile, though, but proud, because she gave me a quick smile a moment later.

As we stopped at the unpainted door of a tall house she said, 'My name is Elva.'

54

She opened the door and stepped inside.

I was about to follow her when I noticed that a numeral had been painted crudely on the bare wood of the door: 14. It caught my attention because ever since my illness I had developed distinct colour associations with numerals. The number 14 had a firm synaesthetic association with pale blue, but the number on the door was painted in a yellowish white. For some reason it disconcerted me and as I looked at it the painted number seemed to change from white to blue, to white again. I knew then that another attack was beginning. Anticipating the worst I stepped quickly into the house behind the young woman and closed the door behind me, as if putting the numeral out of my sight would put off the attack.

It seemed to do the trick. As the woman switched on the light my mind cleared and the synaesthetic attack faded. I recoiled from the disturbing images but they were now a part of me. I followed Elva up a flight of uncarpeted stairs (she went slowly, placing one foot beside the other on each step) and I remembered the waves of vermilion arousal Slenje had inadvertently awakened in me as I lay helpless in the hospital. I tried perversely to will the attack to return, or continue, as if the synaesthesia would add an extra dimension to the act of sex.

We came to a small bedroom which was entered through a door by the top of the stairs. Although the room was close and airless in the heat it was tidy and smelt faintly of furniture polishing materials. It was a lit by a single light bulb, glaring harshly in the white-painted room.

Elva said, 'I want the fifty now.'

It was the first time she had faced me as she spoke and in doing so she revealed her teeth. Like those of the dark-haired woman, Elva's teeth were broken and jagged. I recoiled inwardly from the sight, this sudden fastidiousness making me feel uncertain of what I had been wanting or expecting from her, other than the obvious. Elva must have noticed my reaction, because she raised her face more directly towards me and smiled in such a way as to make a humourless rictus that pulled back her lips from her teeth:

55

I saw then that they were not broken by decay or by neglect, but that each tooth, upper and lower, had been filed down to a triangular, sharply pointed section.

She said, 'The Faiandlanders did it.'

'Just to you? And your sister?'

'To all whores.'

'And Slenje?'

'No, Slenje they killed.'

I could not think what to say so I reached into my back pocket and took out my wad of banknotes. Most of the money was still in the high denomination notes I had been given when I left the hospital.

'I only have a hundred,' I said after searching through the notes, holding it out to her and returning the rest to my pocket.

'I have change,' she said. 'Women who work always have coins.'

She took the note from me and opened a shallow drawer. She searched through it and while her back was turned I stared appraisingly at her body. In spite of what had been done to her legs, which made her move and walk like an old person, she must still have been in her early twenties. Her back was slender and her backside curved appealingly under her thin clothes. I felt sorry for her, because of what she had suffered, but I also felt the first surges of sexual energy.

At last she turned and showed me five silver ten-piece coins. She placed them in a neat pile on the top of the dresser.

I said to her, 'Elva, you can keep the money. I think I will leave.'

I was shamed by the state she was in, ashamed of the intentions I had for her.

Her only reply was to lean down by the side of the bed and throw the switch of a power-point attached to the base of the wall. An electric fan whirred round, sending a welcome draught through the stuffy room. As she straightened, the stream of air momentarily pressed the flimsy fabric of her blouse across her breasts, and I saw her dark nipples were erect.

She began to undo the buttons of her blouse.

'Elva, I cannot stay with you.'

She paused then, her blouse now fully open with the sides hanging loosely across her breasts.

'You don't like me? What did you want?'

Before I could answer, before I had to produce lame words in reply, we both heard a thud coming suddenly from near at hand, followed by a childish cry of pain. Elva turned away from me at once and went to a door on the far side of the room. She went through, leaving it open behind her.

I saw that beyond the door there was another room, small and dark, insects whining in the stuffy air, and in it was a tiny cot made of wicker. A child had fallen from the cot and lay on the floor crying, an arm curled under its chest. Elva picked up the child, and swiftly pulled the diaper from its loins. She dropped the soggy fabric on the floor. She held the little boy against her, cradling his head and trying to soothe him. For several minutes the boy was inconsolable, his face red with crying, tears and saliva glossing his little face. Elva kissed him again and again.

I realized that the boy, in falling from the cot, must have landed on his hand. When Elva took the little clenched fist in her fingers he screamed with extra pain. Elva kissed the hand.

She kissed the fingers and she kissed the palm, and she kissed the tiny, puffy wrist.

Elva opened her mouth and some trick of the bright light in the main bedroom made her white filed teeth shine out momentarily. She brought the little boy's hand up to her lips and took the fingers into her mouth, sucking and working her lips forward until at last the whole hand was inside her mouth. All the while she caressed his arm, making tender, soothing noises in her throat.

At last the little boy stopped crying, and his eyes finally closed. With one hand she smoothed the covers in the cot, then leaned over and laid him carefully on the mattress. With deft movements she wiped him clean with a small cloth, then slipped a fresh diaper on him. She tucked the single cover under the mattress. Her naked breasts swung maternally over his head.

She pulled the two sides of her blouse together as she straightened, then she walked back into the room where I was still standing. She closed the door behind her.

Before I could say another word Elva pointed at the belt of my trousers and with a swift motion of her hand indicated that I should start undressing.

'The child ...' I said.

'The child has to be fed. To feed him I work.'

She pulled the blouse off and dropped it on the floor, then slipped out of her skirt. When she was naked she sat on the bed, leaning back against the pillow with one knee raised, so that I should see all of her. I undressed rapidly and lay beside her on the bed. We began foreplay at once. Elva kissed me passionately as we roused, and I tentatively explored her mouth with my tongue. The edges and points of her serrated teeth were sharply dangerous and she made play with her mouth, pretending to savage me. Soon tiny weals were appearing on my arms, my chest, as she snarled in her throat and lightly dragged her teeth across my flesh, my tongue, my lips.

She bit me, though, with the same great tenderness she had shown to her child.

When we had finished the act of lovemaking she began to cry and lay beside me in the bed with her back to me. I stroked her hair and shoulders, again thinking about leaving. I was embarrassed by being there; I had not often been with whores. Our union had been brief, but for me, after months of forced abstinence, it was satisfying enough. There had not been the vermilion passion that Slenje's words stirred up in my mind, but Elva was an expert and exciting lover. I lay tensely but with my eyes closed, wondering if I should ever see her again once I had left.

From the next room there came a quiet whimpering noise, and Elva moved away from the bed at once and opened the interconnecting door. She peered at her baby but apparently the little boy had only stirred in his sleep. She closed the door again. She returned to the bed, where I was already sitting up, preparing to put on my clothes.

'Don't leave yet,' she said.

'I've had my time with you,' I said.

'You were not here for time,' she said, and pushed me with both hands flat against my chest. I allowed myself to fall back across the mattress. 'You paid for what you wanted, and what you have had. Now this is what I want for myself.'

She crawled on me in mock ferocity and straddled me, kissing my neck and chest, again running her frightening teeth across my skin. She licked the weals she had raised earlier, then created some more. I tingled with pain, with the anticipation of more. Her lovely body pressed against me in many exciting and erotic ways.

I was quickly aroused again and tried to roll her over on the bed beside me, but she stayed above me. She went on kissing and sucking at my skin, teasing me with her pin-sharp teeth. Her head moved lower, across my stomach.

It seemed to me, as her mouth at last found my rigid organ and took it deep inside, that there was a sense of lemon pleasure, and the liquid, sucking sounds of her mouth became like a hot pool of stagnant voices, endlessly circling ...

I was in terror of the synaesthetics, knowing that I became unable to tell reality from falsity. I had a vision of Elva's mouth, lined with tiny knife blades, closing around me, slicing into me. Her tongue, eagerly licking and stroking my shaft, had the consistency of mercury. I looked down at her: I saw her bobbing head, her hair tangled and strewn across my stomach, and in my synaesthetic torment I visualized her as some monstrous animal, chewing into my gut. Struggling against the madness of my visions I reached down with my hand and laid it on the back of her neck. Her hair fell slinkily across my hand, like the shaggy fur of an immense animal, but I stroked her, feeling the shape of her head and neck, concentrating on the reality of her.

And soon reality returned. She was sucking me with the greatest of gentleness. I remembered the tender way she had mouthed the hurting hand of the little boy, the light touch of those deadly teeth as she played them across my chest. I began to love her in a way and watched as she moved back a little, lifting her head so that I could see what she was doing. Her lips were around the end of my shaft, her cheeks concave as she sucked so steadily. I could feel her lightly gripping me with her pointed teeth, holding my glans across her quivering tongue. As she looked up towards me I climaxed violently and happily.

I said, when I had dressed, 'You must take the whole hundred.'

'We agreed fifty.'

'Not for that, Elva.'

She was lying where I had left her, face down on the bed, her head turned so that she could watch me. Her hair was blowing in the cool stream of air from the electric fan. I noticed that the skin on the back of her legs had been damaged in some way. There was a pattern of recent scars high on each thigh, and on the soft skin across the joint behind her knees.

'You paid for once. We agreed the price.'

'You need the money,' I said.

'I wanted you again,' she said. 'No charge.'

I looked at the five silver coins, lying where she had placed them on the top of the dresser.

'I'll leave them there anyway,' I said. 'Buy something for the boy.'

But she sat up at once, then levered herself upright with a stiff movement. Her pale skin was faintly blotched with pink from where she had lain. She took the five coins and slipped them into the breast pocket of my shirt.

'Fifty.'

That had to be the end of it.

I heard the sound of her child again, waking in the next room. Elva glanced briefly in that direction.

'You don't have to leave,' she said. 'I have to feed him, then maybe ...'

'Who is the boy's father?'

60

'My husband.'

'Where is he?' I said.

'The whores took him.'

'Whores?'

'The Faiandlanders. They took him when they left, the fucking bitches.'

She told me that there had been sixteen hundred troops in Winho Town during the second occupation, all of them women. Every man in the town had been taken into custody by them. When our troops relieved the town the men had been taken away as the enemy withdrew. Only males who were extremely old, or pre-pubertal boys, were left behind.

'Do you suppose your husband is still alive?' I said.

'I think he is. There have been no reports of massacres and there are known to be prisoners. But how would I know otherwise? Anything could have happened.'

She was sitting, naked still, on the edge of her bed. I expected her to cry again but her face had a hard, resistant expression and her eyes were dry.

The child had started to cry in the next room.

'Why do you want me to stay?' I said. 'Are you frightened of something?'

She opened her mouth wide, laid one of her fingers on her tongue. Her teeth held back, like the cutting edges of saws. She rubbed her finger to and fro on her tongue, then pretended to suck on it.

'You like that?' she said.

'Well, of course.'

'Stay with me,' she said. 'I like you.'

I stood there facing her for a few moments, torn between my conscious wish to escape from the tragic young woman's life, and a deeper sense that I should stay and protest falsely that she had been more than a way of passing time. I would then have to try to help in some way.

'I don't know,' I said helplessly.

'Then go. That means you have decided what you want to do.'

I had.

'Shall I come again?' I said.

'If you wish to. It will be fifty every time. No extras.'

She turned away from me. She put on a long shift-like garment, pushed one foot into a slipper and searched around for the other, peering down at the floor. I opened the door, and a few moments later I was standing in the scumbered street that ran steeply outside her house.

The next morning I learnt that one of the infrequent ferries would be calling at Winho Town before midday and I decided to leave the island. While I was waiting for the boat to arrive I walked slowly through the narrow streets of the town, wondering if I would see Elva.

It was hot and humid again, so I undid the buttons at the front of my shirt to let some air in and try to stay cool. It was then I noticed that a tracery of fine scratches had appeared on my chest and I remembered the way Elva had teased me with her sharpened teeth. I touched one of the longer scratches. There was no pain to speak of but the weal was now a much brighter red than before. I wondered if some kind of infection had set in. As I walked along I kept my eye open for a pharmacy, thinking it might be sensible to buy some antiseptic cream.

The town, languid under the pressure of the windless heat, felt moist and soft, and the air around me was like the intimate embrace of female flesh. I felt I was suffocating and as I walked along I repeatedly turned my head to and fro, trying to gulp in some oxygen. It was only when I reached the harbour and stood on the pier where the ferry was expected that I realized I was suffering yet another synaesthetic attack. It seemed to be a mild one. With the consolation of having identified the problem I immediately felt a little better.

I paced up and down the pier, trying to detect the real substance of the hard concrete surface through the rubbery, imprecise texture that my distorted sensations were lending it. My mouth and throat were sore, tasting synaesthetically scarlet, my back and legs were stiff and my genitals were hurting as if trapped in a vice. The feeling of physical agony was so real that I thought again that I should go and search for a pharmacist, or even a doctor, but I did not want to miss the ferry.

Glancing down, I saw that several of the scratches on my chest were beginning to open. Blood was smearing where my unbuttoned shirt flapped against me.

At last the ferry hove into sight. After it had docked I walked the short distance to its berth with the other passengers. Knowing I should have to pay a fare again, I reached for the notes in my back pocket but then remembered the repeated difficulties I had been having with the high-value notes. I still had the five silver coins that Elva had given me and I reached into the breast pocket of my shirt.

Something soft and warm wrapped itself about my two searching fingers, and I snatched them out at once.

There was a hand gripping my fingers!

It was a small, perfect hand. A child's hand. It was pink in the bright daylight, severed at the wrist.

I stepped back, shaking my hand in wild horror.

The child's hand gripped me more tightly.

I let out a cry of fright and swung my arm frantically, trying to throw off the little hand, but when I looked again it was still there. I turned away from the throng of other waiting passengers on the quayside and took hold of it with my free hand, trying to wrench it away. I pulled and pulled, perspiring with horror and anxiety, but nothing I could do would make it relax its hold. I could see the effect of the tight grip on itself: the tiny knuckles were white with tension and the ends of the fingers, around the minute nails, were bright red. The two fingers it was gripping were beginning to throb, so great was the pressure on them.

No one on the quayside was taking any notice of me, because there was much confusion caused by the arrival of the disembarking passengers. Everyone was trying to get on and off the boat at once and people were shoving each other in the crowd. I had moved to the edge of the mêlée, obsessed with the horror of what was happening to me. I stared round in anguish, feeling I should never be released from the nightmare of the child's severed hand.

I made one more attempt to free myself by pulling with my other hand, but then resorted to desperate measures. I put my trapped fingers on the concrete surface of the quay and pressed down on the child's hand with my boot. I leaned forward, putting on as much weight as possible. The child's hand tightened more. I shifted position, raised my foot, stamped down. As agony coursed through me the child's hand relaxed a little, and I snatched my fingers away.

Suddenly I was free, and I jumped back.

The child's hand lay on the quay, the little fingers still tightly clenched into a fist.

Then the fingers opened, and the hand began to crawl quickly towards me, like a bloated pink spider.

I dashed forward and brought my boot down on it with all my weight. I stamped again, then again, and again …

The large banknote caused another argument on the ferry, and to bring it to a swift end I let the ferryman keep it without paying me change. I was in no condition to argue. I was shaking convulsively and the scarlet pains in my throat and mouth, and the larger searing agonies of my chest and genitals, were growing worse with every minute. I was almost unable to speak.

When the business of the fare had been settled I went to the stern of the ferry and sat alone, trembling and frightened. The voyage was already under way and we had passed through the concrete arms of the harbour walls. Behind me the angular shapes of Winho's mountain range stood darkly against the sky, a silent valediction. The sea was calm. When I looked to the side of the boat, away from the white turmoil of the wake, I could see the rays of sunlight shafting down through the green depths.

I had no idea where the boat was taking me.

My shirt was stained with blood in several places and I took it off. I felt on the outside of the breast pocket to see if the coins were still inside. I was terrified of slipping my fingers into it once again. I could not feel the coins. I held the pocket upside down over the deck of the boat, but nothing fell out.

As the ferry moved further out to sea, and Winho became distant behind us, I sat bare-chested in the glaring sunshine, watching one scratch after another ooze blood down my chest. At intervals I used my shirt to clean myself up a little. I dared not try to speak to anyone because my mouth was an open pit of pain. I could feel streams of blood slipping down through the unshaved bristles on my chin. When I used the lavatory I discovered that my groin was a mess of gore and blood.

Back on the deck, as I crouched in agony, the other passengers stayed away from me.

The boat went from one island to the next, making brief stops at each port, but I did not leave it until night was about to fall. By this time we had reached the island of Salay and I went ashore. That night I slept in the local garrison, having to share a room with sixteen other officers, more than half of whom were women. My dreams were rich and textured with agony, and lurid colours, and an uncontrollable and unfulfilled sexual desire. Images of Elva's mouth haunted me. I awoke in the morning with what I thought was an erection, but instead the sheets of the bed were stiff with the blood from my wounds.

The
Trace of Him

•

The study was lodged high beneath the eaves of the house, and it was imbued with traces of him. It had not changed much in the twenty years since she was last there – it was more untidy, a mess of papers and books, standing on, lying beside, heaped below the two tables and a desk. It was almost impossible to walk across the floor without stepping on his work. The room was otherwise much as she remembered it. The window was still uncurtained, the walls unseeable behind the crowded bookcases. His narrow divan bed stood in one corner, now bare of everything except the mattress, although she had never forgotten the tangle of blankets she had left behind when she was here before.

The intimacy of the room was a shock to her. For so long his study had been a memory, a hidden joyful secret, but now it had become tragic, bereft of him. She could detect the scent of his clothes, his books, his leather document case, the old frayed carpet. His presence could be felt in every darkened corner, in the two squares of bright sunlight on the floor, in the dust on the bookshelves and on the volumes that stood there in untidy leaning lines, in the sticky ochre grime on the window panes, the yellowed papers, the dried careless spills of ink.

She gulped in the air he had breathed, paralysed by sudden grief. It was incomprehensibly more intense than the shock she had felt on receiving the news of his illness, his imminent death. She knew she was rocking to and fro, her back muscles rigid beneath the stiff fabric of her black dress. She was dazed by the loss of him.

Trying to break out of the grief she went to his oaken lectern, where he had always stood to write, his tall shape leaning in an idiosyncratic way as his right hand scraped the pen across the sheets of his writing pad. There was a famous portrait of him in that stance – it had been painted before she met him, but it captured the essence of him so well that she had later bought a small reproduction of it.

Where his left hand habitually rested on the side, the invariable black-papered cheroot smouldering between his curled knuckles, was a darker patch, a stain of old perspiration on the polish. She ran her fingertips across the wooden surface, recalling a particular half-hour of that precious day, when he had turned his back on her while he stood at this lectern, absorbed suddenly by a thought.

That memory of him had haunted her as she set out on her desperate quest to reach him before he died. The family had delayed too long in telling her of the illness, perhaps by choice – a second message she received *en route*, while waiting on an island, had broken the final news to her. She had travelled across a huge segment of the Dream Archipelago with the unchanging mental image of his long back, his inclined head, his intent eyes, the quiet sound of his pen and the tobacco smoke curling around his hair.

Downstairs the mourners were gathering, awaiting the summons to the church.

She had arrived later than most of the others, after four anxious days of hurriedly arranged travel to this island of Piqay. It was so long since she had made the journey across the Archipelago. She had forgotten how many ports of call there were on the way, how many lengthy delays could be caused by other passengers, by the loading and unloading of cargo. At first the islands charmed her again with their variety of colours, terrains and moods. Their names had memories for her from her last journey, all those years ago: Lillen-cay, Ia, Junno, Olldus Precipitus, but they were reminders of breathless anticipation on the voyage out or of quiet thoughts on the journey home, not actual recollections of events or experiences ashore.

The remembered charm soon faded. After the first day on the ship the islands simply seemed to be in her way. The boat sailed slowly across the calm straits between islands. Sometimes she stood at the rail, watching the arrowing wake spreading out from the sides of the vessel, but it soon came to be an illusion of movement. Whenever she looked up from the white churning wake, whichever island they happened to be passing still seemed to be in exactly the same relative position as before, across the narrows. Only the sea-birds moved, soaring and diving around the superstructure, and at the stern, but even they went nowhere that the ship did not.

At the port on Junno she left the ship, trying to see if there was a quicker passage available. After an hour of frustrated enquiries in the harbour offices she returned to the ship on which she had arrived, where the protracted unloading of timber was still going on. The next day, on Muriseay, she managed to find a flight with a private aero club: it was only a short hop by air but it saved visits to the ports of three intervening islands. Afterwards, most of the time she saved had slipped away, while she was forced to wait for the next ferry.

At last she arrived on Piqay, but according to the schedule of funeral arrangements that arrived with the news of his death, there was only an hour to spare. To her surprise, the family had arranged for a car to meet her at the quay. A man in a dark suit stood by the harbour entrance, holding a large white card with her name written in capitals. As the driver steered the car swiftly away from Piqay Port and headed into the shallow hills surrounding the town and its estuary, she felt the commonplace anxieties of travel slipping away, to be replaced at last by the complex of emotions that had been kept at a distance while she fretted on ships.

Now they returned to her in force. Fear of the family she had never met. Apprehension about what they might have been told about her, or what they might not. Worse, what they intended for her now, the lover whose existence might undermine his reputation, were she to become known to the public. The bottomless grief still sucking her down as it had done from the moment she heard the news about his illness, then latterly his death. Defiant pride in the past. The untouchable sense of loneliness, of being left only with memories. The hopes, the endless hopes that something might yet live for her. And the confusion about why the family had sent the messages to her. Were they motivated by concern for her, by spite at her, or by just the dutiful acts of a bereaved family? Or perhaps, and this was what she clasped to herself, he had remembered her and had made the request himself?

But above all these, that endless grief, the loss, the feeling of final abandonment. Those twenty years without him, holding on to an inexpressible hope, and now the rest of the years to come, finally, absolutely without him.

The driver said nothing. He drove efficiently. After her four days aboard ships, with engines and generators constantly running, the bulkheads vibrating, the car's engine felt smooth and almost silent. She looked out of the dark-tinted window by her side, staring at the vineyards as the car sped along the lanes, glancing at the pastures, at the rocky defiles in the distance, at the patches of bare sandy soil by the roadside. She must have seen these the last time, but she had no memory of them. That visit was a blur of impressions, but at the centre were the few hours she had spent alone with him, brilliant and clear, defined for ever.

She thought only of him, that time. That one time.

Then, the house. A huge crowd at the gates, pushing aside to make a way for her car. People stared curiously. One woman waved, leaning forward to try to see her. The gates opened to an electronic signal from the dashboard of the car. They closed behind, as the car moved at a more stately pace up the drive. Mature trees in the park, mountains behind, glimpses of the cerulean sea and dark islands, far away. Her eyes remained dry, but she found it painful to look around at a view she had once thought she would never forget.

On arrival she stood silently with the other mourners, knowing no one, feeling their silent disdain. Her suitcase stood on the floor outside the room. She moved away from the cluster of people and went to an inner door, from which she could see across the main hall towards the wide staircase.

An elderly man detached himself from the group and followed her. He glanced up the stairs.

'We know who you are, of course,' he said, his voice unsteady. His eyelids fluttered with apparent distaste, and he never looked directly at her. She was struck by a facial similarity. Surely not old enough to be his father? There was a brother, probably the right sort of age, but he had said they were alienated. Years ago. 'He left clear instructions for us to pass on to you,' the man said. 'You are free go up to his room if you wish, but you must not remove anything.'

So she had made her escape, went quietly and alone up the staircase to this room beneath the eaves. But now she was trembling.

A faint blue haze remained drifting in the room, a vestige of his life. This room must have been empty for several days, yet the light mist of the air he had breathed remained.

With a sudden flowing of renewed unhappiness, she remembered the only time she had lain with him, curled up naked on the bed beside him, glowing with excitement and contentment, while he sucked in the acrid smoke of the cheroots and exhaled it in a thin swirling cone of blueness. That was the same bed, the one in the corner, the narrow cot with the bare mattress. She dared not go near it now.

Five of the cheroots, probably the last ones he ever bought, lay in an untidy scrambled pile on a corner of one of the tables. There was no sign of a packet. She picked one up, slid it beneath her nostrils, sensing the fragrance of the tobacco and thinking about the time she had shared one with him, relishing the damp-ness of his saliva transferred to her lips. A delirious exhilaration moved through her, and for a moment her eyes lost focus on the details of the room.

He had never travelled away from the island during his lifetime, even after the prizes and honours began to be bestowed. While she lay naked in his arms, exulting inwardly over the touch of his fingers as they rested on her breast, he tried to explain his attachment to Piqay, why he could never leave to be with her. It was an island of traces, he said, shadows that followed you, a psychic spoor that you left behind if you departed the island, but if you did you would become diffuse in some way that he could not explain. He would never be able to return, he said. He dared not try, because to do so might mean he would lose the trace that defined him to Piqay. For him, the urgency to leave was less powerful than the urgency of staying. She, feeling a different and less mystical urge, quietened him by caressing him, and soon they were making love again.

She would never forget that one day they had spent alone together, but afterwards, in the years of silence that followed, she had never been sure if he even remembered her.

Too late she had had the answer, when the messages arrived. Twenty years, four days.

She heard large cars moving slowly on the gravel drive outside the house, and one by one their engines cut out.

The blue haze was thicker now. She turned away from the lectern, aroused by her memories, but despairing because memories were all they could ever be. As she looked away from the dazzle of the window it seemed to her that the blue air was denser in the centre of the room. It had substance, texture.

She moved her face towards it, her lips puckering. The haze swirled about her, and she darted her face to and fro, trying to detect some response from it. Streaks in the old residue of smoke, denser patches, coalesced before her eyes. She stepped back to see them better, then forward again to press her face against them. Smoke stung against her eyes, and tears welled up.

The swirls took shape before her, making a ghostly impression of his face. It was the face as she remembered it from two decades before, not the one the public knew, the famous grizzled countenance of the great man. No time had passed for her, nor for the trace he had left. There were no features painted in the smoke, just the shape of his head and face moulded in the blue,

71

like a mask, but intimately detailed. Lips, hair, eyes, all had their shapes, contoured by the smoke.

Her breath halted momentarily. Panic and adoration seized her.

His head was tilted slightly to one side, his eyes were half closed, his lips were apart. She leaned forward to take her kiss, felt the light pressure of the smoky lips, the brush of ghostly eyelashes. It lasted only an instant.

His face, his mask, contorted in the air, jolting back and away from her. The eye shapes clenched tightly. The mouth opened. The lines of smoke that formed his forehead became furrowed. He jerked his head back again, then lunged in a spasm of deep coughing, rocking backwards and forwards in agony, hacking for breath, painfully trying to clear whatever obstructed him below.

A spray of bright redness burst out from the shape that was his open mouth, droplets of scarlet smoke, a fine aerosol. She stepped back to avoid it, and the kiss was lost for ever.

The apparition was wheezing, making dry hacking coughs, small ones now, weak and unhoping, the end of the attack. He was staring straight at her, terrified, full of pain and unspeakable loss, but already the smoke was untangling, dispersing.

The red droplets had fallen to the floor and formed a pool on one of his discarded sheets of paper. She knelt down to look more closely, and trailed her fingertips through the sticky mess. When she stood again, her fingers carried a smear of the blood, but now the air in the study had cleared. The blue haze had gone at last. The final traces of him had vanished. The dust, the sunlight, the books, the dark corners remained.

She fled.

Downstairs she stood once again with the others, waiting in the great hall to be allocated to one of the cars. Until her name was spoken by one of the undertaker's staff, no one acted as if they knew who she was or acknowledged her in any way. Even the man who had spoken to her stood with his back against her. The family and the other mourners spoke quietly to each other, clearly daunted by the seriousness of the occasion, by the thought

72

of the crowds waiting in the road at the end of the long drive, by the passing of this man.

She was given a seat in the last of the cars, bringing up the rear of the cortège. She was pressed against the window by the large bodies of two serious and unspeaking adolescents.

In the crowded church she sat alone to one side, steadying herself by staring at the flagstone floor, the ancient wooden pews. She stood for the hymns and prayers but only mouthed the words silently, remembering what he had said were his feelings about churches. The tributes to him were formal, grand, spoken sincerely by illustrious men and women. She listened closely, recognizing nothing of him in their words. He had not sought this renown, this greatness.

In the churchyard on a hill overlooking the sea, standing near the grave, back from the main group of mourners, hearing the words of committal distorted by the breeze, she was again alone. She thought about the first book of his she had ever read, while still at college. Everyone knew his work now, but at that time he was unknown and it had been a personal discovery.

The persistent wind from the islands buffeted against her, pressing her clothes against her body on one side, sending strands of hair across her eyes. She smelt the salt from the sea, the promise of distance, departure, escape from this place.

Members of the public and the cameras of the media were only just visible, kept in the distance beyond a cordon of flowers and a patrol of policemen. In a lull of the wind she heard the familiar words of the committal uttered by the priest, and saw the coffin being lowered into the ground. The sun continued to shine but she could not stop shivering. She thought only of him, the caress of his fingertips, the light pressure of his lips, his gentle words, his tears when she went away at the end. The long years without him, holding on to everything she knew of him. She barely dared to breathe for fear of expelling him from her thoughts.

She held her hand out of sight beneath the small bag she carried. The blood had congealed on her fingers, cold, an encrustation, eternal, the final trace of him.

The
Miraculous
Cairn

•

The offshore island of Seevl lies like a dark shadow of regret over my memories of childhood. The island was always within view, sprawling across the sea opposite Jethra's shore, in the offing. Sometimes it was blurred or obscured by the low clouds of storms. At other times it seemed only a ball's throw from the shore, standing out with its black and rugged outline against the southern sky. Because it shared rock strata with the mainland, Seevl's landscape was not unlike that of the mountains around Jethra, but Jethra and this island were close in other ways. As if we were members of the same family we told stories about each other. We said for instance that when our ancestors had no use for chunks of rock they threw them out to sea, and there were soon so many of them that Seevl was formed.

The nearness of Seevl to Jethra created an inevitable and trad- itional bond – there were real family ties, trading agreements, old alliances – but although to the Jethrans Seevl was an offshore island, politically it was a part of the Dream Archipelago. After the war began journeys between mainland and island were forbid- den, unless there was permission from the Seigniory, but a ferry ran every day in defiance of the ban, openly and commercially. Officialdom turned a blind eye because trade was important to Jethra and crucial to Seevl. I myself travelled to Seevl on many occasions during my childhood. Three or four times a year, throughout my childhood, we made the short sea crossing to Seevl to visit my aunt and uncle.

*

Now it was twenty years since I had last been to Seevl, and sixteen years since I had lived in or even visited Jethra. The last time I saw the city was when I left to go to university in Old Haydl and with nothing to return for I had stayed away ever since.

The twenty years had produced mixed luck, the successes being only superficial, I felt. I shone without depth. I had had a good education, though, and I was in teaching, a career I found interesting. I had so far been able to avoid war service, and now, at the age of thirty-eight, was probably beyond the age of call-up. As a teacher I was exempted from service under the present rules and even when I searched my conscience I knew that I was more useful doing that than I would have been in one of the armed services.

So my professional life was more or less secure. My private life, though, was less certain. It was returning to Jethra, with Seevl out there in the sea, that brought the memories and doubts to the forefront.

Jethra was the old capital of our country but because of the war the government and most of the civil service had been dispersed to the newer, less exposed cities inland. There was still a token government presence in Jethra, but the Monseignior's palace was unoccupied, and the Senate House was one of those buildings that had been badly damaged by enemy bombing at the beginning of the war. There remained the inshore fishing, some light industry, a railhead, hospitals, organizational bodies, international bureaux, but many of the civilians inessential to the war industries had moved out. Jethra had become a large, desolate ghost of a city.

Any return to a place of childhood involves reminders. For me, Jethra meant memories of life at home with my father and mother, schooling, friends with whom I had later lost contact … and the regular visits to Seevl.

These memories reminded me of what I once had been and so, inevitably, they also underlined to me what I had since become. It started to become clear to me as I sat on the train to Jethra, thinking about the past. I was curious to see the old town again,

75

and nervous of travelling to Seevl once more, but since the reason for the journey had arisen, I felt it was an opportunity, after two decades away, to go back and confront the past.

When I was a child the closeness of Seevl had a foreboding quality for everyone, and certainly for school-age children. 'Send you to Seevl,' was the greatest of childish threats. In our alternate world of invented myth, Seevl was populated by bogeymen and creeping horrors, while the actual landscape of the island was thought to be a nightmare terrain of crevasses and volcanic pools, sulphurous mists, steaming craters and shifting rocks. This vision was as true for me, in an imaginative sense, as it was for all the other children, but I had the child's unconscious ability to see the world from a number of simultaneous and different viewpoints.

I knew Seevl for what it really was. It was no less horrifying in reality, but its horrors were not the commonplace ones of children's books or folklore.

I was an only child. My mother and father, both native Jethrans, had given birth to another child before me, but she died a year before I was born. I therefore came into a world where I was eagerly welcomed and protectively loved. I was shielded and guarded with almost fanatical thoroughness, for reasons I could not begin to understand until I was almost grown up. Now that I do understand I have some sympathy with what my parents did, but the closeness of their protection meant that until I was in my middle teens I was still being treated as some precious object which might break, or be stolen, or become instantly corrupted in some way the moment their guard relaxed. While youngsters of my own age were hanging around on the streets after school, or getting into scrapes, or experimenting with sex or alcohol or drugs or general misbehaviour, I was expected to be at home, sharing my parents' friends and interests. I was not a rebel: I went along with what they wanted, possibly because I knew little better. There were some filial duties, though, that I carried out only with numb acquiescence and from a sense of obligation, suppressing the urge to evade them altogether. Chief amongst these duties was to accompany my parents on their regular visits to my father's brother at his house on Seevl.

My Uncle Torm was a few years younger than my father but had married at about the same time: there was a photograph in our living room of the two young men with their brides. Although I recognized the youthful versions of my father, mother and uncle it took me years to realize that the pretty young woman holding Torm's arm in the photograph was my Aunt Alvie.

In the picture she was smiling and I had never seen Aunt Alvie smile. She was wearing a gay, flowery dress and I had never seen Aunt Alvie in anything except an old nightgown and a patched cardigan. Her hair was short and wavy, cut attractively about her face, while Aunt Alvie's hair was long and greasy and grey. The girl in the picture was standing beside her new husband, raising one leg to show her knee flirtatiously to the camera, and my Aunt Alvie was a bedridden cripple.

Soon after their marriage Torm and Alvie had moved to Seevl. Torm had been appointed to a clerical job at a Catholic seminary situated in the remotest part of the Seevl mountains. I assume the priests had been finding it impossible to employ someone, because otherwise I have never found out why Torm would have been offered the job, or even why he – a man of only vaguely defined beliefs – had applied for it in the first place. I do know that taking the job caused a bitter if short-lived row between him and my father.

Torm and Alvie were there with their new baby on Seevl when the war suddenly worsened and made it impossible to return to Jethra. By the time the hostilities had eased again and the war had returned to the long sequence of attritional skirmishes – during which a certain amount of travel between the mainland and the islands was again possible – Aunt Alvie had been taken ill and was not to be moved.

It was during this long period of her illness that my parents made their weekend visits to see Torm and Alvie, taking me with them.

For me they were occasions of unrelieved dreariness and

depression: a voyage to a bleak, windswept island, then a long car drive to a cramped and dark house on the edge of a moor, a house where a sickbed was the centre of attention and where the conversations were at best about other adult relatives and at worst about sickness and pain and false hopes of a miraculous recovery.

My only relief from all this, and ostensibly why I was dragged along, was Torm and Alvie's daughter, my cousin Seraphina. We were supposed to be friends. Seri was about fifteen months older than me, plump and rather stupid, narrow in her ideas and experience and concerned in nothing I knew anything about. We were not in fact at all interested in each other, yet we were forced into each other's company for the duration of these visits. The prospect of being with her did nothing to relieve those long days of dread before a trip, and afterwards the memory of our sullen hours together was one more reason to want never to go again.

As I left the station in Jethra a policewoman wearing the familiar Seigniorial uniform climbed out of a marked police car and walked across to me. My first impression was that she had a stiff, authoritarian manner. She barely looked at me as she spoke.

'Are you Lenden Cros?' she said to me.

'Yes.'

'I am Serjeant Reeth.' She produced a leather-bound ID card, and held it out for me to see. I glimpsed a colour photograph, an official stamp, a printed name, rows of numbers, a scrawled signature. 'I am to accompany you.'

'I was told to report to the police,' I said, confused by her. 'I was planning to do that tomorrow before I left.'

'You're leaving the country.'

'Only temporarily.'

'You cannot travel without an escort.'

'It's only family business. There's hardly any need—'

She glanced at me with what I took to be an uninterested expression. I supposed she had orders, and anything I said was irrelevant to her.

'So what's the first step?' I said, disconcerted by this development. I had been planning to stay overnight in the town, and was intending to walk down to the dock area to see if I could find inexpensive overnight lodgings. A colleague at the school had given me the name of a street where he said I would find some cheap hotels. After that I had more general plans to see if I could make contact with one or two of my old friends I thought might still be in the city.

'Arrangements have been made for you,' she said. 'Jethra is a war zone.'

'I know that of course. How does it affect a short trip to Seevl?'

'All travel by civilians is restricted.'

'That's not what I was told before.' I looked in my wallet. 'Look, I've been given a visa to leave Jethra, and another to re-enter within seven days. In fact, I shall probably only need to be there for a day or two—'

Again, I saw the lack of interest in her eyes.

'Get in the car, please,' she said.

She opened the back door and I placed my bag on the seat. I wondered if I was expected to sit there at the back with it, but I had no intention of being driven around looking as if I was under arrest. I closed the rear door and went to the front. I let myself in and sat down. It seemed to make no difference to the policewoman. She climbed in and started the engine.

'Where are we going?' I said.

'The ferry does not sail until the morning. We are staying overnight at the Grand Shore Hotel.'

'I was planning to find somewhere less expensive,' I said, with some alarm.

'It has all been booked in advance. The decision wasn't mine.'

She drove out of the station square and turned into the main road that led towards the city centre. I watched the buildings go past.

My family had lived in the suburbs, a place called Entown, along the coast to the east of the city. I therefore remembered the centre of Jethra only in parts and then from the perspective of a child. I recognized buildings, names of streets, certain parks or squares. Some had vague but poignant and subtly disturbing associations for me. As a child I had thought of the city centre as the place where my father worked, where my mother sometimes went shopping. The street names were landmarks from their territory, not mine. The city today looked disused and unloved: many of the buildings had unrepaired bomb and blast damage to them, and hundreds more were boarded up. There were of course several complete areas flattened into rubble by the enemy bombing. The streets were not busy with traffic: there were trucks, buses, some cars, no new models of any vehicles. Everything looked shabby and patched up. I saw a surprising number of horse-drawn vehicles.

We were held up for a few seconds at an intersection.

Into the silence that lay between us I said to Serjeant Reeth, 'Do you live in Jethra?'

'No.'

'You seem to know which way to drive.'

'I arrived this morning. I've had time to familiarize myself. Police training.'

That last phrase seemed to me to bespeak a certain unfamiliarity with the job, as if that training had not been too long in the past. I stole a glance across at her, saw how young she looked. The traffic around us moved on, she engaged gear and the police car accelerated away. The short conversation ended.

I had never stayed at the Grand Shore Hotel, had never even been through its doors. It was the largest, most expensive hotel in town. In my childhood it had been the scene of society weddings, business conferences and glittering civic occasions. All these must have been before the evacuation to the country areas began in earnest.

We drew up in the car park outside the main entrance, with its imposing and solid façade of soot-dirtied red brick.

Serjeant Reeth stood back as I registered. The clerk pushed across two pieces of white card for my signature: one was for a room in my own name, the other, with an adjacent number, was for the policewoman. A porter took my bag and led us up the wide, curving staircase to the next floor. There were mirrors and chandeliers, a plush carpet on the stairs, gold paint on the plaster ceiling mouldings. The mirrors were unpolished, though, the carpet was worn and the paint was peeling. The muted sounds of our feet as we climbed were poor substitutes for those distant parties that surely must survive as memories somewhere.

The porter opened the door to my room and went in ahead of me. The policewoman went to her own door and inserted the key. As she went inside she did not look back at me.

I tipped the porter and he left. I took my clothes from my bag and hung them in the wardrobe. Because I had been travelling on the train all day I showered, and put on clean clothes. Then I sat on the edge of the bed and looked around at the old room.

It was an unexpected moment of inaction from which to contemplate my past life. I had not anticipated having to spend so much time in the company of someone I had never met before. How was I to pass the evening? Alone, or with the policewoman? Did her escort duties include eating dinner with me? Was she the only officer sent to accompany me, or would she be replaced later this evening when her shift came to an end?

As soon as I thought this I realized that almost from the first moments of our meeting I had been hoping that she was not going to share the escort duty with other officers. For all her cold manner, and the unyielding words we had exchanged, I had found the young policewoman physically attractive. I wondered what chance, what sequence of events, had led to this good-looking young woman being assigned to such a task as escorting someone like me on a journey. Intriguingly, she was already reminding me of someone I had been involved with several years before: they were about the same age, had the same fair colouring. She, Lelian, was one of several lovers I had been with during those years, many of whom I had known only casually. Perhaps if I had met Serjeant Reeth then, different times, different matters, she might have become another of them.

I was older and supposedly wiser now, though. I had learned that casual affairs almost inevitably ended badly. I had made no pick-ups for years, preferring the less concentrated sorrows of abstinence. Serjeant Reeth reminded me of the past in much the same way Jethra itself was doing. I had moved on from both, I thought.

There were no drinks in the room and I was feeling thirsty, so I decided to visit the bar downstairs. I left my room and headed for the stairs. On the way I passed an elevator which I had not noticed on the way up to the room: a printed sign attached to the door explained that it could not be used by hotel guests. When I reached the head of the grand staircase I thought I should, out of politeness, ask the policewoman if she would like to join me for the drink.

She answered my knock at her door after only a moment's delay, as if she had been standing there, waiting for me. She was still wearing her uniform, but she said she would enjoy a drink, and thank you. We went downstairs together.

The door was locked and there were no lights showing inside. In the lounge I rang a bell and after a short delay an elderly waiter came to serve us.

When he had taken our order and left the lounge the two of us sat awkwardly at the table, avoiding each other's eyes.

Making conversation, I said, 'Is escort work something you do often, Serjeant Reeth?'

'No. This is the first time.'

'Do people need escorting often?'

'I don't know. I've been serving the Monseignior for less than a year.'

'So how did you come to be assigned to me?'

She shrugged, laid her fingers on the surface of the table and stared down at them.

'Duty rotas are worked out, jobs go up on the noticeboard in the corridor. We're expected to put our names forward. I saw this assignment coming up so I volunteered for it.'

Just then the waiter returned with our drinks.

'Will you be dining in the hotel this evening?' he said to me.

'Yes.' I realized I had spoken for us both so I looked at Serjeant Reeth for confirmation. 'Yes,' I said again.

When he had gone, and while another silence between us endured, I looked around the lounge. We were the only people there, perhaps the only guests in the whole building. I liked the airy, gracious feeling in the room, with its tall windows and long velvet drapes, the high Consortship light shades and the broad-backed wicker chairs grouped around the low tables. There were dozens of potted plants, great cascading ferns and tall parlour palms, lending a feeling of growth and life to an otherwise decaying old building. All the plants were green and thriving, so someone must still be looking after them, dusting them, watering them.

The policewoman's awkward silences gave me the opportunity to try to assess my companion. I guessed her age at about twenty-two or three. She had not brought her cap with her from her room, but the uniform – crisply starched, deliberately asexual in appearance – effectively neutered her. She wore no make-up and her light-coloured hair was drawn back into a bun. She seemed shy and uncommunicative, and unaware of my regard.

At last it was she who broke the silence.

'Are you from Seevl?' she said.

'No ... I was born here in Jethra.'

'Then do you know Seevl well?'

'I haven't been there for many years. What about you?'

'No. I've never been out of the country.'

'Do you have you any idea what Seevl is going to be like?'

'I'm told it's barren. Mountainous, with not many trees. Wintry all year round. I've heard about the wind.'

'It's not quite as bad as that,' I said. 'I can't claim to know it well, although the scenery won't have changed much.' I took more of my drink, intending to swallow only a sip of it but finding myself almost emptying the glass. I needed something to ease the stiffness of our conversation. 'I used to hate going across there. I always dreaded being there.'

'Why?'

'The mood of the place, the scenery,' I said vaguely, avoiding specific memories. Back there in my mind were thoughts of the feeling of being inside the seminary, of Alvie and her depressing bedroom, the open moors, the constant wind, the dead towers. All these were inexpressible to a stranger. 'It's bleak, but that's not all. I can't describe it. You'll probably feel it as soon as we land on the island tomorrow.'

I said this last sentence deliberately, leaving it open for her to tell me that she was sharing the duty with other officers, but she did not pick up on it. I found that rather pleasing.

Instead, she said, 'You sound like my brother. He says he can tell if a house is haunted.'

'I didn't say the place was haunted,' I said, quick to its defence. 'But you're right about the wind,' I added.

Jethra itself was built in the shadow of the Murinan Hills, but to the west of the city was a wide, straight valley that led northwards into the foothills of the polar range some distance away. For all but a few short weeks at the height of summer, a stiff wind came down that valley and vented out to sea, whining across Seevl's treeless fells and moors. Only on the eastern side of the island, the part closest to Jethra, were there villages of any size. The only north-facing port, Seevl Town, was there.

One of my clearest childhood memories of Seevl was seeing it in the springtime. I could look to the south from my bedroom window and see the blossoms shining pink and white and bright red on the trees along the roadsides and in the boulevards of Jethra, while beyond, out in the Midway Sea, there would be Seevl, still with its wintertime crust of snow.

Serjeant Reeth's mention of a brother gave me the first glimmer of information about her background, so I asked her about him. He was also in the Seigniory, she said, serving with the Border Police. He had been serving in the mountains, but now he was hoping for promotion. His unit had recently embarked for a spell of duty on the southern continent. The war was still confused to those taking part and confusing to those who were not: from the point of view of civilians remaining in the north, following the progress of the military campaigns was difficult, because of the unfamiliarity of the landscape and geography of the southern lands and the lack of identifying place names that people could recognize.

At least the islands remained neutral for the time being, although in my own case it was a mixed blessing. If Seevl had been annexed to Faiandland – as for a time it had been mooted it might be – getting across to it from the mainland would have been a straightforward matter. As things stood, the island's neutral state meant that it was technically foreign territory.

News of Torm's death had taken more than a month to reach me. Arriving with it was a request from the Father Confessor's office at the seminary that I should visit my uncle's house as soon as possible to sort out his effects. Both of these messages had reached me through the medium of the Seigniorial Visa Department in Jethra. If it had come direct to me and not through official channels, if the priests at the seminary had had my address, I could have slipped across unofficially. But that was not to be. Government officials knew of my visit in advance and therefore I was to be escorted.

I was telling Serjeant Reeth about the reasons for my trip – the need to sign documents, to permit furniture to be given away or destroyed, to decide which of his papers should be kept – when the waiter returned to the lounge. He was carrying two menus, discreetly implying that the dining-room staff were ready for us. While we perused the menu he drew the curtains across the tall windows, then led us down the corridor to the dining room.

My last visit to Seevl. I was fourteen.

There were examinations coming up at school and I was trying to concentrate on them, but I knew that at the end of the week we were going to visit my aunt and uncle and cousin. It was summer and Jethra was dusty and windless, with a great blank heat pressing down on the city. Sitting by my bedroom window, unable to concentrate on my revision, I looked frequently out across the roofs towards the sea. Seevl was green then, a dark, tough green. It was a coloured lie, a deceit about lushness.

The days crept by and I thought about evasion tactics I had tried in the past: a migraine attack, a sudden bout of gastroenteritis, an obscure ailment allegedly picked up from a passing stranger ... anything that I thought might delay the next visit. At last the day arrived, though, and there was no more avoiding it. We were out of bed and away from the house before dawn, hurrying down in the breaking light, cool and lovely at that time of year, to catch the first tram of the day.

What were these visits for? Unless my parents spoke in some adult code I have never been able to decipher, they went out of a combination of habit, guilt about Alvie's illness and broader family obligations. Torm and my father seemed to have nothing in common any longer. I never heard them discussing anything of interest, in the way I now know educated adults can discuss matters (both my parents were educated and so was my uncle, although I cannot be sure about Aunt Alvie). There was news to impart but it was always stale news, trivial family events and remarks and experiences, not even interesting when fresh. Everything that passed between the four adults was familial or familiar: an aunt or cousin who had moved house or changed jobs, a nephew who had married, a great-uncle who had died. Sometimes, photographs were passed around Alvie's sickbed: Cousin Jayn's new house, or this is us when went to the mountains, or did you know Kissi, your sister-in-law's daughter, had given birth to another baby? It was as if they had no ideas they could externalize, no sense of the abstract, no conception that there might be a larger world of events outside the narrow one they presently inhabited. I was serious about such matters at that age. I was trying to learn to think for myself. I came to the mature conclusion, at the age I was, that they used these banal exchanges as a levelling device. It was almost as if they were instilling a sense of mediocrity into themselves, to bring themselves to Alvie's level, to make her seem, that is, no longer ill.

It made sense to me then.

And where were their recollections of each other? Did they have no past together they could reminisce about? The only hint of their forgotten past was the photograph taken before I was born, the one in our living room at home. I was genuinely fascinated by it. When had it been taken and where? What were they doing that day? Who took the photograph? Was it a happy day, as it seemed from the picture, or did something occur later to mar it? Why did none of them ever mention those times?

What occurred in the years after that photograph was almost certainly the swamping effect of Alvie's illness. It spread over everything in past and present. She knew only her pain, her discomfort, the treatments she endured, the doctor who understood nothing, the lack of a proper hospital, the absence of regular nursing, the medication with its innumerable side-effects.

The disease was creeping through her. Every time we visited she was a little worse. First her legs lost all sensation. She became incontinent. She could not take solid food. But if her decline was steady it was also slow. News of further deterioration usually came by letter between visits, so that whenever I saw her I did so with the prospect of seeing her arms withering or her teeth falling out or her face decaying away. The ghoulish imaginings of childhood were never satisfied, disappointed even, once I had resigned myself to having to visit her again. There was always an inverse surprise, based on morbid fears: how well she looked by comparison with what I expected! Only later, as the depressing news was handed out to us, would we hear of new horrors, new agonies.

Yet the years dragged by and Alvie was still there in her bed, propped up by eight or nine pillows, her hair in a lank skein over one shoulder. She grew fatter and paler, more grotesque, but these changes would show in anyone who never took exercise, who never went outside. Her spirit was unfailing: her voice was pitched on one note, sounding sad and dull and dreary, but the things she said were self-consciously everyday. She reported her pain and setbacks factually, she did not complain about them. She knew the disease was progressively killing her, but she spoke of the future, even if it was a future of the narrowest vision (what would I like for my next birthday? what was I going to do when I left school?). She was a stalwart example to us all, a model of stoicism in distress.

Whenever we made our visits one of the priests would come in to see Alvie. I cynically believed that no one ever called round from the seminary unless there was someone there from the outside world to take note of it. Alvie had 'courage', they told us, she had 'fortitude', she 'bore her cross'. I loathed the priests in their black soutanes, waving their white hands sanctimoniously over the bed, blessing not only Alvie but me and my parents too. I sometimes thought it was the priests who were killing her. They were praying not for a cure, I decided, but for a lingering death and they were doing it to make a point with theological content to their students. My uncle was godless, his job was to him just a job. There was hope in religion, and to prove it to him the priests were going to kill Alvie slowly.

I remember too many of the wrong things. Feelings not facts, impressions not information. How little I knew and how little I still know.

The last visit. Yes.

The boat was late docking in Jethra. The man in the harbour office told us the ship's engine was undergoing emergency repairs. For a joyful moment I thought the trip would have to be cancelled, but then at last the ferry appeared at the harbour mouth and moved slowly to the quay to collect us. There was a handful of other passengers waiting too. I've no idea who they were or why they were making the crossing.

It seemed to me that we were almost upon Seevl as soon as the boat left Jethra harbour. The grey limestone cliffs were dead ahead, and the clear marine air had an illusory foreshortening effect. It was a whole hour's voyage to Seevl Town, though, because the boat had to swing far out to sea to avoid the shoals beneath Stromb Head, before turning in again to take the sheltered deep-water passage beneath the Seevl cliffs. I stood apart from my parents, staring up at the cliffs, watching for occasional glimpses of the high moors beyond, feeling the onset of the real, stomach-turning dread I invariably suffered as we arrived. It was cool out at sea and although the sun was rising quickly the wind came curling down from the cliffs above. My parents went into the bar to escape the chill wind, and I stood alone on the deck with packing cases, trucks loaded with livestock, bundles of newspapers, crates of drink, two tractors.

The houses of Seevl Town, built up in terraces on the hills around the harbour, were constructed from the grey rock of the island, their roofs whitened around the chimney stacks by bird droppings. An orange lichen clung to the walls and roofs, souring the houses, making them seem more decrepit. On the highest hill, dominating the town, stood the derelict remains of a rock-built tower. I never looked directly at the tower, fearing it.

As the boat glided in on the still and sheltered water of the harbour my parents came out of the saloon and stood beside me, one on each side, like a military escort, preventing flight.

There was a hired car to be collected in Seevl Town. Such a thing was an expensive luxury in Jethra but it was a necessity for the wild interior of the island. My father had booked it the week before but it was not ready and we had to wait an hour or more in a cold office overlooking the dismal harbour. The ferry departed on its return trip to Jethra. My parents were silent, trying to ignore me as I fidgeted and made fitful attempts to read the book I had brought.

Around Seevl Town were some of the few farms on the island, rearing their scrawny animals and growing their hybrid cereals on the barren soil of the eastern side. The road climbed up through these smallholdings, following the perimeters of the fields and turning through sharp angles and steep climbing corners. The surface of the road had been metalled once but now it was breaking up, presumably under the effect of the harsh winters and the general economic malaise. The car lurched uncomfortably in the potholes and the wheels frequently spun on the gravelly sides. My father, driving, stayed tight-lipped, trying to master not only the dangerous road but also the controls of the unfamiliar vehicle. He went too fast on the level stretches, braked too late for corners. He was constantly having to correct his mistakes. My mother sat beside him with the map, ready to direct him, but we were forever lost on Seevl, we never seemed able to find the same way twice. I sat in the back of the car, cold and uncomfortable, thinking of home, ignored by them both except when my mother would turn to see what I was doing. I was always doing nothing, staring out of the window in mute suspension of visible reaction, wishing I could dream.

It took nearly half an hour of such driving to reach the first summit of the fell road, by which time the last farm, the last hedge, the last tree, were miles behind us. There was a far-distant glimpse of Seevl Town as the road went over the crest, and a wide, unwelcome view of the gun-metal inner sea, flecked with islets and rocks. Across the strait the unfamiliar aspect of the mainland coast, bathed in sunlight.

On the moors the road rose and fell at the whim of the country, winding through the scrub-covered land. Sometimes the car would emerge from a high pass, where on each side great crags of limestone loomed over the scree slopes and the blast of wind from the north would kick the car to the side.

My father drove jerkily, trying to avoid the loose rocks on the road and the unpredictably positioned potholes. The map lay unconsulted on my mother's knee because Father claimed he knew the way from memory, pointing out supposedly familiar landmarks as we passed them. Yet he frequently made mistakes, took wrong turnings or drove up a side road that led nowhere. Mother would sit quietly at his side until he realized. Then the map would be snatched from her lap, the car would be reversed or turned and we would go back the way we had come to the place where he had made the error. Sometimes he drove past without realizing it, doubling the problem.

I left it all to them, although, like my mother, I usually knew when we took a wrong turning. My own interest was not with the road but the landscape through which it passed.

I never failed to be appalled and impressed by the gigantic

emptiness of the Seevl moors. Father's wrong turnings had the double advantage of not only putting back the time of our eventual arrival at the seminary, but also of opening up more island vistas to my eyes.

The road passed several of the dead towers of Seevl, frightening me every time. I knew the islanders would never go near the towers, but I did not know why. Whenever the car passed one I could scarcely look towards it for the fear it aroused in me, but my parents never even noticed. If we passed slowly I would cower in my seat, tensed up, trying not to move, anticipating some ghoul of legend making a rush for the car. I never really worked out why these old buildings should scare me so much. I knew only what I saw: they were abandoned, they were unexplained, they were like nothing I had ever seen at home.

Later in the journey the surface of the road deteriorated still further, becoming a rough track consisting of two gravel paths divided by a strip of long, coarse grass that scraped against the underside of the car.

Another hour or two passed on the moors before the track led down briefly into a shallow valley, one I always recognized. Four of the dead towers stood like sentinels along the ridge. The valley was almost treeless but there were many sprawling thorn bushes and in the lowest part of the valley, beside a wide stream, was a tiny hamlet with a view of the sea and the mainland. A part of Jethra could be seen from here. It spread blackly against the side of the Murinan Hills and it seemed simultaneously close and foreign. Already by this time you had started looking and seeing like an islander might.

Outside the village we climbed up to the high fells again and I looked forward to passing one of the scenic surprises of the journey. The island was narrow for a distance and after crossing the moors the road briefly ran along the southern side. For a few minutes we had a view of the Midway Sea to the south of Seevl, a sight never possible from Jethra, nor indeed from most parts of the coast near to where we lived. Island after island cluttered the sea, spreading southwards towards the horizon. Because of its closeness and cold climate I had never really considered Seevl to be a part of the Dream Archipelago. That was a different kind of place, as I imagined it: a lush, tropical maze of islands, hot and tranquil, forested or barren, but always dozing under the equatorial sun and peopled by strange races with customs and languages as bizarre as their food, clothes and homes. Seevl was a cold offshore island, geologically if not politically part of our country. This elevated view across part of the girdling sea, with its temptations of the tropics, was an almost cruel glimpse of a world I could never enter, away from the north, under a marine sun. The rest was dream.

I saw airplane condensation trails high in the sky, spiralling away towards the south.

Another valley, another hamlet. The road led the car back inland once more.

I knew we were approaching the seminary at last and in spite of myself I was staring ahead, looking for the first sight of it.

After dinner Serjeant Reeth and I returned to our separate rooms, she because she said she wanted to take a bath and wash her hair and I because I could think of nowhere else to go and had nothing else to do. I tried to telephone one of the friends I had been intending to look up, but the outside line for guests would not connect. I sat for a while on the edge of my bed, resting my feet on my suitcase and staring at the carpet, then found the letter I had received from the Father Confessor at the seminary.

It was strange to read his ponderous, circumlocutory sentences, full of a stiff intent – meant not only to engage my sympathies but also, it seemed, to intimidate me – and to try to reconcile it with my adolescent bitterness about him and his priests.

I remembered one occasion of many. I had been walking on a lawn at the seminary, innocently close to one of the flower-beds, and a priest had appeared and reprimanded me severely for endangering the garden. I didn't deserve it but I took it meekly. None of them could leave a reprimand to stand alone: they had insights into the universe and I did not, and so I was warned of hell and my imminent and irreversible destiny. In the intervening years that priest had quite possibly become this reverend father, and the same implied threat was there in his letter: you must attend to your uncle's affairs or we will fix the fates for you and God will get you.

I lay back on my bed, thinking about Seevl and wondering what it would be like to be there again.

Would it depress me as Jethra had ever since I arrived? Or would it scare me all over again? The priests and their heavenly machinations no longer held any terror for me. Alvie was long dead and now so too was Torm, both joining my parents, and a generation was gone. The island itself interested me – as scenery, as a place – because I had only ever seen it through a child's eyes, but I wasn't looking forward to crossing its empty moors again, seeing the bare views of rock and marsh. Then there were the dead towers: they were another matter, one I did not know how to think about. Do childish superstitions survive into adulthood?

I knew, though, that this trip was not going to be the same as before. Perhaps earlier that morning, when I had set out from home, I might have thought it would be the same without actually articulating the words. But everything had changed when Serjeant Reeth appeared.

She told me at dinner that her name was Ennabella but that I should call her Bella. She had instructed me in this when we ordered our second bottle of wine. I, with much of the wine inside me, had been unable to stop myself smiling. I had not known that policewomen had names like Bella, but there it was. She drank quickly and the wine was unstiffening her too: she forbade me from calling her by her rank again, yet even as she sat across from me, in the starched khaki shirt of her rank, I found it difficult to believe that she meant it. But thinking of her as Bella did help. The mask she hid behind began to slip. She told me the Seigniory training had been a hard, testing experience but she had done well, made friends, gained achievement points. She had not been a serjeant long because she had been promoted quickly, while still young. She didn't say as much but I assumed it meant that she was an achiever, earning the respect of her superiors. She had a quality of innocence, a wide-eyed ingenuousness which showed many times. I couldn't decide if it was a natural mannerism, or something she was using to try to influence me in some way. I spent most of that meal trying to work her out. It was the uniform that confused me, those drab-looking clothes which came attendant with so many associations of Seigniory repression of nonconformist ideas and official interference with civil liberties.

Bella. She wanted me to call her Bella. It took some doing. She didn't laugh often, but when she did she was uninhibited, throwing back her head, wrinkling her eyes, smiling across the table at me afterwards. I liked it, and I liked the feelings about her that rose within me, but she made me feel my age. I could not shake off the idea that our roles were reversing – that I, being older, more experienced, was becoming her guardian, an escort for the journey. In spite of the severe uniform, the austere hairstyle, it became easy to forget that she was a member of Seigniory, with immense powers of authority residing behind those dancing eyes and girlish smiles.

A few minutes after I had given up trying to contact my friends the room telephone rang, but with a cracked, intermittent bell sound. It made me wonder if something on the line had short-circuited. I picked up the receiver.

'Yes?'

'It's me next door. Bella Reeth. I'm sorry to trouble you.'

I said nothing, wondering indeed what to say.

After a few more moments she said, 'My hairdrier isn't working. The plug doesn't fit. Do you have an adapter, or another drier I could use?'

'Yes,' I said straight away. 'I can take a plug off something in here.'

'Shall I come to your room, then?'

'Yes.'

'Are you sure?' she said. 'It wouldn't be inconvenient?'

'No. I'll unlock the door for you now.'

94

So she came, appearing at my door with her damp hair wrapped up in a towel. She had her electric drier in one hand. She was wearing a calf-length silken robe, one that was tied at the front by a belt made of the same fabric, but which had no buttons. It was thin and white, hardly concealing her body. She clasped the front of it together between her breasts with her free hand. Her nipples beneath the flimsy fabric were visibly erect.

She numbed me with surprise. Tentative fantasies about what might follow from meeting such an attractive young woman had been flickering distantly all evening, but I had not expected her to come to my room on what seemed like a pretext. The hesitant, awkward relationship we had had until that moment was overtaken by the implications. It was late in the evening, she was wearing hardly any clothes, we were practically strangers. I invited her in, asked her to close the door. I had moved the hotel easy chair close to the bed as soon as I had put down the phone, and now I indicated she should sit on it. The seat was low, making her knees rise above her lap as she sat down. She kept them pressed close together. I searched around for my penknife, and for something from which I could borrow a plug. I used the bedside light, bent my head over it while I undid the little screws holding the wires in place.

While I did this she removed the towel from her head and shook out her hair, letting it fall in damp ringlets around her face. A delicate fragrance of shampoo or soap wafted towards me.

'I have to dry my hair straight away after washing,' she said. 'It goes frizzy unless I do.'

I was fumbling with the plug, trying to hurry, trying not to show my nervousness. My head was close to one of her knees, where it poked out nakedly through the opening at the front of her robe. I was so close I could see the fuzz of tiny soft hairs growing on her calf. A thought was circling repetitively: I had not sought or created the situation, it was she who was making herself available by coming to my room like this, I was not to blame, I was free to respond, but I did not want it to happen, although I had not sought it, I found her so tempting, but surely I was not to blame, which gave me freedom to respond, but—

She was leaning forward while she waited. I could not look up at her, so conscious was I of her presence, her radiant cleanliness from the shower, her young body, her casually revealing robe.

The plug came off the end of the lamp's flex.

'Give me the drier,' I said, looking up at her long enough to hold out my hand to take the appliance. There was still the existing plug to remove, then the other to put in its place. My hands could remain busy a while longer.

I could feel her watching me as I bent over the simple task.

'Do you think we're the only guests in the hotel?' she said.

'We haven't seen anyone else, have we?'

The closed bar, the silent lounge. We had been alone at dinner, with lights on around our table, but the rest of the large room had been in darkness. The attentive waiter had swept in and out of our circle of light, responsive and polite.

'I looked in the register this morning, when I arrived,' Bella said. 'No one else has checked into the hotel for more than a week.'

Her foot was resting beside my leg as I knelt on the carpet to change the plugs. When I had to twist around to reach for one of the bits I allowed my leg to move over slightly and press down on her naked foot. She did not move away.

'It must be the quiet season,' I said, making the last connection.

'I tried room service just now, to see about the plug. No one answered.'

'Maybe we really are alone in the building, then,' I said. 'The staff have gone home for the night.'

'That's what I was thinking. We could do anything we liked.'

'Yes, we could,' I said, not looking at her. I screwed the back on the plug and passed the drier up to her. 'That's fixed it,' I said.

She shook her head again, ran a hand through her still-damp hair. I was surprised how long it was, now she had released it from the severe bun.

She reached down past where I was kneeling and slipped the plug into the wall socket. As the hot air began to whine, she played the flow across her hair, teasing it out with a comb she had taken from her large loose pocket. I was still on the floor at her feet. I watched the way the thin material of her wrap stressed and pressed against her nipples as she moved her arms.

She was awakening feelings in me that had been dormant for years, feelings I had repeatedly suppressed. I yearned to have her. With her hair loose she looked so young! As she dried her hair she was looking directly down at me, with her head cocked on one side. She combed out several strands, holding them away from her head in the hot stream of air, and as the hair dried it fell in a light cascade about her shoulders.

'Why don't you wear your hair like that during the day? You look better with it loose.'

'Would you like me to?'

'Yes, I would.'

'Regulations. The collar must be seen.'

'Tomorrow we'll be going across to the island. No one from the Seigniory will be there, or even on the boat.'

She gasped in mock outrage. 'Are you trying to get me into trouble?'

I pressed my leg harder on her foot. Still there, still touching.

'Perhaps,' I said. 'You know.'

'I'll still be on duty,' she said. 'I couldn't risk it.'

That, I felt, was the unambiguous admission of her feelings that I had been waiting for. Risk what? Risk being seen with me, with her hair down? Risk stirring up my emotions to the point where I could no longer control them? No, she said. No, she was saying, she couldn't risk it, not that, nor anything else.

Her hair was dry. After touching it quickly with her fingers, then combing it through a few times, she switched off the drier. The room was suddenly silent.

'Are you on duty now?' I said. 'I mean at this moment.'

'What do you think?'

'Obviously you're not,' I said, feeling dull for having asked the question. But it had reflected the confusion she had created all evening: the conflict between the uniform of the constabulary, the sexually available young woman.

'Right.'

'So risk doesn't come into it at the moment.'

'Everything's a risk. Isn't it?'

She bent forward again to unplug the drier. For an instant as she leaned over, the top of her robe fell loosely open and I glimpsed most of the soft mound of her breast. It was probably an accident – she hadn't meant that to happen. As she sat up again she pulled the wrap together across her chest, holding it primly against her with her hand. But she was regarding me with an open, unguarded expression.

'What next?' I said.

'What do you think?' she said. 'Are you going to ask me to stay?'

The words seemed to echo around me. I turned away from her, not wanting to put what I was feeling into words that I would have to hear myself say. I stared back at her, hardly breathing. She stood up, and the flex of the hairdrier dangled by her legs. I was beside her. The bed was next to both of us.

I said nothing.

'Well?' she prompted. 'It's what you'd like, isn't it?'

'I don't know,' I said in the end, lamely, inadequately. In reality I did know. I wanted to thrust her forcefully back across the top of the bed, slip my hands under that silken wrap, cover her face and shoulders with kisses, smother her with the weight of my body on hers ...

'We've only just met,' she said. 'I'm too young for you, you have someone else waiting at home, you're not ready for an affair, you're scared of what it might lead to. That's what you're thinking, isn't it?'

'No, it's not. None of those. I'm just not sure.'

'I thought perhaps you'd like me to stay.'

'I feel a terrible compulsion to explain,' I said. 'But you wouldn't want that. It's not your fault.'

98

'I made a mistake, I guess.' She tried to express a laugh, but it sounded insincere. I realized I was embarrassing her, and it was all without good reason.

'No, I'm not ready. I can't say why. I think I'm nervous. The trip and everything.'

'All right.' She held up the drier. 'Thanks for this. We can change back the plug later.'

She went quickly from the room, her robe swirling around her legs. She closed the door quietly behind her. I went to it, pressed my ear against the crack. I heard her moving outside in the corridor, heard her key go into her door, heard the door open and close. Then silence.

I knew that I should follow her now. Call her back now. Explain now. Knock on her door now. Don't let any more time slip by. Tomorrow she will be back on duty, her hair tied up again. The chance was vanishing even as I stood there, listening.

The silence endured. I made no move to follow her.

At last, when I could bear to, I went to the mirror in the tiny bathroom and stood looking at myself for a long time. I pulled at the loose skin around my eyes, smoothing the tiredness there, making the wrinkles temporarily vanish. But doing so pulled down my eyelids, gave red rims to my eyes, made me look worse.

I undressed and went to bed. I woke at intervals through the night, straining to hear some sound of Bella, urging her mentally to come back to my room.

It would have to be that way: she must come back to me. It could not be the other way round, because if she were to reject me the way I had just rejected her I wouldn't have been able to bear it.

It made me reflect on what her feelings about me must be, after what I had done. It was arrogant to assume she might return to me during that night, but if she had done so it would have resolved an uncertainty. Through everything that had happened in those brief minutes – the nearness of her, the banal and evasive conversation, the little glimpses of her young body – I had been attracted to her more powerfully than I had been attracted to any woman in years. I wanted her with a passion that made me turn restlessly and tensely in the unfamiliar hotel bed, tormented by frustration.

Even so, deep down I was terrified she would return. The struggle between sexual attraction and sexual repulsion had dogged my life. Ever since Seri.

The ticking clock by Alvie's bed and the wind gusting against the window in its loose frame – these were the only sounds in the pauses between conversations. I sat by the draughty window, looking down into the gardens and watching a black-robed priest tending one of the flowerbeds with a weeding tool. Why did they bother to grow flowers in such an inhospitable place? The lawns and the beds of the seminary's grounds were incongruous on Seevl, an island within an island, constantly watered and fertilized and prodded. When we went to visit in the winter months only the lawns survived but today there were clusters of tough-looking flowers, the sort you found in mountain passes, gripping the paltry earth with shallow roots. If I craned my neck I could see the huge vegetable garden where the theological students sometimes worked. On the other side of the grounds, invisible from my position at Alvie's window, was a small livestock farm. I knew that the seminary was not self-sufficient in food, because it was part of my uncle's job to organize the supplies from one of the south-coast harbours, a day's drive away across the mountains.

The priest at the flowerbed had glanced up at me when I first sat by the window, but since then he had ignored me. How long would it be before he, or one of the others, came to visit Alvie in her sickroom?

I looked across to the rising ground beyond the seminary walls. The skyline was a long, straight crag, with slopes of scree beneath it. Below the scree was the rank wild grass of the lower moors. There was a dead tower out there, a short way from the seminary, but it was one of the less conspicuous ones on Seevl, standing not against the sky but against the duller background of the crag.

My parents had started to discuss me. Lenden was getting

ready for exams, Lenden had not been studying properly, Lenden was not doing well. I sometimes wished I had the sort of parents who boasted about their child, but mine apparently believed that humiliating me in front of other people would goad me to greater efforts. I loathed them for it, of course. I glanced at Seri, who was sitting by herself at a table in the corner of the room, apparently reading a book. Naturally she was listening while pretending not to. When she saw me turn in her direction she looked back with a blank stare. No support there.

After the humiliation came the ordeal.

'Come here, Lenden,' said Aunt Alvie.

'What for?'

'Go to your aunt, Lenden,' said my father.

Reluctantly I left my seat by the window and went to stand beside the head of the bed. She stretched out a palsied hand and took mine. Her fingers were smooth and weak.

'You must work harder,' she said. 'For the sake of your future. For me. You want me to get well, don't you?'

'Yes,' I said, although I didn't see the connection. I was acutely aware of my parents watching me, of Seri's feigned indifference.

'When I was your age I won every prize at school,' Aunt Alvie said. 'It wasn't as much fun as being lazy, but in the end I was glad I'd tried. I know what it's like to have to be lazy now, lying here all day. You do understand, don't you?' I understood all too well. She wanted my future to be like her present. She wanted to inflict her illness on me. I shrank away from her but the soft pressure on my hand increased. 'Now kiss me,' she said.

I was constantly having to kiss Alvie: when we arrived, before and after every meal, as we departed ... and at special occasions, like this. It was part of the dread these visits held for me. I leaned forward, presenting my cheek to her cyanotic lips, but I was reluctant and delayed a little too long. She pulled my hand towards her. As her lips touched coldly against my cheek I felt her pressing my hand against her breast – her coarse wool cardigan, the thin nightdress, the surprisingly soft flesh below. I was at that age when other people's bodies are matters of endless curiosity. I was astounded by the feel of her breast.

I turned my face, quickly kissed her cold white cheek, then tried to move away. She was still clasping my hand against her soft chest.

'Promise me you'll try harder from now on,' Alvie said.

'I promise.'

I tugged my hand away. Released at last I stumbled back from the bed and returned to my chair by the window. My face was hot with the indignity of the interview but I could still feel the ghost of the flaccid breast in my hand.

I stared out of the window, waiting for them to find another subject to discuss. But they would not leave me.

'Why don't you go out for a walk, Lenden?'

I said nothing.

'Seraphina, do you think Lenden would like to see your den?'

'I'm reading,' Seri said in a voice that tried to convey pre-occupation.

Uncle Torm came into the room then, carrying a tray with cups and glasses. He put it down on the table where Seri was reading, covering her book.

'Take your cousin for a walk, Seri,' he said brusquely.

We were clearly being dispatched – something adult was about to be discussed. I should not have minded hearing whatever it was.

Seri and I looked at each other with expressions of resignation. We were at least at one on something. She led me out of the room, down the gloomy and damp-smelling corridor and out of the house. The wind immediately gusted around us. We crossed the small garden attached to Uncle Torm's house and emerged through a gate in a brick wall into the main grounds of the seminary.

Here Seri hesitated. 'What do you want to do?'

'Do you really have a den?' I said.

'No. That's what they call it.'

'What is it then?'

'My hideout.'

'Can I see it?' I sometimes climbed a tree in the garden at home to be by myself but I had never had a proper hideout. 'Is it secret?'

'Not now. But I don't let anyone in I don't want there.'

We walked along a gravel path edging one of the lawns. From an open window there came the sound of voices chanting a psalm. I walked with my feet scuffing up the gravel to try to drown the sound, because it reminded me of school.

We came to one of the wings of the seminary building. Seri led me towards some railings beside the base of the main wall, behind which were some narrow stone steps leading down to a basement. A priest, hoeing a flowerbed, paused in his work to watch us.

Seri ignored him and went down the steps. At the bottom she crouched down on her hands and knees and crawled through a low, dark hatchway. When she was inside she turned around and stuck out her head to look back at me. I was still waiting at the top of the steps.

'Come down here, Lenden. I'll show you something.'

The priest was working again but glancing back over his shoulder in my direction. I went quickly down the steps and crawled in through the hatchway. It was a smaller opening than I had expected and I had to squeeze through the narrow wooden frame. The space behind was dark, lit by two candles. As I stood up in the confined space Seri lit a third candle.

The hideout had apparently once been some kind of store or small cellar, because there were no windows and the hatch was the only way in or out. The ceiling was high enough for us to stand erect and although the space was narrow I could see that it extended away beyond the range of the weak candlelight. It was cool down there and the sound of the wind did not penetrate. Seri lit a fourth candle, high on a shelf running along the narrow room. The tiny cell smelled of match phosphor and candle wax and soot. There were two upended boxes on which to sit, and from somewhere Seri had found an old mat for the floor.

'Do you come here alone?' I said.

'Usually.'

'What do you do?'

'I thought I might show you.'

The candles cast a weak, fluttering light but as my eyes began to adjust from the bright daylight it seemed adequate. I sat down on one of the boxes.

I had been expecting Seri to sit on the other box but she came and stood close in front of me. She seemed deliberately to be hemming me in against the wall.

She said, 'Do you want to do something with me, Lenden?'

'What sort of thing?'

'How old are you?'

'Fourteen.'

'I'm fifteen. Have you done it yet?'

'Done what?'

'This is a dead secret. Between you and me.'

Before I realized what she was talking about Seri quickly raised the front of her skirt. With her other hand she pulled down the front of her pants. I saw a tangly black bush of hair at the junction of her legs.

I was so surprised by the suddenness of the revelation, and recoiled so sharply, that I almost fell sideways off the box. Seri let go and the elastic in her pants snapped them back into place, but she did not release the skirt. She held it high against her chest, looking down at herself. Her pants were dark coloured and woollen. The elastic bit into the plump flesh of her belly.

I was acutely embarrassed by what she had done, but also excited and curious.

'Do that again,' I said. 'Let me see.'

She stepped back, almost as if she were about to change her mind, but then she came forward again.

'You do it,' she said, thrusting her abdomen towards me. 'You pull them down. All the way down.'

I reached forward tentatively and took the top of her pants

104

in my fingers. I pulled the cloth down until I could see the first growth of her hair.

'Further!' she said, knocking my hand out of the way. She pulled the pants down, front and back, so that they clung to her legs above the knees. Her triangle of hair, curling and black, stood unambiguously before me. I could not stop staring at her, feeling hot and prickly, a strange yearning in my loins.

'Do you want a feel?' Seri said.

'No.'

'Touch me. I want you to feel.'

'I'm not sure I should.'

'Then let me look at you. I'll feel you.'

I didn't want that, not then, shyness and fright rising in me unmanageably, so I reached out and touched her hair with my fingers. Seri moved forward, pressing herself against my fingertips.

'Lower down, Lenden,' she said. 'Feel a bit lower down.'

I turned my hand so that the palm was up and reached for the junction of her legs. There was less hair, a fold of skin. I snatched my hand away.

Seri came forward even more.

'Touch me again. Go right inside.'

'I can't!'

'Then let me touch you!'

'No!' The thought of that happening, of someone, anyone at all, touching and exploring, was inconceivable. I was still growing. Too much of all that had never been explained to me. I was ashamed of my body, of growing up.

'All right,' Seri said, sounding excited. 'Put your finger in me. Right inside. I don't mind.'

She seized my wrist and brought my hand up against her. She was damp now, and when my fingers reached forward they slipped easily over the soft flaps of skin and slid into the warm recess behind. That intimacy took me beyond hesitation. I pushed forward, trying to go further in, wanting to sink my fingers, my hand, into that exciting wet hollow. But then she stepped back smartly, and pushed down her skirt with her hand.

I said, 'Seri—'

'Ssh!'

She bent low and listened beside the square of shadowed daylight that was the hatch. Then she straightened and hoisted up her pants with a sinuous movement of her hips.

'What's going on?'

'I think there's someone outside,' she said. 'I heard something fall.'

'Let me touch you again,' I said.

'Not now. Not if there's someone listening.'

'When?'

'In a minute. We'll have to go somewhere else. Is that what you want?'

'Of course I do!' It was difficult to believe that this was Seri, my detested cousin!

'I know somewhere safe,' she said. 'Outside the seminary ... a short walk.'

'And then I can ...?'

'You can go the whole way if you like,' she said casually, but the words had such power I almost fainted.

She made me crawl first through the hatch and she blew out the candles. I scrambled through. As I did so, a shadow falling from above moved quickly. The priest we had seen earlier was at the top of the steps but he was now backing away rapidly. I went up the steps and saw him hurrying across to where he had dropped his hoe on the path. By the time Seri had joined me outside he was leaning over his work on the garden again, hoeing the soil with quick, nervous movements.

He did not look up as Seri and I walked hurriedly along the gravel path, but I glanced back as we passed through the gate. He was standing upright with the hoe in his hand, staring towards us.

'Seri, he was spying on us.'

She said nothing but took my hand and led me, running, through the long wild grass outside the seminary walls.

*

106

A rental car was waiting for us outside a side street office in Seevl Town, a Seigniory pass already attached to the windscreen. I took the front passenger seat beside Serjeant Reeth. We were crammed close together by the narrow body of the old car, the two bucket seats at the front divided only by a floor-mounted parking brake. She drove slowly through the narrow streets towards the hills.

After a long restless period I had finally fallen asleep at some point in the small hours of the morning. I had woken up at day-break in a complex, contradictory mood. I was still giddy with the sexual desire the young woman had awakened in me, but I was also feeling embarrassed, apologetic, introspective, ashamed, fatigued. I winced inside whenever I remembered the way I had turned her down. As we drove out of Seevl Town I was coping with this stew of feelings by keeping still, forcing myself to appear calm and by saying as little as possible. Bella said she would be needing me to direct her across the island, so I sat, as once my mother had sat, with the map open on my knee.

Bella had appeared at breakfast in the hotel dining room, crisp in her uniform, once more the policewoman. Uniforms are of course symbols of the organizations they represent, and Serjeant Reeth when dressed as a policewoman was not the same sort of person as damp-haired Bella Reeth had seemed to be, in her scanty silken robe, sitting on the low hotel chair with bare knees poking up, while I crouched in a torment of indecision beside her. That image of her, which for a few minutes had been literally within my reach, now became a vision of fantasy and impossible allure. Why I had not accepted the invitation she threw down I could no longer imagine.

I had hoped that she would appear in the morning wearing civilian clothes and dress in her uniform only once breakfast was over, giving me a chance to align what had happened with the fact of spending the day ahead with her. That was not to be.

I knew that the events of the evening before could not be pretended away by silence, or denied by her wearing her starchy uniform. While we waited on Jethra dockside for the ferry, while we sat together in the unheated saloon of the boat, while we walked through Seevl Town in search of the car rental company, the words unsaid hovered in the space between us like a physical barrier. The longer I was with her the more I became obsessed with her physical presence, haunted by my memory of her young body in the loose silk wrap and frantic about the way I had undermined everything at the end.

I was still paralysed by my need to explain, but the years of silence I had observed had created a habit it was almost impossible to break.

Now we drove. Sometimes, as she shifted gear in the elderly car, her hand or sleeve would brush lightly against my knee. To see if it was accidental, as it seemed to be, I moved my leg unobtrusively a little to the side and it did not happen again. Later, I allowed my leg to move back, because her touch excited me.

Once, at a junction on the higher slopes of the moors, we went to the map for guidance. Her head bent down beside mine. I longed for her to turn her face towards me.

Watching the sombre green of Seevl's fells my thoughts turned by imperceptible degrees away from that intrigue to the other, the old dreads and fears: my feelings about the island and the seminary.

My memories of the moorland road were unreliable, but the mood induced by the scenery was a familiar companion, instantly recognizable after twenty years away. To someone seeing it for the first time, as Bella was seeing it, Seevl would appear wild, barren, grossly empty, but probably lacking in undercurrents of threat. The moors and rocks were rounded by centuries of harsh winters and unrelenting gales: where the rock was exposed no plant life clung to it except in the most sheltered corners and then it was only the hardiest of mosses or the lowliest of lichens. There was a violent, uncompromising splendour to Seevl, a scenic ruggedness unknown in Faiandland. Yet the bleak scenery was to me merely a context. The moors were neutral but they contained a menace. My feelings were always influenced by awareness of that menace.

As Bella drove us along the narrow road I was already imagining

108

ahead, thinking about the crag-enclosed valley at the other end of the island, with its cluster of grim, limestone buildings, the lawns and the incongruous flowerbeds.

Bright sunlight did not suit Seevl. Although on this day the sky was clouded, the sun broke through from time to time, casting for brief periods a bright unnatural radiance on the landscape. We had the car windows closed and the heater on, yet still the cold reached us. On the higher stretches, the sideways blast of wind against the car buffeted and rocked it as it lurched on the broken surface of the road. I shivered every now and then, shaking my shoulders, pretending to feel the cold more than I really did, because it was the whole island that was chilling me and I did not want Bella to realize that.

She drove slowly and expertly, steering more cautiously along the rutted tracks than ever my father had. The car was in low gear for much of the time, the engine's note fast and high, constantly changing. Still we said hardly anything to each other, only a few occasional remarks about which way to go. I watched for familiar landmarks – a cluster of standing stones, the village in the valley from where you could see part of Jethra's coastal suburbs, a fall of water, the dead towers – and sometimes I could direct her from memory without referring to the map. My knowledge of the landscape was erratic: there were long sections of the road that felt new to me and I would be sure we had lost our way, but then some landmark I remembered would finally appear, surprising me.

We stopped for a midday meal at a house in one of the little hamlets. There was planning involved: it turned out that we were expected, a meal was ready. I saw Bella sign a document, a form that would reimburse the woman for her expense and trouble.

When we reached the narrow part of the island and travelled along the road above the southern cliffs, Bella pulled the car over to the side and stopped the engine. We were shielded from the wind by a high, rocky bank and some bushes, and the sun warmed us. We stood by the car, looking in shared silence across the glistering seascape, the huge dark mounds of the islands, the silver-clouded sky with its beams of brilliant sunlight striking down, the view that as a child I had only been able to glimpse from my parents' moving car. They never stopped to look.

'Do you know the names of any of those islands?' I said.

Bella had removed her cap, leaving it on the driver's seat in the car. Wisps of hair blew lightly around her face.

'I can't identify them from here,' she said in a moment. 'But Torquin must be one of them. We have a base there and my brother sent me a letter while he was staying on Torquin. He said it wasn't far from home. If Torquin's one of them then Derril must be another, because that's part of the Serque group of islands, isn't it? Where the Covenant was drawn up?'

'You seem to know a lot about the islands,' I said.

'You've just heard every fact I know.'

'So you've never been in the Archipelago?'

'Only here, with you.'

Only Seevl, the offshore island.

As the clouds moved and the chiaroscuro of sunlight swept slowly across the view, we could see that the islands were many different shades of green. It was impossible to discern details from such a distance, only shapes and broad areas of colour. Like Bella, I knew little about the islands I could see. I did know that most of the islands close to Jethra were part of the Serque Group, that they were primarily dependent on dairy farming and fishing, and that most of the indigenous people spoke the same language as I did. It was school knowledge, half-remembered, all but useless. I wished now, as I had done so many times in the past, that I had travelled out to the islands when I was younger, when the restrictions weren't so severe. The war we were fighting was ultimately about the neutrality and domain of the islands in the Archipelago. Like so many people I was ignorant of not just the issues but the actual islands and seas that were the essence of the conflict and was thus ignorant of the ultimate dispute of the war.

'Have you been thinking about yesterday evening?' Bella said suddenly, leaning forward and hunching her shoulders so that she appeared to be looking down at the rocks and the surf so far below us at the base of the cliff.

My heart lurched. I had been bracing myself to say something. I was not expecting her to bring up the subject. I kept staring at the sea, the sky, the islands.

In the end I felt my silence was becoming more significant than any words, so I said, 'Yes. Ever since.'

'I can't stop thinking about it either. Was I wrong about you?'

'No,' I said, quickly. 'I simply wasn't ready. I'm so sorry. I felt terrible afterwards.'

'I did too. But what you wanted is probably best. You know, when you've only just met someone, it's probably better—'

'To hold back a little?' I filled in gratefully.

'I only want to be sure I hadn't made a mistake.'

Silence fell again. I was thinking, Mistake about what? Does she mean what I think she means, or does she mean something else, or am I imagining everything? Nothing was any clearer for what she had said.

At least we had spoken about it, however evasively.

I said finally, 'We'll have to stay tonight at the seminary. You know we won't have time to get back to Seevl Town today?'

'Yes, I know.'

'They'll probably have guest rooms in the college.'

'That's all right,' she said. 'I went to a convent school.'

She went round to the driver's door and climbed inside the car. We drove on. I knew it took at least another hour from here and the daylight hours were running out. Bella said nothing after our short break, concentrating on the difficult drive. I stared out of the window at my side, surrendering reluctantly to my memories and to the oppressive mood of the island.

Seri held my hand in hers, not affectionately but in the way a determined parent will hold a child's. We leapt and ran across the rough ground, the coarse grasses whipping against our legs. It was the first time I had ever ventured outside the seminary grounds. Never until then had I realized how the stout walls acted as a bulwark against the rest of the island. Out here the wind already seemed stiffer and colder.

'Where are we going?' I said, gasping because I was breathless.

'Somewhere I know.'

She released my hand and went on ahead.

'Can't we do it here?' I said. Some of the sexual tension that had built up in her hideout had been dissipated by our sudden decision to flee and I wanted to carry on where we had left off before she changed her mind.

'Out here in the open?' she said, rounding on me. 'I told you it was secret.'

'There's long grass,' I said lamely. 'No one would see.'

'Come on!'

She set off again, leaping down a shallow slope towards a stream. I held back for a moment, staring guiltily towards the seminary. I could see there was someone there, outside the walls, walking in our direction. I guessed at once that it must be the priest with the hoe, although he was too far away for me to be sure.

I ran after Seri and jumped across the narrow stream to join her.

'There's someone following us. That priest.'

'He won't follow us where we're going!'

It was now obvious where Seri was leading me. The ground sloped up steeply from the stream, rising eventually to the high rocky crag ahead. Long before that eminence and a short way from us, built from the ubiquitous limestone of the island, was the dead tower.

I looked back and saw that even if the priest were still following us we had moved temporarily out of his sight. Seri marched on, already a long way ahead of me, scrambling up the hillside through the windswept grass.

The tower appeared to be much like the others I had seen around the island, although I had never been as close before: it was about as tall as a four-storey house, hexagonal in shape and with window frames higher up which might once have contained

112

glass but which were now vacant squares in the stonework. There was an unpainted wooden door in the base, hanging open on its hinges, and all around in the grass were pieces of broken stone facing and fallen tiles. There had once been a roof, built in the shape of a candle-snuffer cone, but now most of it had collapsed and only two or three beams remained to declare its old shape.

Seri was waiting for me by the open door.

'Hurry, Lenden!'

I stepped over a heap of fallen masonry and looked up apprehensively at the ruined tower as it loomed over me.

'You're not going inside, are you?'

'It's been here for years.'

'But it's falling down!'

'Not any more.'

The only thing I knew for sure about the dead towers of Seevl was that no one went near them. Yet there was Seri, standing by the door as casually as if it were just another hideout. I was torn between my dread of the tower and what Seri would let me do with her inside.

'Aren't these towers dangerous?' I said.

'No, they're only old. This one was something to do with the college, when it was still a monastery.'

Seri went through the door. I hesitated only a few seconds longer before following her. She pushed the door closed behind us.

It was surprisingly gloomy inside after the harsh light outside. There was an almost intact upper floor above us. Joists and plank flooring were still in place up there and two small windows set a short distance below this ceiling admitted the only daylight. A fallen beam lay at an angle across the room, propped up against the wall. The floor was littered with broken fragments of glass and plaster, as well as many large pieces of stone.

'See, there's nothing to worry about.' Seri used her foot to push several pieces of stone out of the way, roughly clearing a space on the wooden floor. 'It's just an old dump the priests will never come to.'

113

'That priest we saw in the garden was definitely following us,' I said.

Seri turned away from me, swung the door open part of the way and peered out. I stood behind her, looking over her shoulder. We could both see the priest. He had reached the stream and was walking along the bank, apparently trying to find somewhere he could cross.

Seri closed the door again.

'He won't come here,' she said again. 'Not to the tower. None of the priests will come here. They say the tower has evil in it, which is why it's safe for us.'

I glanced around in the dim half-light nervously.

'What's evil about it?'

'Nothing. It's their superstitious beliefs. They say something wicked happened a long time ago, but they never tell you what it was.'

'He's still coming towards us,' I said. 'Whatever you say.'

'You wait and see what he does.'

I went back to the door and again eased it open so that there was a slit of daylight. The priest had moved across to the side but was still the same sort of distance away from the tower as he had been when we last looked. He was standing with his hands on his hips, staring up the slope towards us. I closed the door and told Seri.

'You see?' she said.

'But he'll wait until we come out. What will happen then?'

'Nothing will happen,' Seri said. 'What I do is none of his business. I know who that is: it's Father Grewe. He's always following me around, trying to find out what I'm doing. I'm used to him. Shall we start?'

'If you want to,' I said. The mood had left me.

'Get undressed, then.'

'Me? I thought you—'

'We both undress.'

'I don't want to.' I stared down at the rubble-strewn floor. 'Not yet, anyway. You do it first.'

'All right. I don't mind.'

She reached up under her skirt and pulled her pants down her legs. She tossed them on the floor.

'Your turn,' she said. 'Take something off.'

I hesitated, then complied by removing my pullover. Seri undid two buttons on the side of her skirt and it slid down her legs. She turned away from me to drape the garment over the fallen beam and for a moment I saw the pinkness of her buttocks, slightly dimpled.

'Now you,' she said.

'Let me feel you again first,' I said. 'I've never done ...'

Some compassion softened her determination to make me undress with her. She sat down on the floor, keeping her knees together and reaching forward to rest her hands on her ankles. I could see none of her secret places, just the pale curve of her thighs as they rounded towards her buttocks. Her sweater finished at her waist.

'All right,' she said. 'But you have to be more gentle. You were jabbing at me before.'

She leaned back and rested her elbows on the floor behind her. She parted her legs. I saw the black thatch of hair, the whorl of pink that was below, revealed but mysterious. Staring at her I moved forward, crouching down.

I was suddenly as sexually aroused as I had been before: it switched on like a powerful motor, compelling me towards her almost against my will. I felt a tightness in my throat, a sweatiness in my palms. That passive, lipped organ, lying between her thighs like an upright mouth, waited for my touch. I reached forward, ran my fingertips across the lips, felt how warm they were, felt how moist it was between them. Seri sucked in her breath. She was as tense as I was.

Something small and hard whacked against the door, startling us both. Seri twisted away from me, turning to one side. My hand brushed against the top of her thigh, then she was gone from me. She scattered small pieces of rubble as she swung around.

115

'Don't move,' she said to me. She went quickly to the door, eased it open and peered out.

I heard distantly, 'Seri, come out of that place. You know it is forbidden.'

She closed the door.

'He won't come near you, so long as you stay in here.' She picked up her skirt and stepped into it, buttoning it again at the waist. 'I'll have to go and talk to him. I want him to leave us alone. Wait in here and don't let him see you.'

'But he knows I'm here,' I said, impatiently. 'He followed us from the college. I'll come with you. We ought to be going back anyway.'

'No!' she said, and I saw the familiar quick-tempered Seri of whom I had always been a little frightened. 'There's more to do than just touching.' Her hand was on the door. 'Stay here, keep out of sight and I'll be back in a few moments.'

The door slammed behind her, shaking on its loose old hinges. I peeped through the crack, saw her running down through the long grass to where the priest was waiting. He spoke to her with angry gestures, waving his hand towards my hiding place, but she was uncowed. She stood near to him, kicking idly at the grasses while he berated her.

There was a faint, musky fragrance on my fingertips. I drew back from the door and looked around at the filthy, broken interior of the tower. Without Seri I felt ill at ease in the old ruin. The ceiling was sagging – what if it fell in on me? The constant wind blustered around the tower and a piece of broken wood, hanging by the window aperture, knocked to and fro.

Minutes passed. I began to wonder guiltily about the possible consequences of being caught here. Suppose the priest told Torm and my parents that we had been up to something, or that we were gone long enough for them to guess anyway? Would they smell the musk on my hand? If they suspected the truth, or even a part of it, there would be a terrible scene.

I heard the priest's voice in a freak silence of the wind. He said something in a sharp tone of voice, but Seri's response was

116

laughter. I returned to the door, put my eye to the slit and looked out at them. The priest was holding Seri by the hand, tugging her, but she was pulling back from him. To my surprise I realized that they were no longer arguing but seemed to be playing. Their hands slipped apart, but it was an accident because they joined again immediately. The playful pulling went on.

I stepped back from the door, puzzled and confused.

We were in a part of the seminary to which I had never been before: a large office situated behind the main entrance. We had been greeted by Father Confessor Henner, who was thin, bespectacled and younger than I had expected from his letter. He tried to be tactful and solicitous: he enquired after my well-being following the long journey from Jethra, he gave me his condolences on the death of my uncle, a tragic loss, a hard-working servant of God. He handed over the key to the house and then pointed out that we were in time for a meal in the refectory. Father Henner told us we could eat with the students but when we arrived at the large room we were directed to a small table in the corner, away from everyone else. Many curious glances came our way. Night was falling beyond the stained-glass windows.

I could hear the wind, made louder by the airy space above us, the high, vaulted roof of the refectory.

'What are you thinking?' Bella said, over the sounds of the students clattering their dishes on the other side of the hall.

'I'm wishing we didn't have to stay here tonight. I'd forgotten how much I loathe this place.'

We returned to Father Henner's office. After a delay he took us across the grounds to the house, leading the way with a battery flashlight. Our feet crunched on the gravel pathway, while the misshapen trees moved blackly against the night sky. The vague shape of the moors beyond loomed around us. I unlocked the door and Father Henner turned on a light in the corridor. A dim, low-wattage bulb shed yellow light on the shabby floor and wallpaper. I smelled damp rot and mould.

I remembered walking along this corridor: there was a kitchen on the left, another room next to it, opposite the kitchen on the right was my uncle's former office. At the end of the corridor was the flight of stairs to the next floor. By the bottom of the stairs was the dark-varnished door to Alvie's room.

'You understand that while your uncle was still alive we weren't able to maintain the house?' Father Henner said. 'The whole place has to be renovated.'

'Yes,' I said.

'You'll find that we have already removed much of the furniture,' he went on. 'Your uncle naturally bequeathed the more valuable pieces to the college, and some of the other effects belonged to us already.' He indicated a long handwritten inventory he had given me earlier, which I had not yet had a chance to examine. 'You may take with you any of the remaining pieces, or arrange to have them destroyed. We have tried to trace the daughter, but without success. As far as we are concerned you are his only next of kin. We really must ask you to finalize everything while you are here.'

'Yes, I will,' I said, thinking of Seri, the daughter. The priest had suddenly made me wonder, where are you now, Seraphina?

'What about my uncle's papers?' I said.

'They're all here in the house. Again, we ask you to take what you want when you leave. The rest will have to be incinerated.'

I opened the door into the office and switched on the overhead light. The room was completely empty, with pale squares on the walls where pictures had hung and impressions on the old linoleum where his desk, chair, filing cabinet, and so on, had stood. A dark patch of rising damp spread up from the floor, covering half of one wall.

'As I said, most of the rooms have been emptied,' said Father Henner. 'Everything has been moved to the kitchen, and of course there's your dear aunt's room. Your uncle left it as it had been while she was still alive.'

Bella had moved to the end of the short corridor and was standing by the door to my aunt's room. Father Henner nodded to her and she turned the handle. I felt a sudden compulsion to back away, fearing that Alvie would still be there in the room, waiting for me, and would somehow burst out upon us as soon as the door was released.

'I'll wish you goodnight and God bless,' said Father Henner, moving back to the main door. 'I shall be in my office tomorrow, should you need any more information. Otherwise, if all is well you may deposit the key to the house with the secretary, when you leave.'

I said, 'Father, before you go – where are we sleeping tonight?'

'Has that not been arranged already?'

Bella said, 'Yes, through the Chamberlain's office.'

'The Chamberlain?'

'At the Seigniory.'

'I know nothing of that,' Father Henner said, frowning. He opened the door and his black soutane ballooned in the sudden wind gusting in from outside. 'You may use the house, of course.'

'The Chamberlain arranged for there to be guest rooms for us tonight. Under warrant from the Seignior.'

Father Henner shook his head.

'In the college?' he said. 'We would never have agreed to that. We have no facilities for women.'

Bella looked at me questioningly. I, stricken with a dread of spending a night in the house, shook my head.

'Isn't there somewhere else we could go to?' I said. 'There must be an inn somewhere near, or even a house—'

'Are there any beds here?' Bella said, pushing Alvie's door wide open and peering into the room. My aunt's folding screen was still there, making a temporary corridor into the room and blocking the view of the rest.

Father Henner was outside in the windswept dark.

'You'll have to make do,' he said. 'It's only for one night, after all. May God be with you.'

He went. The door slammed behind him. Relative quiet fell. The stone walls muted the wind, at least while we stood here in

119

the corridor in the centre of the house, away from the windows.

'What are we going to do?' Bella said. 'Sleep on the floor?'

'Let's see what they've left for us.'

We went into Aunt Alvie's room; my dear aunt.

Pretending to myself that it was an ordinary room, pretending to Bella, I went past her and walked in. The central light was beyond the folding screen so the way was shadowed. At the end, facing us, someone from the seminary had stacked two huge piles of old documents. Tomorrow I should have to go through them. Dust lay in a gritty film on the top sheets. Bella was behind me. I reached the end of the screen, looked round it into the rest of the room. The narrow double bed, Alvie's sickbed, was still there, dominating everything. Tea chests had been brought into the room, two extra chairs were crammed against the wall, books lay in uneven piles on the table beneath the window, picture frames rested on the mantelpiece ... but the bed, piled high with pillows, was the focus of the room, as it had always been. By its head was the bedside table: dusty old pill bottles, a notebook, a folded lace handkerchief, a telephone, a bottle that had once held lavender water. These I remembered, these had remained here ever since her death. So long ago. Uncle Torm had not removed anything.

Alvie's presence still occupied the bed. Only her body was absent.

I could smell her, see her, hear her. Above the bed, on the wall behind the top rail of the brass headboard, were two darker marks on the time-darkened wallpaper. I remembered: Alvie had a characteristic gesture, reaching up behind her to grip the rail with both hands, perhaps to brace herself against pain. Her hands, those long years of her hands gripping the brass rod like that, had left the marks.

The windows were black squares of night. Bella pulled the curtains across and dust cascaded down. I could hear the wind again and I thought, Alvie must have known this wind, every night, every day.

'There's a bed, at least,' Bella said.

'You can use it,' I said at once. 'I'll sleep on the floor.'

'There must be another bed somewhere. In one of the rooms upstairs.'

But we went to look and there was not. The upper storey of the house had been cleared. Not even the electric lights worked up there.

Back in Alvie's room I stood alone, breathing that musty air, while Bella went to collect the car from where she had first parked it. I tried not to look around me but everywhere I laid my eyes were reminders of what this room had meant to me when I was a child. When I heard the sound of Bella's car returning I was starting to shake with fear, and I practically rushed outside to find her. I helped her carry in our bags, concealing my fears with activity, then once again we stood together in Alvie's room, facing the inevitable.

Neither of us could sleep on the stone flags of the downstairs rooms, neither of us was prepared to sleep alone in the dark upstairs. There was a bed, and it was large enough for two to share. Proprieties, instincts, wishes, curiosities, all faded in the face of the factual state of affairs. Whatever we had planned or had been uncertain about the previous evening, it was now plain that Bella and I were going to have to sleep in the same bed now. We were both worn out after the long day of travelling and the cold house was chilling us. There was literally nothing else to do but go to bed.

Together we stripped the bed of the ancient sheets and blankets and took them through the main door into the night to shake out what dust we could. Next we took out the mattress and pillows for the same treatment. Bella made up the bed quickly, smoothing the sheets and blankets, getting me to help straighten them out.

I busied myself, trying to be useful, distracting myself from the thoughts: this is Alvie's bed, this is where she lay, this is where she died and this is where I'm going to make love to Bella. In Alvie's bed.

At last it was ready. We took it in turns to use the bathroom on the floor above, going up the stairs with the flashlight Father Henner had left for us. I went first. When Bella went after me – we said nothing, our eyes did not meet as we passed on the stairs – I sat on the edge of Alvie's bed listening to the sounds of Bella's footsteps on the bare boards upstairs.

I had spent all day with her but barely felt anything for her. I was swamped by memories and obsessed with my own impressions of the island. That tentative first intimacy the night before – her hair, the silken wrap, the accidental glimpses of her body, the clean bedroom, the quietness of the empty hotel – now felt a lifetime away. It was that brief incident that had started to arouse these memories but being on the island had done the rest. Now the focus had tightened even more: here, in Alvie's room, all my fears met. The shadow of my past and how it was barring me from Bella, the memories of Alvie and the winds and darkness that surrounded the house, the dead tower and the fumbled sexual contact with Seri. Now Bella, with me in Alvie's room, alone together, our interest in each other declared, soon to be in bed with each other.

I heard her upstairs, walking again across the creaking floorboards. I realized that she was about to return to the room. I was not ready! I made a sudden decision: I stripped off my outer clothes and while still wearing my underclothes I slid quickly under the sheets. I pulled them up to my chin.

Bella switched off the room's central light as she entered the room. When she reached the end of the folding screen she looked straight at the bed and saw me lying there. I said nothing but returned her stare. She had loosened her hair from its bun, but she was still wearing the police uniform.

I said, 'Nothing need happen tonight. We're both tired.'

I was trembling. The sheets were unwashed in years, sticky to the touch, smelling like something that had been buried for a decade, cold and old and touching me all over. I longed to have her there in the bed beside me.

'Is that how you want it to be?' she said.

'I'm freezing cold,' I said evasively.

'I am too.'

She stood there, dressed like a cop, with her long fair hair loose on her shoulders and a toothbrush in her hand. She made no move to come to bed.

'I could still sleep on the floor,' she said.

'No. It won't be like last night. I'd like you with me.'

I watched, and did not watch, as Bella undressed in the glow from the table lamp. With her back towards me she took off the uniform with care, folding the garments and laying them precisely over the back of one of the chairs. She removed her jacket first, then the thick khaki blouse and the dark serge skirt. Underneath she was wearing suspender belt, stockings, black pants and a strong, sensible bra. She took everything off, without performance but also without coyness. Still with her back to me she stood naked, and blew her nose on a paper tissue.

Before she turned round I said, 'Do you want me to switch off the light?'

'No,' she said, turning towards me. She crossed to the bed, raised the sheets and slipped in beside me. The bed was not wide and the mattress sagged readily, so our bodies were in contact from the first moment she was there. Her flesh was icy cold. 'Will you hold me?' she said, her voice against my face.

My arm went easily around her – she was slim and her body shaped itself comfortably against mine. I could feel the plump weight of her breast on me, the prickle of her hair against my thigh. My hand rested lightly and naturally on one buttock. I was getting aroused already but did not move, not wanting to declare it yet.

She ran her free hand lightly over my stomach, then up to my breasts.

She said, 'You're still wearing your bra.'

'I thought—'

'You're so shy, Lenden. You don't have to do anything. Let me.'

She slipped her hand inside my bra and found my nipple, then kissed me on my neck. Pressing herself against me she slipped the bra strap down from my shoulder and bared one breast. She cupped it in a hand, and took my nipple gently in her mouth.

Soon she had me naked and was crouching over me, her breasts lightly stroking my bare skin, her hand resting intimately between my legs. I stiffened, aroused and terrified.

Then she was astride me, creeping forward with her legs wide open, brushing herself over me. She guided my hand to her sex, thrust my fingers in, clamped down on me. One of her breasts filled my open mouth.

She left the table lamp alight, and although the room remained cold she soon had thrown back all the covers and was making love to me on top of them.

It ended at last. While Bella lay back on the bed, propped up against a pillow with a single sheet covering her, I went to the window and stared out into the night. The dark was impenetrable. My breathing steadied. I heard Bella moving in the bed, rearranging the bedclothes over herself.

'Lenden, you're still confusing me,' she said.

'How?'

'Was that the first time you've been with another woman?'

'No, of course it wasn't.'

'You seemed so nervous.'

'I'm sorry. I can't explain. Perhaps it was because it was the first time we were with each other.'

'Why do you make it so difficult for yourself?'

'I didn't mean to.' I was clutching one of the smelly old blankets around my body, the ancient woollen material feeling stiff against my skin. 'Bella, I have to ask you something. It's been bothering me.'

I turned back to face her and saw her reaching back to grip the brass bedhead behind her, her fists holding on to the rod almost exactly where Alvie had made dark marks on the wallpaper. Her long hair was trailing down across her shoulder. I looked away quickly.

'What is it?' she said.

'You said you'd volunteered for this job. You seemed to know about me, the kind of woman I am. Is that right?'

'Yes.'

'Then how did you know before you met me?'

'Lenden, I'm a cop. There are files on everyone these days. It's not difficult for me to access them. You've never asked about my life, so you wouldn't know. But last year I split up with my lover, and I've been alone ever since. You don't know how difficult it is to meet the right people. Or maybe you do. I was getting lonely, really lonely. Then I realized I had been in the police long enough to be eligible for escort work. I thought it might be a way of meeting people.'

'So you make a habit of this.'

'No ... it's the first time. I promise you. When I met you yesterday, at the station, as soon as I saw you I was – attracted to you.'

I said, 'They have that about me on file? That I'm homosexual?'

'They're more circumspect than that. They list known partners or lovers. The file said that you had had lovers, and I could see their files too. They were all women. Of course. So I—'

'Why are the police interested?'

'It's not only the police. The files are compiled by the Seigniory, and we can get access to them. I know I shouldn't have done it. And I shouldn't have told you.'

The cold was seeping into me and although I clutched the clammy blanket more tightly it did no good. I sat down on the end of the bed, feeling Bella's leg close beside me.

'Are you angry?' she said.

I thought about that, searching my feelings as frankly as I could. In the end I said, 'No, not angry. Certainly not with you, not even with the government. I've gone past caring.'

'But you still weren't certain of me?' Bella said.

'No.'

'What's the problem?'

'I can't tell you.'

'Are you involved with a man now?' she said.

'No.'

'Another woman, then?'

'No, not that either.'

'I wish I knew what it was.'

'If we stay together maybe I'll find a way of telling you,' I said. 'I don't want to make a mystery of it. I'm glad we've made love, but we still hardly know each other. Don't rush me.'

'How do I slow down?'

'You could tell me you'd like to see me again. After this, I mean. When we're back on the mainland.'

'Come back to bed, Lenden. We're both cold. We can hold each other. I want you with me. We can meet again after this trip, whenever you like.'

So I crawled under the bedclothes and this time she turned out the table lamp. We kissed affectionately, then lay still for a while. When we were feeling warmer she made love to me again. I tried not to stiffen against her. I tried to yield, tried to enjoy, tried to feel not only the urging of lust but also the release of it. It was easier the second time, but not by much. I was beginning to learn her body, as she was learning mine. Some time later she fell asleep, curled up comfortably against me. I was sitting up against the pillows, leaning my head on the brass rails behind me, my hair falling down and covering one of my breasts. The bed smelt of bodies.

Something happened to me inside that dead tower while Seri was outside with the priest. I can describe what it was, but I cannot explain it. There was no warning of it and I had no fearful premonition. It is simply what occurred and it is that which has remained to haunt my life ever since.

I was irritated with Seri and curious about what she was doing out there with the priest who had followed us. She had suddenly awakened my sexuality, filled my heart with promises and hopes, but then she twice denied me. I wanted the knowledge she had seemed to be offering and although I did not realize it at the time I craved the consequent knowledge of myself.

She had told me to wait, though, to stay out of sight. I was prepared to do both, but not for long. I had expected her to get

126

rid of the priest as quickly as possible, but instead she was still out there with him.

Thinking of what was going on outside I barely registered the sound of a low snuffling that came to me over the noise of the wind.

I was picking up my pullover, retrieving Seri's pants. I was about to go outside to join her because I wanted to know what she was doing.

I was stuffing her pants into my skirt pocket when I heard the noise again. It surprised me. I had heard it the first time without really thinking about it and had ignored it, but then it happened again. It was like nothing I had ever heard before. It was animalistic but there was a human quality to it too, as if some beast had managed to form half a spoken word before reverting to a grunt. It did not frighten me. I thought for a moment that Seri might have returned and was playing some kind of joke on me.

I called her name, but there was no answer.

I stood in the centre of the floor of the crumbling tower, looking around, thinking for the first time that perhaps some large beast was in the vicinity. I listened, trying to screen out the persistent noise of the wind so that I could hear the sound again.

A beam of Seevl's bright cool sunlight was striking in through one of the high windows, illuminating the wall beside the door. Like much of the rest of the tower this part of the wall was crumbling away. A jagged hole, about the size of a man's head, had formed in the inner wall. Beyond, the cavity of the tower wall was revealed, with the great grey stones of the main outer structure dimly visible behind. It was one of several such holes in the wall that I could see, but I was suddenly certain that this one was the source of the animal noise.

I stepped towards it, still thinking that Seri must be behind it somehow, fooling around outside the door.

Something moved deep inside the cavity and although I was staring straight at the place I saw only a dark, quick movement. The sun went in as one of the clouds passed in front of it. It suddenly seemed much colder. Moments later the sun came out again but the feeling of cold remained. I knew then that the chill was in me.

I placed my hand on the brickwork, leaning towards the hole, trying to peer down into it. I did not want to go too close but I was convinced someone, or something, was in there. I could sense a gentle heat, as of a living body. I reached down tentatively, into the dark.

There was a violent noise, a shocking burst of movement and something inside the wall grabbed my hand.

It pulled me, dragging my arm down into the hole until my shoulder scraped painfully against the stonework. I screamed in surprise, gasping in terror. I tried to pull back to free myself, but whatever it was that had taken hold had sharp claws or teeth and they were biting into my skin. My face was jammed sideways against the wall, the skin of my bare upper arm grazing agonizingly against the broken stones around the edge of the hole.

'Let go!' I shouted helplessly, trying to tug my arm away.

As the thing grabbed me I had instinctively balled my hand into a fist. Now I could feel it contained in something wet and warm, hard on one side, soft on the other. I pulled again and the grip of the teeth tightened. Whatever it was in there was no longer dragging me down but was holding me. When I pulled back against it the sharp teeth tightened around me. Many of them felt as if they were backward-pointing, so that to pull against them dragged my flesh against their sharp edges.

I unballed my fingers slowly, painfully aware that to loosen them was to expose them. The tips pressed against something soft and I again clenched my fist reflexively. I shuddered, wanting to scream again but lacking the breath to do so.

I had been seized by something with a mouth.

I knew that from the moment it took hold, yet it was too horrible to accept. Some animal crouching in the wall cavity, some huge, rank animal had taken my arm in its mouth and was holding me. My knuckles were jammed against the hard roof of its mouth, my tightly balled fingers were against the coarse surface

128

of the tongue. The teeth, the fangs, had closed about my arm, just above the wrist.

I tried turning my arm, attempting to twist it free, but the teeth closed more tightly on me the instant I moved. I shouted in pain, knowing that the flesh must have been torn in many places and that I was surely bleeding down into the animal's mouth.

I shifted my feet, trying to balance, thinking that if I could only stand more firmly I would be able to pull harder. The animal, though, had dragged me over at an angle as it drew me down. Most of my weight was consequently on the shoulder jammed against the wall. I moved a foot, shifted some of my weight on to it. The fangs tightened on me again as if the animal sensed what I was doing.

The pain was awful. The strength I was using to hold my fingers closed was draining away and I could feel my fist loosening. Again my fingertips touched the hot, quivering surface of the tongue and drooped towards the throat. Miraculously I still had the sense of touch. I could feel the hard glossy gums, the slick sides to the tongue. It was the most disgusting thing I had ever felt in my life.

The animal, having a firm hold of me, was trembling with some kind of unfathomable excitement. I could feel the head shivering and the breath rasping in and out over my arm, cold against the wounds as the animal inhaled, wet and hot as it exhaled. I could smell its stench now: it was sweet with the saliva of animalism, rancid and foetid with the smell of carrion.

I tugged once more in desperate, disgusted terror, but the agony of the gripping teeth redoubled. It felt as if it had almost bitten through me. A ghastly image flashed into my mind of being able to withdraw my arm at last and seeing it severed through, the sinews dangling from the stump, the blood pumping away. I closed my eyes, gasping again with horror and revulsion.

The animal's coarsely textured tongue started moving, working around my wrist, stroking my palm. I felt as if I was about to faint. Only the pain, the intense, searing agony of torn muscle and crushed bone, kept me conscious to suffer longer.

Through the veils of pain I remembered that Seri was some-where outside the tower, not far away. I shouted for help but I was weakened. My voice came out as a hoarse whisper. The door was only a short distance from me. I reached over with my free hand and pushed at it. It swung outwards and I could see down part of the slope, across the long grass. The brilliant cold sky, the dark rising moors, the long crag above, but no sign of Seri.

Staring through tear-filled eyes, unable to focus, I stayed help-less, leaning against the rough stonework as the monster in the wall cavity ate my arm.

Outside, the wind made shifting light-coloured patterns on the thick, waving grass.

The animal began to make a noise, an iteration of the first sound it had made. It growled deep inside its throat; beneath my helpless fingers the tongue was quivering. The animal sucked in its cold breath and I felt the jaw tense. It growled again more loudly. Somehow, the sound made my fevered imagining of the animal more detailed: I saw a huge wolf's head with deep-set eyes, a long fur-covered snout, flecks of foam on a dark muzzle. The pain intensified and I sensed the animal's increased excite-ment. The noises from its throat were coming regularly now, in a quick rhythm, faster and faster as its hold on my arm tightened. The agony was so acute that I was certain it must have almost bitten through me. I tried once again to pull away, resigned to losing my hand if that was what it was going to take to gain my release. The animal held on, chewing more viciously, snarling at me from within its hidden den below. The pain was intolerable. The animal noises were coming so quickly they joined into one continuous howl.

Then, inexplicably, the jaw sagged open and I was released.

I slumped weakly against the wall, my arm still dangling inside the cavity. The pain, which throbbed with every heartbeat, began to recede. I was sobbing with relief and agony, but also from terror of the animal which was still there below me in the wall cavity. I dared not move my arm, believing that even one twitch of a muscle would provoke another attack. However, I knew it was my chance to snatch away what was left of my arm.

My tears ceased because I was more afraid than upset. I listened carefully: was the animal breathing, was it still there?

I could no longer feel the breath moving across me. Was it because my arm had lost all sensation? Certainly the pain had ceased. My arm was numb. I imagined rather than felt my fingers hanging uselessly from my mangled hand and wrist, blood pulsing down into the animal's snout below.

A deep revulsion stirred me at last. Not caring if the animal should attack me again I stood away from the wall, withdrawing my shattered arm from the cavity. I staggered back and supported myself by resting my good hand against the fallen beam. I looked at the injuries done to me.

My arm was whole, my hand was undamaged.

I held my arm before me, disbelieving what I saw. The sleeve of my blouse had been torn as I was dragged through the hole in the stonework, but there were no marks on the skin itself, no lacerations, no indentations of teeth marks, no torn flesh, no blood.

I flexed my fingers, bracing myself against the expected pain, but they moved normally. I turned my hand over, looking at it from all sides. Not a mark, not even a trace of the saliva I had felt running over me. My palm was moist but I was sweating all over. I touched the arm gingerly, feeling for the wounds, but as I pressed down on the sore areas the only sensation I could feel was of my own fingertips pressing against unhurt flesh. There was not even a ghost of the pain I had suffered. There was a faint, unpleasant smell on my hand, but as I sniffed at the backs of my fingers, at my palm, it faded away.

The door was still open.

I snatched at my pullover, which had fallen to the floor, and I lurched outside. I was holding my wounded, undamaged arm across my chest, as if I were in pain, but it was only a subconscious reflex.

The long grass swept around me in the wind, and I remembered Seri.

131

I needed her. I needed someone I could tell what had happened, someone who might explain, or soothe or calm me. I wanted to see another human being to give the reassurances I could not give myself. But Seri seemed to have gone and I was alone.

Even as I looked around to find Seri I saw a movement. At the bottom of the slope, near the stream, a figure in black clothes suddenly stood up from the concealment of the long grass. His soutane was caught in the belt at his waist and he was pulling it as he turned, freeing it so it would hang normally. I ran towards him, rushing through the grass.

He turned his back on me as soon as he saw me and strode away. He took the stream at a leap, then went quickly back towards the seminary across the undulating ground.

'Wait, Father!' I shouted after him. 'Please wait for me!'

I came to the place where the grass had been flattened. In its centre lay Seri. She was naked and her clothes were scattered around her.

'Do you still want to touch me, Lenden?' she said, giggling. She twisted round so that she raised her knees and parted them. Her laughter became more hysterical.

I stared at her, disbelieving what I was seeing. In my naïvety I still wanted only human comfort, but the blatant invitation she was making finally broke through my own sense of overwhelming needs. I realized what she and the priest must have been doing.

I kept a distance from her, waiting for her to calm down, but something about the way I was standing there must have aggravated the madness that had taken hold of her. She was screaming with laughter, having difficulty getting her breath. I remembered that I had her pants in the pocket of my skirt. I found them and threw them at her. They landed on her naked belly.

That sobered her. She rolled to one side, coughing and wheezing.

I turned from her and ran away, towards the seminary, towards the house. I sobbed as I ran and the torn sleeve of my blouse flapped around my upper arm. I stumbled when I crossed the stream, drenching my clothes as my feet kicked up spray, and when I was crossing the last patch of rough ground towards the house I slipped several more times. I cut my knee when I fell, I tore the hem of my skirt.

Bloodied, hysterical, bruised and soaked through, I ran into the house and burst into my aunt's sickroom.

My uncle and my father were supporting Alvie above a chamber pot. Her white, withered legs dangled like bleached ropes. Drops of orange urine trickled from her. Her eyes were closed and her head lolled.

I heard my uncle shouting. My mother appeared and she slapped her hand over my eyes. I was dragged, screaming, into the corridor.

All I could say, again and again, was Seri's name. Everyone seemed to be shouting at me.

Later, Uncle Torm went out on the moors to search for Seri, but my parents and I had already left before he returned and were driving through the evening and night, towards Seevl Town.

It was the last time I went to Seevl with my parents. I was fourteen. I never saw Seri again.

We burned my uncle's papers in the yard behind the house. Charred fragments floated up like tiny patches of black silk, then were whisked away by the wind. Gradually we added to the blaze, carting everything burnable out from the house: piles of old clothes, some wooden chairs and a table, my uncle's desk. Everything was damp or mildewed and even the wooden furniture burned only slowly. I stood by the fire, watching the flames, watching the cinders funnelling in the wind across the bleak countryside.

The priests wanted us to take away the furniture we could not burn: an ancient gas cooker, a filing cabinet, a metal table, Alvie's brass bedstead. It was impossible even to contemplate. A van would have to be brought over from one of the ports, or even from Seevl Town, taking a day or two to arrive. Then there was the cost to consider. I tried to reason with Father Henner's secretary, but he was adamant. In the end I managed to negotiate with him, to the effect that the seminary would make all the practical arrangements after we had left. I would be sent the bill.

Bella was standing in the doorway behind me. She must have checked that there was no one from the seminary in the house, because for the first time that morning she spoke intimately and quietly to me.

She said, 'Why do you keep staring up at the moors?'

'I wasn't aware that I was.'

'There's something out there. What is it?'

'I was watching the blaze,' I said. As if to prove it I jabbed at the base of the fire, sending up embers and half-burnt scraps of paper. A chair leg rolled out and I kicked it back towards the fire. Sparks flew. Something in the fire spat and a cinder shot across the yard.

'Have you ever walked out on the moors?' Bella said.

'No.'

Not to the moors, I thought. Just as far as the tower on that one day. Never further, never up the long scree slopes to the over-hanging crag and the high barren plain that lay beyond its crest.

'I keep thinking you must have known someone here. In the days when you used to come. Someone special. Isn't that right?'

'Not really,' I said, realizing for the first time that Seri had in her way been special to me. 'I mean, yes.'

Bella walked across to me, and stood by my side, staring with me into the heart of the blaze.

'I was right, then. Was it a woman?'

'A girl. We were both teenagers.'

'And she was your first?'

'In a sense. There was nothing really between us then. We were too young.' I was trying to visualize Seri from an adult viewpoint, something I usually found difficult. She had left such an impression on me that it was as if my knowledge of her was frozen in time. 'What she did was ... wake me up.'

Thinking of Seri, being with Bella, had made me remember. Not only about the catastrophe with Seri but also about the search I had been drawn into during the years that followed. It had taken me a long time to discover that the knowledge I sought was impossible for me to learn.

I thought back to the people I had known and loved in some of those years. There were men as well as women, but many more women than men if I made mental lists and counted the names. I had only been to men in desperation, when loneliness reached a seeming crisis. I sought but I did not strike: when I was close enough I was invariably the passive lover, the recipient of passion, stealing it secretly from other people's actions. I envied other people their lack of inhibition, their frankness. They excited me with their relish in caressing my body, of holding me, of penetrating me. I moved from one partner to the next, determined that the next one would be different, that I would not repeat old mistakes and then I would take the initiative and be an active, loving partner. In that sense Bella Reeth was no different from any of my other lovers. I had not in fact changed. Before Bella I had thought a few years' abstention, a gaining in maturity, could have cured me of the irrational fears. I should not have allowed her to put me to the test. I had been weak, thinking that the return to Seevl would in itself be a kind of passage from past to future, that in the process I would emerge renewed. I had been misled by Bella's youth, her pretty body, her unassertive manner. These had drawn me once again to loveless sexual activity, shorn of feelings. The years had gone by while I waited and I had not known that I had started to dry, that I was becoming a husk.

'I'm only trying to understand,' Bella said.

'So am I.'

'We're completely alone here,' she said. 'No one can hear us. Speak honestly to me.'

'I am, I think.'

'I would like to see you again. What about you?'

'I think so,' I said, prevaricating.

'I can travel freely when I'm not on duty. Let me visit you in your home.'

'If you'd like to.'

It seemed to satisfy her but she stood beside me with her hand on my arm. The fire glared at us, burning our faces.

I didn't know what she wanted. What was it she saw in me? Surely she had friends of her own age? I, a frigid woman, entering middle age, already lonely and unfulfilled, largely bereft of close friends. I was so many years older than Bella. I tried to imagine what her personal life must be like. I had asked her hardly anything about herself. The brother – I knew she had a brother. Parents still alive? She must have friends, and some of them must be ex-lovers or even would-be lovers. How did she live when not in uniform, when not on police duty, when her hair was not pinned back? I could so easily imagine her with a group of friends on her nights off, dining out, going to parties, drinking too much, using personal slang and knowing each other and going to clubs that I would probably not like. Even during wartime there must be a life of that kind in Jethra that could be lived. Maybe that was untrue, that she was as solitary as she said. Anyway, I had nothing like it, by choice. I was usually alone. I had many grey hairs appearing, my breasts had started to sag, my belly to bulge, my waist was full, my thighs were thick. I spent most of my time alone in my apartment, or at the school, teaching, marking, coping with the school's paperwork, then at home again with the music I listened to, the books I read, but mostly with my memories. I was to Bella the older woman, more mature and presumably more experienced, yet it was she who pursued me, she who took the initiative, she who made the love.

If it had been anywhere else or at any other time – not on the way to Seevl, not on Seevl itself, not in Alvie's bed – would it have been any different?

For me the failure was inevitable, as were the excuses I could find.

The real excuse, if there was any at all, lay out there under the crags of Seevl's moors.

That morning I had risen before Bella was awake and climbed from Alvie's bed. I went to the window. From there I had been sure I should be able to see the dead tower where the incident with the animal had happened, but I looked and I had not been able to see it. The seminary gardens were still much as I recalled them, as was the view across to the high, limestone crag. I had always been able to see the tower from this window, but there was no sign of it now.

Bella was right. All that morning, as I worked through my uncle's papers, as I tried to decide about the furniture, as I argued with Father Henner's secretary, I had been glancing over towards the moors, wondering where the tower had gone.

There must be a rational explanation. It had been demolished, it had fallen down, or even that it was not in the direction I remembered.

Or that it had never been there. I could not think about the significance of that.

Bella was still holding my arm, her shoulder pressing gently against me. We waited until the fire burned down low. There was an old broom in the yard, so worn that virtually all the bristles had fallen out or rotted down. I used it to sweep the charred pieces of wood and the ashes into a smaller, neater heap. They flared up briefly, would probably go on smouldering for hours, but the fire was now effectively safe.

Bella returned to the house and in a minute emerged with our bags. She carried them by herself to the car and began to stack them in the tiny luggage compartment at the back. I stared at the back of her severely stockinged legs as she bent forward into the car, her skirt stretching across her backside, and I was thinking how easy it would be to let go of the past, to fall in love with a lonely, attractive young woman like her, to make a decision and act on it.

I took the house key to Father Confessor Henner's office and left it with his secretary. Walking back through the seminary grounds, alone, I made one last attempt to locate the dead tower. I retraced the way Seri had taken me that day of the last visit and found the gate in the high wall that led outside the grounds. It was unlocked and opened readily, so I went through.

Immediately, what I could see with my own eyes was starkly

137

different from my memories. I distinctly, vividly remembered that the rough ground outside came up as far as the wall of the grounds, and once through the gate one entered a trackless waste of undulating ground covered in long grass. But now I saw that beyond the gate was another yard and two or three decrepit buildings that looked as if they might have been stables in years gone by. I had no memory of them at all. They hadn't been there that day. I crossed the cobbled yard but there was no way through the ancient constructions. I walked to the end, found a passage that led to the back, but beyond the stables was a paved yard and a long flight of steps down to more buildings. The view of the moors seen from here was quite different from anything I remembered.

I went back into the main seminary grounds, looking for another way out through the surrounding wall, the way that Seri had led me that day. The wall was solid and old, with no other gates on this side. I walked around, found no others.

I went back to the wing of the building where Seri had made a hideout in the basement. That I also remembered clearly, but the hideout too, when I looked, was no longer discoverable. Where I remembered steps down to a half-hidden hatch there was just a concrete path leading past the doors and windows at ground level, a path that looked as if it had been in place, untouched, for many years.

Could everything have been rebuilt, changed around, in the two decades since my last visit? Everything looked solid, enduring, permanent.

I headed round to the other side of the building, thinking that perhaps in my memories I had somehow reversed the layout of the place.

On my way to the front of the building I passed our rented car. Bella was standing beside it, leaning back against the metal bodywork.

She said, 'Lenden—'

'A few more moments,' I said. 'There's something I've got to work out.'

138

The front of the building was built so that it looked down a shallow slope: there were no grounds or gardens here. There was a drive, several parking places, a concrete hardstanding, a disused outhouse of some kind. But no encircling wall, no gate, no access to the wild moorland I remembered so clearly. The front of the seminary faced a shallow valley. There were moors visible a long way to one side, but the dominant view was across open pasture to a distant vista of the sea.

'Lenden?'

Bella had walked up behind me.

'All right, I'm ready to leave,' I said, and set off towards the car.

'Are you going to tell me about it?' she said, following.

'Not now. I'm still not sure.'

'You mean you're not ready. What you keep saying to me.'

'It's not about being not ready,' I said. 'It's about being not sure. Everything I am, that I have been as an adult, began here at the seminary. I gained my identity here. If I hadn't come back I would still feel that I had that identity, but now it's gone. I'm not sure of anything.'

In the car, driving slowly down the hill to find the road that led back across the island to Seevl Town, Bella's hand brushed against my knee.

'But something else happened here once, didn't it?' she said.

I nodded, then because I realized she was looking at the road and would not have seen that, I laid my hand on hers and squeezed it lightly.

'Yes.'

'The girl you mentioned?'

'Yes.'

'So it was a long time ago.'

'Twenty years at least,' I said. 'I'm not sure what it was. I think I might have imagined it. This is what I meant. Everything seems different now.'

'I was just a child, twenty years ago,' Bella said.

'So was I.'

But as we drove back across the dreary moors, I fell into intro-spection again.

I wanted to ask Bella to turn the car around and go back to the seminary. I should have found out the truth about the tower, what it was, why it had been built, what it was supposed to mean, why it had been removed since my last visit. I should have con-firmed my memories, made sense of them in adult terms. Because I had not they were still unresolved and the haunting of that day would remain. I thought again about Seri, Seraphina. Bella obvi-ously wanted to know about her, but there was nothing I wanted to say. Nothing I could say, in fact. The only sure thing I knew about Seri was the mystery she had created when she ran away from home, years and years ago. Where had she gone, and where was she now? Was she too surrounded by uncertainty?

We drove on, halting for lunch in the same house as before. We were going to be early for the ferry and Bella asked me if I would like her to stop the car somewhere in the lonely countryside, so we could be alone together again before we returned to Jethra. I said no, still locked in my past. She had not unshaped me from the pattern.

We talked, though, and we made plans. In the car, waiting on the harbour for the ferry to come in, sitting in the saloon of the ship, we made our plans for future meetings. I told her the dates of weekends in the near future when I should be free and when she might visit me. She gave me an address; I gave her mine. We made no firm arrangements, but parted on the quay at Jethra and I have not heard from her since.

The
Cremation

.

It was the first time Graian Sheeld had been to a private cremation. In his own country cremations were unusual, performed
for technical reasons of some kind, available only by court order.
All ordinary family funerals were interments and burning a body
was held to be shocking. What you grow up with you accept as
standard. In his short time in the islands he had already noticed,
without taking a special interest in the subject, that there were
several large burial grounds on other islands in the Dream
Archipelago and until today had assumed the practice of burying
the dead was widespread and normal. What happened at Corrin
Mercier's funeral therefore surprised him.

The chapel itself was surrounded by a graveyard, again a fact
that did not give any hint that something unusual was about to
occur. The short funeral service also seemed unexceptional to
Sheeld, given that he had only ever been to two funerals before
and that this one was conducted in a language he did not speak.
The significance of the words, the general mood of loss and
mourning, were comprehensible to him.

As the tributes came to an end he supposed a graveside ritual
would follow. Instead, the casket was wheeled out on a large trol-
ley and taken to an unobtrusive building a short distance away,
set discreetly among ornamental trees. The mourners followed
in a quiet, straggling line, then stood in silence for a while in a
paved yard outside the louvred doors. Soon, the casket was taken
inside the building and the doors were closed. After a few more

141

moments of contemplation the funeral party began to disperse and moved across the grounds to where a line of carriages was waiting.

The whole event was another reminder to him of the differences between his old life in the Federation and his new one as an expatriate in the Archipelago.

He felt isolated and cast adrift in the islands – he was missing his family, his home, his friends, and regrets about his move were for the time being predominating. Everything in the Archipelago seemed exotic and difficult, riddled with rules where none seemed necessary, yet almost anarchic in other ways. Every social contact, every business meeting, every venture into a restaurant or visit to a shop, was fraught with potential for misunderstandings, actual as well as imaginary. Although he had started to adjust to the way of life on Foort – the island where he had settled six weeks earlier – this first real visit to another island, other than short transits while on ferries, had revealed to him the diversity and complexity of life on the hundreds of inhabited islands. He had only been here on Trellin for a few hours but he was already suffering from culture shock.

For instance, when he arrived at Corrin Mercier's substantial residence that morning he had been disconcerted to discover that most of the other guests, as well as all the members of the family, spoke to each other in island patois. He had been introduced to a few of Mercier's close family – his widow Gilda, his young adult sons Fertin and Tomar – and they had spoken to him politely in his own language, but immediately afterwards Tomar Mercier had taken him aside and explained that at funerals on Trellin the mourners were expected to speak the language preferred by the deceased. 'It is difficult even for us,' Tomar said apologetically, but soon afterwards Sheeld heard him speaking the patois fluently to someone else.

There were no flowers, because in certain cases, of which Corrin Mercier's death appeared to be one, flowers were deemed to be in bad taste. Sheeld had been asked to put the offering he had brought at the back of the house, out of sight. None of

142

the many servants was prepared to handle the flowers. No one, man or woman, sat down either before the funeral or during the service. Everyone wore black clothes – at least he had got that right – but also covered their heads. Sheeld had been lent a scarf of dark, heavy material by one of the dead man's sons before they departed to the chapel. He was still wearing it and intended to go on doing so until he saw other men remove theirs.

Now as they drove back to Mercier's house in a long slow procession of carriages, Sheeld was wondering how soon he could depart without giving offence to anyone.

He had been given a place in one of the leading carriages of the cortège. When they returned to the Mercier house Sheeld and the handful of elderly mourners with whom he had travelled walked through a series of open rooms – the expensive furniture set back in areas behind ropes, as if in a palace temporarily opened to the public – on their way to the rear of the mansion. Here the grounds consisted of a wide expanse of parkland created by reclaiming part of the rainforest, which otherwise covered this part of Trellin. The grounds were landscaped in the immediate neighbourhood of the house into a series of large ornamental gardens and shallow lakes, but looked less formal further away. There was little time to admire the view. The servants politely but firmly indicated that everyone should walk along a gravelled pathway that ran through a rose garden, then alongside a small lake, to a walled garden some distance from the main house. Here the servants had set out a feast on three long tables on the lawn.

The garden was a sheltered, oppressive place, surrounded as it was on three sides by high walls overgrown with climbing plants. On the fourth side the garden was unwalled but met the dark crush of trees of the tropical jungle in a sudden transition to the wild.

There had been a heavy, drenching rainstorm while they were at the service, but now the sun was beating down from a cloudless sky. As the ground quickly dried the air was moist and sweltering and Sheeld felt over-dressed in his formal suit. Beneath the thick scarf he could feel his hair pressing down wetly against his scalp.

Sweat ran in tiny streams from his temples. While he waited for the rest of the funeral party to arrive he walked slowly around the garden, trying to look more at ease than he felt.

Alongside one of the walls there was a raised, balustraded verandah, with vines growing on an overhead trellis. Sheeld stood there for a few moments, grateful for the shade, until one of the servants handed him a glass of white wine and requested him to wait in the centre of the garden with everyone else.

Fertin and Tomar Mercier eventually arrived, sweeping off their head-coverings with evident relief. Fertin shook his head and scrambled his fingers through his curly, sweat-matted hair. Sheeld thankfully removed his own scarf and laid it on the floor in the corner of the verandah. He mopped his face.

Most of the mourners were middle-aged or elderly, apart from Mercier's sons. But there was one other conspicuous exception. Sheeld had noticed a certain young woman during the service, or more accurately, he had felt himself being noticed by her.

While the chapel filled with mourners he had been looking curiously around, untouched by the grief that clearly consumed so many of the older relatives. The young woman had walked in unaccompanied. Sheeld had looked at her directly, and she returned his look with a stare of such shocking intensity and frank curiosity that he had turned away in confusion. A few minutes later, as the service began, he had glanced again in her direction and found himself still the subject of her forthright, unwavering scrutiny. It was the sort of look whose covetous meaning could not be mistaken. Coming from a complete stranger, in the subdued surroundings of a family funeral, it was at once incongruous, intriguing and dangerous.

It was also, as far as Sheeld was concerned, entirely uninvited and unwanted. He had not run away from his tangled relationships with women at home only to walk straight into a new one. His short stay on Foort, a self-imposed exile into sexual abstinence, had already begun to pay rewards. Free of emotional demands he was feeling able to address his own future. Even the letters from the three lawyers who most persecuted him were beginning to take on a mollifying tone.

Looking across at the young woman in the funeral chapel he sensed trouble, a familiar kind, the sort of trouble he had until a few months ago found irresistible. Even now, appraising the way she stood, and her physical stance, the way she held her shoulders and head, the physical invitation that seemed implicit in her behaviour, he felt a lustful craving for her. It was not only wildly inappropriate in these circumstances, but the social and cultural distances that stood between them made any contact with her all but impossible. He tried to ignore her. Afterwards, though, as they stood in silence around the furnace house, she had contrived to stand next to him. Although they had neither looked at each other nor spoken, Sheeld had perceived that she was in an almost tangible state of tension.

He did not want her, did not want to get involved with anyone. But waiting there in the humid heat, while the unseen but enigmatic ceremony of cremation went on, Sheeld knew he was thinking about her and not about the man whose death he was supposed to be mourning.

As they moved to the carriages, Sheeld had heard one of the older women speaking to her and he heard the name 'Alanya'.

Now he walked slowly around the long tables on the lawn, inspecting the place cards beside each setting. He found his own quickly enough, in a suitably unimportant position towards the end of one of the smaller tables, but hers was on the head table. She was one more Mercier amongst many: Alanya Mercier.

Sheeld drank his glass of wine quickly, then took a second from a tray being carried by one of the servants. He stood near the bottom of the verandah steps, watching as the other guests arrived back from the service. At last Alanya Mercier came through the gate in the wall, holding the arm of Gilda, Corrin Mercier's widow. The two women spoke quietly in patois for a few moments, then separated to find their places at the tables. Alanya walked along the head table, peering down at the place cards. When she found hers she straightened and looked towards Sheeld.

Once again he saw that disconcertingly candid expression and once again it was he who first averted his eyes.

Sheeld could not help thinking that these direct stares from the young woman, intriguing as they were, only helped to cut him off further from the other guests. Already separated from them by age, language and culture, he suspected that if he were to show any response to her at all then his alienation would be complete. How could he, an outsider and intruder at this private celebration of grief, possibly meet and strike up some relationship with a member of the bereaved family? Even should he want to, which he did not.

He tried again to put her out of his thoughts. He had no place in this tragic family gathering: he had been called upon at the last minute to represent his uncle, who had been at university with Corrin Mercier and who was unable to attend in person because of the wartime restrictions on travel from the mainland. Sheeld knew no one here.

After the meal, during which Sheeld, against his own volition, had several times glanced again in the direction of the veiled young woman on the head table, the guests stood about on the lawn in small informal groups, chatting in patois. The mood was noticeably lighter than before. What Sheeld at last recognized as the usual social process of a funeral party was taking place as the sense of mourning adjusted. He stood alone, though, feeling conspicuous and nervous in his isolation. He had already made one effort to depart, trying to slip away from the garden purportedly to find a toilet, but one of the servants had pointed out that temporary facilities were available in a marquee in one of the corners of the garden. He had noticed how several of the servants were not actually involved in offering the guests drinks and canapés, but stood around not only by the gated entrance to the garden but at several strategic points inside. They were impeccably dressed, and their manner was quiet and respectful, but they gave off the aura of bodyguards or minders. His chosen alternative to leaving was to drink as much wine as he could, as quickly as possible and get through the rest of the party painlessly.

Alanya Mercier was on the far side of the lawn, speaking to a woman Sheeld recognized as one of Corrin Mercier's sisters. She was now appearing to ignore him altogether, which complicated the idea that she might have been sending him a message of some kind earlier, but it was nonetheless a relief.

Time passed and he drank more glasses of wine. Once he thought he heard his name being mentioned, but when he turned to see who it was the two men conversing behind him were facing the other way. He wondered what the word 'graiansheeld' meant in patois and why they said the word or words so frequently.

He decided again that it was time to leave and looked around for somewhere to deposit his empty glass. Alanya Mercier was no longer speaking to anyone, but walking with apparent casualness along the side of the table where he had been sitting. When she reached his seat she looked closely at his place card.

She knew he was watching her because she looked up. For an instant their gaze met again. She smiled briefly, then went across to him.

'I'm going for a walk, Graian Sheeld,' she said, without pre-amble. 'As far as the Trellin cliffs. You've probably heard of them. Perhaps you'd like the chance to enjoy the view. There's a private guesthouse we could visit, with an excellent position over the sea. We'll be alone together for a while.'

She turned from him before his astonishment could register and walked slowly down the lawn, apparently admiring the im-mense tropical blooms planted in the flowerbeds at the side.

Sheeld stood for a few moments longer in an acute crisis of indecision: amazement at her effrontery, the general paralysis of his culture shock and social alienation, the intrigues of his curios-ity about her and the unmistakable physical attraction he felt, the ambiguities of language, the uncertainties of meanings or customs or conventions, the slight daze of too much alcohol on a humid afternoon. All these were tugging him in different directions.

He delayed still more, while she walked as far as the end of the lawn and stepped over the patch of uncultivated ground to the edge of the forest, then at last he followed. He walked across the lawn at the same easy pace as hers, admiring the same exotic blooms, trying to make it appear as if he was not following her.

The forest was rich with the damp perfumes of the tropics. The sun which had blazed down on them in the garden was now filtered by the thick canopy of tree foliage and the lower leaves were still dripping after the rain of two hours before. A great warmth, sticky and sweet-fragranced, permeated the trees. Birds and animals clamoured invisibly around them.

Sheeld found a well-trodden path that wound through the undergrowth and glimpsed Alanya Mercier in her jet-black dress a short distance ahead. She did not turn or otherwise acknowledge his presence, but she must have known he was behind her because it was difficult to walk without brushing noisily past the sprawling bushes and plants.

In a while he caught up with her, but still she did not turn to look at him.

Then she said, 'Who are you?'

'You looked at my place card and you know my name.'

He could not help but admire the fullness of her figure from behind. He watched her hold the long black dress at the side to lift it away from the damp soil and so stretch the fabric across the backs of her legs.

'What are you doing at our funeral, Graian Sheeld?'

'I'm representing my uncle.' He explained briefly about the telegram that had arrived two days before and how he had been travelling for most of a day and a night.

'Graian Sheeld,' she said. 'That's not an island name.'

'No.'

'What are you? A draft dodger? A tax evader?'

'Nothing like that.'

'Fugitive from the law?'

'There are other reasons for coming to the islands.'

'So they say. Some of us were born here.'

'I realize that.'

All through the exchange she had continued to walk, without

looking back at him. She was brushing through the thick shrubbery on either side and the droplets of rainwater that did not fly back at Sheeld attached themselves to her dress like tiny jewels.

'Then you don't know anyone here today?'

'I've spoken to Mme. Mercier. And both of the sons.'

'That's what I thought.' She looked back quickly at him over her shoulder and for a moment Sheeld glimpsed those eyes that earlier had sent such unmistakable signals to him. This time, though, it was a spontaneous, less calculated look. She had raised her veil and laid it across her hat and her face was pale and exposed.

'Why should you think anything about me?' he said.

'I'm trying to find out something about you. After all, you seem anxious to accompany me to a private meeting.'

'At your invitation. I shouldn't have thought, under the circumstances, that knowing anything about me would matter at all.'

'It always matters, Graian Sheeld.'

She kept saying his full name like that, with a hint of parody in her voice. Was there some meaning in it, or was it simply her accent? Perhaps his name, fortuitously, sounded like something else in their patois – whatever it was those two men had been talking about, for instance. More to the point, perhaps, what was she doing by leading him away from the main party and what had those looks implied, back there at the house? Suddenly, he wondered if he had misunderstood everything that had been happening that day. Perhaps it was not a funeral at all, he thought sarcastically, as he stumbled behind her, his foot stubbing against a half-buried root. What he had interpreted as a blatant sexual invitation, as blatant as any he had ever known in his life, was another misunderstanding, based on his ignorance of island manners.

In the heat of the afternoon he began to regret having followed her into the forest, to be led along a winding path through encroaching vegetation while answering small-talk questions. In particular, he was growing tired of following her like a pet dog, unable to see her expression when she spoke to him. When they came to a wider stretch of the path he caught up with her and walked at her side. She did not even glance at him, but strode on. Ahead, the path narrowed again and Sheeld decided to stop walking. Alanya Mercier went on for a few more paces, evidently intending that he should continue to follow her, but when she realized he had no intention of going any further she turned to face him.

'You've never attended one of our funerals before, have you?' she said.

'No. But I've been to others on the mainland.'

'You'd never been to a cremation, though,' she said. 'I could tell. You didn't know what was going to happen when they took the coffin to the furnace.'

'That's true,' he said.

'It was something of a novelty for us all. The whole family has found it an unusual experience.'

'Then why was it done?' Sheeld said.

'The law of the island. On Trellin the manner of disposal depends on the cause of death and in this case my cousin had to be cremated. You know how he died, of course?'

Sheeld shook his head. He had not known how to ask anyone what had caused the death, nor indeed, until this moment, had he been especially interested. As Mercier must have been the same age as his uncle, in his late seventies or early eighties, Sheeld had assumed he had been suffering from some degenerative disease related to age.

'He was bitten by an insect,' Alanya said. 'A thryme.'

She tossed out the information in a factual way, but the words had a profound effect on Sheeld. A faint nausea passed through him, a swimming sense of light-headedness and disgust. He felt the air around him smothering him, suddenly warmer.

'A thryme?' he said stupidly.

'You must know what that is.'

'Yes, but I didn't think they attacked humans,' he said, his voice sounding ineffectual. He wanted to disbelieve what she had said.

'They don't usually. But this one had come into the house. One of the servants discovered later that an insect screen had worked loose. We think the thryme must have got into the upholstery of the chair Corrin usually sat in. That's where he was found, with the bite on his back. The insect had managed to penetrate his clothes. The consultant at the hospital said he'd never seen a wound like it before. Thrymes normally only attack exposed skin.'

Sheeld shuddered.

'This is terrible!' he said. 'I wish you hadn't told me! I'm terrified of those things.'

He was trying to make himself sound reasonable, practical, adult, but he could hear the tremor in his voice. The news struck at the deepest phobia in him.

'You'd better be careful while you're here,' Alanya Mercier said and a smile flickered across her face. 'They're all over the place. There are more thryme colonies here than on most of the other islands.'

She's deliberately tormenting me, Sheeld thought, but he said, 'Let's go back to the house.'

'You won't see any out here. They stay underground during the day and anyway a thryme will only attack if it feels cornered.'

'I wish you hadn't mentioned this!'

'I thought you were interested in why it was a cremation.' She was looking at him intently again, the bland, greenish light of the forest making her lips and eyes look dark and her face the more pale. 'You can go back to the house if you like, but I thought you had agreed to come with me.'

'Is that true what you said, that we won't see any?'

'Yes. Thrymes nest underground and they stay there until after nightfall. You almost never see one during the day. Anyway, where we are now isn't the sort of environment they like. This forest looks like untamed jungle but in fact it's a managed timber resource. You won't find fallen trees with exposed roots around here and the ground under those is the thryme's natural habitat. Stay on the path and you'll be as safe as you would be in a town.'

151

She appeared to grow bored with explaining and she turned away from him and continued along the path. Sheeld followed, but now his mind was reeling and he felt his nerves jangling. She had made him feel like a small child, nervously demanding reassurance about bogeymen. But every unexplained sound or sudden movement in the forest had become a moment of potential horror for him, a suggestion of menace. He looked anxiously at the ground as he walked, watchful for anything that might be moving.

Many people, most people, had a phobia about thrymes and until this moment Sheeld had never felt that his own dread was in any way unusual or remarkable. For most of his life the phobia had anyway been academic, as the only place in the Federation you were likely to see a live thryme was in a glass case in one of the zoos. Even so, the insects held a peculiar and particular horror for him, as they did for many others. In reality Sheeld had never seen a thryme, not even in a zoo, preferring not to go near any place where they might be found.

During the long period in which he had been trying to decide whether to relocate to the islands, the prospect of moving to a place where the thryme was native had played no small part in his agonizing indecision. Finally, other considerations had overcome the phobia, made it peripheral, but he had never conquered it.

Both male and female thrymes had a stinging tail and the sting was venomous, but there was at least an antidote for that. If it was applied quickly enough the antidote would normally enable the victim to recover, albeit after a short but nasty period of illness. The sting was therefore something to be wary of, but not to fear unduly. The bite was a different matter.

It was the bite that made fear of the thyme into a rational thing: one bite from a fully grown female thryme would kill any human being, child or adult. This was because the female had a marsupial pouch inside her mandible and after her eggs had hatched she would collect the grubs and carry them in her jaw. She would then seek a host in which to place them as parasites. Although the host would normally be an animal cadaver, or a fallen fruit, or even a heap of mouldering vegetation, it could also be a living host. Usually, the host was an animal; sometimes, rarely, it was a human being.

You treated a thryme with extreme caution if you came across one, exactly as you would a venomous snake, or a hunting panther, or an angry bear. The fear was a rational one, because the harm it could do you was real and deadly. Even professional handlers, keepers at zoos, entomologists, treated the thryme with elaborate care, always wearing protective clothing, never working alone, always making certain that emergency measures were ready in case a bite was inflicted.

None of this explained the phobia, the uncontrollable dread.

Most people found the thryme loathsome in appearance, could not bear to look at one without shuddering or shrinking away. It was the most common phobia of all, hugely exceeding in number those of all the other familiar irrational fears, such as spiders, ladders, confined spaces, cats, foreigners and so on.

The thryme was a large insect: most adults of the species grew to about fifteen centimetres in length, but some achieved twice that or more. It was also a tall insect. Its cantilevered legs lifted the main thorax to about ten centimetres above the ground when the insect was running or attacking. It was coloured dark brown or black. Like all insects it was six-legged, but the legs were thick and covered with long fine hairs. The touch of even these hairs against unprotected skin was said to produce a painful rash. The thryme had vestigial wings, which, although never used for flight by the adult, were flared in attack and helped cocoon the baby insects when they first metamorphosed from the grub. The head was hard and shiny, covered in a chitinous shell, but the body was in effect one large thoracic muscle. It made the main body soft and resilient, like that of a garden slug. Because of its extreme pliancy, the thryme was supposed to be difficult to kill: even if you whacked it hard with a stick it would keep scuttling towards you. It could instantly huddle into a defensive ball, dangerous to touch because of the hairs, then quickly resume its shape and continue to charge. It moved horrifyingly quickly: at full speed

153

a large thryme could for short distances keep up with a running man.

During Sheeld's short stay in the Dream Archipelago he had never seen a thryme, nor had he met anyone else who had. Thrymes could be found in theory anywhere in the islands, but they were supposed to prefer the wet tropical forests of the large islands in the Aubracs and the Serques. Trellin was one of the Greater Aubracs and about seventy-five per cent of its surface was covered in rainforest.

Sheeld had selected Foort as his destination for a number of different reasons, but principal amongst them was the fact that unlike Trellin it had a dry climate, with much of its surface made up of lava rock or sand. There were known to be some thryme colonies on Foort, but his new friends on the island dismissed the insect as an unlikely threat. Occasionally, a few might be found living peaceably in a wall cavity, or in a patch of wild ground, but they were almost never seen in the towns, never came into houses, rarely represented any kind of serious threat.

After a couple of nervous weeks, Sheeld had started to accept that it might actually be true and eventually he was able to put the unpleasant little creatures out of his mind.

Alanya Mercier was continuing to stride on ahead of him, but it appeared that at last the heat was getting to her. Sheeld could see a darker patch of perspiration spreading down between her shoulder blades and in the clefts of her arms. She suddenly removed her hat and with an abandoned movement tossed it aside. It skimmed unevenly through the air, until caught on a broad-leafed frond. Sheeld noticed everything she did, worrying about her behaviour.

Further along the path widened again, with a harder, rockier surface. Alanya slowed to allow him to catch her up and walk at her side. From time to time Sheeld glanced covertly at her face, wondering what was going on in her mind. In the shadowless light of the forest her face was devoid of the subtlety that the discreetly lit chapel and the veil had lent it. She had a wide mouth with generous lips and her eyes were recessed and dark. Her hair, tightly drawn back and worked into a bun, was deep brown in colour. She was not conventionally beautiful, but what she undeniably had was animal sexual magnetism with a charge greater than any Sheeld had ever known. To be this close to her was an extraordinary experience and she dominated all his awareness.

Ahead, the sky visible through the trees was brightening and the path began to slope down.

As the forest thinned they emerged on to a narrow strip of scrubland and rocks and approached the edge of the cliffs cautiously. The ground was broken and littered with loose stones and boulders, hard and barren. Sheeld's oppressive fears about thrymes began to fade away.

From the clifftop he was confronted with an unexpectedly magnificent panorama across the sea and he stood for a few moments to stare at it. Alanya continued along the path by the edge of the cliff.

'The house is down here!' she called.

He was invigorated by the stiff breeze from the sea and the sensational and dizzying view from the clifftop, but Alanya was hurrying away. With some reluctance he followed her down a steep slope along the face of the cliff itself to where some steps had been fashioned out of the rock. After these the path curved with the face of the cliff, descending at a more shallow angle to a natural hollow. Here, on ground which had been partly levelled, supported on wooden piles, was a wooden cabin with broad picture windows facing the view. Behind, another lane led up a natural shallow acclivity, winding up to where it was soon lost in a burst of vegetation, another route back into the forest.

The front of the cabin had a wide balcony and on it was a long upholstered swing chair with a coloured canopy. Alanya had gone straight to it and was now rocking to and fro, with her legs raised and tucked under her body. She was watching him with a coquettish expression.

Sheeld had seen something of these cliffs from the sea, as his ferry approached Trellin Town shortly after dawn. They ran along part of the south-western coast of the island, where the inland range of mountains met the sea. They were a famous sight, much painted and photographed. There had in fact been a large painting of the cliffs in the saloon bar of the ferry Sheeld had crossed in. As a vantage point for viewing this part of the Archipelago the Trellin cliffs were unrivalled. The view was privileged, a sight not seen by many, as only a few houses were allowed along the coast and the cliffs and the territory surrounding them were the private property of a select few.

Before Sheeld was a dazzling sea- and island-scape. There were something like nine or ten large islands in view, each one rising darkly from the turquoise sea and bordered with a dazzling strip of surf and beach. In the perfect visibility of the afternoon he could see the closer islands in stark detail, even in spite of the distances they must have been from him, but the ones on the horizon were only just visible in the oceanic haze.

Sheeld was still unfamiliar with the topography and configuration of the islands, but he knew that most of the ones he could see were part of the Aubracs and that one of them, probably the large one out towards the westerly horizon, was Grande Aubrac itself. That had been his last port of call during the overnight voyage. Learning the names of the islands, even the relatively few that lay in the vicinity of Foort, was a continuing problem for Sheeld. He had expended much time trying to obtain an accurate or up-to-date map of the Archipelago, but because of the war these were almost impossible for civilians to obtain.

There were several thousand inhabited islands in the Archipelago and an incalculable number of smaller rocks, crags, islets and reefs. The Midway Sea formed a wide, continuous belt around the world, but it was not an unbroken ocean. It was said that nowhere in its extent could you sail in a straight line for more than two hours without being forced to change direction to avoid a landfall. There were so many islands in the Archipelago that from any coastal point on any one island you could see at least seven other inhabited islands, or part of either continental mass, with the naked eye.

Sheeld was one of tens of thousands of new young expatriates in the islands. Many of the émigrés were avoiding military service – for the time being, exile to the islands was still a legal alternative to the draft. Although in his country there was a law that the exile, once chosen, would be permanent – the Archipelago was designated as a cultural development zone and public revenue was attached to incoming migrants – most of the draft dodgers assumed that when the war was over there would be an amnesty.

But not all émigrés were avoiding the draft. A combination of the precarious state of neutrality and the fact there were more than two hundred democratically elected parliaments in the Archipelago, all of widely differing size, type and constituencies, made the islands into a more or less ungovernable maze of laws, juridical systems and social conventions. Anyone who could get out of the warring countries of the north and escape to the islands was effectively free to travel and live exactly as they pleased. The Dream Archipelago was therefore a haven for anyone who wanted to disappear from an old life, or take on a new identity, or simply to start again. Sheeld's own reason was to do with women, or rather with one particular woman called Borbellia. He and Borbellia had lived together for three years, but all through that time Sheeld had been having secret affairs with two other women. Eventually, inevitably, he had been found out. In the mounting confusion and emotional fallout that had surrounded his activities he had come to believe that his only recourse was to flee. He knew that he was making excuses for his betrayals, that were he stronger in character he would have stayed and taken responsibility for his actions, but once the idea of exile and a new life had taken hold he found it impossible to resist.

Not unnaturally, the native islanders had profoundly mixed feelings about the arrival of so many immigrants from the north. There were good reasons to make the newcomers welcome: most émigrés brought money or other kinds of capital with them, in addition to the state grants that they made available. They also brought ideas and technology from the more sophisticated countries in the north. As a consequence a modern technological infrastructure was rapidly spreading through the islands. Health facilities, schools, commerce, housing, the arts, communications, all these were enjoying a thoroughgoing renascence, with apparent living standards throughout the Archipelago improving every year. But the whole island way of life was in jeopardy: languages, customs, traditions and family structures were undergoing drastic changes and there were many who resented the process of change and tried to resist it.

Exacerbating all this was the constant movement of the military through the islands, the troopships calling into ports where until a few years before fishing had been the only activity, the military flights needing landing strips, the islands made over into rest and recreation facilities for the troops, the increasing number of military camps and garrisons, the refuelling and provisioning of the armies, the recruitment of non-combatant support staff.

In spite of everything large stretches of the Archipelago were still in most senses unspoiled and even in those areas where there were the greatest concentrations of outsiders it was still possible to find the traditional way of island life going on as it had done for centuries.

The process of change had undoubtedly begun, though, and as certainly would continue. Resentments grew. There had been acts of sabotage at some of the military establishments, there were reports of émigrés' houses being burnt down in their absence, social movements were emerging that were set up to protect local languages, religions and customs. Laws prejudicial to the interests of immigrants were often enacted by the smaller islands.

Much of it had so far passed Sheeld by, presumably because as an expatriate himself he was insensitive to the concerns of the native islanders, or at least would remain so at first. Foort itself was also relatively untouched by the effects of the war, although he had soon encountered a small colony of fellow expatriates in Foort Town. He had so far seen few of the other islands, but he had often heard people talking about Muriseay, the largest of all the islands. There were two huge army camps on Muriseay, one for each side, at opposite ends of the island. Because of the size of Muriseay Town, as well as its cultural and entertainment attractions, there were also more exiles there than anywhere else. Life in most of Muriseay was said now to be indistinguishable from that in many of the northern countries.

From behind Sheeld, Alanya called, 'Come and sit beside me. If you want to look at the scenery, you can do it as well from here.'

He turned back to face her and saw that she was reclining in the shade of the canopy, as if having laid herself out across a bed. The sun was beating down on his uncovered head and it was tempting to move into the shade to be with her, if only for that reason.

But he said, 'What are you doing, Alanya?'

'I thought you wanted to be with me. Why else did you follow me?'

'The wake was almost over. I was about to leave, but you made me curious. And these cliffs—'

'Just a view of the sea. Who cares?'

'Your family presumably does. Otherwise why should they live here? Why should they build this villa?'

'You know how it is,' she said dismissively. 'You should ask them if you want to know. Like you, I'm only visiting. You didn't leave the party with me to look out there at the view.'

'I thought I did. You suggested I follow you. I followed you.'

'We're alone here. Come and sit with me.'

Because of the bright sunlight beating down painfully on his unprotected head, and only for that reason, Sheeld went up the four wooden steps to the balcony and sat down on the end of the swing chair. It rocked back, moving unevenly. An expanse of cushion lay between them.

Alanya reached up and released her hair, swinging it free with a movement that reminded him of Borbellia. She too had kept her hair tied up for formal occasions, and made a play of shaking it out when she wanted some fun.

'Come nearer to me,' Alanya said.

'Why?'

'Do I need to tell you?'

She swung her legs down, and slid purposefully across the cushioned seat towards him, smiling invitingly.

Sheeld moved smartly, stood up and stepped away from her. He stood at the rail of the balcony, looking out towards the sea, embarrassed by her. He wished again that he had left the funeral immediately after the service at the crematorium.

That should have been a sign to him. Something unusual was going on, even by their standards. The Mercier family were magnifying his feelings of alienation, with the patois they spoke, the customs they observed. He was aware of Alanya behind him, the seat still rocking to and fro as a result of their sudden movements. He glanced back at her and saw she was again reclining full length along the seat, resting her head on her hand, looking up at him with a coy smile. She did not seem in the least annoyed or angered by his reaction.

Again, he was reminded by her behaviour of how little he knew of island ways. Where he came from women did not act in their relationships with men the way Alanya had been doing. That was not at all to say the women were sexually submissive, but Sheeld could not think of anyone he had known in the past who would throw herself so blatantly at a man she had only just met. Indeed, in this case she appeared to have approached him with the sole motive of throwing herself at him.

Everything here in the islands was still too strange to him to enable him to make safe generalizations about what he saw or encountered. For all he knew Alanya Mercier was acting as any other island woman might towards a man she had met only an hour or two earlier. On the other hand, she might be abnormally impulsive and demanding, known by her close friends and family for going in for such overt sexual behaviour, a social embarrassment to them.

'I'm going to walk back to the house now,' he said, the last thought having helped him to the decision.

'You'd never find the way on your own.' A touch of scorn.

'I don't see why not. I'll go the way we came.'

'Come and make love to me, Graian Sheeld.'

He was briefly tempted: the animal magnetism she radiated was still there, but there suddenly came to him a factual presentiment of what it would be to take advantage of her. He imagined going to her, kissing her, touching her, pulling her clothes off, feeling her doing the same to him ... then later, not long from now, twenty minutes from now, half an hour away, a familiar feeling of regret and shame and loss. Just sex with a stranger. There had been too many times before in his own life: thoughts of the aftermath had a proactively detumescent effect on him, unless the woman was someone he really wanted to be with.

'I don't want what you want,' he said simply.

'How do you know what I want?'

'I thought you said you needn't tell me.'

'Now you're humiliating me,' she said, and she pouted. He stared at her, thinking of pre-teen children and how little he wanted any of this.

'I don't intend to humiliate you,' he said. 'I'm sorry if it seems that way, but you surprised me. We don't know one another. I'm in a strange country—'

'But you must realize what happens at funeral ceremonies like this.'

'What happens? No, actually I don't.'

'Then why did you come? It's a family occasion. Outsiders ...'

'Outsiders what?'

'They normally stay outside.'

'I came on behalf of a member of my own family. I'm here to represent—'

'Yes, yes. Your uncle,' she said. 'You told me all that.'

He was beginning to dislike her – perhaps he should have done so from the start. Almost everything she said had an implied second meaning, a riddle. Sheeld detested riddles. Alanya Mercier rarely spoke directly. He walked down the wooden steps and crossed the short strip of levelled ground towards the edge of the cliff. He glanced back only once, to see Alanya still sprawling as

161

he had left her. She looked slightly ridiculous, an amateur vamp denied her reward.

He retraced his steps, intending to return to the house as quickly as possible, then depart. There was no point remaining.

He walked along until he came to the sloping path. He climbed it and the steps beyond and followed the ledge as it regained the top of the cliff. The vertiginous drop to the sea dizzied him, but he climbed briskly. Without a backward look at the view he strode into the forest.

Almost at once he was uncertain which way to go.

It was clear that three separate tracks diverged from this point. When he had walked along here with Alanya a few minutes earlier he had not noticed it, as a convergence passed when coming the other way. The route they had walked by, the one he seemed to remember and which looked the most direct way through the trees, was the central path, striking away from the cliff at approximately a right angle. He started along it but almost at once he came to a halt. Two large trees had fallen across the path and he was sure they had not had to clamber past them on the way here. He went back.

The left-hand path went nowhere. It started promisingly, but curved around after a short distance and led to another viewing position on the edge of the cliff. Sheeld was certain he had not passed this. He went back. The third path, the only one remaining and the one that went to the right, again seemed at first to be the one he and Alanya had walked along, but after following it for about five minutes he was no longer sure. The path twisted several times, then came to a deep, overgrown gully where the only way down was by way of a flight of steps hewn out of the ground.

He returned to the junction of the three, close to the clifftop, and stood there in agonized indecision.

As he passed in front of the cabin he saw Alanya standing by the door, working a key in the lock. It turned with a faint scraping noise and she went inside without acknowledging him.

A narrow alley ran alongside the cabin, created by the proximity of the wall to the rising face of rock. Sheeld walked through the alley, then as the ground immediately widened he scrambled up the slope beyond. A clear path lay ahead, winding up through the trees and striking away from the sea. He strode along feeling optimistic, because although it was not the way he had come the path was wide and it had clearly been created to lead somewhere. He imagined that if it did not take him back to the house or the grounds, then returning to a public road would be as good. He could presumably find a lift into Trellin Town.

However, after five minutes of easy walking he saw that the path ahead began to narrow and soon he was moving along a dirt track hemmed in with thorns and leaves which brushed stiffly past his legs. The texture of the path softened, and he saw that his feet were squeezing up outlines of muddy water around the soles of his shoes. Because he could see the track winding on ahead he continued along it, hoping that it would widen again.

At one point he had to clamber around another fallen tree, one with its roots pointing jaggedly across the path. Keeping an eye on the ground, to make sure he didn't lose his footing, Sheeld noticed how the soil had been worked into a loose scattering of muddy mounds, as if something small had been burrowing through it.

He stepped back at once, until he was standing on firmer ground. The thought of exactly what might have been burrowing around exposed tree roots was enough to change his mind about everything. The tree completely blocked the path. Its fallen branches extended a long way to the side, buried in the massing foliage of the forest. On the other side, the ground fell away into a swampy morass. To continue would mean clambering through the roots, unavoidably stepping where burrows had been made.

He hesitated a little longer, then with real reluctance began to retrace his steps. At first he walked slowly, not wanting to see Alanya Mercier again, but it was not long before he realized that without her he could spend many wasted hours trying to find his way out of the forest.

He walked more quickly, climbing the slope back towards the cliffs, sweltering in the long tropical afternoon.

As he emerged from the forest and walked through the narrow alley between the cabin and the rocky face, Sheeld saw Alanya pacing along the levelled area of ground in front. She heard him approaching and turned at once.

'I said you would not find the way. You were thinking about me, and what you wanted to do with me, as we came here. You should have been remembering the route we took.'

'I was being polite. I was following you to see where you would take me.'

'Yes, so you were. And you were frightened of our large insects, and you were thinking about having sex with me, and the money my family owns, and all the things you no doubt came here today to take from us.'

'What did you say?'

'Isn't it true? You came after me because you thought I would be easy to seduce, and afterwards you would blackmail me for my family's money.'

He gestured with irritation and despair.

'Nothing could be further from the truth,' he said. 'I want none of it. If you would show me how to retrace our steps to the house, or show me the way to a public road, all this can end.'

'So you feel nothing for having humiliated me.'

'I'm sorry. I meant no harm.'

'Was that true in the past?'

'The past? My past? What do you know of that?'

'Everyone leaves traces behind them,' she said. 'The profession of the Merciers has been to follow such traces. You do not come to our islands with clean hands, Graian Sheeld. We know about you, knew about you before you arrived today. I thought you would try with me what you have done in the past with others.'

'You set me up? You were trying to provoke something from me?'

'Your words.'

164

'I came here on family business,' he said.

'Our family too has business. Still, I think you will be fortunate today. You have done well.'

'I've passed some test of behaviour.'

'You know what we normally do with people like you, on the island where I was born?'

'I don't.' Nor, he thought, did he much care.

'We're interested in revenge.'

'This is so ridiculous.'

'That is what many of us also say, because we're not primitives. I'm one of them. Revenge is ridiculous, uncivilized. What our ancestors used to do to their enemies is embarrassing to those of us who are living in the modern world. But the custom of the islands is also for us to speak our minds.'

Sheeld stared around. The high fringe of the forest, the dizzying narrowness of the paths at the top of the cliffs, the heady view of the sea and the islands. A place to die, perhaps.

He felt unable to form words that were not clumsy, so used those anyway.

'You and I both made a mistake,' he said. 'You wanted something, I was unsure. We are both adults. Can't we share the responsibility?'

'You are no islander!'

'You know that. What difference does it make?'

He felt himself still to be floundering, a caricature of an expatriate mainlander, falling back on irrelevant manners and reasonableness to try to negotiate around some obscure island custom. Friends had warned him of it before he left, the way hostilities could be accidentally aroused: there was a long history of island exploitation by the north, and old memories and grievances had been revived by the war.

Sheeld had thought before he left: I can avoid all that. I'm young, free-thinking, unassertive, self-controlled. I can live a quiet life, not aggravating the island people I meet, not letting them aggravate me. I can slip imperceptibly past the memories, be who I am and what I am without having to explain or defend myself.

Thus his rationalization of himself to himself, but it was all untested theory. It had worked after a fashion while he lived on Foort: the islanders there seemed incurious about him and he felt he had started to assimilate quietly into their way of life. Then came the visit to Trellin and the first test of his theory. When he agreed to attend the funeral he had not thought, had never expected, to be confronted by a situation like the one Alanya Mercier had created.

He was out of his depth in manners and traditions and habits in which he was unpractised.

But how significant could such matters be? This was a funeral. A man dies suddenly; his family mourns; friends and acquaintances from a wider circle are moved to pay their last respects at the man's funeral. One of them asks a proxy to attend on his behalf. There is a service, a wake. All these were surely universals, amongst civilized people?

They were still standing there, locked in the impasse that had arisen between them. He wanted only to find an end to it. She wanted ... what? He couldn't imagine. An apology, an abasement, some symbolic island gesture to appease the wrong she imagined he had done her?

'I show you the way back,' she said. 'It's not difficult.'

'I couldn't find the path on my own. It looks as if I do need you.'

'That's why I waited.'

He glanced up at the sky: the sun was still high, and the hot air beneath the trees seemed immovable. He was dressed unsuitably for the climate, another matter that had revealed his ignorance.

'Is there any fresh water in the cabin?' he said. 'I'm thirsty.'

'There is a little. I'm dry too. But I was going to show you, on the way back. We have a fruit that grows here. It's in season now. To eat it at this time of year is more refreshing than cold water.'

'I'd rather have water. May I have some of that first?'

'Of course.'

She led him back to the cabin, unlocked the door. She left him on the porch while she went inside but returned a few moments later with an unsealed bottle of mineral water. It was cold, from an icebox, but there were only a couple of fingers of water at the bottom. He removed the cap and emptied the mouthful of water into his mouth.

'Do you always swallow water like that?'

'Like what?'

'You drank it in one gulp.'

'I was thirsty! You only gave me a mouthful.'

'In a hot climate it is better to sip over a long period of time.' She locked the door. 'Now we return to the house,' she said. 'If you want more water to gulp, you will find it there.'

Seething with irritation, Sheeld followed her along the path up the face of the cliff.

The mystery of the apparently lost footpath was soon revealed: the first path he had tried was the right one, but the real way forward involved stepping over some spreading shrubbery at a point where a levelled path forked to one side. Beyond the wildly growing shrub, the path continued on, heading more or less directly towards the main house. Looking back he remembered going that way, but as she had reminded him, he had been thinking about Alanya, watching the back of her body as he walked.

Now beside her, Sheeld began to regret his bad temper with her, realizing that he was as much the initiator of the problem as she was. He should simply have made a token appearance at the funeral and left immediately it was over. He should not even have returned to the house for the wake. Why he had followed her at all was now a mystery to him, however clear it had seemed to him at the time.

The path led uphill and Sheeld felt increasingly hot and thirsty. He became intent only on returning to the house, finding something to drink, then leaving as quickly as possible. He no longer even cared if he gave offence by doing so. Once away he would never see any of these people again.

Somewhere along the way Alanya's dress was snagged by a thorny bush. She turned, bent, unpicked the thin material from

167

the tiny spikes. He stood behind her, waiting patiently. When she had finished she did not straighten but for some reason stood that short distance in front of him with her head and shoulders bowed. She twisted her head and smiled up at him. The angle of her face made her mouth look as if it had distorted into an unpleasant rictus. There was something so odd and perverse about her posture that a tremor of fear ran through him.

She held the expression.

He said, 'What is it?'

'What is what?'

'Why are you looking at me like that?'

'Do you know what is on the ground beside you?'

Instantly he looked down, but could see nothing. 'What are you talking about?'

'I thought I saw a thryme.'

He leapt back in a reflex. Then, as he realized exactly what she had said, he stepped back again.

'Where is it?'

He hopped and stumbled across the path, beating at his shins and ankles with his hand, shuddering in terror. He could so easily imagine its soft repellent body pressed against him, the thick black legs scuttling over him, the mandible sinking into his skin, the loathsome larvae flowing into his bloodstream ...

Alanya had not moved, other than to give up her perverse angular stance. Now she was standing erect, watching him with frank interest.

Shuddering, he said, 'Are you lying to me?'

'What do you think?'

'Don't do this! Is there really a thryme near me?'

'You're terrified, aren't you?'

'Yes.'

'You spurned me. You humiliated me. Now I have to go back to my family, and they will know what has happened, what has not happened.'

'Is that what you're doing?' Sheeld said. 'You lied about the insect?'

'You pretended you wanted me. You allowed me to show you how much I wanted you. Then you said no. Now all you are thinking about is the damned insect.'

Sheeld was standing in the centre of the path, where no vegetation was overhanging, where the ground was not broken. He looked on all sides, peering into the long grasses and ferns on each side of the path, trying to see past bushes.

'You said islanders no longer took revenge,' he said, and he shuddered. Sweat was pouring down his face, through his shirt, wetting the palms of his hands. His throat was drier than ever.

'That's true. You seem to know nothing about women, though.' She bent down, close to where they had been standing a few moments before. 'I'll show you what I saw on the ground.'

She picked up a dark, round object, covered in leaves. Sheeld felt an instinct to step further back from her but she calmly unfolded the outer leaves and tossed them aside. Inside was a dull-green sphere about the size of a large grapefruit.

'What is it?'

'Just a fruit,' she said. 'I told you. The juice is refreshing to drink.'

She broke the outer skin and peeled off a part of the fruit. She put it into her mouth, and chewed and sucked at it noisily.

'It's perfect,' she said, swallowing. She held out a second piece towards him. 'Want to try it?'

'No.'

'I thought you were thirsty.'

'Not for that. What is it?'

'A fruit,' she said. 'It grows on most of the islands, but it doesn't travel well. You pick it and eat it as you find it.' She held up another segment. 'In an hour or two it will have started to ferment because I broke the skin, so I eat it now.'

'What sort of fruit is it? What's it called?'

'If I told you that you wouldn't taste it even if it was the last food in the world.'

'You might as well tell me, because I've no intention of having any of it.'

169

'It's called a puthryme,' she said, smiling at him again.

'That sounds like ...'

'It's called a puthryme because it grows on a tree where the thryme will sometimes nest. Some people will never try the fruit, for the same reason as you. They fear the insect more than they want to experience the taste.' She held out one of the long green segments. 'Why don't you try it?'

'I'd rather not.'

'Because of its name? Because of what I told you?'

'I don't want it.' It was as much truth as he felt like admitting, that he did not like the look of it.

'In the islands two people who are no longer friends eat the puthryme together to show forgiveness.'

'Another charming custom.'

'You have offended me, and soon you will be leaving. Probably, we shall never see each other again. We are no longer friends. It would be a way of parting on even terms.'

'We were never friends, Alanya. We have barely met.'

'But I feel a grievance against you.'

'Let's leave things as they are.'

'If you wish,' said Alanya.

Soon afterwards they reached the edge of the forest and walked out on to the lawn of the walled garden. Many of the guests appeared to have left, or at least had moved away from the garden. The servants had cleared away all traces of the earlier meal, but now were resetting the long tables for another. There was no food or drink in sight.

A group of women stood by the verandah. As soon as they noticed Sheeld and Alanya returning there was a reaction. One of the women headed out of the garden and walked off in the direction of the house. Another came over to speak to Alanya.

Ignoring Sheeld, she said, 'Alanya, Fertin has been asking for you.'

'I can't talk to him now.'

'He said you and M. Sheeld were to go and see him as soon as you returned from your walk.'

'I'm busy, Maëve. He can wait.'

Alanya turned away and went slowly across the lawn to the two long tables. She took another piece of fruit. Juice welled from her mouth and rolled down her chin, but she caught it expertly with a napkin she picked up quickly from the table.

'Who did she mean?' said Sheeld.

'Fertin is Corrin Mercier's elder son,' she said. 'You were introduced to him when you arrived.'

'I remember now. A relative of yours.'

'Of course. We are all relatives here.'

'Why should he want to see both of us?'

'He thinks he is so important.' She gestured in an irritated way towards where the women had been. Only Maëve and one other remained by the verandah. Both were watching them. 'You and Fertin are the same, you know. When I am not here, I have a career, a life. I travel on business, representing a large company. They pay me well, they commit huge sums of corporate money on the basis of my decisions. Yet when I am in the family, as here, you would think that I have no life beyond the one of a sexually subservient woman. Men treat us so. Fertin wants my soul, you want my body. But then Fertin rejects my soul, you reject my body. Here ... you need this.'

She thrust the fruit towards him.

'I don't want it.'

'Take it. There's no water.'

Reluctantly, he did. He was convinced now she was deranged in some way. Nothing made sense, except that the longer he stayed in the environment of the house the more vulnerable he felt. But vulnerable to what? He had done nothing wrong, hardly even in his thoughts.

'It's time I left.'

'Goodbye,' she said without looking at him. 'Eat some fruit with me before you go. It is a symbol that would mean much to me.'

'Not to me.'

But as he headed towards the gate out of the walled garden, he was still holding the fruit.

171

A servant said, 'May we oblige you in any matter, sir?'

'No, I have to leave now. But thank you.'

'Mme. Mercier is resting at present. She has asked not to be disturbed until the evening meal is ready.'

'Yes, I understand.' Sheeld was disturbed by the way the man was standing, ostentatiously barring his way. 'Would you kindly give Mme. Mercier my condolences once more, and please explain that I was not able to stay for dinner as I have to catch the evening ferry.'

'Yes, sir.' He did not shift.

'Then do you require anything else of me?'

'Of course not, sir. But do you wish to remain here in the garden, or would you prefer to join some of the other guests in the house?'

'No, I'm leaving.'

'That's not possible, sir. I have explained about Mme. Mercier.'

'And I have explained about the ferry.' Sheeld wanted the conversation to end.

'We are well aware of the ferries from the island, sir.'

'Yes, indeed.'

Sheeld pushed past the man and headed for the gateway. Two other male servants appeared from beyond the wall and closed in on him the moment he appeared in the gap. This time there was no appearance of courtesy. They brusquely manhandled him back through the gateway into the walled garden.

Since she was the only person he had spoken to, from whom he might expect the least part of understanding, Sheeld looked for Alanya. He had left her beside one of the long tables, but when he went back there was no sign of her.

He looked around in surprise. The garden was well filled with shrubbery and trees and ornamental beds, but there were few if any places anyone could disappear into. Yet not only Alanya but the group of women, of whom Maëve had been one, had also vanished. It was a mystery, because apart from the path into the rainforest, the only apparent way out of the garden was through the gateway where he had been speaking to the servant. He did not remember anyone passing while he was there, and he would certainly have noticed Alanya if she had left that way.

With a great deal of apprehension he walked back to the servant, who visibly stiffened as Sheeld approached.

'Where is Alanya Mercier?' Sheeld said.

'As I told you, sir, Mme. Mercier does not wish to be disturbed until later.'

'But you meant Mme. Gilda Mercier, did you not?'

'No, sir. I spoke of Mme. Alanya Mercier.'

Sheeld took that in, but could not comprehend its meaning.

'But Alanya Mercier was here just now. Not in the house!'

'I am expected only to convey messages, sir. That is what I have done.'

'Where is everyone else?' Sheeld said.

'They have returned for the time being to the house. But my instructions are that you are to remain here. May I oblige you in any other matter, sir?'

'No!'

Sheeld walked back into the walled, ornamental garden. Apart from the servants, who appeared to be taking no notice of him, he was now the only person there. He walked around, feeling as if he was being watched from every corner. The sun beat down on him relentlessly.

A jet aircraft went by high overhead, wheeling to the right in a broad circle, tracing a line of curving condensation across the bright blue sky.

An hour later Sheeld was feeling seriously uncomfortable. He had sat for as long as possible in the shade beneath the verandah, but the air was stifling hot and he was desperate for liquid. The only servants remaining were the two who guarded the gateway and although the tables had been reset for the next meal there was still no food or drink. The toilet marquee had been removed. There was not even a faucet for a garden hose or sprinkler. How

Alanya and the others had left the garden without him seeing remained a mystery. Obviously there must be another way out of the garden and back to the house, but although he walked slowly round the entire garden he found no clue of it.

There was still the rest of the fruit Alanya had picked, with her promise that it was refreshing to eat, but the irrational fear in him had made him put it off until the last possible moment.

The moment had, however, arrived. When his thirst finally became too much for him Sheeld went across to the gate guards and asked them to let him have some water, but they ignored him.

It was this, as much as his real sense of confinement for the last hour or more, that convinced him he had become a prisoner.

He returned to the table where he had placed the fruit, and retrieved it. He remembered how Alanya had been eating it earlier and so he stripped off some of the remaining outer leaves to reveal the segments beneath. He broke off one of these and bit into it before he could change his mind.

Because he had not known what to expect the combination of the fruit's flavour and texture, both of which were unexpected, made him want to spit it out again. The fruit was dry and crisp, like a sliver of fried potato, not at all the refreshing treat Alanya had described. When he bit into it, though, the crispness yielded as a green apple will yield, and the inside turned out to be attractively firm and moist. The flavour was extraordinary: it spread out to fill his mouth like a distilled liqueur, and had a sweet muskiness to it that was more surprising than unpleasant. He chewed it cautiously, quickly deciding that he did not after all dislike it. On the contrary, as he chewed the pieces in his mouth into smaller morsels, the taste became positively pleasant and imparted a feeling of wonderful freshness to his mouth.

When he had finished the first segment, he took another, wishing now that Alanya had left more of it for him.

He walked to and fro across the walled garden, eating the fruit, enjoying it, forcing himself to take it in steady portions so as to make it last a little longer. Alanya had been right: for some reason that was hard to pinpoint it was more refreshing than cold spring water.

Removing the segments revealed the central core of the fruit, yellow and spherical. As he finished the last of the segments, Sheeld toyed with the kernel in his hand, wondering if it too was edible. It had roughly the colour and surface texture as a ripe apricot, and had the same furry feel to it. At the bottom, where the segments had broken off, there were the remains of the stalk, but apart from that the surface was unblemished. He sniffed it, rubbing the surface with his thumb. He smelt a mild sweetness, like that of the fragrance of the segments.

He went to one of the long tables and took a knife from where it had been set. He cut the yellow fruit in half, then laid both parts on a porcelain plate and looked carefully at them.

The inside was yellow, moist and fibrous, with dozens of tiny black pips suspended in the flesh. Sheeld prodded it with his finger, found that the fruit was cool and firm, and a cautious sniff confirmed that it was much the same as the segments, and therefore probably safe to eat.

He slipped one of the hemispheres into his mouth, and pressed it gently with his tongue.

It was sweet and delicious, like a ripe orange. Once again the sensation of flavour spreading around his mouth was irresistible, but as soon as he broke through the soft fibres the flesh of the fruit became rubbery and tended to stick to his teeth and the roof of his mouth. He wished he had not taken so much at once.

He could feel the pips inside the fleshy mass, small and hard. He looked around for somewhere he could spit the fruit out, because he was no longer enjoying it. He tried to work the mass into a small bulk, so he could slip it out into his hand, but in doing so he accidentally crushed one of the pips between his teeth. He felt it break apart. At once a stronger flavour, bitter and putrid, overwhelmed the rest. Disliking it intensely he swallowed quickly, trying to get rid of the fruit. Some of it went down, the rest remained gummily around his teeth. He worked at it with his tongue, feeling the little hard pips everywhere. He was careful not to bite any more of those.

Gradually he managed to swallow the rest, then he cleaned around his gums with his tongue and fingers. There were pips in many of the crevices between his teeth, and either he removed these with a fingernail or swallowed them. He succeeded in not breaking any more. He spat on the grass several times.

Now he stood in the garden, working his tongue, swallowing frequently, trying to banish all last remnants of the taste of the fruit. The bitterness remained, sour and disgusting, entirely removing the earlier pleasant effect of the rest of the fruit.

When he looked up and turned around, the garden had filled again with funeral guests.

Two servants walked towards him from the entrance. Fertin Mercier followed them. A short distance behind him, Alanya followed.

Sheeld stepped back, feeling threatened by their approach. The long table was behind him and he retreated until he felt his backside pressing against the edge. He put a hand back to steady himself, and it fell on the hemisphere of fruit he had not tried to eat.

'Is this the man?' Mercier said to Alanya.

'Yes, you know it is.' She flashed a look at Sheeld, but what meaning or intent it contained was lost on him.

'When you came to the Dream Archipelago,' Fertin Mercier said to Sheeld without preamble, 'you exercised an option to become an islander. You accepted our customs as you found them and you therefore took them to yourself. The law for one island is respected by all the others, and island law demands justice for what you did here today.'

Sheeld said, 'I've done nothing, and I've done nothing wrong.'

'That's an arguable point, and it is what I want you to tell me. According to what I witnessed for myself, and what many other members of my family also saw, you left this garden alone with my wife and were absent with her for more than an hour. What were the two of you doing together?'

'Nothing occurred between us.'

'Nothing?' Fertin Mercier looked at Alanya beside him, but she made no perceptible response.

'Say it again, M. Sheeld.'

'Nothing of any kind happened. We simply took a walk to the clifftop to admire the view, then we returned.'

Mercier nodded. 'That much at least seems to confirm what my wife has said.'

'Well, then—'

'But you see, Graian Sheeld, I know what my wife had in mind when you left together, because she has acted like this many times before, with other men. She has as good as admitted it.'

'I'm not answerable for your wife's behaviour. In my view, based on what I've seen of her behaviour, she needs—'

'My wife is sexually responsible, M. Sheeld. Her behaviour, as you call it, is not your concern but mine. She has her rights as an adult, but so too do I.'

'I assure you nothing at happened between us,' Sheeld said again, painfully aware not only that Alanya was hearing every word, but that the other members of the family were listening too.

'You did not make love to my wife, rape her, seduce her, debauch her, ravish her? Is she not attractive to you?'

'She is extremely attractive, of course,' Sheeld said, thinking back to the few minutes when she had seemed so to him, and wondering whether his position was made worse or better by admitting it.

'Yet you say you resisted the temptation she laid before you.'

'Yes.'

'That is what she says too. You concur.'

'All I can say, M. Mercier,' Sheeld said, with sudden sincerity. 'All I can do now is apologize to you if I have somehow trans-gressed either your hospitality or your traditions. I am a stranger

177

here, I meant no harm and I am embarrassed that I have caused you anger or upset.'

'Yes, you are a stranger here, aren't you?'

'I can't help that.'

'Nor it seems can you help the fact that either you have embarrassed me in front of my family, should you have had knowledge of my wife, or you have humiliated my wife by refusing her. Which is to be?'

'I've already apologized to your ... to Alanya.'

'So she tells me.'

The rest of the family were now grouped in a loose semicircle around the quiet confrontation. He thought: what culture is it where a man publicly confronts another man he suspects of having cuckolded him, while he does not know the truth? Sheeld felt again a powerful wish to be away from the place, back in the town, in the port, waiting for a ferry, enjoying the safety of the cosmopolitan company of fellow travellers, all intent on their own destinations.

'You can't hold me here against my will,' he said. 'I've done nothing wrong. I've offended no one. I've apologized for the offence I gave. I meant nothing by it.' But the words were coming out too loudly, revealing the fright that was beneath the calmness he was trying to project. Fertin Mercier was as composed as if he were reading from a script, and Sheeld had felt himself speaking with the same semi-formal stresses, but his own image of self-control was slipping. He tried to moderate his words. 'Let me leave and I will have nothing to do with any of you again.'

'That is our intention,' Mercier said. 'But how can I be sure you mean it?'

'I'm planning to catch the evening ferry. Two days from now I will be at home.'

'And your home is?'

'Foort.'

'It would take you only a day or two to return here.'

Alanya spoke for the first time.

'He could eat the puthryme, Fertin.'

178

'That old superstition again!' But he looked thoughtful. 'Would you accept that?' he said to her.

'Now I would. He knows what it signifies.'

'Forgiveness,' Sheeld said cynically.

'If it is eaten together,' Mercier said, turning on him swiftly. 'Did you do that with my wife as well? Have you forgiven each other too?'

'Fuck you,' Sheeld said. The sheer unreasonableness of what was happening had finally reached critical.

'Profanity won't help you.'

Sheeld looked towards the gateway out of the garden, wondering what would happen if he simply tried to dash away. Most of the relatives looked fairly old and many of them were obviously feeble, but Mercier and his brother were fit and youthful. Then there were the servants. Four of them were standing in front of or near to the gate.

'What is it you actually want of me?' he said to Fertin Mercier.

'Let us say you could do as my wife has suggested. Eat the puthryme, then you may go.'

'I can't believe you said that.'

'We are too influenced by the past here,' Mercier said, with a sudden edge of reflectiveness in his voice. 'I myself sometimes wish we could throw it off. But the funeral today has been a great family occasion, and not everyone here thinks like me.' There was the sound of assent from some of the people watching. 'As my wife has said, eating a puthryme traditionally signifies forgiveness between two people. You may feel you have nothing to forgive, but that is not so. Forgiveness has to embrace both sides of a dispute. You slighted my wife. To gain her forgiveness, and therefore mine, and therefore that of the rest of us, you should do as I say. The puthryme is a tradition with us. Isn't that so?'

Fertin Mercier turned unexpectedly, looking around at the rest of the family to include them in what he was saying. Sheeld heard more sounds of agreement. One of the men said something quickly in patois, glancing towards the people immediately to his

179

side, seeking their concurrence. Sheeld heard again the word that sounded like 'graiansheeld'.

'Then I can satisfy you,' he said. 'I have already eaten some of your disgusting fruit.'

'You said you wouldn't touch it,' Alanya said.

'I was thirsty. I tried some of it.' Sheeld still had the sour aftertaste in his mouth. He indicated the plate on the table behind him, where he had left the uneaten hemisphere of orange fruit. He noticed that several of the black pips were lying on the surface of the plate beside the fruit. How had they made their way out of it? 'I ate some of what you left.'

Both Alanya and her husband looked intently at the fruit.

'My God, he did!' Alanya said.

The other people were pressing forward to see. Sheeld felt a distinct jab of fear. Fertin Mercier lifted up the plate for everyone to see, then put it down quickly. He wiped his hand against his leg and stepped back and to the side, clearly making way for Sheeld to depart. The relatives were also moving back, now they had seen.

A servant stepped up to Mercier's side, presumably responding to some unseen signal.

'Deal with it quickly!' Mercier said. He turned to Sheeld. 'You should watch this before you leave, Graian Sheeld.'

Mercier moved further back.

The servant was carrying a small silver bowl, with a lid. He removed the lid and inside the bowl could be seen a quantity of a transparent liquid. It sloshed around with quick movements, suggesting that it was not water or water-based. The servant poured the liquid on to the plate where Sheeld had put the remains of the fruit, then stepped back.

Fertin Mercier took a cigarette-lighter from his pocket and handed it to the servant. The man flicked the flint wheel, then put the flame to the fruit. There was a flash and a popping sound, barely visible or audible in the open daylight, and a yellow flame guttered around the half-eaten puthryme.

'In the islands,' Mercier said to Sheeld, 'there are some things

180

we always cremate. But you probably know that by now.'

Sheeld stared at the fruit as it burned. He saw the yellow flesh turning brown, sizzling and charring inside the flame. The pips curled and wriggled as the heat reached them, squirming like the maggots he suddenly knew they were. Then they abruptly frizzled up and died.

They made a pungent smell, disgusting and foetid.

Sheeld looked desperately at Mercier, at Alanya. Someone in the semicircle of relatives spoke loudly in patois, and a woman fainted. Most of the people began to back away.

Sheeld thrust two fingers into his mouth, reaching down into his throat, trying to make himself vomit. He gagged, then belched. Foul fumes eructated up from his gut. Alanya was watching him. Her eyes were half closed and her lips were moist. She held the arm of her husband, pressing one of her breasts rhythmically and sensuously against him.

Sheeld stepped away from her, felt his back arching as a spasm of excruciating pain coursed through him. He stared up at the sky. Two jet aircraft, high in the blue, reflecting silver sunlight, were heading towards the south on converging courses. Behind them, their condensation trails stretched away across the sky in huge curling spirals.

The
Watched

•

Sometimes Jenessa was slow to leave in the mornings, reluctant to return to her frustrating job, and when she lingered in his house Yvann Ordier had difficulty concealing his impatience. This morning was one such. He lurked outside the door of the shower cubicle, fingering the smooth leather case of his binoculars.

Ordier was alert to Jenessa's every movement, each variation in sound giving him as clear a picture as if the door were wide open and the plastic curtain held back: the spattering of droplets against the curtain as she raised an arm, the lowering in pitch of the hissing water as she bent to wash a leg, the fat drops plopping soapily on the tiled floor as she stood erect to shampoo her hair. He could visualize her glistening body in every detail. Thinking of their lovemaking during the night he felt a renewed lust for her.

He knew he was standing too obviously by the door, too transparently waiting for her to emerge, so he put down the binoculars case and went to the kitchen. He used the microwave oven to warm up some coffee left over from the night before. Jenessa had still not finished in the shower. Ordier paused again by the door of the cubicle and knew by the sound of the water that she was rinsing her hair. He could imagine her with her face tilted up into the spray, her long dark hair plastered flatly back above her ears. She often stood like that for several minutes, letting the water run into her open mouth before it dribbled away, coursing down her body. Twin streams of droplets would fall from her nipples, a tiny rivulet would snake through her pubic hair, a thin film would gloss her buttocks and thighs.

Again torn between desire and impatience, Ordier went to his bureau, unlocked it, and took out his scintilla detector.

He checked the batteries first. They were sound but he knew he had recharged them too many times and that he would have to replace them soon. He used the detector regularly: a few weeks earlier he had discovered by chance that his house had become infested with a large number of the microscopic scintillas and since then he had been systematically searching for them every day.

Today there was a signal the instant he turned on the detector. He walked through the house listening for the subtle changes in pitch and volume of the electronic howl. He traced the scintilla to the bedroom, where he switched in the directional circuit and held the instrument close to the floor. He found the scintilla moments later. It was in the carpet, near where Jenessa's clothes were folded over a chair.

Ordier parted the pile of the carpet and after a brief search picked up the scintilla with a pair of tweezers. He took it through into his study. It was the tenth he had discovered this week. Although there was the usual chance that it had been brought into the house accidentally lodged in someone's hair or clothes, or stuck to the underside of a shoe, it was always unsettling to find one. He placed it on a slide then peered at it through his microscope. There was no serial number engraved on the silicon-mounted lens.

Jenessa had finished her shower and was standing by the door of the study.

'What are you doing?' she said.

'Another scintilla,' Ordier said. 'This one was in the bedroom.'

'You're always finding them. I thought they were supposed to be undetectable.'

'I've got a gadget for locating them.'

'You never told me.'

183

Ordier turned to face her. She was naked, with a turban of golden towelling around her hair. A few curling, tangled skeins of wet hair framed her face.

'I've made some coffee,' he said. 'Let's drink it on the patio.'

Jenessa turned and walked away, her legs and back still moist from her shower. Ordier watched her, thinking of another woman, the young Qataari woman in the valley below his house. He wished that his response to Jenessa could be less complicated. In the last few weeks they had become at once more intimate and more distant, a process that had begun when he realized she was satisfying desires that the Qataari woman could arouse but never fulfil.

He turned back to the microscope and pulled the slide gently away. He tipped the scintilla into a quiet-case – a soundproof, lightproof box where nearly two hundred more of the tiny lenses were already being kept – then went back to the kitchen. He collected the pot of coffee and some cups and went outside to the glare of sunlight and the rasping of crickets.

Jenessa stood in the morning heat, combing the tangles from her long, fine hair. As the sun glared down at her she talked about her plans for the day.

'There's someone who's recently started in our department,' she said. 'I'd like you to meet him. I said we'd have dinner with him and his wife this evening.'

'Who is it?' Ordier said, disliking any interruption of his routine.

'A professor. He's recently arrived from the north.'

Jenessa sat down on the low wall that surrounded the patio, positioning herself so that her shadow fell towards him. The sunbright garden glared behind her. She was at ease when naked in the open air, showing herself off, knowing he was looking at her.

'Another anthropologist? Here for the usual reason?'

'Of course. There's nowhere else to observe the Qataari. Why else would someone like him come to the island? He knows the difficulties, of course, but he's been given a research grant so I suppose he should be allowed to spend it.'

'Why should I have to meet him?'

'You don't have to,' Jenessa said. 'But I'd like him to meet you.'

Ordier was idly stirring the loose white sugar in the bowl, watching it heap and swirl like a viscid liquid. Each sugar grain was larger than the biggest, most powerful of scintillas. A hundred or more of the tiny spy transmitters mixed in with the sugar would probably go unnoticed. How many scintillas were left in the dregs of coffee cups, how many were accidentally swallowed?

Jenessa leaned back on her elbows along the low wall. Her breasts spread across her chest, the nipples erect. She raised a knee and shook her long hair out so that it fell behind her. She checked to see if he was still looking at her. He was, of course.

'You like to stare,' she said, giving him a candid look from her dark eyes. She raised herself restlessly, turning towards him, so that her large breasts rounded out again. 'But you don't like being watched, do you?'

'What do you mean?'

'The scintillas. You go quiet when you find one.'

'Do I?' Ordier said, not aware that Jenessa had been noticing. He usually tried to make light of them and assumed they didn't bother her. As a natural exhibitionist maybe she liked the idea of unknown eyes watching her every movement. 'There are so many of them,' he said. 'All over the island. But there's no evidence anyone is planting them in the house.'

'You don't like finding them, though.'

'Do you?'

'I don't look for them.'

'The one I found this morning was in the bedroom. It was concealed in the carpet, on your side. If it was switched on someone could have been watching you get undressed last night. From below.'

'They could be watching me now,' she said. She briefly opened her legs a little further, as if inviting a spying camera to move in closer. She picked up her cup and took a sip of coffee. She was perhaps not so calm as she pretended because her hand trembled

185

as it held the cup and a tiny trickle of coffee ran down the side of her mouth and over her chin. It plopped down on to one of her naked breasts. She rubbed it with her fingers.

'You wouldn't like it any more than anyone else,' Ordier said. 'No one likes being spied on.'

'True.'

Jenessa stood up and brushed away the particles of grit that had attached to her backside from the top of the wall. The granules of sand and crumbled plaster scattered like grains around her. Some of them caught the sun as they fell, and glistened like microscopic jewels.

Ordier took her move to be a signal that she was about to get dressed then drive to her job at the university, but instead she took a dry towel from under the table on the patio. She placed it along the top of the low wall and draped herself along it. She raised her face to the sun.

In common with most of the expatriates in the Dream Archipelago, Ordier and Jenessa did not often speak about their past lives, either between themselves or to other people. In the islands past and future were effectively suspended by the Covenant of Neutrality. The future was sealed, as were the islands themselves, because until the conclusion of the war on the southern continent no one was officially permitted to leave the Archipelago. No one, that is, except the crews of ships and the troops of the combatant sides. And the airmen who flew overhead; the missionaries and consultants and medical supervisors; the government functionaries and the administrators of the military matériel warehouses; the whores and the con men and the drifters; all of these came and went without apparent hindrance. Most people stayed in the islands because they had to, or because they wished to. Neutrality was official, but it could only be enforced with broad consent.

With a sense of future removed, the past became irrelevant and those who came to the Archipelago, choosing the permanence of neutrality, made a conscious decision to abandon their former lives. Yvann Ordier was one amongst thousands of such émigrés.

He had never told Jenessa the details of how he had made his fortune, how he had paid for his relocation to the islands. All he had told her was that he had been successful in business, connected with scintillas, enabling him to take early retirement.

Jenessa, for her own part, had also said little about her background. He had thought when he first met her that she was a native islander, but he learned later that her parents had brought her from the north when she was a small child and had raised her on the island of Lanna. Technically, she was as much an expatriate as he, although in his eyes she was almost indistinguishable in her attitudes, accent and looks from true islanders. She was now a lecturer in anthropology at the University of Tumo, a member of one of several teams who were attempting, unsuccessfully, to study the refugee Qataari.

What Ordier did not want to reveal to Jenessa was how he came to possess a scintilla detector.

A few years before, in the full blood of opportunistic youth, Ordier had seen a chance to make a great deal of money and had snatched at it. At that time the war on the southern continent had lapsed into stalemate that was proving expensive in both lives and money. The enterprises sections of the armed forces had been raising money by unconventional means, using as an excuse the need to break the deadlock. One of the schemes was the selling of private commercial franchises to some of the hitherto classified matériel. Ordier had swiftly obtained exploitation rights to the spy scintillas.

His formula for commercial enrichment was simple: he sold the scintillas themselves to one side of the market and the detectors to the other. Although once the technology was out in the world it could be copied and emulated, by a clever system of patents and trademarks Ordier had ensured that a flood of royalties continued to come to him. In any event his business remained the market leader and his company was the prime distributor of the scintillas and the digital image-retrieval equipment. These sold more quickly than the army ordnance factories could produce them.

Within a year of Ordier opening his agency the saturation use of the scintillas meant that no room or building was closed to the eyes and ears of others, whether they were enemies, jealous spouses, criminals, commercial interests, government agencies or the merely voyeuristic.

For the next three and a half years Ordier's personal fortune had accrued. During the same period, paralleling his rise in wealth, a deeper sense of moral responsibility grew in him. The way of life in the civilized northern continent had been permanently altered. Scintillas were used in such profusion that nowhere was entirely free of them. They were in the streets, in the gardens, in the houses, in shops, offices, airports, doctors' surgeries, schools, private cars. You never knew for sure that a stranger was not listening to you, recording your words, watching your every action. Social behaviour changed. Away from home people moved with neutral expressions, said or did nothing that was not bland or apparently harmless. At home, not because they assumed they were unwatched but simply because they were at home, they broke free and acted without restraint. Everyone knew about what went on behind closed doors, because, of course, you could buy scintilla-sourced videos of ordinary people acting uninhibitedly in their homes. A mirror-image industry quickly arose as a reaction to the spread of the scintillas: hotels advertised rooms that were guaranteed scintilla-free; offices and conference suites were routinely cleared before important meetings or seminars; houses were sold on the basis that they had been scanned and cleared and could be maintained scintilla-free; code languages and signs were developed that were claimed to be untranslatable through the fish-eye lenses that otherwise saw everything. Naturally, nowhere was entirely safe from the scintillas. Wherever you went you were one of the watched.

At last, with guilt overwhelming every other feeling, Ordier sold the business to one of the major electronics corporations and took himself and his fortune to exile in the Dream Archipelago. He knew that his departure from the world of eavesdropping commerce would make not a jot of difference to its booming growth, but he himself wanted no more part in it.

He chose the equatorial island of Tumo from one of many that the island property brokers offered to him, and purchased a large tract of land in the remote eastern part, well away from the populous mountain region in the centre of the island. Many years before, the land had belonged to a noble Tumoit family, but the last of them had died decades earlier and the property was mostly derelict. Ordier had paid for the old ruins to be razed and removed, and the land made suitable for building. With this done he had commissioned the erection of a large, modern, barricaded house beside the edge of a long valley, while he lived in suspension of activity in a secure hotel in Tumo Town. When the house had been completed and furnished, the services connected, the security systems tested and certified, and when all the grounds and buildings had been repeatedly swept and cleared of stray scintillas, Ordier moved in.

He lived for some time in what he believed was a scintilla-free environment but he was finally forced to face up to the fact that nowhere was truly safe from them. His first use of the detector had turned up a scintilla infestation on what the trade would call a randomized cover basis. In other words, his house and grounds were only lightly covered and therefore did not appear to have been targeted. After he had located and removed all those scintillas – a task which took him several weeks – Ordier regularly checked his property. Until recently, the spread of scintillas had continued to be sporadic and accidental.

A few weeks ago, though, Ordier had discovered that scintillas now appeared to be infesting his house and grounds on an organized basis. The possibility of random cover remained, but not only did the number of scintillas increase, they were turning up where most people would seek privacy: the bedroom where he and Jenessa usually made love, the rooms where they played or relaxed, the shower cubicles, the toilets, the walled garden, this patio where Jenessa customarily sat around naked after her morning showers.

There were other features of the infestation that were just as alarming.

In the first place Ordier had no idea how the scintillas were actually being placed around his property. No one could enter or leave except by the main gates, which could only be opened by direct control from within the house, or by using a portable radar key; he and Jenessa were the only two who had such keys. All other access to the house was closed, so the scintillas were either being sown from the air, or intruders were finding a way into the grounds when the house was unattended.

Squinting up at the sky, against the bright sunshine, Ordier could see the familiar swirls of aircraft condensation trails, spiralling in towards the overhead position. Scintillas were often distributed from the air, but only in saturation quantities. How could a single one, placed by air, be hidden in the tufts of a carpet beside his bed? Somehow, intruders must be gaining access.

The other feature of the scintillas that concerned Ordier was the matter of their source. There seemed no discernible pattern: some were coded to sections of the belligerent forces in the south, which meant that their presence on any of the islands was a breach of the Covenant. Both sides, of course, were using them. Most of them, though, were from commercial marketing or lobbying companies, and many of these were licensed to organizations Ordier could identify. In an irony not lost on him, the scintillas were most likely to be part of consignments he himself had once sold. But there was a third group, and these scintillas were uncoded and thus untraceable. It was a new and worrying development for Ordier. In his day scintillas had invariably carried internal markings.

Ordier's life now was ostensibly centred on his casual but well-established relationship with Jenessa, on his house and garden, on his growing collections of books and antiques. He often made journeys to other parts of Tumo, an island rich in archaeological treasures, and during Jenessa's long vacations they sometimes travelled together to other islands in this part of the Dream Archipelago. Until the beginning of the summer he had felt reasonably happy, secure and relaxed, and coming to terms at last with his conscience. But at the end of the short Tumoit rainy season, with the first spell of really hot dry weather, the apparently planned placing of scintillas in his house had begun. At the same time, by chance, he had made a certain discovery about the Qataari refugees and it had created an obsession which had grown ever since.

It was focused on the ancient, castellated folly that had been built centuries before on the ridge of the eastern border of his grounds. On taking over the property the folly had struck him as so odd and beautiful that he had not had it demolished with the other buildings. Exploring the folly one day, clambering around in the sun-warmed granite walls, he had come across the discovery that quickly became his obsession.

There in the folly he had gained his first sight of the young Qataari woman, had uniquely witnessed the Qataari rituals. There he had listened and watched, as hidden from those he watched as the men who decoded the mosaic of digital images broadcast by the ubiquitous scintillas.

Jenessa lounged in the sun. She drank her coffee, then when Ordier made a fresh pot she poured herself another. She asked him to collect her bottle of sun blocker from the bathroom and spread it slowly across her body like a cat grooming itself. She asked Ordier to rub it on her back. This sometimes turned out to be a preliminary to sex but today she didn't seem interested in that. She lay back in the hot sunshine, glistening with the cream, the dazzling sunlight making irregular streaks of brilliance on the curves of her naked body.

Ordier, while pretending to sit contentedly with her, wondered if she was intending to stay with him all day, as sometimes she did. He enjoyed their lazy days together, alternating between swimming in the pool, making love and sunbathing. The previous evening she had been talking about some assignments she had to collect from her office at the university, and the presence of her new colleague. Now, though, because she seemed to be settling in for a day of sunbathing he wasn't sure what she was really planning.

191

At last though she collected up her things and walked through to the nearest bathroom. She showered again, this time wearing a shower cap for her hair and staying in only long enough to rinse off the sun blocker. A few minutes later she appeared on the patio fully dressed and they walked together down to where she had left her car. There were last words and perfunctory kisses before she drove away.

Ordier stood under the shady edge of the grove of trees that grew beside the main drive and watched the gates open and close for her as she drove through. The car turned on to the track that led down to the main road crossing the island. The white cloud of dust thrown up by her tyres hovered long after the car had driven away.

Ordier waited, knowing that sometimes she returned to pick up something she had forgotten.

When the dust had settled and his view across to the mountains was interrupted by nothing more than the shimmering of the heat haze, Ordier turned back to his house and walked up the sloping drive to the main door.

Once inside he made no further attempt to conceal the impatience he had been suppressing while Jenessa was there. He hurried to his study and found his binoculars, then went through the house and left by the side door. A short walk took him across to the high stone wall that ran laterally along the base of the ridge. He unlocked the padlock on the stout wooden gate and let himself through. Beyond was a sandy, sun-whitened courtyard, surrounded on all sides by walls and already breathlessly hot in the windless day. Ordier made sure the gate was locked on the inside then climbed steadily up the slope towards the angular height of the castellated folly on the summit of the ridge.

It was the presence of the folly that had made Ordier want to buy this piece of land in this part of the island, an area that was inconveniently remote from most of the other people who lived on Tumo. He had intended to find somewhere outlying to live, but perhaps not to this degree. Whatever, the presence of the

192

folly, an act of inspired foolishness by whoever had built it three centuries before, had decided him to make the purchase.

The ridge that marked the eastern boundary of his property ran more or less due north and south. For most of its length it was unscalable, except by someone properly equipped with climbing boots and ropes. It was not so much that it was high – on the side facing Ordier's house it was never more than a couple of hundred feet above the plain – but that it was broken and jagged with many small, sharp and friable rocks loose underfoot. In the geophysical past there must have been a tumultuous seismic upheaval, compressing and raising the land along some deep-lying fault, the crust snagging upwards like two sheets of brittle steel rammed with overwhelming force against each other's edges.

It was on the summit of the ridge that the folly had been precariously built, although at what risk to the lives of the builders Ordier could not imagine. It balanced on the broken rocks, seemingly in permanent danger of collapse.

When Ordier had first been shown the folly the valley which lay beyond the ridge had been a wide tract of semi-desert, alternately muddy and dusty depending on the time of year, studded with rank vegetation. But that had been before the arrival of the refugees and the changes that followed.

A flight of stone steps had been built across the inner wall of the folly, leading to the battlements. Before Ordier had moved into the house he had paid his own builders to strengthen many of the lower steps with steel rods and concrete stanchions, but the upper ones had been left in their original state. It was still possible to reach the narrow battlements but only with difficulty and at some peril.

About halfway up, before the last of the reinforced steps, Ordier reached the tiny hidden cell that had been contrived inside the main wall.

He glanced back, staring down from his vertiginous position across the land beneath. There was his house, its evenly tiled roofs glittering in the sunlight. The constantly watered gardens that surrounded it were a verdant green, almost uniquely so in the whole visible landscape. Beyond the house lay the huge untamed stretch of scrubland, reaching as far as the brown and purple heights of the distant Tumoit Range, with their evidence of human habitation. Behind the first range of peaks, invisible to Ordier from here, was Tumo Town, nestling in its blue bay, a sprawling modern settlement built on the ruins of the seaport that had been sacked in the early days of the war.

To north and south Ordier could see the splendent silver of the sea. Somewhere to the north, a strip on the horizon, with most of it below the curvature, was the island of Muriseay. It was not in sight today because of the haze.

Ordier turned away from the view and stepped through into the cell, squeezing between two overlapping slabs of masonry which had clearly been positioned to conceal the presence of the cavity behind. Even from just outside, standing on the perilous steps, it was not immediately obvious that there was a way in. However, as Ordier had discovered by chance the first time he had explored up here, there was a warm, dark space within, high enough and wide enough for a man to stand. Ordier wriggled through the gap and stood inside on the narrow ledge, still out of breath after his brisk climb.

The brilliant sunshine had dulled his eyes and the tiny space was at first a cell of blackness. The only light came from a horizontal crack in the outer wall, a slit of shining sky.

When his breathing had steadied and his eyes had adjusted, Ordier stepped up to the ledge where he generally stood, feeling with his foot for the slab of smooth rock. Beneath him was the whole of the inner cavity, plunging between the jagged rocky walls to the foundations far below: Ordier had shone a bright torch down there on one of his first visits and realized that if he slipped and fell there would be little hope of escape.

He braced himself with his elbow as he transferred his weight and at once a sweet fragrance reached his nostrils. As he brought his second foot up to the slab he glanced down and saw in the dim light a pale, mottled colouring on the ledge where he was standing.

The smell was distinctively that of Qataari roses. Ordier remembered the hot southerly wind that had been blowing all day yesterday – the Naalattan as it was called on Tumo – and the whirling vortex of light and colour that had risen from the valley floor as the fragrant petals of the Qataari roses scattered and circled. Many of the petals had been lifted by the wind as high as his vantage point here in the cell. Some had seemed to hover almost within reach of his fingers, were he to stretch through the slit and try to grab them. He had had to quit his hidden cell to meet Jenessa when she was due to arrive at the house and before he left he had not seen the end of the warm blizzard of petals.

The fragrance of the Qataari rose was known to be narcotic. The cloying smell released as his feet crushed the petals was sweet in his nose and mouth. Ordier kicked and scuffed at the petals that had landed on the shelf, sweeping them down into the wall cavity.

At last he leaned across to the slit that looked outwards into the valley. Here too the wind had deposited a few petals. Ordier brushed them away with his fingers, careful that they fell into the cavity beneath him and not out into the open air.

He raised his binoculars and leaned forward until the metal hoods over the object lenses rested on the stone edge of the horizontal slit. With rising excitement, he focused the glasses and began scanning the Qataari in the valley below.

In the evening Ordier drove to Jenessa's apartment in Tumo Town. He went reluctantly, out of a sense of loyalty to her. He usually disliked having to make conversation with strangers, but in addition he knew that the talk on this evening was unavoidably going to centre around the Qataari refugees.

Since his discovery in the folly Ordier found all discussion of the Qataari difficult and unpleasant, as if some private part of himself was being invaded. For this and other reasons Ordier had never told Jenessa what he knew. Like her main dinner guest that evening she was a cultural anthropologist. She too had spent most of her working life trying to solve the enigma represented by the Qataari. He did not know how to tell her that he thought he was in the process of solving the mystery, partly because he did not want to reveal how he was doing it but also because to tell her would mean he would have to reveal the guilty and illicit pleasures he was experiencing.

The other dinner guests had already arrived when Ordier walked in.

Jenessa introduced them as Professor Jacj Parren and his wife Luovi. Ordier's first impression of Parren was unfavourable: he was a short, overweight and intense man who shook Ordier's hand with nervous, jerky movements, then turned away at once to resume the conversation with Jenessa that Ordier's arrival had interrupted. Normally, Ordier would have bridled at such grace-less behaviour but Jenessa flashed him a soothing look.

He poured himself a drink and went to sit beside Luovi.

During the apéritifs and main course the conversation stayed on general subjects, with the islands of the Archipelago the main topic. Parren and Luovi had only recently arrived from the north and were anxious to learn what they could about some of the islands where they might make their home. The only places they had so far been to were Muriseay – which was the island where many immigrants disembarked when heading for this part of the Archipelago – and Tumo itself.

Ordier noticed that when he and Jenessa described any of the other islands with which they were familiar it was Luovi who showed the most interest. She always asked how far such-and-such an island would be from Tumo, how long it might take to commute from there.

'Jacj must be close to his work,' she said to Ordier.

'I think I told you, Yvann,' Jenessa said conventionally. 'Professor Parren is here to study the Qataari.'

'Yes, of course. Then why don't you simply move here to Tumo?'

'Naturally, we've thought of that,' said Parren quickly. 'But among the theories I've been developing about the Qataari, and it will come as no surprise to Jenessa, is the proposition that

196

they are acutely sensitive to smell. There are of course essential background odours associated with every location, the product of soil, vegetation, agriculture, industry, all that sort of thing, and it occurs to me that part of the sensory warning apparatus used by the Qataari might be olfactory recognition of place. If we were to make our home here, we would become identifiable in the same way as everyone else who approaches them with the dust of Tumo, so to speak, on them. Our ideal location would therefore be one that is within reasonable commuting distance of Tumo, yet which has a completely different olfactory signature.'

'I think you might have something there,' said Ordier, sipping his drink, and sensing an inconsistency in the argument.

'So which island would you suggest?' Luovi said to him.

'Let me think about it.'

Parren was regarding him aggressively.

'I think I know what you're thinking, Ordier,' Parren said. 'Why should I succeed where others have failed?'

'The Qataari represent a substantial challenge to researchers,' Ordier replied neutrally.

'I wouldn't have given up my career in Jethra if I'd thought it was a challenge I couldn't respond to.'

'Of course not.'

'There are a number of ways that haven't been tried before.'

'Can you give an example?'

'I can give you the main one. I make no secret of my ideas.' Parren was sitting forward intently. 'There is one feature of the Qataari settlement that no one seems to pay any regard to. It's so obvious, in fact, that like everyone else involved in the subject I almost missed it. The Qataari habituate the equator.'

'Almost the whole of Tumo is on the equator,' Jenessa said, but she sounded intrigued.

'The island does indeed straddle the equator, but the valley where the Qataari have made their settlement is exactly on the line itself. Have you ever wondered why that might be so, Ordier?'

'It's happenstance, surely? I assume they were installed in the valley by the authorities after they left their homeland. Presumably it was one of the few places large enough to accommodate such an influx of homeless immigrants.'

'No, sir,' said Parren. 'The Qataari went to that valley because they asked to go there, indeed demanded to go there.'

'Tumo isn't the only island on the equator. Why should they choose this one?'

'Because the other islands either didn't want them or weren't for one reason or another suitable. I've looked into it closely, Ordier, and I can tell you that the settlement on Tumo wasn't found for them straight away. The Qataari were relocated many times around the Archipelago, and for several years, before they settled on Tumo. In all that time they never strayed more than a degree or two away from the equator.'

'They were from the south originally, weren't they?'

'Yes, but you must surely know the position of the Qataari Peninsula.'

At last Parren's remarks began to make sense to Ordier. The Qataari Peninsula was part of the southern continental landmass, the long northernmost tip of a huge triangular plain reaching into the Midway Sea at what was consequently its narrowest point. This subcontinental promontory, known as the Tenkker Wilderness, extended so far to the north that part of it, the Qataari Peninsula, actually crossed the equator. As a result some of its land lay, uniquely for the southern continent, in the northern hemisphere. Although most of the Tenkker was uninhabited except by nomads, the mountainous portion beyond a swampy, mangrove-ridden isthmus – which virtually created an island – was where the Qataari originated.

'With respect, Jacj,' Jenessa said, 'all this has been known for years. It's one of the features of the Qataari that makes them of interest, but no one has ever shown what effect the equatorial source has on their culture.'

'That's right. And no one has ever tried observing them from the air.'

Jenessa looked back at him blankly.

'From the air,' she repeated.

'I intend to fly over them. The temporal vortex enables stationary flight above any point on the equator. I intend to observe them from above.'

Jenessa reached across the table to start collecting the empty dishes, stacking them up before her with an absent expression.

'Surely that would never work, Professor Parren,' she said.

'I fail to see why.'

'Because the presence of any aircraft flying low enough for you to observe them would induce the same reaction as always.'

'The temporal vortex crosses their settlement twice a day,' Parren said. 'The sight of aircraft overhead is one they're accustomed to, which enables anyone flying overhead to observe them with a fair chance of not being noticed. Anyway, it's never been tried.'

'Possibly with good reason. The vortices pass over here too, of course. The stationary flight is an optical illusion. Flying through the vortex doesn't gain you a better view of the ground.'

'So you say. Have you tried it yourself?'

'I haven't,' Ordier admitted.

'There you are, then.' Jacj Parren looked at the two women as if for support.

Jenessa would not meet his gaze, and took the plates she had collected to the hatch that led to her small kitchen.

'You lack ambition, Jenessa, my dear,' said Parren.

'Probably,' she replied.

Ordier rarely saw Jenessa in the company of her academic colleagues and because of the condescending way Parren was speaking to her he suddenly felt sympathy for her. He knew that the frustrations of trying to study the Qataari had already wrecked several of her departmental colleagues' careers. Somehow she had stayed on, but not through personal ambition.

'Ambition is the foundation of achievement,' Luovi Parren said, smiling first at her husband then at Ordier.

Ordier said, 'For a social anthropologist?'

'For all scientists. Jacj has taken leave of a brilliant career to study the Qataari. But of course you would know his work already.'

'Of course.'

Ordier was wondering how long it would be before Parren or his wife discovered that one never took leave to visit the Archipelago. Maliciously, it amused Ordier to think that Luovi probably imagined, in anticipation of her husband's success, that completed research into the Qataari society would buy them the ticket back to Jethra, where the brilliant career would be resumed at a higher level. The islands were full of exiles who had once nurtured similar illusions. The few ways there were back to the north were not ones someone like Professor Parren might ever find.

Jenessa returned to the table with a large glass bowl containing the chilled dessert she had prepared earlier. Ordier looked covertly at her, trying to work out exactly how she was taking all this. He and she had spoken on the telephone during the afternoon, when she made it clear that Jacj Parren was one of the most influential academics in her field. It might be in her career interests to be patronized by him, at least on social occasions like tonight. She had spoken truly when she accepted her lack of personal ambition, but that was not the whole story.

Because Jenessa had lived for so much of her life in the Archipelago she had a sense of island nationalism that Ordier himself lacked. She sometimes spoke to him about the history of the Archipelago, of the distant years when the Covenant of Neutrality had come into being. A few of the islands had put up resistance to the enforced neutralization. For some years there had been a unity of purpose amongst these rebels, but the big northern nations had overcome the resistance. The whole Archipelago was said to be pacified now, but contact between many of the islands, and between nearly all of the island groups, was restricted. Jacj Parren might for the time being delude himself that he could choose the island on which he wished to live, but he would find, soon enough, that in practice his choice was severely restricted.

Jenessa often said that in spite of the frustrations there

remained a definite purpose to her work. It was nothing like Jacj Parren's single-minded ambition. There were many Qataari artefacts available for study now that there had been a military resolution to the Peninsula occupation, and these were providing a steady stream of research projects. Some of them were starting to bear fruit. On a larger ambit, Jenessa and other scientists saw their work as a step towards the Dream Archipelago's eventual assimilation into the modern world. She had no illusions about the immediate worth of studying Qataari fragments – because without access to the culturally dominant societies of the north, her research could never produce definitive results – but it was nonetheless scientific intelligence that would in the end contribute to the store of knowledge.

'Where do you fit into all this, Mr Ordier?' Jacj Parren said, filling a pause that had appeared in the conversation. 'You're not an anthropologist, I gather?'

'That's correct.'

'So your line of work is ...?'

'I'm retired.'

'So young?' said Luovi Parren.

'Not so young as perhaps it appears.'

'Jenessa was telling me you have a house up by the Qataari valley. I don't suppose it's possible to see their settlement from there?'

'You can climb the rocks,' Ordier said. 'I'll take you up there one day if you like. It's not an easy climb, though.'

'That's all there is to it? As simple as that? Clambering up a few rocks?'

'It's one of the ways of seeing the Qataari. It's no better than any of the others. You won't actually witness anything. The Qataari usually post guards all along the ridge.'

'Then I could see the guards!'

'Of course. But you wouldn't find it satisfactory. They'll turn their backs as soon as they realize you're there.'

Parren was lighting a cigar from one of the candles on the table. He leaned back with a smile and blew smoke into the air.

'A response of sorts,' he said.

'The only one,' Jenessa said. 'It's worthless as an observation because it's responsive to the presence of the observer.'

'But it fits a pattern.'

'Does it?' Jenessa said. 'How does anyone know what their behavioural patterns are? The few glimpses we've had are completely insufficient for serious study. We should be concerned with what they would do if we weren't there.'

'Which you think is impossible.'

'And if we weren't here at all? If there was no one else on the island?'

'Now you have ceased to theorize, and are fantasizing instead. Anthropology is a pragmatic science. We are as concerned with the impact of the modern world on isolated communities as we are with the communities themselves. If we must, we intrude on the Qataari and evaluate their response to that. It's a better study than no study at all.'

'Do you think no one's tried that?' Jenessa said. 'There is simply no point. The Qataari wait for us to leave, and wait, and wait ...'

'As I said. A response of sorts.'

'But it's a meaningless one!' Jenessa said. 'It becomes a trial of patience.'

'In which you say the Qataari must necessarily prevail?'

'Look, Jacj ... Professor Parren.' Jenessa, visibly irritated now, was leaning forward across the table. Ordier noticed that strands of her long hair were falling across the uneaten dessert on her plate. 'When the Qataari were first settled here a team from our department went into the camp. They were testing exactly the kind of response you're talking about. They made no secret of their presence, nor of what they wanted. The Qataari simply waited for them to go away. They sat or stood exactly where they had been when the team arrived. They did *nothing* for seventeen days! They didn't speak, move, eat, drink. If we give them food or water they take it, but will do nothing to find them for themselves. When they had to sleep they lay down wherever they happened to be. If that happened to be in a muddy pool, or in their own mess, or on rocky ground, then it made no difference. When they woke up they resumed the position they'd been in before.'

'What about the children?'

'Children too. Like the adults.'

'And bodily functions? And what about pregnant women? Did they sit down and wait for the team to leave?'

'Yes, Jacj. Except that they were only sitting down if they had happened to be doing that when the team arrived. It's interesting you should mention the pregnant women. It was because of the medical condition of two of them that the experiment had to be called off. In the event both women had to be treated in hospital. One of them lost her baby.'

'Did they resist being taken away?'

'No ... the Qataari resist nothing.'

'What about later attempts?'

'Exactly the same. Details are different of course, but in essence the Qataari act in such a way that ethnological study is impossible. I was on several entry teams myself before the field work was called off. These days almost nobody from outside is allowed in.'

'Who decides that? The Qataari?'

'No ... the authorities here.'

Luovi suddenly said, 'Nothing you've told us contradicts what Jacj has said. What the Qataari do when intruders arrive can be seen as a response to the outside world.'

'It's no response at all!' Jenessa said, turning towards the other woman with almost truculent speed. 'It's the opposite of response, it's the stopping of *all* activity. You must know the photographs ...'

'I have seen the photographs,' Jacj Parren said dismissively.

'Then you can appreciate the problem. We have hours of video footage in the department: there's a lot you probably haven't seen. You'll see: the people don't even fidget. After ten days, twelve days, they are still stationary, watching us, waiting for us to leave.'

'Then they might be in some kind of trance.'

203

'No, they are *waiting*! There's no other possible interpretation.'

Watching Jenessa's animated expression Ordier wondered if he recognized in her some of his own dilemma about the Qataari.

Jenessa maintained that her interest in them was a professional and scientific one but in every other part of her life she was rarely unemotional in her dealings with people. And the Qataari were special people, not simply to anthropologists.

They were simultaneously the best and the least known of all the races in the world. There was not a single nation on the northern continent that did not have a social or historical link with the Qataari. For one nation there would be the warrior tradition: the Qataari who turned up in times of war and fought with fanatical bravery for their side. For another country there would be the heritage of public buildings or palaces, designed by Qataari architects and built by itinerant Qataari masons and artisans. There were the Qataari doctors who mysteriously arrived in times of plague. The Qataari rescuers who materialized unbidden at scenes of natural disasters. The Qataari playwrights, artists, dancers who performed, excelled, then departed. The athletes, nurses, mathematicians. All came, made their mark, left afterwards.

Physically, the Qataari were a beautiful people. It was said in Ordier's own country, for example, that the model for Edrona – universal symbol of male potency, wisdom and mystery, captured in marble sculpture and famous throughout the world – had been a Qataari. Similarly, a Qataari woman, painted by Vaskarreta nine centuries before, embodied sensual beauty and virginal lust. Her face, pirated in the cause of commerce, adorned the labels of dozens of different products: cosmetics, cereals, underwear, household paints, electrical appliances.

For all the visited history, the persistence of the legends and the revered traditions, the civilized world still knew almost nothing of the Qataari or their homeland.

Where the mangrove swamps gave out, where the first hills of the Qataari Peninsula rose thick with tropical forest, there stood a line of guards. They were guards like no other. The Qataari never prevented others from entering, but the guards were in place to send a signal warning of the intrusion back to their people. In reality, few outsiders had ever tried seriously to gain access to the peninsula. The Tenkker Wilderness was huge and trackless. At the south it was desert and mountains; further north on the long approach to the Qataari Peninsula it was covered with dense and uncharted rainforest. Even the swampy, infested isthmus defied transit. Approaches from the sea were equally difficult, as landing places were few along the steep, rocky coast. By virtue of their lack of contact with the outside world the Qataari were assumed to be self-sufficient in most matters, but practically nothing was known about their customs, culture or social structure.

They were believed, though, to be of unique cultural importance in the world. Their society apparently represented an evolutionary link between the civilized nations of the north, the myriad peoples of the Archipelago and the barbarians and nomads of the south. Certainly, evidence of their skills and intellectual abilities could be found everywhere. Several ethnologists had tried to visit the peninsula over the years, but they had all been frustrated in their work by the silent waiting and watching that Jenessa had experienced and described.

There was only one aspect of Qataari life that was known with any confidence: they dramatized their lives. Aerial photographs and the reports of the few visitors revealed that there were open-air auditoria beside every village or community. People were always present. Theories about the auditoria abounded, but it was now widely accepted that the Qataari depended on drama as a symbolic means of action: it was used in some way for decision making, for the exercise of the law, for the resolution of problems, for celebrations.

What few pieces of Qataari literature had reached the world's libraries were baffling to a non-Qataari readership. Although it was couched in the form of drama or declamation, the prose and verse were impenetrably and maddeningly elliptical. Many characters were given names, but they seemed to play a symbolic role as well as being referred to by an apparently endless list of contracted, familiar or formal names. Semiotic deconstruction of Qataari texts was a major academic activity in the northern universities.

The few Qataari who travelled, who visited the northern countries for one reason or another, invariably spoke obliquely of such matters. One Qataari woman, a linguist who had arrived unexpectedly to help mediate a political summit conference, had obligingly agreed afterwards to discuss Qataari life in a public forum. She memorably explained to an audience of postgraduate students that she was a mere actor in cultural exposition, a mouthpiece for words that were not her own. Everything she said, including the content of her present speech, had been pre-ordained by improvisation workshops and teams of collaborative writers. She answered all other questions by reformulation of this exegesis. The transcript of the meeting was still being studied, interpreted and argued over by experts.

The war came eventually to the Qataari Peninsula when the troops from Faiandland had begun constructing a deep-water refuelling base on one side of the peninsula. As Qataari territory was a hitherto undisputed area it constituted a breach of whatever neutrality the Qataari had enjoyed until then. Soon the Federated States had mounted a full-scale invasion of the peninsula and the Qataari duly suffered the shattering totality of the war, with its neural dissociation gases, its scintillas, its scatterflames, its acid sprays. The villages were flattened, the rose plantations burned, the people killed in thousands. Within a few weeks the Qataari society was destroyed.

A relief mission was sent from the north and during a short ceasefire the surviving Qataari were evacuated unresisting from their homeland. After living in many temporary colonies they had been brought finally to Tumo, where a refugee camp was built for them in the remote valley at the eastern end of the island. At first they were supplied by the Tumoit authorities but within a remarkably few days the Qataari had begun asserting their own individuality. They erected huge canvas screens around the perimeter fence and set their guards at every access point. Conditions within were said to be primitive and unsanitary and the authorities did what they could to deal with these problems, but everyone who entered the camp after the screens first appeared – medical teams, agricultural advisers, builders, social workers – returned with the same report: the Qataari were waiting.

It was not polite waiting, it was not impatient waiting. It was a simple cessation of activity, a long silence.

In time, many but not all of the screens had come down as the Qataari refashioned the buildings inside the camp to their own choosing and the settlement had gradually expanded across the wide area they had been allocated. Today, the outward appearance of much of the refugee camp, seen from a distance, was not exceptional, given the landscape, the building materials that were available, and so on. But the impossibility of making contact with the Qataari remained. Large screens still shrouded many parts of the settlement.

Ordier realized that Jacj Parren and Jenessa were continuing to argue and that Jacj was addressing him.

'... you say that if we climbed the ridge by your house we should see Qataari guards?'

'Yes,' Jenessa answered for him, apparently realizing that Ordier had been letting his thoughts wander for a few moments.

'But why are they there? Along the ridge? I thought they never left the camp.'

'The whole valley has been given over to the Qataari,' Jenessa said. 'Much of the land is under cultivation.'

'Subsistence farming, presumably.'

'No,' she said. 'They grow roses in the valley. The Qataari roses.'

Parren looked satisfied. 'Then at least they can be studied doing that!'

Jenessa looked helplessly across the table at Ordier. He stared back at her, trying not to reveal anything with his expression. He was sitting forward with his elbows on the edge of the wooden table, his hands linked in front of his face. He had taken a shower before driving to Jenessa's apartment this evening but even so a certain fragrance was still present on his skin. He could smell it as he looked back at her, experiencing a trace of the pleasant sexual arousal that was induced by the smell of the petals of the Qataari rose.

Jacj Parren and his wife were staying in one of the hotels down by the harbour in Tumo Town. Jenessa went to see them the next morning and Ordier left her apartment at the same time. They walked together as far as his car, embracing coolly. It was no hint of the night they had just spent together, which had been unusually wakeful and passionate.

Ordier drove slowly back to his house, thinking about lovemaking and Jenessa. He was more reluctant than he could remember to succumb to the temptations of the cell in the folly wall, but at the same time he was more intrigued than ever about what he might see. Talking about the Qataari had renewed his interest. When it had all begun he had made the excuse to himself that what he saw was so insignificant, so fragmentary, that it was only of mild curiosity value. But as the weeks went by his knowledge of the Qataari had grown and with the knowledge so had the secret. A bond between him and the refugees had been tacitly tied. To speak of what he knew would be to betray a trust he had created in his own mind.

As he parked the car and walked up to the house Ordier added further justification to his silence by reminding himself how much he had disliked Parren and his wife. He wanted to say nothing to encourage the man. He knew that prolonged exposure to the seductive laziness of Tumoit life, not to mention the general laxity of Archipelagian ways, would change Parren in the end but until then he would be an abrasive influence on Jenessa. She would seek the Qataari more eagerly, take a closer interest in their affairs.

The house was stuffy from being closed for the night. Ordier walked around the rooms, opening the windows, throwing back the shutters. There was a light breeze and in the garden that he had been neglecting all summer the overgrown flowers and shrubs were waving gently. He stared at them while he tried to make up his mind.

He knew that the dilemma was one of his own making and could be resolved by a simple decision never to climb up to the folly again. If he did he could thereafter ignore the Qataari, could continue with his life as it had been until the beginning of this long equatorial summer. But he was a man with an addiction who thought that quitting was simply a matter of deciding when to do it. The lure of that hidden cell was still acting powerfully upon him. The conversation the evening before had heightened his awareness of the mystery of the Qataari, reminded him of the special and intense curiosities they aroused.

It was not for nothing that the romantic and erotic impulses of the great composers, philosophers, writers and artists had been stimulated by the Qataari, that the legends and daydreams persisted, that the societies of the north had been so thoroughly permeated by the enigma that there was not a work of art that did not directly or indirectly summon Qataari-inspired images. Even down at the level of the gutter there was hardly a graffito that did not hark back to Qataari influence, nor a pornographic fiction that did not perpetuate the myths.

Voluntary abstention from his obsession was an agony to Ordier. He occupied himself by taking a swim in his pool. Later he opened one of the long-neglected chests he had had sent over from the mainland and set the books it contained on shelves in his study. By midday, though, the curiosity was like a nagging hunger and so he found his binoculars and walked up the ridge to the folly.

More petals had appeared in the cell in his absence. Ordier carefully brushed them away from the slit with his fingers, then raised the binoculars to his eyes and inched them forward. As he reached the stone wall he felt the metal lens hoods grating gently. He minutely shifted his position, using the tiny ledge as a way of balancing himself.

The Qataari camp lay on the further side of the shallow valley. Several of the familiar canvas screens had been raised again, this time in the area Ordier had learned from Jenessa's textbooks was

209

thought to be where the children were schooled. The breeze was moving through the valley from the south, stirring the screens. Great slow ripples moved laterally across the canvas blinds. His glasses lacked the necessary magnification to bring them close in his vision, but Ordier nevertheless felt a sense of intrigue, hoping that the wind would momentarily raise the skirt of screens so that he might glimpse what lay behind.

In front of the camp, spreading across the irrigated floor of the valley, was the plantation of Qataari roses: so closely were they planted that from Ordier's elevation the plants made a sea of scarlet and pink and green.

He stared intently for several minutes, panning the glasses slowly across the view, relishing the privilege of having this undetected look.

It was the workers in the rose plantation he had first observed from the hidden cell. Last night, listening to the dinner conversation, he had heard Parren speak with some awe of the possibility of glimpsing the Qataari at work in the rose beds. Remembering his own initial excitement of discovery, Ordier had felt a tiny tremor of sympathy for the man.

None of the Qataari he could see had gone into the stance of patient waiting. He knew from this that he had not been detected.

A small group of Qataari were standing amongst the roses, arguing volubly amongst themselves. After a while two of them walked away and collected large panniers. Pulling the huge baskets behind them they left the others and began patrolling slowly between the long rows of bushes, plucking the largest and reddest flowers and tossing them into the trailing panniers.

The weeks during which he had been spying on the Qataari had taught Ordier to be systematic, so he looked with the binoculars at each of the rose pickers in turn. Many of them were women and it was at these he looked most carefully. There was one young woman in particular he was seeking. She had been one of the rose pickers the first time he had discovered he could look at the Qataari without being noticed. He had no name for her, of course, not even a familiar one he used to himself as shorthand. She did remind him in some ways of Jenessa, but after much soul-searching Ordier had privately admitted these reminders were only the product of guilt.

She was younger than Jenessa, taller, undeniably more beautiful. Where Jenessa was dark in hair and complexion, attractively combining sensuality and intelligence, the Qataari woman had fragility and vulnerability trapped in the body of a sexually mature woman. Sometimes, when her work in the plantation had brought her closer to the folly, Ordier saw a captivating expression in her eyes: knowingness and hesitation, invitation and caution. Her hair was golden, her skin was pale and she had the classic proportions of the perceived Qataari ideal. She was, for Ordier, the embodiment of Vaskarreta's avenging victim.

Jenessa, though, was real. Jenessa was available. The Qataari woman was remote and forbidden, forever inaccessible to him.

When he had made sure that she was not working in the rose plantation, Ordier lowered the binoculars and leaned forward until his forehead was pressing against the rough rock slab. With his eyes placed as near as possible to the slit, he looked down towards the arena the Qataari had built at the foot of the folly wall.

He saw her at once. She was standing near one of the twelve hollow metal statues that surrounded the cleared and levelled circular area. She was not alone; Ordier had never seen her alone. She was one of a large group of both men and women making the arena ready, but she stood slightly apart from the others. They were tidying up and preparing the arena: the statues were being cleaned and polished by the men, while the women swept the gravelly soil of the arena floor and scattered handfuls of the Qataari rose petals in all directions.

The young woman was watching the activity. She was dressed as usual in red: a long, enfolding garment that lay loosely and lightly on her body like a gauze toga, made up of several different panels of diaphanous fabric overlapping each other.

Silently, taking great care not to draw attention to himself,

Ordier raised the binoculars to his eyes and focused them on her face. The magnification at once lent him the illusion he was nearer to her. As a consequence he felt much more exposed to her.

Seeing her so closely, Ordier noticed that the garment was tied loosely at her neck and was slipping down from her on one side. He could see the curve of her shoulder, the junction of her arm with the shoulder and the first hint of the rising of her breast. If she turned quickly or leaned forward the garment would undoubtedly slip away to reveal more of her body. Ordier stared at her, transfixed by her unconscious, almost careless, sexuality.

There was no observable signal for the beginning of the ritual. The preparations led imperceptibly to the first transactions of the ceremony. The women scattering rose petals turned from casting them across the ground to throwing them over the young woman. The men who had been cleaning the statuary each moved round to the rear of individual figures. The backs of these were hinged. The men pulled them open and stepped inside, closing the hatches behind them.

The rest of the people, roughly the same number of men and women, took up positions around the edge of the small arena, standing in the spaces between the various statues.

The woman stepped forward to take her place at the centre.

This much was familiar to Ordier; soon the chanting would begin. Each time he watched the enigmatic ritual unfold Ordier was certain that the events had been slightly developed beyond the ones he had witnessed the time before. If not, then the events were mounted to convey the idea that he was about to see more. The dual possibilities of the woman's sexual role became increasingly tantalizing.

The chanting began: soft and low, inharmonious. The woman rotated slowly where she stood, swaying slightly as she shifted the position of her feet, scuffing at the petals around her, the garment swinging loosely about her limbs. It slipped lower on her shoulder as Ordier had anticipated and as the panels lifted and fluttered Ordier saw glimpses of ankle, elbow, breast, hip. It was obvious that she was naked beneath it. As she turned she looked briefly but intently at each of the men standing at the edge. It could have been a challenge, a dare, an invitation, a selection. It was impossible for Ordier to decide which it was.

More petals were thrown and as the young woman turned in the small arena her feet trampled and crushed them. Ordier fancied he could smell the scent as it rose towards him, although he knew that most of the intoxicating fragrance came from the petals he had found in the cell.

The next stage was also one Ordier had witnessed several times before. One of the women who had been throwing the petals put down her basket and stepped directly towards the centre of the arena. As she stood before the young woman she tore at the front of her own bodice, pulling aside the fabric to bare her breasts. Another woman stepped forward, shouldering aside the first. She too bared her chest. Then a man ran into the arena, seized both women and dragged them backwards out of the arena, clearly admonishing them. While this was going on a third woman dashed forward, tearing at her clothes. Another man went quickly to her and pulled her back.

The young woman at the centre was starting to respond, moving her hands voluptuously across her own body and tugging with short, impatient motions at the light fabric that covered her. Gradually, the panels of thin fabric were working loose.

Ordier watched it all, wondering, as he often wondered, where it was to lead. He was impatient to see the rest of the ritual because in the past the ceremony had never proceeded much beyond this point. He lowered his binoculars and leaned forward again, watching the whole scene.

He was obsessed with the beautiful young woman. In his fantasies he could easily imagine that the ceremony took place here, beneath the wall of the folly, for him, for him exclusively. He dreamed that she was being prepared for him, readied for him, that she was a sexual offering.

But those were the fantasies for later, for his solitude. When he was here, actually watching the Qataari ritual unfold, he was acutely aware of his role as a secret intruder into their world, an observer as incapable of affecting the proceedings as was, it seemed, the young woman herself.

Ordier's passivity, though, concerned only his lack of intervention. In another more basic way he was becoming deeply involved, because whenever he watched the events below his hiding place in the cell he was sexually aroused. He could again feel the tightness in his groin, the swelling and hardness of physical excitement. He stared down at the familiar scene, watching what was for him the secondary interest of the brief naked displays of the other women.

Then the young woman in the centre moved, and Ordier snapped back his attention on to her. As one of the women went across to her, already pulling at the strings of her bodice, she moved to meet her. She snatched at one of the long hanging panels of her scarlet garment, tossing it away from her. It fell lightly like a veil on the petals.

Ordier, with the binoculars once again jammed against his eyes, saw an infuriatingly brief glimpse of the nakedness beneath, but then she turned away and her flimsy garment swung across to cover most of her once again.

She took two halting steps; she stumbled, then fell forward. She collapsed into the part of the central area where the petals had been laid the deepest. A flurry of them flew up around her. Before they had settled a man strode across to her and stood above her. He prodded her with his foot, then used all his strength to push her, lifting and rolling her over on to her back.

She appeared to be unconscious. The flimsy gown was in disarray, its loose panels spreading and twisting about her supine body. Her legs and arms were bare and where she had torn the veil away a strip of diagonal nakedness was revealed. It ran between her breasts, across her stomach, across one hip. Through his binoculars Ordier could see the pale pink aureole surrounding one nipple and a few curling strands of her pubic hair.

The man stood over her, apparently ready to take her. He was

214

half crouching and his hand was at his groin, energetically rubbing his genitals.

Ordier watched, surrendering at last to the excitement of sexual pleasure. As he came to physical climax, releasing wetly into his clothes, he saw through the shaking lenses of the binoculars that the young woman had opened her eyes and was staring upwards with a dazed expression, her lips apart, her head shaking slightly to and fro.

She seemed to be looking straight at him.

Ordier moved back from the crack in the wall, ashamed and embarrassed.

Two days later Jacj and Luovi Parren came to Ordier's house in the early morning. After breakfast the two men set off towards the ridge, leaving Jenessa to entertain Luovi.

At Ordier's suggestion Parren had brought with him a pair of strong boots. They climbed roped together, but Parren was overweight and a novice and he slipped almost as soon as they began the ascent. He slithered down the crumbling face of a large slab, brought up short when Ordier managed to take his weight on the rope.

Ordier secured the rope then scrambled down to him. The portly little man had regained his feet and was looking ruefully at grazes on his arm and leg, showing through rents in his clothes.

'Do you want to go on?' Ordier said.

'Of course. Give me a minute. Nothing serious.'

But the challenge of the climb seemed to have waned, if only temporarily, because he was obviously in no hurry to continue. The bulk of the ridge rose above them.

Parren looked to the side, where the folly loomed high on the ridge.

'That castle belongs to you, doesn't it?' he said.

'It's not a real castle. It's a folly.'

'Couldn't we climb up to the battlements? It looks like it would be easier than these rocks.'

'Yes, it's easier,' Ordier said. 'But also more dangerous. The folly's partly ruined and the steps are reinforced for only some of the way up. In any event, the view is better from the ridge, I assure you.'

'So you have been up to the battlements?'

'Only the first time I looked round the property. But I wouldn't risk it again.' Ordier decided to take a chance. 'But you could go up there alone, if you like,' he said.

'Maybe not,' Parren said, rubbing his arm with his fingertips. 'Let's do it this way.'

Ordier again ran through the list of precautions, showing Parren how to use the rope, how to find footholds and handholds, how to shift his balance as he climbed. It was not a steep or a high ascent but the rocks were so broken and brittle that any careless movement could bring disaster to them both.

They resumed their climb. All went well until about two-thirds of the way to the top when Parren slipped again. He cried out as he fell against a boulder jutting out beneath him.

'You're making too much noise,' Ordier said, when he had climbed down to the man and saw that he was unhurt. 'Do you want the Qataari to hear us even before we reach the top?'

'You've done the climb before. It's different for you.'

'I was alone the first time I climbed up here. I didn't make such a song and dance about it.'

'You're younger than me, Ordier.'

The recriminations ceased when Ordier climbed away from him and resumed his position with the rope. He sat down on a slab and stared at Parren, waiting to see if the man wanted to go on with the climb. The anthropologist continued to sulk for a few more minutes, then appeared to realize that Ordier was doing his best for him. At last he climbed slowly up. Ordier took in the slack of the rope.

'You were right, Ordier,' Parren said, speaking quietly. 'I'm sorry I made a fuss.'

'That's all right.'

'Do you suppose the Qataari know we're here?'

'It's impossible to be sure until we actually reach the top.'

216

'So you think they heard me?'

'I've been wondering about that,' Ordier said. 'The wind's noisy today. Maybe you'll get away with it. They don't have super-human faculties, as far as anyone knows. Be as silent as possible from now on.' He pointed up. 'We'll head for that dip there. It's not exactly where I went last time, but close to it. If the Qataari haven't changed their guard positions since you'll find that the nearest guard is some distance away from you. With any luck you'll have a few minutes before they spot you.'

Ordier crawled forward, placing his feet on the best holds he could find, pointing them out mutely to the other man. Up here towards the summit of the ridge there were fewer pieces of broken and fallen rock, so it was possible to move with less risk of dislodging anything. Parren followed in silence. At last Ordier reached a broad slab just beneath the crest of the ridge and lay face down across it while he waited for Parren to climb up to join him.

They both lay in silence for a couple of minutes, letting their breathing steady. The face of the rock was sun-hot, burning their hands and faces as they rested.

'If you'll take more advice from me,' Ordier whispered, 'don't use your binoculars at first. Take in the general view, then use the glasses on the nearest subjects.'

'Why's that?'

'Once they spot us the cry will go up. It radiates outwards from here.'

Parren had his binoculars out and hanging around his neck. Ordier took out his own from their case.

'Are you ready?' he said softly.

Parren nodded and they inched forward and upward, until they could peer over the ridge into the valley beyond.

A group of five Qataari guards stood in the valley immediately beneath them, staring patiently up at the exact place where they were looking over.

Ordier reflexively ducked down again, but in the same moment he heard the Qataari shouting and knew there was no more chance of surprising them.

When he moved back up to look again he saw that the warning was fanning outwards. The guards along the valley side of the ridge were turning their backs on Ordier and Parren, and in the rose plantation, along the banks of the narrow river, on the approaches to the camp, the Qataari were halting in whatever they had been doing. They stood erect, passively waiting.

Parren was holding his binoculars awkwardly, trying to see but trying to keep his head down at the same time.

'There's no point concealing yourself any more,' Ordier said. 'You might as well stand up. You'll see better.'

Ordier himself sat up and settled as comfortably as possible on the edge of the slab. In a moment Parren sat down beside him. The two men looked across the valley, the sun beating down on their faces. They both scanned to and fro, using their binoculars.

Ordier had his own concerns. While Parren searched for whatever it was he wanted to see, Ordier scanned the rose plantation systematically, looking with the powerful glasses from one person to the next. Most of them stood with their backs turned away from him. At such a distance it was difficult to see clearly, even under magnification. His heartbeat was causing the glasses to judder in his hands, making the image leap. There was one Qataari who was unmistakably female. Ordier stared at her, unable to be certain it was not the young woman he saw in the arena.

While Parren was still busy with his own observations Ordier swung his glasses to the side, towards the part of the ridge where the folly was. Because of the lie of the land it was not possible to see the actual arena but two of the hollow encircling statues were visible. He had had no hopes of seeing if a ritual might be in progress – anyway, the distance was too great – but he wanted to find out if there were any people in that part of the valley. Apart from one of the guards standing close to the folly, though, there was no apparent activity over there.

Their silent observations of the unmoving valley continued for several more minutes. Parren produced a notebook, made sketches of the view and wrote two pages of notes in small, tight handwriting. Ordier watched him with eyes half-closed against the brilliant sunlight, feeling the top of his head starting to burn in the heat.

Scattered around the rock on which they were sitting were several rose petals, curled up and dried by the sun. As they ascended Ordier had noticed petals all over the lower part of the ridge, but those, perhaps for being better sheltered from the sun, had still been soft and pink. He picked up one of the dried ones, curled and crushed it between his fingers. It broke into dust, and drifted lightly to the ground when he brushed his hands together.

When he completed his notes Parren again scanned the valley through his glasses, then said that he had now seen everything he wanted.

'Have you any idea when they'll break out of that?' he said.

'They'll wait until they think the coast is clear. Whatever else you can be sure of, none of them will move a muscle until a long time after we've left.'

Parren stared off into the distance: Ordier's house, the dusty landscape that lay all about, the heat-hazed mountains in the background.

Eventually he said, 'Would it be worth waiting here out of sight for an hour or two? I have the time.'

'The Qataari have more. They know we're here now. We might as well go back.'

'They seemed to be expecting us, Ordier.'

'I know.' He glanced apologetically at the other man. 'That's probably because I brought you to the same part of the ridge that I climbed before. We should have tried somewhere else.'

'Then we could do that next time.'

'If you think it's worth it.'

They began to make their way down, Ordier taking the lead. With the greater power of the sun the descent quickly became physically unpleasant. They were tempted to take shortcuts so as to cut short the climb, but the unstable surfaces and the jagged edges of the rocks were a constant reminder of the dangers.

It was Parren who called a halt first. He squatted down in the shade of an overhang. Ordier climbed back up to him and crouched beside him. They both drank water from their bottles, wiping their mouths with the backs of their hands. Below them and slightly to the side, seemingly close at hand, Ordier's house and grounds stood out against the dun landscape like a brightly coloured plastic model. They could see the figures of Jenessa and Luovi basking beside the pool, side by side in the shade of a large canopy.

Parren said, 'Jenessa tells me you once worked with scintillas.'

Ordier glanced at him in surprise. 'Why did she tell you that?'

'I asked her outright. Your name was familiar. We both come from Faiandland, after all. Once she told me I remembered your story, what the press had said about you.'

'Well, at least you know why I came to the islands,' Ordier said. 'I've nothing to do with scintillas any more. I've left all that behind me.'

'Yes, but you still know more about them than most people.'

'What use is that sort of knowledge here, in the islands?'

'To me, it could be extremely useful. I need to consult some- one with specialized knowledge. In other words, I need to consult you.'

'What would you want to know?' Ordier said, resignedly.

'Everything you can tell me.'

'Professor Parren, I think you've been slightly misinformed about me. I was never technically involved with the scintillas. I was simply an expediter, a merchandising agent.'

'I know what you did. But I also know you're not being com- pletely candid with me. If you're not an expert in scintillas, no one is.'

'I've told Jenessa only a little about what I used to do. She shouldn't have said anything. I truly know little about scintillas that isn't common knowledge by now. Techniques were improv- ing. The equipment I was selling is years out of date.'

'Then that's not a scintilla detector I saw in your house?'

'Look, I don't see why you're interested.'

Parren was sitting forward away from the shade of the over- hang. His manner had changed.

'Let's not mince words, Ordier. I need some information and you're clearly the best person to give it to me. I want to know for instance if there's any law in the Archipelago that prohibits the deployment of scintillas.'

'Now why should you need to know that?'

'Because I want to use scintillas to observe the Qataari. I'd like your opinion on that. And because of what we've both just seen, I want to know if you think the Qataari might have any way of jamming the signals from scintillas.'

'I can tell you there's no law against using them. Or at least, no enforceable law. There's only the Covenant of Neutrality, but I've never heard of it being invoked against the use of scintillas. Planting them is generally considered to be a breach of the Covenant, but I've never heard of any prosecutions. Some of the islands might have their own local laws. Tumo, as it happens, doesn't.'

'What about the rest of what I asked?'

'Obviously, the scintillas could be deployed if you could think of some way of planting them without the Qataari knowing.'

'That's actually the easiest part. I've already told you that I'm planning to use an aircraft. There's a company in Tumo Town that says it can supply the equipment for releasing scintillas at night.'

'You're ahead of me, you see,' said Ordier mildly. 'Why do you suppose the Qataari would know how to jam scintillas?'

'They've had experience of them. Both sides were using scintillas when the Peninsula campaign was going on. The military overdo everything. Scintillas must have been ankle-deep around the Qataari. It wouldn't have taken much for even a relatively backward race to work out what the scintillas were for. Anyway, as we both know, the Qataari are not backward.'

'I was under the impression that you thought they might be. Anthropologists don't usually spend much time studying scientifically literate people.'

'The Qataari are different. They're of interest to researchers precisely because they won't allow research. As you say, social

221

anthropology normally concerns itself with primitive peoples, but the Qataari aren't primitives. We categorize societies in groups of soft and hard. That's our jargon for the degree to which they impact on the world around them. The Qataari look like a classic society of the soft kind: they're not warlike, they grow flowers, they're passive to a fault. But there's something deep and subtle and worked-out going on. It's obvious to anyone. I think of the Qataari as decivilized but hard. As hard as any society can be. Their technological skills must be a match for anything of ours.'

'How do you know that?'

'An intelligent guess. They're obviously trying to conceal something. But what's your opinion about the scintillas, Ordier? Do you think they could jam scintilla output?'

'No one else can, so far as I know. They couldn't be jammed when I was working with them, and the conventional wisdom was that they probably never would be. Limitations on wavelength and signal compression, apparently. But you know how it is with technology. It's always improving.'

'That would also be true of Qataari technology, of course.'

'I don't know, Parren. I imagine so.'

'Look at this.' Parren reached into a pocket and pulled out a small box. Ordier recognized it at once: it was a scintilla quiet-case, similar to his own. Parren opened the lid and reached inside with a pair of tweezers he took from a mounting inside the lid. 'Have you seen one of these before?'

He dropped a scintilla into the palm of Ordier's hand.

Ordier, guessing, said, 'It doesn't have a serial number engraved on it.'

'Right.' Parren leaned over and picked up the scintilla again with the tweezers. He dropped it into the quiet-case and closed the lid with an emphatic click. 'Do you know why?'

'Do you?' Ordier said.

'I've never encountered it before.'

'Neither have I,' Ordier said. 'Except here on Tumo. My guess is that they're military.'

'No, I've checked. They're required by the Treaty of Yenna to mark them. Both sides have abided. Anyway, the imprinted serial number is used digitally in decoding the images. The scintillas are supposed not to be able to work without it.'

'Then it's a bootleg?'

'They're usually marked too, for the same reasons. A few of the pirates might leave them blank, some kind of perverse virus mechanism. But the numbers of unmarked bootleg scintillas would be tiny, because there's no point in anyone using scintillas unless they can acquire the signals. These little devils are all over the place. I've found hundreds since I've been on Tumo.'

'You've checked them all?' Ordier said.

'No, but nine out of ten of the ones I've found in the town have been blank.'

'Then whose are they?'

'I was hoping you'd tell me, Ordier.'

'I think we've already established you're better informed than I am.'

'All right, then I'll tell you what I think. They're connected with the Qataari.'

Ordier waited, expecting more to follow, but the other man was looking at him expectantly, waiting for a response.

He said in the end, 'So ...?'

'Someone,' Parren said with emphasis, 'is spying on the Qataari.'

'With what purpose?'

'The same as mine, obviously.'

Ordier heard again the ambitious note in Parren's voice he had heard at Jenessa's dinner party. For a moment Ordier felt the same stab of guilt, thinking that Parren had somehow learnt that he was spying on the Qataari from the folly. But Ordier's own guilt was nothing beside Parren's ambition, which was so bright behind his eyes that it blinded him.

He said after a moment, 'Then perhaps you should join forces with whoever it is. Or else you'll end up getting in each other's way.'

'That's it precisely. As I don't know who it could be I'm forced to compete with.'

'You have your own scintillas?'

Ordier had intended the question sarcastically, but Parren said at once, 'Yes. I can get hold of a new version, the latest thing. They were still being tested only a few days ago. They're a quarter the size of existing scintillas, so to all practical purposes they're invisible. At the same time they have digital networking capacity, which means that for the first time saturation coverage produces a holistic image, instead of hundreds of thousands of separate digital channels that have to be decoded.'

'Then there's your answer,' Ordier said, mentally recoiling from the surprising information. 'You would clearly have the edge.'

'I know. But there's one unavoidable problem. The cost is going to be immense. I can't commit my university budget if it transpires the Qataari can jam my scintillas.'

Ordier smiled grimly. 'As I said, I can't help you. Technology moves too swiftly. But if you want my opinion I think a technical ability to detect scintillas is irrelevant, when we're talking about it in the context of the Qataari. You've seen how sensitive they are to being watched. It's like a sixth sense. My guess is they'd find out about your scintillas somehow.'

'But they're not superhuman, as you said.'

'As a lot of people say. They just go on acting as if they are. Look, I need a proper drink. We can talk about this back at the house.'

Parren concurred, reluctantly it seemed to Ordier, and in a few moments they resumed their clumsy descent of the rocks. When they reached the house half an hour later, their skin burnt red wherever it had been exposed to the sun and their clothes drenched in perspiration, they found the place empty. Two unoccupied sun loungers lay beside the pool. Ordier fixed some iced drinks while Parren took a dip in the pool, then he showered and changed his clothes.

He left Parren on the patio and went in search of the women. He located them in the rough ground behind the house, walking from the direction of the gate in the courtyard wall. He waited impatiently until they reached him.

'Where have you been?' he said to Jenessa.

'You and Jacj were gone so long I took Luovi to see your folly. The gate was unlocked so we assumed it would be all right.'

'You know it's not safe up there!' Ordier said.

'What an interesting building it is,' Luovi said to him. 'Such eccentric architecture. All those concealed faults in the walls. And what a view there is from higher up!'

She smiled at him patronizingly, then shifted the strap of her large leather bag on her shoulder. She walked past him towards the house. Ordier looked at Jenessa, hoping for some explanatory expression, but she would not meet his eyes.

Parren and his wife stayed at the house for the remainder of the long, hot day, lazing in the shade beside the pool.

Ordier was a passive listener to most of the conversation that occurred, feeling excluded from it. He found himself privately wishing that he could involve himself in Jenessa's work to the same degree that Luovi worked with her husband, but whenever he ventured an opinion or an idea into the endless discussion of the Qataari he was either ignored or corrected. The consequence was that while Jacj was outlining his elaborate scheme – there was an aircraft to be hired and a place to be found where the scintilla decoding equipment could be installed – Ordier fell into an introspective mood and grew increasingly preoccupied with thoughts of his secret voyeuristic relationship with the young Qataari woman.

From the summit of the ridge it had been possible to see that no ritual was taking place at that moment, which was consolation of a kind. It reinforced his inner belief that he, by acting as a silent watcher, was actually taking some kind of part in the event. The need for this burned in him, but he did not know why. But it was disturbing for other reasons to suspect that the business with the arena and the statues did not go on except when he happened to be present to see it.

225

And there was the other uncertainty of what Jenessa and Luovi might have seen or done while they were in the folly.

Guilt and curiosity, the conflicting motives of the voyeur, were rising in Ordier again.

Towards the end of the afternoon, as the heat was starting to fade a little, Parren announced that he had another appointment in the evening. Jenessa promptly offered to drive them back to Tumo Town. Ordier, uttering the platitudes of a host to departing guests, saw it as a chance to satisfy his curiosity. He walked down with the others to Jenessa's car and watched as they drove away. The sun was already hanging not far above the Tumoit Mountains.

As soon as the car was out of sight Ordier hurried back to the house, collected his binoculars and a torch and set off for the folly. As Jenessa had told him, the padlock on the gate was open. He must have forgotten to close it the last time he left the folly. As he went through he made sure of locking it, as he usually did, on the inside. He did not want anyone coming up to the folly, for whatever reason, while he was there.

The period of twilight on Tumo was virtually non-existent because of its equatorial position, the sun vanishing swiftly behind the mountains without afterglow and throwing this part of the island into sudden darkness. As Ordier went up the slope to the folly wall his shadow on the ground was spreading long. Nightfall was only minutes away.

Once inside the hidden cell Ordier wasted no time and put his eyes to the slit. Beyond, the Qataari valley was stark with deep colours and long shadows. All was still: there was no one in sight out there, and the familiar screens across parts of the settlement were hanging motionlessly in the calm evening air. All the Qataari people had returned to their homes. It was obvious that the alarm raised when he and Parren peered over the edge of the ridge had passed.

Extremely relieved, Ordier returned to the house in the new darkness, shining the torch across the uneven ground. He tidied up the patio, put away the loungers and took in the glasses and

226

plates they had been using. He had just finished washing everything when Jenessa returned.

She was looking excited and beautiful and she kissed Ordier as
soon as she came in.

'I'm going to work with Jacj!' she said. 'He wants me to be his
personal assistant and adviser.'

'Advise him? How?'

'About the Qataari. He says he can pay me the same money as
I'm getting now and that when he returns to the north there'll
be a vacant position for a research fellow in his department. He'll
want me to go with him, he says.'

Ordier nodded, and turned away.

'Aren't you pleased for me?' Jenessa said.

'What are the strings?'

Jenessa had followed him as he walked out on to the patio.
From the doorway she turned on the coloured lights concealed
amongst the grapevines hanging from the overhead trellis.

'Why should you think there strings to anything I want to do
on my own?' she said.

'And where's he getting the money from? You know the situation as well as I do. He isn't on leave of absence from a university.
It's not possible any more to make a temporary trip to the islands.
There's no way back for anyone, and so everything he's telling
you is demonstrably a lie.'

'It's really got to you, hasn't it?' she said.

Looking back at her he saw the multi-coloured lights glowing
on the olive skin of her face, like the reflection from flower petals
of sunlight. He always found her lovely to look at, never more
so than now. He said nothing, wishing the exchange had not
started.

'Let's have a drink,' he said.

'We've had enough.'

She apparently wanted it to go on. He said, 'Why don't you tell
me more about going north with him?'

'Jacj has a way.'

'I doubt it. Why haven't you told me this was going on?'

'I'm telling you now. The first opportunity I have. Nothing's been agreed definitely. I can still pull out if I want to.'

'But you don't want to.'

'Don't I?' Jenessa said. 'And, by the way, nothing's going on, as you put it.'

'You're making me wonder.'

'Why do you say that? Do you think I'm having an affair with him?'

'No.'

'It's just a job, just the work I've always done. You know how I feel about what we're doing in the department! It's a dead end. We haven't made any measurable progress since the Qataari were first settled.'

'It's always the bloody Qataari, isn't it?' Ordier said. 'That's what it is. You're as obsessed with them as he is.'

'I can't deny it. From a career point of view—'

She took his arm then. He snatched it away angrily and turned from her, but she persisted and grabbed hold of his arm again. She held his hand in hers. He stood there, feeling as if he was being treated like a petulant adolescent; he also had a feeling that perhaps he deserved it.

He was angry, though, and it usually took time for his moods to subside. Jenessa knew him well. It was irrational, of course, these things invariably were. Parren and his wife, ever since their arrival, had seemed set on changing the settled, placid way of life he enjoyed, guilty conscience and all. The thought of Jenessa going over to them, collaborating with them, was just one more intrusion. Ordier was incapable of dealing with it in any way other than emotionally.

Much later, when they had made some supper and were drinking wine together on the patio, enjoying the warmth of the dark and insect-loud night, Jenessa said, 'Don't fly off the handle again, but I think Jacj would like you to join his team as well.'

'Me?' He had mellowed as the evening progressed and his laugh now was not a sardonic one. 'I doubt if there's much I could do for him.'

228

'I don't know about that. He seems to like you.'

'He can't be all bad, then.'

'He said he would like to rent the folly from you.'

'Whatever for?' Ordier said, taken by surprise.

'It overlooks the Qataari valley. Jacj wants to build a hide in the wall. Set up some cameras there, or something like that.'

'Tell him it's not available,' Ordier said abruptly. 'It's structurally unsound.'

Jenessa was regarding him with a thoughtful expression.

'It seemed safe enough to me,' she said. 'We climbed as far as the battlements without any problem.'

'I thought I told you about the folly—'

'What?'

'It doesn't matter,' Ordier said, sensing another row on the way. He lifted the wine bottle to see how much was left. 'Want me to open another bottle?'

Jenessa yawned, but she did it in an affected, exaggerated way, as if she too had seen the way the conversation was going and welcomed the chance to drop the subject.

'Let's finish the bottle, then go to bed,' she said.

'You'll stay the night, then?'

'If you want me to.'

Four more days passed. Although Ordier stayed away from his cell in the folly wall his curiosity about the young Qataari woman would not leave him. He was also growing more uncertain about what the ritual signified, and it was compounded by the unwelcome presence of Parren and his wife.

The morning after their last visit, Ordier had been waiting for Jenessa to leave when a disquieting thought came to him. It was what Parren had said to him on the ridge, about the unknown origins of the unmarked, unidentified scintillas. Parren had linked them to the Qataari, construing their presence to mean that someone else was trying to observe them.

Ordier, listening to Jenessa's movements in the spraying water

229

of the shower cubicle, suddenly realized that there could be an altogether different explanation.

It was possible, as Parren suggested, that someone else might be spying on the Qataari. But what if it were the Qataari themselves who were watching?

With their obsessive desire for privacy, it would be in their interests to observe the movements of those people outside their community. If they had access to scintilla equipment – or had been somehow able to manufacture it themselves – then it would be one way of building a defence against the outside world.

It was not impossible. As Parren had said, no one who had contact with the Qataari made the mistake of thinking they were tribal primitives. The Qataari men and women who had in the past travelled to the northern nations had revealed a brilliant inductive understanding of science and technology. Parren himself had said that Qataari science was sophisticated. If so, they could have discovered how to duplicate the scintillas.

If the Qataari were watching anyone they would be watching Ordier. He was their closest neighbour, with property that directly overlooked their settlement. He remembered the unmarked scintillas he kept finding in his house.

Later that day, when Jenessa had departed, Ordier took his detector and scoured every room of the house. He found another ten or so around the rooms, but when he went outside and searched the patio, pool area and garden he turned up literally hundreds more. He put them all into the quiet-case, closing the lid quickly. The space inside was now more than two-thirds filled.

He had spent most of that day in thought, troubled that this conjecture, if accurate, led to the conclusion that the Qataari knew he was spying on them from inside the folly.

If that was so, then it would account for something he found naggingly strange: his unshakeable inner conviction that the ritual was being put on for his exclusive benefit.

He had invariably been scrupulously secretive about what he was doing. In ordinary circumstances he would have had no reason to suppose the Qataari had any suspicions he was there.

But the young woman had become a central figure in the ritual after he had noticed her in the plantation and had watched her through his binoculars. Why should she be the one they made the focal figure? Pure chance, or by looking at her had he in effect picked her out for himself?

Then there was the fact that the ritual itself invariably started after he went to the cell. He had never once found it in progress. And the ceremony, although staged in a circular arena, was not only within his sight, it appeared to be mounted so that he had a clear view of it. The woman, for instance, was always facing towards him. Nothing went on that he could not watch.

Until now, Ordier had not tried to think of a rational explanation. If the Qataari were watching him, though, were waiting for him, were staging it for him ...

But all this denied one fact: the famous dislike the Qataari had of being watched. They were hardly likely to encourage someone to spy on them.

It was this new thought, and its attendant enigmas, that had kept Ordier away from the folly for four days. In the past he had fantasized that the young woman was being readied for him, that she was a sexual lure, but that was the stuff of erotic imaginings. To convert fantasies into reality was something for which he was not ready.

To do so would be to accept something else that had once been an element in his fantasies: that the woman knew who he was, that she desired him and that the Qataari had selected him for her.

So the days passed.

Jenessa was involved with Parren's preparations and she didn't seem to notice Ordier's abstracted state of mind. He prowled the house by day, sorting through his books and trying to concentrate on domestic matters. By night he slept as usual with Jenessa, sometimes when she came to his house, sometimes when he went to her apartment, but during their lovemaking, especially in those moments just before reaching climax, Ordier's imaginings were of the young Qataari woman. He envisaged her sprawling

231

across the bed of scarlet petals. Her flimsy garment was torn away or crumpled beneath her naked body, her legs were spread and her knees were raised, her mouth was reaching to meet his, her eyes stared submissively at him, her body was warm and soft to the touch.

She had been offered to him and Ordier knew that she was his for the taking.

On the morning of the fifth day Ordier awoke to a new realization: he believed he had resolved the dilemma.

Jenessa was still asleep beside him in his bed. As the first sunlight spread through the bedroom, Ordier watched the play of light on his walls and ceiling as it reflected from the barely shifting surface of the pool outside. He had sensed all along that the Qataari had selected him, but he had always denied it to himself. It was only now that he accepted and believed it.

It was also only now that he realized why. He had met several Qataari in the north before he left, and at that time there had been no point in making a secret of his involvement with surveillance scintillas. They knew then who he was, so they would know now who he was; they knew where he lived; they knew everything about him.

There was more. Until this waking moment Ordier had feared the idea because it implied that he was a prisoner of the Qataari will. But this new understanding actually freed him.

There was no further basis for his obsessive curiosity. He need never again agonize about missing the ritualized ceremony, because, he now realized, nothing of any interest would happen until he was present to observe it. He need never again return to the airless, narcotically drenched cell in the wall, because the Qataari would wait.

They would wait for his arrival as they would wait for the departure of others.

Lying in his bed, staring up at the mirrored ceiling, Ordier realized that the Qataari had liberated him. The woman was an offering which he could accept or decline as he wished.

Then Jenessa, waking beside him, turned over and said, 'What's the time?'

She was gazing at him with half-opened eyes. Ordier glanced at the clock, told her the time. She pressed herself affectionately against him, making Ordier think she wanted to make love while she was still half-asleep. It was something he knew she loved. But after a moment she moved away.

'I have to hurry this morning,' she said, kissing his chest lightly.

'What's the rush?'

'Jacj's catching the ferry to Muriseay today. The aircraft will be ready for him.'

'Aircraft?'

'The one he's renting to scintillate the Qataari. It's likely to be done today or tomorrow.'

Ordier nodded. He watched Jenessa as she rolled sleepily from the bed and walked naked to the mirror attached to the bedroom wall. She stared into it, looking drowsily at the reflection of her face, running her fingers tentatively through her hair. Ordier stared appreciatively at her back view: the generous curve of her bare buttocks, her long shapely legs, her smooth skin, her breasts drooping forward as she leaned towards the mirror.

When she walked into the shower he climbed out of bed and followed her. He waited outside the cubicle, imagining her voluptuous body moving sinuously through the energetic spray as she pressed her soapy hands across her limbs and chest. Later, when she had snatched a slice of dry bread for her breakfast, he walked with her to her car and watched her drive away. He returned to the house.

Reminding himself of his newly liberated state he percolated some coffee, then took it out to the patio. The weather was sweltering again, and the vibrant scraping of the crickets seemed especially loud. A new crate of books had arrived at the house the previous day and the swimming pool looked clean and cold. He could make it another long day of pleasant idling.

He wondered if the Qataari were watching him now; if their

scintillas lay between the paving stones, in the branches of the vines, in the soil of the overgrown flowerbeds.

'I'll never spy on the Qataari again,' he said aloud, into the imagined aural pick-ups.

'I'll go up to the folly today, and tomorrow, and every day,' he said.

'I'll move away from this house,' he said. 'I'll rent it to Parren and I'll move into town and live with Jenessa.'

'I'll watch the Qataari,' he said. 'I'll watch them until I have seen everything, until I know all their secrets, until I have taken from them the last thing they have.'

He left the cushioned sun lounger and roamed around the patio, playing to an imagined invisible audience, gesturing and waving, miming elaborate postures of deep thought, of sudden decision, of abrupt changes of mind.

It was an act but not an act. Free will liberates the purposeful and traps the undecided.

'Am I interrupting anything?'

The voice broke into Ordier's ridiculous charade, startling him. He swung around in anger and embarrassment. It was Luovi Parren, standing by the open door to his lounge. Her large leather bag was slung as usual across her shoulder.

'All the doors were open,' she said. 'I tried knocking but there was no answer. I hope you don't mind.'

'What do you want?'

It was impossible for Ordier to keep the incivility out of his voice.

'If you don't mind, I would like a drink.'

'I'm drinking coffee. I'll get you another cup.'

'I'd prefer water. I've walked a long way.'

'All right.'

Furiously, Ordier went into the kitchen and found a clean glass. He took a bottle of mineral water from the fridge and filled the glass, clinking in two ice cubes. Before he took it through to her he stood by the sink, resting both hands on the edge and staring down angrily into the bowl. He hated being caught off guard.

How had she got through the electronically controlled gates?

Luovi was sitting in the shade, on the steps that led down to the patio from the verandah. As he passed her the glass Ordier briefly stood over her. He saw that she was sitting with her knees wide apart, stretching the fabric of her dress across her legs. Dark stains of sweat spread beneath her armpits. The front of her blouse was mostly unbuttoned and he had a momentary view of two large, unsupported breasts hanging loosely inside the garment, vertical stretch marks along her sunburnt chest indicating the sag. Had she undone those buttons while he was in the kitchen? He didn't recall noticing that they were undone when she arrived. She smiled flirtatiously up at him as he gave her the glass.

'I thought you might be swimming in the pool today,' she said to him. 'It's so hot in the sun.'

'Maybe later.'

'It looks wonderful to me. Shall we take a dip together?'

'If you'd like to take a swim, feel free,' he said. 'I might be going out shortly. You could use the pool while I'm away.' He was beginning to recover from the surprise of her unwelcome arrival, at least to the point where he felt able to say polite things. 'I thought you'd be with Jacj today.'

'I didn't want another trip to Muriseay,' Luovi said. 'There's nothing for me to do while I'm there. Is Jenessa with you?'

'Isn't she with Jacj?' Ordier said. 'She said something about going to Muriseay. Catching a ferry?'

'You think Jenessa is with Jacj? I don't believe so. Jacj left two days ago.'

Ordier frowned, trying to remember what Jenessa had actually said about her plans for the day. Although he didn't recall her saying she was going on the ferry herself, she had distinctly said that Jacj was travelling across to Muriseay. Since she had been working for Parren she accompanied him on most of his short trips. How had Luovi reached his house? It was surely too great a distance for anyone to walk all the way from Tumo Town, yet she had arrived without a car. Had someone given her a ride, all or part of the way?

'Jacj has gone to Muriseay to charter an aircraft, I take it?' he said.

'Of course not. The Qataari camp was scintillated two nights ago. Didn't you hear the plane engine?'

'No, I didn't! Does Jenessa know about this?'

'I'm sure she must,' Luovi said, and smiled the same sparse smile he had seen the day she came back from looking at the folly.

'Then what's Jacj doing in Muriseay at the moment?'

'Collecting the monitoring equipment. Do you mean Jenessa hasn't told you anything?'

'Jenessa told me—'

Ordier hesitated, regarding Luovi suspiciously. Her manner was as sweetly polite as that of a suburban gossip breaking news of adultery. She sipped her water, then tipped her fingers into the glass and pulled out one of the ice cubes. She ran it over her mouth and lips, then around the sides of her face and finally over the skin of her neck and chest. Droplets of meltwater ran down into her blouse, trickling into the loose chasm between her drooping breasts. She took another sip of water, apparently waiting for his reply.

Ordier turned away, took a breath. He had to make up his mind whether to believe this woman or to trust the words and behaviour of Jenessa, who in the last few days had done or said nothing that roused any suspicions about what Jacj might be doing, or what her knowledge of that might be, or indeed of anything else.

As he turned back to face her Luovi said, 'I was hoping I would find Jenessa here today so that she and I could talk things over.'

Ordier said, 'Maybe you should talk things over somewhere else, Luovi. I don't know what you're trying to do, or what you mean by coming to my house today—'

'You do know a lot more about the Qataari than you've admitted.'

'What's that got to do with it?'

'Everything, as far as I know. Isn't the folly the whole reason you bought the house?'

'The folly? What are you talking about?'

'Don't think we don't know! It's time Jenessa was told.'

Five days earlier Luovi's insinuations would have struck straight through Ordier's defences to his guilty conscience. That was five days ago, though, since when everything had become more complex. His own feelings of guilt now made him less vulnerable to attack, because they had become part of what was obviously a larger intrigue.

'Look, it's time you left, Luovi,' he said.

'Very well.' Luovi put down her glass. She stood up with an athletic motion, scooping up her leather bag and turning away from him all in one movement. 'You presumably realize there'll be unpleasant consequences for you.'

'I haven't the least idea what you're talking about. But I don't wish to know, so kindly—'

She had already stepped away from him, into his house. He followed her through the cool rooms, making sure she left by the main door. She walked down the sloping drive towards the gate. In spite of his protestations to her, now that she was actually leaving the house Ordier was far from uncomprehending of what she meant. The main gates were open. Perhaps they had failed to close behind Jenessa's car when she left earlier. Ordier followed Luovi through the gates, then used his radar key to close them.

He watched her walking angrily away.

Clearly, she must know as much as she was implying: that he had been spying on the Qataari. He felt a surge of defensiveness, a need to deny or explain, but he knew it was already too late. Anyway, there was nothing he wanted to say to Luovi about that. Meanwhile, had she really come to the house simply to find Jenessa, or was it to confront him with what she knew about him? Then there were those implications she had made that Jenessa had been lying to him. Why should she do that? What could her motives conceivably be for that?

The sun was high. White light glared down across the dusty

237

countryside. In the distance, the Tumoit Mountains were shimmering in the haze. Luovi was striding angrily away from him, through the heat, across the radiant landscape. He could see her heavy shoulder bag banging against her thigh with every other step she took.

He noticed that she had somehow taken a wrong turn and was not heading back along the road that would lead eventually to Tumo Town. She was moving across the hillside parallel to the ridge. Ordier knew that there was nothing in that direction: no other houses, no more road. Not much further along from where she was walking the terrain became extremely rough and broken, dangerous for anyone to try to walk across, never mind someone ill-equipped for walking and seething with anger into the bargain.

He ran after her. She had gone further than he thought and he had to run fast to catch up with her.

'Luovi!' he called breathlessly, as soon as he thought she was within earshot. 'Luovi, please wait!'

Finally she either heard him or decided to wait for him. In a moment he caught her up. She glared at him interrogatively as he went up to her, out of breath and tormented by the dazzling sunshine.

'I can't let you walk all the way back to town,' he said. 'It's a huge distance. You mustn't do that now, not in heat like this.'

'I know what I'm doing,' she said.

'Come back to the house. I'll drive you to town.'

She shook her head, then turned away and walked on.

'I know exactly where I'm going,' she said grimly. She glanced up at the high ridge as she stumbled along.

Ordier marched into his house and slammed the door behind him. Motes of dust billowed in his wake.

He went out to the patio and sat down on the cushions scattered across the sun-hot paving stones. A bird fluttered away from where it had been perched on the grapevine and Ordier glanced up. The verandah, the patio, the rooms of the house – they all had their hidden scintillas, making his home into a stage for an unseen audience.

He was hot and breathless after running after Luovi so he stripped off his clothes and dived into the pool. He swam to and fro for a long time, trying to calm his thoughts. Afterwards, dried and dressed in fresh clothes, he paced around the pool's edge, trying to organize his thoughts and replace ambiguity with certainty. He was not successful.

The unmarked scintillas. He had almost convinced himself that they were being planted by the Qataari but the possibility remained that someone else was responsible.

Jenessa. According to Luovi she had deceived him, while according to his instincts she had not. Ordier continued to trust her, but Luovi, annoyingly, had succeeded in placing doubt in his mind.

The trip to Muriseay. Parren had travelled to Muriseay (today? or two days ago?) to charter an aircraft, or alternatively to collect the monitoring equipment. According to Luovi the aircraft had already done its work. But would it have been carried out before the eager and ambitious Jacj Parren was standing by with the decoding equipment to receive the images?

Luovi. Where was she now? Was she returning to the town, or was she still somewhere close to the house, in the area next to the ridge?

Jenessa, again. Where was she now? Had she gone to the ferry, as she had implied she would, was she at her office, was she with Parren, or might she be returning to his house?

The folly. How much did Luovi know about his visits to the hidden cell? Had she been guessing and hoping that questions might prompt him to reveal inadvertent information? What did she mean about the folly having been built for something 'in the first place'? Had she managed to find out more about its past than he had? Why *was* there in fact an observation cell in the wall, with its view across the valley?

All these were the recent doubts, the additional ones created by Jacj and Luovi. The others, the old ones, remained.

The Qataari. Who was watching whom? He had thought he had known; now he wasn't so sure.

The young Qataari woman. Was he a free observer of her, hidden and unsuspected, or was he a chosen participant playing a crucial role in the development of the ritual?

In his confusion between free will and determinism, Ordier recognized that by paradox it was the young woman who provided the only certainty.

He was convinced that if he went to the folly at any time, on the spur of the moment or after hours of deliberation, it made no difference, if he went there and placed his eyes to the crack in the wall, then for whatever reason or combination of reasons she would be there waiting for him ... and the ritual would recommence.

He knew that the choice was his. He need never again climb up to the cell in the wall. It was over if he wanted it to be.

Without further thought, Ordier went into the house, found his binoculars and started to climb up the slope of the ridge towards the folly.

He went a short distance then turned back, pretending to himself that he was exercising his freedom of choice. In fact he was collecting his scintilla detector, and as soon as he had the instrument under his arm he left the house again and climbed towards the courtyard gate.

He reached the bottom of the folly wall in a few minutes, then went quickly up the steps to his hidden cell. Before he went inside he put down the detector and used his binoculars to scan the countryside around his house.

The track down to the road into town was deserted, as was the road itself along the stretch of it he could clearly see. There was not even any drifting dust to show that a car might have driven recently in either direction. He then scanned along the parts of the ridge visible from his position, searching for a sight of Luovi. Where he had last spoken to her, though, was dotted with high, free-standing boulders. He could see no sign of her, but knew she could still easily be in that area.

Ordier stepped back, squeezed between the two projecting slabs and went through into the cell. At once he was assailed by the sickly, pungent fragrance of Qataari roses. It was a smell that he had come unambiguously to associate with the woman in the ritual, with the feeling of spying on the valley, with the watching of the ritual, and with the sense of sexual provocation and illicit promise.

He placed his binoculars on the shelf and took the scintilla detector from its case. He paused before switching it on, apprehensive of what it might reveal. If there were scintillas here, inside the cell, then he would know beyond any more doubt that the Qataari had been aware of his presence for some considerable time.

He pulled the antenna to its full height and threw the switch. At once the speaker gave out an electronic howl that faded almost instantly to silence. Ordier, whose hand had jerked back reflexively when the device went off, touched the directional aerial and shook the instrument but no further sound came from it. He swept his hand across the switch, wondering what was wrong.

He took the detector out into the sunlight and turned on the switch again. In addition to the audible signal, the detector normally indicated its response through several LEDs and a row of calibrated dials on the side of the housing. The LEDs glowed, albeit dimly, presumably because of the bright ambient sunlight, but the dials remained at zero. The speaker was silent. Ordier shook the instrument but the circuits stayed dead. He breathed noisily in exasperation.

When he checked the batteries Ordier found they were dead.

He cursed himself for forgetting to recharge them and put the detector on the steps. The thing was useless to him. Another uncertainty had appeared. Was his hiding place seeded with scintillas, or was it not? That sudden burst of electronic noise: was it dynamic overload, or the dying gasp of failing batteries?

He returned to the confining cell and picked up his binoculars.

Qataari rose petals lay thickly on the slab where he normally

241

stood and as he stepped forward to the observation slit Ordier saw that more petals lay there, piled so thickly that the aperture was all but blocked. Uncaring whether they fell back into his cell or fluttered down into the valley, Ordier brushed them away with his fingers and shuffled his feet to kick them from the slab. The fragrance rose around him like a cloud of pollen. As he breathed it he felt a heady sensation: sexual arousal, physical excitement, intoxication.

He tried to remember the first time he had found the petals here in his cell. There had been a strong, gusting wind. They could have blown in through the slit by chance. But last night? Had there been a wind? He could not remember.

Ordier shook his head, trying to think clearly. There had been all the confusions of the morning, then Luovi. The dead batteries. The perfumed petals.

It seemed to him, in the suffocating darkness of the cell, that events were being contrived by greater powers to confuse and disorientate him.

If those powers were real, he thought he knew whose they were.

As if it were a light seen wanly through a mist, Ordier focused on the knowledge and blundered mentally towards it.

The Qataari had been watching him all along. He had been selected by them, he had been led to the hiding place inside this cell, he had been intended to watch. Every movement he made in the cell, every indrawn breath and muttered word, every voyeuristic intent and response and thought, they had all been monitored by the Qataari. They were decoded and analysed, and tested against their own actions, so that they knew his every response. The Qataari behaved according to their interpretations of the data they collected from him.

He had become a scintilla to the Qataari.

Ordier gripped a piece of stone jutting out from the wall, trying to steady himself. He could feel himself swaying as if his thoughts were a palpable force that could dislodge him from the cell. He sensed the dark wall cavity that lay dangerously beneath him.

The first day he had found the cell, the beginning of all this. He had been *concealed* and the Qataari had been *unaware* of him. That was surely axiomatic? He had found the land, paid for the house to be built, taken over ownership of the folly, by a process, a sequence of events, that must be considered random. He had always watched the Qataari in secret, gradually realizing the nature of his stolen privilege. He had spied out the young woman, watched her moving through the rose bushes, plucking the flowers and tossing them into the pannier on her back. She had been one amongst dozens of others but he focused on her because some physical chemistry, based on his perception of her appearance and manner, made her extremely attractive to him. He had said nothing, except in his thoughts, and the Qataari could not have noticed.

They could not have noticed, any more than they could have contrived the whole thing.

The rest was chance and coincidence. It had to be so.

Reassured, Ordier leaned forward and pressed his forehead against the slab of rock above the slit. He looked down, into the circular arena below.

It was as if nothing had changed. The Qataari were waiting for him.

The young woman lay back on the carpet of rose petals, the garment lying loosely and revealingly across her body. There was the same visible crescent of pale aureole, the same few strands of pubic hair. The man who had kicked her was standing back from her, looking down at her with his shoulders hunched and stroking himself in the groin. The others stood around: the women who had thrown the petals and bared their bodies, the men who had been chanting.

The restoration of the scene was so perfect, as if the image of his memory had been photographed and reconstructed so no detail should be omitted, that Ordier felt a shadow of the guilt that had followed his spontaneous ejaculation.

He raised his binoculars and looked at the woman's face. Her eyes, although half closed, were looking directly at him. Her expression too was identical: the abandonment of sexual antici-pation, or satisfaction. It was as if he was seeing the next frame of a film being inched through a projector gate. Fighting the feeling of associative guilt Ordier stared down at her, meeting her gaze, marvelling at her beauty and the lust in her expression.

He felt a tightness in his crotch, a new tumescence.

She moved suddenly, shaking her head from side to side. The ritual immediately resumed.

Four of the men stepped forward from the edge of the circle, picking up long ropes that had been coiled beside the statues. As the men moved towards the woman, their feet stirring the petals, they uncoiled the ropes. Ordier saw that the other ends were tied around the bases of four of the statues. At the same time, the women picked up their panniers of rose petals and came forward with them. The others began to chant.

In the rose plantation beyond, the Qataari were moving about their tasks, tending and plucking and watering. Ordier was sud-denly aware of them, as if they too had been waiting for the ritual to resume, had taken up their movements at the same time.

The men were tying the woman by her wrists and ankles, the ropes being stretched taut and the knots tied forcefully about her. Soon her arms were stretched out on both sides and her legs were held wide open. She struggled against the men, but ineffectually. She was writhing as best she could: a circling of her pelvis, a slow turning of her head.

The garment had worked almost completely from her body: while she struggled against being tied the flimsy robe had slipped away from her. One of the men stepped over her, temporarily blocking Ordier's view. When he moved back he had rearranged the garment so that she was covered again.

Through all of this – the tying of the ropes, the throwing of the petals – the solitary man stood before her, working his hand across his genitals, waiting and watching.

When the last rope was secured the men withdrew. The chant-ing came to a sudden end. All the men, except the one who stood

244

before the woman, walked away from the arena, towards the plantation, towards the distant Qataari camp.

The spreadeagled young woman writhed helplessly in the hold of the ropes. The flower petals were falling on her like snow, drifting across her and burying her. Ordier could see the petals landing on her face, her eyes, into her open mouth. Helplessly, she shook her head from side to side, trying to clear the petals from her face. Still they landed on her. As she pulled desperately against the ropes, Ordier could see the mound of petals heaving with her struggles, could see the ropes flexing and jerking.

At last her efforts ceased and she stared upwards again. Looking at her through the binoculars, Ordier saw that in spite of her violent writhing her expression was relaxed and her eyes were wide open. Saliva brightened her cheeks and jaw, and her face had a healthy, ruddy flush, as if reflecting the colour of the flowers. Beneath the petals her chest was rising and falling quickly, as if she was breathless.

Once more she was seeming to look directly back at Ordier, her expression knowing and seductive.

The stilling of her body signalled the start of the next stage in the ceremony, as if the victim of the ritual was also its director, because no sooner was she staring lasciviously upwards than the man who stood before her leaned down. He crouched beside her, reaching into the heap of petals. He began stripping the panels of her loose garment from her, tearing them up and away, tossing them behind him. Petals swirled around him. Ordier, staring eagerly down, saw tantalizing glimpses of her body, but the petals were flying too densely above her. The other women closed in, throwing more petals, concealing the nakedness so briefly revealed. The last part of the garment, the piece that had been beneath her, came away with difficulty. As the man snatched it away the young woman's body bucked against the restraint of the ropes: bare knees and arms, a naked shoulder, heaved moment-arily from the mound of petals.

Ordier watched as more and more of the petals were heaped on top of her, completely burying her. The women were no longer

245

throwing the petals with their hands but now upended the panniers on top of her, letting the scarlet flower petals pour on to
her like liquid. As the petals fell the man knelt beside the young
woman's body, shaping and smoothing them over her with his
hands. He pressed them down against her body, heaped them
over her arms and legs, pushed them into her face.

Soon it was finished and the man stepped back. From Ordier's
viewpoint above, the small arena now looked like a smooth lake
of petals, with no hint of the shape of the woman's body beneath.
Only her eyes were uncovered.

The man and the women with the panniers moved away from
the arena. They walked back towards the distant camp.

Ordier lowered his binoculars and took in the general scene.
Throughout the plantation the work had stopped. The Qataari
were returning to their homes behind the dark canvas screens of
the encampment, leaving the woman alone in the arena.

Ordier looked down at her again, using the binoculars. She
was looking back at him steadily. To Ordier it seemed she was
making a frank, explicit enticement, a steady stare, challenging
him, inviting him.

There was a suggestion of darkening around her eyes, like the
shadows left by recent grief. As her steady gaze challenged and
beckoned him, Ordier, partially drugged by the narcotic fragrance
of the roses, saw a familiarity in her eyes that froze all sense of
mystery. That bruised look of the sensitive skin around her eyes,
that confident stare ...

Ordier looked back at her for a long time. The longer he stared
the more convinced he became that he was gazing into the eyes
of Jenessa.

Intoxicated by the roses, sexually aroused by their fragrance,
Ordier fell back from the slit in the wall and lurched outside.
The brilliance of the sunlight, the heat of its rays, took him
by surprise and he staggered on the flight of narrow steps. He
regained his balance by resting one hand against the main wall

246

of the folly, then went past his discarded scintilla detector and started to descend the steps towards the ground.

Halfway down there was another narrow ledge, which ran unevenly across the wall as far as the end of the folly. Obsessed with the urgency of his need, Ordier walked precariously along the ledge. At the end he was able to climb down to the top of the wall which surrounded the folly's courtyard. Once there he could see the rocks and broken boulders of the ridge a short distance below.

He jumped, landing heavily across the face of a boulder. He had been further away than he thought. He grazed a hand and took a painful knock on one knee, but apart from these, and being winded by the fall, he was unhurt. He crouched for a few seconds, recovering his breath.

A hot, stiff breeze was blowing through the valley and along the ridge, and as Ordier's breathing steadied he felt his head clearing. At the same time, with a sense of regret, he felt the sexual arousal dying too.

A moment of the free will with which he had flattered himself earlier had returned. No longer driven by the enigmatic stimulation of the Qataari ritual Ordier realized that it was once again in his power to abandon the quest.

He could scramble somehow down the overhangs and broken slabs of the ridge and return to his house. He could see Jenessa, who might have returned by now with an easy, plausible explanation of the contradictions Luovi had raised. He could seek out Luovi and apologize to her, then try to find an explanation for Jacj Parren's apparent or actual movements. He could resume the life he had been leading until this summer, before the day he had found the cell. He could forget the Qataari woman and all that she meant to him, and never again visit the folly to spy on her.

So he crouched on his boulder, trying to be clear in his mind.

But there was something he could not resolve by walking away.

It was the certain knowledge that *next time* he looked through the crack in the folly wall – be it tomorrow, or in a year's time, or even in half a century's time – he would see a bed of Qataari rose petals, and staring back at him would be the bruised eyes of a lovely young woman, waiting for him and reminding him of Jenessa.

Ordier scrambled clumsily down the last overhanging boulder, fell to the scree beneath and skidded in a cloud of dust and grit to the sandy floor of the valley.

He stood up and brushed himself down. The gaunt height of the folly loomed beside him and above him. He regarded it with interest, never having seen the building from this angle before. The side that looked out over his grounds was an effective fake, constructed of stone slabs and built to resemble a medieval castellated tower. On the rear no such efforts had been made to forge an appearance. Although the lower part of the main wall was built with stone blocks, from about the height of a man's head upwards the wall had been constructed with a variety of bricks and stone blocks, clearly being whatever materials the builders had had to hand at the time.

Ordier knew there was nobody about because as he had been climbing down the rocky ridge he had an uninterrupted view to all sides. There were no guards visible along the ridge, no other Qataari anywhere. The breeze blew through the deserted rose plantation. Far away, on the other side of the valley, the screens around the camp hung heavy and grey.

The encircling statues of the arena lay ahead of him. Ordier walked slowly towards them, excited again and apprehensive. As he approached them he could see the mound of petals and could smell the heady perfume being given off by them. Here in the shadow of the folly the breeze had little effect and barely stirred the surface of the mound. Now he was at ground level he saw that the petals had not been smoothed to an entirely flat surface over the young woman, but that they lay irregularly and deeply. The flatness had been an illusion caused by his position high above.

Ordier hesitated when he came to the nearest of the statues. It happened to be one of the ones to which the ropes had been tied. He saw the rough-fibred rope stretching tautly across to the mound of petals, vanishing into it.

What was he supposed to do now? What was expected of him?

Should he walk across to the young woman in the mound of petals and introduce himself, formally and conventionally? Should he stand threateningly before her in imitation of the way that the man had done earlier? Should he simply take advantage of the fact that he was alone with her and possess her at last, rape her? Should he release her from the ropes? He looked around helplessly, hoping for some clue as to what to do.

All these possibilities were open to him. He was aware, though, that his apparent freedoms were actually created for him by others. He was free to act as he wished, but whatever he did would have been preordained by the mysterious, omniscient power of the Qataari.

Still he yearned to be with her, to seize her, to know her. She was there, trapped, a short distance away from him. He was free to have her.

But he was also free to leave. That too would have been pre-determined as his choice.

So he stood uncertainly by the statue, breathing the dangerous sweetness of the roses, feeling again the rise of sexual desire. At last he stepped forward but some residual trace of social convention made him clear his throat nervously, signalling his presence, his approach.

There was no audible reaction from the young woman.

He followed the rope until he came to the edge of the mound of petals. He craned forward, hoping that something of her could be seen without him having to push through the piles of petals to reach her. The fragrance of the petals lay heavy – his presence stirred it up like flocculant sediment shaken from the bottom of a bottle of poor wine. He breathed it deeply, embracing the dullness of thought it induced, welcoming further surrender to the mysteries of the Qataari. It relaxed him and aroused him, made

249

him sensitive to the sounds of the breeze, inured him to the great dry heat of the overhead sun.

His clothes were feeling stiff and constraining on him, so he quickly stripped them off. He saw the pile of bright red material where the young woman's torn toga had been tossed aside. He threw his own clothes on top. When he turned back to the pile of petals he crouched down and took hold of the rope. He tugged on it and felt the tautness, knowing that as he twitched it she would feel the pulling on her limb and realize he was there.

He stepped forward and the petals stirred around his ankles. The scent thickened, like vaginal musk of desire.

Then he hesitated again, suddenly aware of an intrusive sensation, so distinct, so intense, that it was almost like pressure on his naked skin.

Somewhere, somebody hidden was watching him.

The realization was so definite that it penetrated the pleasant delirium brought on by the rose perfume. Ordier stepped back again. He turned around, looking first at the high wall of the folly behind him, then across at the plantation of roses. There was no one in sight.

The encircling statues faced inwards, their blank metal visages staring down at the woman trapped beneath the petals.

A memory, surfacing sluggishly like waterlogged timber through the muddy pool of his mind: the statues, the statues. Earlier in the ritual – why were the statues there? He remembered, dimly, the men gathered around the woman, the cleaning and polishing of the statues. And later, as she walked into centre of the arena ... some of the men climbed into the hollow statues!

The ritual had not changed. When he returned to his cell that morning the Qataari were positioned exactly as he had last seen them. But were the men still inside the statues? Were they still there?

Ordier stood before the one nearest to him and stared up at it.

It depicted a young man of great physical strength and beauty, holding a scroll in one hand and in the other a long spear with a phallus for a head. Although the figure was naked from the waist up, its legs were invisible because of a voluminous, loose-fitting garment shaped around them, worked brilliantly by the sculptor to appear to have the texture of cloth. The face of the statue looked forward and downwards, directly towards where the woman lay buried under the petals.

The statue's eyes—

There were no eyes. Just two holes, behind which it would be possible for human eyes to hide.

Ordier stared up, looking at the dark recess behind the eye-holes, trying to see if anyone was there. The statue gazed back vacantly, implacably.

Ordier turned away towards the pile of rose petals, knowing the naked young woman still lay there a few paces away from him. Beyond the petals were the other statues, staring down with the same sinister emptiness. Ordier fancied he saw a movement: behind the eye-holes of one of the statues, a head ducking down.

He stumbled across the arena, tripping on one of the buried ropes (the petals of the mound rustled and shifted; had he tugged at the woman's arm?), and lurched up to the statue. He felt his way round to the other side, groping for some kind of handle which would open the hinged back. His fingers found a knob shaped like a raised disc; one touch, and he recoiled away. The metal was sun-hot, almost unbearable to grip. He tried again, arching his fingers, trying to spread the pain by rolling them as he gripped. He managed to raise it. The hinges squeaked, the back came open, the door slammed into a fully open position. Superheated air billowed out from within.

Ordier looked inside. The statue was empty.

He opened the others, using his discarded shirt to protect his hand from the burning metal. All the statues were empty. Ordier kicked his naked foot against them, he hammered at them with his fists and slammed the metal doors. The statues rang with a hollow reverberation.

But the young Qataari woman was still there, bound and silent beneath the petals. Ordier was growing increasingly aware of her silence, her mute, uncritical presence.

He returned to the mound of petals in the centre of the arena, satisfied, as far as possible in his mental state, that he had done all he could. There was no one about, no one watching. He was alone with her. Even so, as he stood before her, breathing the sickly fragrance of the roses, he could still feel the pressure of watching eyes as distinctly as if it were the touch of a hand on the back of his neck.

An awareness of what he had to do was growing in him. He had to succumb to the fragrance of the flowers. He had dreaded that in the past, but now there was no alternative. He gulped in the hot midday air and the perfume it carried, holding it in his lungs and feeling his skin tingle, his senses dull. He was painfully sensitive to the woman's silent presence, to the promise of her offered sexuality. Images of her bruised eyes, frail body, innocent demeanour, her evident excitement, all swam before him. He kneeled down, reached out with his hands, began to search for her in the mound of petals.

He pushed forward on his knees, wading through. The petals swirled about his sides and his elbows like a light, foamy liquid, scarlet coloured, desire perfumed. He came to one of the ropes beneath the petals and followed it with his hand towards the centre of the arena. He was close to her now, sensing her ahead of him, and he tugged lightly on the rope several times, feeling it yield, imagining it bringing one of her hands nearer to him, or spreading her legs a little wider. He waded forward hurriedly, groping for her.

There was a deep indentation in the ground beneath him. Ordier, leaning forward to put his weight on one hand, fell instead. He pitched forward into the soft, warm depths of the petals. He shouted as he fell and many of the petals entered his mouth.

He reared up like a non-swimmer who has fallen suddenly

into shallow water, showering flowers around him in a pink and scarlet spray, trying to spit the petals from his mouth.

He felt something gritty between his teeth. He reached in with a finger and wiped it around. When he brought it out several petals were clinging moistly to it. He raised it to look more closely at them and Ordier saw a sudden glint of reflected light.

At first he thought it was a bit of his own spittle, but then he saw that all the petals had an identical high spot of reflected light embedded in their fragile material.

He sank down again on his knees and picked up another of the petals at random. He held it before his eyes, squinting at it. He saw a tiny gleam of light, a glittering, shimmering fragment of metal and glass.

Ordier picked up a handful of the petals, felt and saw the same microscopic glitter on every one. He threw them up and let them float away around him.

As they flickered down the sun reflected minutely from the scintillas embedded in all the petals.

Ordier closed his eyes. The scent of the petals was overpowering. He staggered forward on his knees, the petals rippling about his waist. Again he reached the depression in the ground beneath the petals and he fell forward into the lake of flowers, reaching out for the body of the woman. He was in an ecstasy of delirium, desire and tumescence.

He floundered and beat his arms, thrashing the petals aside, sinking deeper into the morass of colour and scent, kicking and struggling against the increasing weight around him, seeking her, seeking her.

But the four ropes met in the centre of the arena, and she was no longer there.

Where she had been bound there was now a large and tightly drawn knot.

Exhausted by the heat, by the tensions coursing through him, by the disappointment, Ordier rolled over on his back and sank into the petals, letting the sun beat down on him.

It was directly overhead; it must be noon. He could feel the hard lump of the knotted ropes between his shoulder blades, supporting him so that he did not sink further into the lake. The metal heads of the encircling statues loomed over and around him. The sky was brilliant and blue. He reached behind himself to grasp the ropes above his head, and spread his legs along the others.

The midday wind was rising and petals were blowing, drifting across him, covering his limbs, spinning above him in a sinuous red twister.

Behind the statues, dominating the arena, was the bulk of the folly. The sun reflected from its many rough surfaces. In the centre of the wall, and about halfway up, was a narrow slit with a small overhang above it. Ordier stared up at the slash of darkness in the sunlit wall. Somewhere within there were two identical glimmers of reflected light. They were circular and cold, like the lenses of binoculars.

The petals blew across him, covering him, and soon only his eyes were still exposed.

He stared up at the sky. Aircraft were spiralling in from all directions, the highest ones trailing long white paths of condensation. The aircraft arrived simultaneously above him, appearing to halt. It was the equatorial vortex, the noonday stasis of time.

Dozens of the flying machines were hovering there, seemingly stacked one above the other, pointing in every direction, flying fiercely through time, blocking the zenithal sun, never moving away from his line of sight. Each was flying at operating speed; each was suspended in the vortex; each appeared from the ground to be unmoving in the air.

The closest plane, the lowest, was a single-engined propeller-powered monoplane. The noise of its engine drummed against him. It seemed to have become trapped in the pink tornado of whirling petals, as the coriolis slowly twisted it horizontally. Then, like an insect laying a clutch of airborne eggs, a dark cloud of tiny particles was ejected from the fuselage of the aircraft. The spinning vortex of petals took them and scattered them in all directions.

The scintillas drummed down around Ordier, on to his face, into his eyes, into his mouth.

The vortex passed, moving on with the noon moment, moving on along the equator. The aircraft, subjectively released from the stasis of the vortex, appeared to shoot away along their many different courses, continuing their spiralling trajectories above the equator, travelling on through their eternal noon, leaving their trails of condensation behind them. Slowly, the tiny particles of condensed moisture dispersed, and the hot sky reverted to its dome of unbroken blue.

Around Ordier's inert body, other tiny particles settled quietly on the ground.

The
Discharge

•

I emerge into my memories of life at the age of twenty. I was a soldier, recently released from boot camp, being marched by an escouade of black-cap military policemen to the naval compound in Jethra Harbour. The war was approaching the end of its three-thousandth year and I was serving in a conscript army.

I marched mechanically, staring at the back of the man's helmet in front of me. The sky was dark grey with cloud and a stiff cold wind streamed in from the sea. My awareness of life leapt into being around me. I knew my name, I knew where we had been ordered to march, I knew or could guess where we would be going after that. I could function as a soldier. This was my moment of birth into consciousness.

Marching uses no mental energy – the mind is free to wander, if you have a mind. I record these words some years later, looking back, trying to make sense of what happened. At the time, the moment of awareness, I could only react, stay in step.

Of my childhood, the years leading up to this moment of mental birth, little remains. I can piece together the fragments of a likely story. I was probably born in Jethra, university town and capital city on the southern coast of our country. Of my parents, brothers or sisters, my education, any history of childhood illnesses, friends, experiences, travels, I remember nothing. I grew to the age of twenty; only that is certain.

And one other thing, useless to a soldier. I knew I was an artist.

How could I be sure of that, trudging along with the other men, in a phalanx of dark uniforms, kitbags, clanking mess tins, steel helmets, boots, stamping down a puddled road with a chill wind in our faces?

I knew that in the area of mental blankness behind me was a love of paintings, of beauty, of shape and form and colour. How had I gained this passion? What had I done with it? Aesthetics were my obsession and fervour. What was I doing in the army? Somehow this totally unsuitable candidate must have passed medical and psychological tests. I had been drafted, sent to boot camp; somehow a drill serjeant had trained me to become a soldier.

Here I was, marching to war.

We boarded a troopship for passage to the southern continent, the world's largest unclaimed territory. It was there that the fighting was taking place. All battles had been fought in the south for nearly three thousand years. It was a vast, uncharted land of tundra and permafrost, buried in ice at the pole. Apart from a few outposts along the coast, it was uninhabited except by battalions.

I was assigned to a mess deck below the waterline, already hot and stinking when we boarded, soon crowded and noisy as well.

I withdrew into myself, while sensations of life coursed maddeningly through me. Who was I? How had I come to this place? Why could I not remember what I had been doing even the previous day?

But I was able to function, equipped with knowledge of the world, with working ability to use my equipment, I knew the other men in my escadron and I understood some of the aims and history of the war. It was only myself I could not remember. For the first day, as we waited in our deck for other detachments to board the ship, I listened in to the talk of the other men, hoping mainly for insights about myself, but when none of those was revealed I settled instead for finding out what concerned them. Their concerns would be mine.

257

Like all soldiers they were complaining, but in their case the complaints were tinged with real apprehension. It was the prospect of the three-thousandth anniversary of the outbreak of war that was the problem.

They were all convinced that they were going to be caught up in some major new offensive, an assault intended to resolve the dispute one way or another. Some of them thought that because there were still more than three years to go until the anniversary the war would end before then. Others pointed out cynically that our four-year term of conscription was due to end a few weeks after the millennium. If a big offensive was in progress we would never be allowed out until it was over.

Like them, I was too young for fatalism. The seed of wanting to escape from the army, to find some way to discharge myself, had been sown.

I barely slept that night, wondering about my past, worrying about my future.

When the ship started its voyage it headed south, passing the islands closest to the mainland. Off the coast of Jethra itself was Seevl, a long grey island of steep cliffs and bare windswept hills that blocked the view of the sea from most parts of the city. Beyond Seevl a wide strait led to a group of islands known as the Serques – these were greener, lower, with many attractive small towns nestling in coves and bays around their coastlines.

Our ship passed them all, weaving a way between the clustering islands. I watched from the rail, enchanted by the view.

As the long shipboard days passed slowly I found myself drawn again and again to the upper deck, where I would find a place to stand and stare, usually alone. So close to home but beyond the blocking mass of Seevl, the islands slipped past, out of reach, this endless islandscape of vivid colours and glimpses of other places, distant and shrouded in marine haze. The ship ploughed on steadily through the calm water, the massed soldiery crammed noisily within, few of the men so much as even glancing away to see where we were.

The days went by and the weather grew perceptibly warmer. The beaches I could see now were white and fringed with tall trees, with tiny houses visible in the shade beyond. The reefs that protected many of the islands were brilliantly multi-coloured, jagged and encrusted with shells, breaking the sea-swell into spumes of white spray. We passed ingenious harbours and large coastal towns clinging to spectacular hillsides, saw pluming volcanoes and rambling, rock-strewn mountain pastures, skirted islands large and small, lagoons and bays and river estuaries.

It was common knowledge that it was the people of the Dream Archipelago who had caused the war, though as you passed through the Midway Sea the peaceful, even dreamy aspect of the islands undermined this certainty. The calm was only an impression, an illusion borne of the distance between ship and shore. To keep us alert on our long southerly voyage the army mounted many compulsory shipboard lectures. Some of these recounted the history of the struggle to achieve armed neutrality in which the islands had been engaged for most of the three millennia of the war.

Now they were by consent of all parties neutral, but their geographical location – the Midway Sea girdled the world, separating the warring countries of the northern continent from their chosen battlefields in the uninhabited southern polar land – ensured that military presence in the islands was perpetual.

I cared little for any of that. Whenever I was able to get away to the upper deck I would stare in rapt silence at the passing diorama of islands. I tracked the course of the ship with the help of a torn and probably outdated map I had found in a ship's locker and the names of the islands chimed in my consciousness like a peal of bells: Paneron, Salay, Temmil, Mesterline, Prachous, Muriseay, Demmer, Piqay, the Aubracs, the Torquils, the Serques, the Reever Fast Shoals and the Coast of Helvard's Passion.

Each of these names was evocative to me. Reading the names off the map, identifying the exotic coastlines from fragments of clues – a sudden rise of sheer cliffs, a distinctive headland, a particular bay – made me think that everywhere in the Dream Archipelago

259

was already embedded in my consciousness, that somehow the islands were where my roots were found, that I belonged in them, had dreamed of them all my life. In short, while I stared at the islands from the ship I felt my artistic sensibilities reviving.

I was startled by the emotional impact on me of the names, so delicate and suggestive of unspecified sensual pleasures, out of key with the rest of the coarse and manly existence on the ship. As I stared out across the narrow stretches of water that lay between our passing ship and the beaches and reefs I would quietly recite the names to myself, as if trying to summon a spirit that would lift me up, raise me above the sea and carry me to those tide-swept strands.

Some of the islands were so large that the ship sailed along parallel with their coastlines for most of the day, while others were so small they were barely more than half-submerged reefs which threatened to rip at the hull of our elderly ship.

Small or large, all the islands had names. As we passed one I could identify on my map I circled the name, then later added it to an ever-growing list in my notebook. I wanted to record them, count them, note them down as an itinerary so that one day I might go back and explore them all. The view from the sea tempted me.

There was only one island stop for our ship during that long southward voyage.

My first awareness of the break in our journey was when I noticed that the ship was heading towards a large industrialized port, the installations closest to the sea seemingly bleached white by the cement dust spilling from an immense smoking factory that overlooked the bay. Beyond this industrial area was a long tract of undeveloped shoreline, the tangle of rainforest briefly blocking any further sight of civilization. Then, after rounding a hilly promontory and passing a high jetty wall, a large town built on a range of low hills came suddenly into sight, stretching away in all directions, my view of it distorted by the shimmering heat that spread out from the land across the busy waters of the harbour. We were of course forbidden from knowing the identity of our stop, but I had my map and I already knew the name.

The island was Muriseay, the largest of the islands in the Archipelago and one of the most important.

It would be hard to underestimate the impact this discovery had on me. Muriseay's name came swimming up out of the blank pool that was my memory.

At first it was just an identifying word on the map: a name printed in letters larger than the ones used for other islands. It puzzled me. Why should this word, this foreign name, mean something to me? I had been stirred by the sight of the other islands, but although the resonances were subtle I had felt no close identification with any of them.

Then we approached the island and the ship started to follow the long coastline. I had watched the distant land slip by, affected more and more, wondering why.

When we came to the bay, to the entrance to the harbour, and I felt the heat from the town drifting across the quiet water towards us, something at last became clear to me.

I knew about Muriseay. The knowledge came to me as a memory from the place where I had no memory.

Muriseay was something or somewhere I had known, or it represented something I had done, or experienced, as a child. It was a whole memory, discrete, telling me nothing about the rest. It involved a painter who had lived on Muriseay and his name was Rascar Acizzone.

Rascar Acizzone? Who was that? Why did I suddenly remember the name of a Muriseayan painter when otherwise I was a hollow shell of amnesia?

I was able to explore this memory no further: without warning all troops were mustered to billets and with the other men who had drifted to the upper decks I was forced to return to the mess decks. I descended to the bowels of the ship resentfully. We were kept below for the rest of the day and night, as well as for much of the day that followed.

Although I suffered in the airless, sweltering hold with all the others, it gave me time to think. I closed myself off, ignored the noise of the other men and silently explored this one memory that had returned.

When the larger memory is blank, anything that suddenly seems clear becomes sharp, evocative, heavy with meaning. I gradually was able to remember my interest in Muriseay, although without learning much else about myself.

I was a boy, a teenager, so it was not so long ago, in my short life. I learned somehow of a colony of artists who had gathered in Muriseay Town the previous century. I saw reproductions of their work somewhere, perhaps in books. I investigated further and found that several of the originals were kept in the city's art gallery. I went there to see them for myself. The leading painter, the eminence within the group, was the artist called Rascar Acizzone.

It was Acizzone's work which inspired me.

Details continued to clarify themselves. A coherent exactness emerged from the gloom of my forgotten past.

Rascar Acizzone developed a painting technique he called tactilism. A tactilist work used a kind of pigment that had been developed some years before, not by artists but by researchers into ultrasound microcircuitry. A range of dazzling colours produced by these pigments became available to artists when certain patents expired and for a brief period there had been a vogue for paintings that used the garish but exciting ultrasound primaries.

Most of these early works were little more than pure sensationalism: colours were blended synaesthetically with ultrasonics to shock, alarm or provoke the viewer. Acizzone came late to the techniques, his work beginning as the others lost interest, consigning themselves to the minor artistic school that soon became known as the Pre-Tactilists.

Acizzone used the pigments to more disturbing effect than anyone before him. His glowing abstracts – large canvases or boards painted in one or two primary colours, with few shapes or images to be seen – appeared at a casual first look, or from a distance, or when seen as reproductions in books, to be little more than arrangements of colours. Closer up or, better still, if you made physical contact with the ultrasonic pigments used in the originals, it became apparent that the concealed images were of a most profoundly and shockingly erotic nature. Detailed and astonishingly explicit scenes were mysteriously evoked in the mind of the viewer, inducing an intense charge of sexual excitement.

I discovered a set of long-forgotten Acizzone abstracts in the vaults of the museum in Jethra and by the laying on of the palms of my hands I entered the world of vicarious carnal passion. The women depicted by Acizzone were the most beautiful and sensual I had ever seen, or known, or imagined. Each painting created its own vision in the mind of the viewer. The images were always exact and repeatable, but they were unique, being partially created as an individual response to the sensual longing of the observer.

Not much critical literature about Acizzone remained, but what little I could find seemed to suggest that everyone experienced each painting differently.

I discovered that Acizzone's career had ended in failure and ignominy: soon after his work was noticed he was rejected by the art establishment figures, the public notables and the moral guardians of his time. He was hounded and execrated, forced to end his days in exile on the closed island of Cheoner. With most of his originals hidden, and a few more dispersed away from Muriseay to the archives of mainland galleries, Acizzone never worked again and sank into obscurity.

As a teenage aesthete I cared nothing about his scandalous reputation. All I understood was that the few paintings of his that were hidden away in the cellars of the Jethran gallery evoked such lustful images in my mind that I was left weak with unfocused desire and dizzy with amorous longings.

That was the whole bright clarity of my unlocated memory. Muriseay, Acizzone, tactilist masterpieces, concealed paintings of secret sex.

Who was I who had learned of this? The boy was gone, grown into a soldier. Where was I when it happened? There must have been a wider life I once lived, but none of those memories had survived.

Once I had been an aesthete. Now I was a foot soldier. What kind of life was that?

We had moored in Muriseay Town, just outside the harbour wall. We fretted and strained, wanting to escape from our sweltering holds. Then:

Shore leave.

The news circulated around us faster than the speed of sound. The ship was soon to leave its mooring outside the harbour and dock against the quay. We would have thirty-six hours ashore. I cheered with the others. I yearned to find my past and lose my innocence in Muriseay.

Four thousand men were released and we hurried ashore. Most of them rushed into Muriseay Town in search of whores.

I rushed along with them, in quest of Acizzone.

Instead, I too found only whores.

There in the dock area, after a fruitless quest that sent me dashing through the streets to find Acizzone's beautiful Muriseayan women, I finished up in a harbourside dancing club. I was unready for Muriseay, had no idea of how to find what I was seeking. I roamed about the remoter quarters of the town, lost in narrow streets, shunned by the people who lived there. They saw only my uniform. I was soon footsore and disillusioned by the foreignness of the town, so I felt relieved when I discovered that my wanderings had brought me back to the harbour.

Our troopship, floodlit in the night, loomed over the concrete aprons and wharves.

I noticed the dancing club when I came across the dozens of troops thronging around the entrance. Wondering what was attracting them, I pushed through the crowd and went inside.

The large interior was dark and hot, crammed to the walls with human bodies, filled with the endless throbbing beat of synthesized music. My eyes were dazzled by the coloured lasers and spotlights flashing intensely from positions close to the ceiling. No one was dancing. At points around the walls, young women stood on glinting metal platforms head-height above the crowds, their naked, oil-glossed bodies picked out by glaring white spotlights. Each of them held a microphone against her lips and was speaking unexcitedly into it, pointing down at certain of the men on the dance floor.

As I pushed my way into the central area I was spotted by them. At first, in my inexperience, I thought they were waving to me or greeting me in some other way. I was tired and disappointed after my long walk around the town and I raised a hand in weary response. The young woman on the platform closest to me had a voluptuous body: she stood with her feet wide apart and her pelvis thrust forward, glorying in the revelation of her nakedness by the intrusive light. When I waved she moved suddenly, leaning forward on the metal rail around her platform so that her huge breasts dangled temptingly towards the men below. The spotlight source instantly shifted – a new beam flashed up from behind and below her, garishly illuminating her large buttocks and casting her shadow brightly on the ceiling. She spoke more urgently into her microphone, jabbing her hand in my direction.

Alarmed by being paid special attention, I moved deeper into the press of uniformed male bodies, hoping to lose myself in the crowd. Within a few seconds, though, a number of women had converged on me from different sides, reaching out through the jam of bodies to take me by the arms. Each of them was wearing a radio headset, with a pin-mike suspended close in front of her lips. Soon I was surrounded by them. They led me irresistibly across to one side.

While they continued to press around me, one of them flicked her fingers in front of my face, her thumb rubbing acquisitively across her fingertips.

I shook my head, embarrassed and frightened.

'Money!' the woman said loudly.

'How much?'

I hoped that money would let me escape from them.

'Your leave pay.' She rubbed her fingers again.

I found the thin fold of military banknotes the black-cap marshals had given me as I disembarked. As soon as I pulled them from my hip pocket she snatched them. With a swift motion she passed the money to one of the women I suddenly saw were sitting behind a long table in the shadowy recess by the edge of the dance floor. Each of them was noting down the amounts taken from every man in a kind of ledger, then slipping the banknotes out of sight.

It had all happened so quickly that I had barely taken in what they wanted. By now, though, because of the close and suggestive way the women were standing against me, there was little doubt what they were offering, even demanding. None of them was young, none of them was attractive to me. My thoughts for the last few hours had been with Acizzone's sirens. To be confronted by these aggressive and disagreeable women now was a shock to me.

'You want this?' one of them said, pulling at the loose front of her dress to reveal, fleetingly, a small sagging breast. I glimpsed a nipple, large and brown.

'You want this too?' The woman who had taken my money from my hand snatched at the front of her skirt, lifting it to show me what was beneath. In the harsh shadows created by the aggravating lights I could see nothing of her.

They were laughing at me.

'You've taken my money,' I said. 'Now leave me.'

'Do you know where you are and what men do in here?'

'Of course.'

I managed to struggle away from them and headed back immediately towards the entrance. I was feeling angry and humiliated. I had spent the last few hours dreaming of meeting, or even of simply seeing, Acizzone's wanton beauties. Instead, these hags tormented me with their withered, experienced bodies.

A group of four black-caps had entered the building while this had been going on. I could see them standing in pairs on each side of the entrance. They had withdrawn their synaptic batons and were holding them in the strike position. While aboard the ship I had already seen what happened to the victim if one of those evil sticks was used in anger. I faltered in my step, not wanting to have to push past the men to leave.

As I did so, another whore forced her way through the crowd and took my arm. I glanced at her in a distracted way, fearing the black-caps more than anything.

I was surprised to see her. This one was much younger than the others. She was wearing hardly any clothes to speak of: a tiny pair of shorts and a T-shirt with a torn neckline that hung low across one shoulder, revealing the upper curve of a breast. Her arms were thin. She was not wearing a radio headset. She was smiling towards me and as soon as I looked at her she spoke.

'Don't leave without discovering what we can do,' she said, tilting her face to speak loudly against my ear.

'I don't need to know,' I shouted.

'This place is the cathedral of your dreams.'

'What did you say?'

'Your dreams. Whatever you seek, they are here.'

'No, I've had enough.'

'Just try what we offer,' she said, pressing her face so close to me that her curly hair lightly teased my cheek. 'We are here for you, eager to please you. One day you will need what whores provide.'

'Never.'

The black-caps had moved to block the doorway. I could see that beyond them, in the wide passageway that led back to the street, more of their escouade were arriving. I wondered why they had suddenly appeared at the club, what they were doing. Our leave was not officially over for many more hours. Was there some emergency for which we had to return to the ship? Was this club, so prominently close to where the ship had berthed, off-limits for some perverse reason? Nothing was clear. I was suddenly frightened of the situation in which I had found myself.

Yet around me the hundreds of other men, all presumably from the same troopship as mine, appeared to show no concern. The racket of the over-amplified music went on, drilling into the mind.

'You can leave this way,' the girl said, touching my arm. She pointed towards a dark doorway placed low, beneath a stage area, away from the main entrance.

The black-caps were now moving into the crowd of men, pushing people aside with rough movements of their arms. The synaptic batons wavered threateningly. The young whore had already run down the short flight of steps to the door and was holding it open for me. She beckoned urgently to me. I went quickly to her and through the door. She closed it behind me.

I was in humid semi-darkness and I stumbled on the unevenly laid floor. The air was thick with powerful scents and although I could still hear the pulsating throb of the bass notes of the music there were many other sounds around me. Notably I could hear the voices of other men: shouting, laughing, complaining. Every voice was raised: in anger, excitement, urgency. At odd moments something on the other side of the corridor wall would bash heavily against it.

I gained a sense of chaos, of events being out of control.

We came to a door a short distance along the corridor – she opened it and led me through. I expected to find a bed of some sort, but there was nothing remotely of the boudoir about the room. There was not even a couch, or cushions on the floor. Three wooden chairs stood in a demure line against one wall, but that was all.

She said, 'You wait now.'

'Wait? What for? And for how long?'

'How long you want for your dreams?'

'Nothing! No time.'

'You are so impatient. One minute more, then follow me!'

She indicated yet another door which until that moment I had not noticed, because it had been painted in the same dull red colour as the walls. The weak light from the room's only bulb had helped disguise it further. She went across to it and walked through. As she did so I saw her reach backwards over her head with both arms and remove the torn T-shirt.

I glimpsed her bare, curving back, the small knobs of her verte-
brae, then she was gone.

Alone, I paced to and fro. By telling me to wait for one minute
had she meant it literally? That I should check my wristwatch or
count to sixty? She had thrown me into a state of nervous tension. What more had she to do in that further sanctum beyond,
other than remove those shorts and prepare herself for me?

I opened the door impatiently, pushing against the pressure of
a spring. It was dark beyond. The dim glow from the room behind
me was not strong enough to help me see. I gained the impression of something large in the room but I could not make out
its shape. I felt around with my hands, nervous in the darkness,
trying to extend my senses against the cloying perfumes and the
endlessly throbbing music, muffled but loud. As far as I could tell
I had come into a room, not another corridor.

I went further in, groping forward. Behind me, the door swung
closed on its spring. Immediately, bright spotlights came on from
the corners of the ceiling.

I was in a boudoir. An ornate bed – with a large, carved wooden
headboard, immense bulging pillows and a profusion of shining
satin sheets – filled most of the room. A woman, not the young
whore who had led me here, but another, lay on the bed in a pose
of sexual abandonment and availability.

She was naked, lying on her back with one arm raised to
curl behind her head. Her face was turned to the side and her
mouth was open. Her eyes were closed, her lips were moist. Her
large breasts bulged across her chest, the nipples lying flatly
and pointing outwards. She had raised one knee, holding it at a
slight angle, exposing herself. Her fingers rested on her sex, the
tips curving down to bury themselves shallowly in the cleft. The
spotlights radiated her and the bed in a brilliant focus of glaring
white light.

The sight of her froze me. What I was seeing was impossible. I
stared at her in disbelief.

She had arranged herself in a tableau vivant that was identical,
not close but *identical*, to one I had seen in my mind's eye before.

It was there in that sole fragment of my past. I remembered the first day I was in the cool semi-darkness of the vault of the gallery in Jethra. I had pressed my trembling teenage fingers, my palms, my perspiring forehead, many times to one of Acizzone's most notorious tactilist works: *Ste-Augustinia Abandonai*.

(I remembered the title! How?)

This woman *was* Ste-Augustinia. The reproduction she was fashioning was perfect. Not only was she an exact replica but also the arrangement she had made of the sheets and pillows – there were folds of satin glinting in the harsh light that exactly matched those in the painting. The long gleam of perspiration running between her exposed breasts was one my lustful imaginings had drooled over a dozen times before.

I was so astonished by this discovery that for a moment I forgot why I was there. Much was immediately and trivially clear to me: that she was not, for instance, the young woman I had seen removing the torn T-shirt; nor was she any of the gaunt women in headsets who had seized me on the dance floor. She was more maturely developed than the skinny girl in the T-shirt and to my eyes many times more beautiful than any of the others. Also, but most confusingly, the deliberate way she had spread herself on the smooth sheets of the bed was a conscious reference to an imagining only I had ever experienced. Or that I remembered in isolation! This was a connection I could not explain or escape from. Was her pose just a coincidence? Had they somehow read my mind?

A cathedral of dreams, the girl had said. That was impossible! Surely it was impossible?

It was madness to think that this had been contrived. But the resemblance to the painting, whose details were clear in my mind, was remarkable. Even so, the woman's real purpose was plain. She was yet a whore.

I gazed at her in silence, trying to find out what I should think.

Then, without opening her eyes, the whore said, 'If you only stand there to look, you must leave.'

'I – I was searching for someone.' She said nothing, so I added, 'A young woman, like you.'

'Take me now, or leave. I am not to be watched, not to be stared at. I am here to be ravished by you.'

As far as I could tell she had not shifted position when she spoke to me. Even her lips had hardly moved.

I gazed at her for a few more seconds, thinking that this was the time and this was the place where my fantasies and my real life could meet, but finally I moved back from her. I was, in truth, frightened of her. I was hardly more than an adolescent, almost completely inexperienced in sex. Not only that, though: in a single unexpected instant I had been confronted in the flesh by one of Acizzone's temptresses.

Lamely, I did as she told me and left.

There was little choice about where I should go. Two doors led into and out of the room: the one I had entered by and another in the wall opposite. I stepped round the end of the huge bed and went to the second door. 'Ste-Augustinia' did not stir to watch me leave. As far as I could tell she had not so much as glanced at me while I was there. I kept my face lowered, not wanting her to look at me, even as I was leaving.

I passed through into a second narrow corridor, unlit at my end but with a low-power light bulb glimmering at the other. The encounter had produced a familiar physical effect on me – in spite of my apprehension I was tingling with sexual intrigue. Lustfulness was rising. I walked towards the light, the door of the room I had left swinging closed behind me. At the far end, just beyond the light bulb, a kind of archway had been formed, with a small alcove behind it.

I came across no doors anywhere along the corridor so I assumed I would find some kind of exit in the alcove. As I lowered my head to pass through the archway I stumbled, tripping over the entangled legs of a man and woman apparently making love on the floor. In the gloom I had not seen them there. I staggered as I tried to keep my balance, uttering an apology, steadying myself by pressing a hand against the wall.

I moved on, away from the couple, but the alcove was a dead end. I felt around in the dim light, trying to find some sign of a door, but the only way in or out was through the archway.

The couple on the floor continued what they were doing, their naked bodies pumping rhythmically and energetically against each other.

I tried to step over them but I was unbalanced by the lack of space in which to stand and I kicked against them again. I murmured another embarrassed apology, but to my surprise the woman extricated herself quickly from beneath the man and stood up in an agile, untroubled movement. Her long hair was falling across her face and she tossed her head to sweep it back from her eyes. Perspiration rolled from her face, dripping down on her chest. The man rolled briefly over. Because of his nakedness I was able to see, with surprise, that he was not at all sexually aroused. Their act of physical love had been a simulation.

The woman said to me, 'Wait! I'll come with you instead.'

She laid a warm hand on mine and smiled invitingly. She was breathing excitedly. A sheen of sweat lay over her breasts; her nipples pointed erectly. I felt a new erotic charge from the light touch of her fingers, but also a surge of guilt. The man lay there passively at my feet, staring up at me. I was confused by everything I was seeing.

I backed away from them, through the archway, back to the long, unlit corridor. The naked whore followed quickly behind me, seizing hold of my upper arm as I blundered along. At the far end of this corridor, past the door which I knew led back into Ste-Augustinia's boudoir, I had noticed yet another door, leading somewhere. I reached it, put my weight against it and forced it open. It moved stiffly. Inside the room that was beyond, the endless throbbing beat of the synthesized music was louder but it appeared to be empty of all people. The musky perfume was intense. I felt sensual, aroused, eager to do the bidding of the young woman who had attached herself to me – but even so I was frightened, disorientated, overcome by the rush of sensations and thoughts coursing through me.

The young woman had followed me in, still holding my arm. The door closed firmly behind us, causing a decompression sensation in one of my ears. I swallowed to clear it. I turned to speak to this whore but as I did so two other young women appeared as if from nowhere, stepping out of the deeper shadows on the side of the room away from the door.

I was alone with them. All three were naked. They were looking at me with what I took to be great eagerness. I was in a state of acute sexual readiness.

Even so, I stepped back from them, still nervous because of my inexperience, but by this time in such a state of excitement that I wondered how much longer I might contain it. I felt the edge of something soft pressing against the back of my lower leg. When I glanced behind me I saw in the pale light that a large bed was there, a bare mattress of some kind, an expanse of yielding material ready for use.

The three naked women were beside me now, their lustful scents rising around me. With gentle pressure of their hands they indicated I should lower myself to the bed. I sat down, but then one of them pushed lightly on my shoulders and I leaned back compliantly. The mattress, the palliasse, whatever was there, was soft beneath my weight. One of the women bent down and lifted my legs around so that I might lie flat.

When I was prone they began to unbutton and remove my uniform, working deftly and quickly, letting me feel the light tattoo of their fingertips. Nothing happened by accident: they were deliberately provoking and teasing my physical response. I was straining with the effort of controlling myself, so close was I to letting go. The girl closest to my head was staring down into my eyes as her fingers worked to slide my shirt from my chest and down my arms. Whenever she leaned across me, or stretched to free my hand from the cuff of a sleeve, she did so in such a way that she lowered one of her bare breasts towards me and brushed the hard little nipple lightly against my lips.

I was naked in a few seconds, in a state of full and agonizing arousal, yearning for release. The women slid my clothes out from

273

underneath me, piled them up on the further side of the mattress. The one beside my face rested her soft fingertips on my chest. She leaned closer to me.

'You choose?' she said, whispering into my ear.

'Choose what?'

'You like me? You like my friends?'

'All of you!' I said without thinking. 'I want you all!'

Nothing more was said or, as far as I could see, signalled between them. They moved into position smoothly and as if in a formation they had rehearsed many times.

I was made to remain lying on my back but one of them lifted my knee that was closest to the edge of the mattress, making a small triangular aperture. She lay down on her back across the mattress so that her shoulders rested on my horizontal leg, while her head went beneath my raised knee. She turned her face towards the space between my legs. I could feel her breath on my naked buttocks. She took hold of my erect penis with her hand, holding it perpendicular to my body.

In the same moment the second woman was astride me with a knee on each side of my chest, her legs wide apart, lowering herself so that her sex touched lightly against, but did not enfold, the tip of my member, which was being held in position by the other woman.

The third one also straddled me but placed herself above my face, lowering herself towards, but not actually against, my eager lips.

Breathing the woman's delicious bodily scents, I remembered Acizzone.

I thought about the most explicit of his paintings hidden away in the gallery cellar. It was called (another title, remembered how?): *The Swain of Lethen in Godly Pleasures*. This one was painted in bold pigment on a stiff wooden board.

All that could be seen of *The Swain* in reproduction, or from a distance, was what appeared to be a smooth field of uniform crimson paint, intriguingly plain and minimalist. One touch of a hand or a finger, though, or even (as I knew I had tried) the light press of a forehead, would induce a vivid mental image of sexual activity. For everyone it was supposed to be different. I myself saw, felt, experienced, a scene of multiple sexual activity, a young man naked on a bed, three beautiful naked women pleasuring him, one straddling his face, one his penis, the third reaching beneath his body to press her face into the cleft between his buttocks. All was bathed, in this intense imagining, in a lubricious crimson light.

Now I had become the swain himself, in godly pleasures.

I was surrendering to the imminent passions the women aroused in me. A lust for physical release was rushing through me even as the extent of the enigma about Acizzone surrounded me. I felt myself hastening to the moment of completion.

Then it ended. As swiftly and deftly as they had taken up their position, the women lifted themselves away from me, deserted me. I tried to call out to them, but my laboured breathing emitted only a series of excited gasps. They stepped quickly down from the bed, slipped away – the door opened and closed, leaving me alone.

I discharged my excitement at last, miserable and abandoned. I could still in one sense feel them, could detect the traces they had left behind of their exquisite and exciting perfumes, but I was alone in that dim-lit, sound-throbbing cell and I expelled my passion as a man alone.

I lay still to try to calm myself, all my senses tingling, my muscles twitching and straining. I sat up slowly, lowered my feet to the floor. My legs were trembling.

When I could I dressed quickly and carefully, attempting to make myself look as if nothing had just happened so that I could depart with at least an appearance of calmness.

As I tucked in my shirt I felt the residue of my discharge, cold and sticky on the skin of my belly.

I found my way out of the room, and walked nervously along the corridor into a large sub-floor area, filled with music and the sound of overhead footsteps. I saw a glint of bright red neon lighting, limned against ill-fitting doors. I struggled with iron handles, pulled the doors open, found a cobbled alley between two massive buildings under the tropical night, sensed the smells of cooking, perspiration, spices, grease, gasoline, night-scented flowers. Finally I emerged into the clamorous street by the waterfront. I saw none of the black-caps, none of the whores, none of my shipmates.

I was thankful the club was so close to the quay. I was soon able to reboard the troopship, check myself in with the marshals, then plunge into the lower decks and lose myself in the anonymous press of the other men who were there. I sought no one's company during my first hours back in the crowded decks. I lay on my bunk and pretended to sleep.

The next morning the ship sailed from Muriseay Town and once again we headed south towards the war.

After Muriseay, my view of the islands was different. The superficial allure of them had diminished. From my short visit ashore in that crowded town I felt myself to have become island-experienced, had briefly breathed the air and the scents, heard the sounds and seen some of the muddle. At the same time, though, the experience had deepened the intrigue of the islands. They still had me in their thrall, but I was careful now not to dwell on it. I felt I had grown up a little.

The whole pace of life on the ship was changing, with the army's demands on us increasing every day. For several more days we continued to cruise our zigzag course between the tropical islands, but as we moved further into the southern hemisphere the weather grew more temperate and for three long and uncomfortable days the ship was buffeted by stiff southerly gales and rocked by mountainous waves. When the storm finally receded we were in more barren latitudes. Many of the islands here, in the southern part of the Midway Sea, were craggy and treeless, some of them only barely rising above the level of the sea. They stood further apart from each other than they had done near the equator.

I still yearned for the islands, but not for these. I craved the insane heat of the tropics. With every day that the islands of the warmer climes slipped further behind me I knew that I had to put them out of my thoughts. I stayed away from the exposed upper decks, with their silent, distant views of fragmented land.

Towards the end of the voyage we were evacuated without warning from our mess decks and while we crowded together on the assembly deck every recruit's kit was searched. The map I had been using was discovered where I had left it in my duffel bag. For two more days nothing happened. Then I was summoned to the adjutant's cabin where I was told the map had been confiscated and destroyed. I was docked seven days' pay as punishment and my record was marked. I was officially warned that the black-cap escouades would be alerted to my breach of the rules.

However, it turned out that not all was lost. Either the search party did not find my notebook or they had not recognized the long list of island names it contained.

The loss of the map obstinately reminded me of the islands we had passed. In the final days on the troopship, I sat alone with those pages from my notebook, committing the names to memory and trying to recall how each of the islands had looked. Mentally, I compiled a favoured itinerary that I would follow when at last I was discharged from the army and could return home, moving slowly, as I planned, from one island to the next, perhaps spending many years in the process.

That could not begin until I had finished with the war, but the ship had not yet even arrived in sight of our destination. I waited on my hammock.

On disembarkation I was assigned to an infantry unit who were armed with a certain type of grenade launcher. I was held up near the port for another month while I underwent training. By the time this was complete, my comrades from the ship had dispersed. I was sent on a long journey across the bleak landscape to join up with my new unit.

I was at last moving across the notorious southern continent, the theatre of the land war, but throughout the three days of my cold and exhausting journey by train and truck I saw signs of neither battles nor their aftermath. The terrain I passed through had clearly never been lived in – I saw a seemingly endless prospect of treeless plains, rocky hills, frozen rivers. I received orders every day: my torment was a lonely one but my route was known and monitored, arrangements had been made. Other troops travelled with me, none of them for long. We all had different destinations, different orders. Whenever the train halted it was met by trucks that either were standing by the side of the rails where we stopped, or which appeared from somewhere after we had waited an hour or two. Fuel and food were taken on at these stops and my brief companions came and went. Eventually it was my own turn to leave the train at one of these halts.

I travelled under a tarpaulin in the back of a truck for another day, cold and hungry, bruised by the constant lurching of the vehicle and at last terrified by the closeness of the landscape around me. I was now so much a part of it. The winds that scoured the bleak grasses and thorny, leafless bushes also scoured me, the rocks and boulders that littered the ground were the immediate cause of the truck's violent movements, the cold that seeped everywhere sapped my strength and will. I passed the journey in a state of mental and physical suspension, waiting for the interminable journey to end.

I stared in dismay at the terrain. I found the dark landscape oppressive, the gradual contours discouraging. I loathed the sight of the grey, flinty soil, the waterless plains, the neutral sky, the broken ground with its scattered rocks and shards of quartz, the complete absence of signs of human occupation or of agriculture or animals or buildings – above all I hated the endless blast of freezing winds and the shrouds of sleet, the blizzard gales. I could only huddle in my freezing, exposed corner of the truck's compartment, waiting for this deadly journey to end.

Finally we arrived somewhere, at a unit which was occupying a strategic position at the base of a steep, broken rockface. As soon as I arrived I noticed the grenade launcher positions, each constructed exactly as I had myself been trained to construct them, each concealed position manned to the right strength. After the torment and discomforts of the long journey I felt a sudden sense of completeness, an unexpected satisfaction that at last the disagreeable job I had been forced to take on was about to start.

However, fighting the war itself was not yet my destiny. After I joined the grenade unit and shared duties with the other soldiers for a day or two, the first frightening reality of the army was borne in on me. Grenade launchers we had, but as yet no grenades. This did not appear to alarm the others so I did not allow it to alarm me. I had been in the army long enough to have developed the foot soldier's unquestioning frame of mind when it came to direct orders about fighting, or preparation for fighting.

We were told that we were going to retreat from this position, re-equip ourselves with matériel, then occupy a new position from which we could confront the enemy directly.

We dismantled our weapons, we abandoned our position in the dead of night, we travelled a long distance to the east. Here we finally rendezvoused with a column of trucks. We were driven in convoy for two nights and a day to a large stores depot. Here we learned that the grenade launchers with which we were armed were now obsolescent. We were to be issued with the latest version, but the entire escadron would need to be retrained.

So we marched cross-country to another camp. So we re-trained. So, finally, we were issued with the latest armament and the ammunition for it and now at last fully prepared we marched off once again to fight the war.

We never reached our reallocated position, from where the enemy was to be confronted. We were diverted instead to relieve another column of troops, five days away across some of the harshest countryside I had yet encountered: it was a broken, frozen landscape of flints and glinting pebbles, devoid of plants, of colour, even of shape.

It didn't sink in straight away, but already the pattern had become established in those first few days and weeks of aimless activity. This purposeless and constant movement was to be my experience of war.

I never lost count of the days or the years. The three-thousandth anniversary loomed ahead of me like an unstated threat. We marched at intervals from one place to the next; we slept rough; we marched again or were transported by trucks; we were billeted in wooden huts that were uninsulated and infested with rats and which leaked under the incessant rains. At intervals we were withdrawn to be retrained. An issue of new or upgraded weapons invariably followed, making more training essential. We were always in transit, making camp, taking up new positions, digging trenches, heading south or north or east or anywhere to reinforce our allies – we were put on trains, removed from trains, flown here and there, sometimes without food or water, often without warning, always without explanation. Once when we were hiding in trenches close to the snowline a dozen fighter planes screamed overhead and we stood and cheered unheard after them; at another time there were other aircraft, from which we were ordered to take cover. No one attacked us, then or ever, but we were always on our guard. In some of the coastal areas of the continent, to which we were sent from time to time, and depending on the season, I was in turn baked by the heat of the sun, immobilized by thigh-deep mud, bitten by thousands of flying insects, swept away by flooding snow-melt – I suffered sores, sunburn, bruises, boredom, ulcerated legs, exhaustion, constipation, frostbite and unceasing humiliation. Sometimes we were told to stand our ground with our grenade launchers loaded and primed, waiting for action.

We never went into action.

This then was the war, of which it had always been said there would never be an end.

I lost all sense of contextual time, past and future. All I knew was the daily marking off of the calendar, sensing the fourth millennium of the war approach ineluctably. As I marched, dug, waited, trained, froze, I dreamed only of freedom, of putting this behind me, of heading back to the islands.

At some forgotten moment during one of our route marches, one of our training camps, one of our attempts to dig trenches in the permafrost, I lost the notebook containing all the island names I had written down. When I first discovered the loss it seemed like an unparalleled disaster, worse than anything the army had inflicted on me. But later I found that my memory of the islands' names was intact. When I concentrated I realized I could still recite the romantic litany of islands, still place them against imagined shapes on a mental map.

At first bereft, I came to realize that the loss of first the map, then the notebook, had liberated me. My present was meaningless and my past was forgotten. Only the islands represented my future. They existed in my mind, modified endlessly as I dwelt on them, matching them up to my expectations.

As the gruelling experience of war ground on, I came to depend increasingly on my haunting mental images of the tropic archipelago.

But I could not ignore the army and I still had to endure its endless demands. In the ice mountains further away in the south, the enemy troops were dug into impregnable defensive positions, lines they were known to have held for centuries. They were so firmly entrenched that it was conventional wisdom amongst our men that they could never be dislodged. It was thought that hundreds of thousands of men on our side, perhaps millions of us, would have to die in the assault against their lines. It rapidly became clear that my escadron was not only going to be part of the first assault, but that after the first attack we would continue to be in the heart of the fray.

This was the precursor to the celebrations of the dawning fourth millennium.

Many other divisions were already in place, preparing to attack. We would be moving to reinforce them shortly.

Two nights later, sure enough, we were put once more into trucks and transported to the south, towards the freezing southern uplands. We took up position, dug ourselves as deep as possible into the permafrost, concealed and ranged our grenade launchers. By now uncaring of what happened to me, made wretched by the physical circumstances and rootless by the lack of mental cohesion, I waited with the others in a mixture of fear and boredom. As I froze, I dreamed of hot islands.

On clear days we could glimpse the peaks of the ice mountains close to the horizon, but there was no sign of enemy activity.

Twenty days after we had taken up our positions in the frozen tundra we were ordered to retreat once more. It was now less than ten days to the millennium.

We moved away, rushing to reinforce major skirmishes then said to be taking place by the coast. Reports of dead and wounded were horrifying but all was quiet by the time we arrived. We took up defensive lines along the cliffs. It was so familiar, this senseless repositioning, manoeuvring. I turned my back against the sea, not wanting to look northwards to where the unattainable islands lay.

Only eight days remained until the dreaded anniversary of the war's beginning and already we were taking delivery of more supplies of armour, ammunition and grenades than I had ever seen before. The tension in our ranks was insupportable. I was convinced that this time our generals were not bluffing, that real action was only days, perhaps hours, away.

I sensed the closeness of the sea. If I was to discharge myself, the moment had arrived.

That night I left my tent and skidded down the loose shale and gravel of the sloping cliff to the beach. My back pocket was stuffed with all the unspent army pay I had accumulated. In the ranks we always joked that the paper was worthless, but now I thought it might at last be useful.

I walked until dawn, hid all day in the tough undergrowth that spread across the high ground behind the littoral, resting when I could. My unsleeping mind recited island names.

During the following night I managed to find a track worn by the tyres of trucks. I guessed it was used by the army so I followed it with immense care, taking cover at the first sign of any approaching traffic. I continued to travel by night, sleeping as I could by day.

I was in poor physical condition by the time I reached one of the military ports. Although I had been able to find water I had eaten nothing solid for four days. I was in every way exhausted and ready to turn myself in.

Close to the harbour, in a narrow, unlit street, not at the first attempt but after several hours of risky searching, I found the building I was seeking. I reached the brothel not long before dawn, when business was slow and most of the whores were sleeping. They took me in, they immediately understood the gravity of my situation. They relieved me of all my army money.

I remained hidden in the whorehouse for three days, regaining my strength. They gave me civilian clothes to wear – rather raffish, I thought, but I had no experience of the civilian world. I did not wonder how the women had come by them, or who else's clothes they might once have been. In the long hours I was alone in my tiny borrowed room I would repeatedly try on my new clothes and hold a mirror at arm's length, admiring what I could see of myself in the limited compass of the glass. To be rid of the army fatigues at last, the thick, coarse fabric, the heavy webbing and the cumbersome patches of body armour, was like freedom in itself.

Whores visited me nightly, taking turns.

Early in the fourth night, the war's millennial night, four of the whores, together with their male minder, took me down to the harbour. They rowed me a distance out to sea, where a motor launch was waiting in the darkly heaving waters beyond the headland. There were no lights on the boat, but in the glow from the town I could see that there were already several other men aboard the launch. They too were rakishly dressed, with frilled shirts, slouching hats, golden bracelets, velveteen jackets. They rested their elbows on the rail and stared down towards the water with waiting eyes. None of them looked at me, or at each other. There were no greetings, no recognitions. Money changed hands, from the whores in my boat to two agile young men in dark clothes in the other. I was allowed to board.

I squeezed into a position on the deck between other men, grateful for the warmth of the pressure against me. The rowing boat slipped away into the dark. I stared after it, regretting I could not remain with those young harlots. I was reminiscing already about their lithe, overworked bodies, their delicious mouths and slithering tongues, their careless, eager skills.

The launch waited in its silent position for the rest of the night, the crew taking on board more men at intervals, making them find somewhere to squeeze themselves, handling the money. We remained silent, staring at the deck, waiting to leave. I dozed for a while, but every time more people came aboard we had to shift around to make room.

They lifted the anchor before dawn and turned the boat out to sea. We were heavily loaded and running low in the water. Once we were away from the shelter of the headland we made heavy weather in the running swell, the bow of the launch crashing cumbersomely into the walls of the waves, taking on water with every lurching recovery. I was soon soaked through, hungry, frightened, exhausted, and desperate to reach solid land.

We headed north, shaking the salt water from our eyes. The litany of island names ran on ceaselessly in my mind, urging me to return.

I escaped from the launch at the earliest opportunity, which was when we reached the first inhabited island. No one seemed to know which one it was. I went ashore in my rakish clothes, feeling shabby and dishevelled in spite of their stylish fit. The constant soakings in the boat had bleached most of the colour from the material, had stretched and shrunk the different kinds of fabric. I had no money, no name, no past, no future.

'What is this island called?' I said to the first person I met, an elderly woman sweeping up refuse on the quayside. She looked at me as if I was mad.

'Steffer,' she said.

I had never heard of it.

'Say the name again,' I said.

'Steffer, Steffer. You a discharger?' I said nothing, so she grinned as if I had confirmed the information. 'Steffer!'

'Is that what you think I am, or is that the name of this island?'

'Steffer!' she said again, turning away from me.

I muttered thanks and stumbled away from her, into the town. I still had no idea where I was.

I slept rough for a while, stealing food, begging for money, then met a whore who told me there was a hostel for the homeless which helped people to find jobs. Within a day I too was sweeping up refuse in the streets. It turned out that the island was called Keeilen, a place where many steffers made their first landfall.

Winter came – I had not realized it was the autumn when I discharged myself. I managed to work my passage as a deckhand on a cargo ship sailing with supplies to the southern continent, but which, I heard, would be calling at some more northerly islands on the way. The information was true. I arrived on Fellenstel, a large island with a range of mountains that sheltered the inhabited northern side from the prevailing southern gales. I passed the winter in the mild airs of Fellenstel. I moved north again when spring came, stopping for different periods of time on Manlayl, Meequa, Emmeret, Sentier – none of these was in my litany, but I intoned them just the same.

Gradually, my life was improving. Rather than sleep rough wherever I went I was usually able to rent a room for as long as I intended to stay on each island. I had learned that the whorehouses on the islands were a chain of contacts for dischargers, a place of resort, of help. I discovered how to find temporary jobs, how to live as cheaply as possible. I was learning the island patois, quickly adjusting my knowledge as I came across the different argots that were used from one island to the next.

No one would speak to me about the war except in the vaguest

285

ways. I was often spotted as a steffer as soon as I landed somewhere, but the further north I moved and the warmer the weather became, the less this appeared to matter.

I was moving through the Dream Archipelago, dreaming of it as I went, imagining what island might come next, thinking it into an existence that held good so long as I required it.

By this time I had operated the islands' black market to obtain a map, which I had realized was perhaps the most difficult kind of printed material to get hold of anywhere. My map was incomplete, many years old, faded and torn and the place and island names were written in a script I did not at first understand, but it was for all that a map of the part of the Archipelago where I was travelling.

On the edge of the map, close to a torn area, there was a small island whose name I was finally able to decipher. It was Mesterline, one of the islands my unreliable memory told me we had passed on the southward journey.

Salay, Temmil, Mesterline, Prachous ... it was part of the litany, part of the route that would lead me back to Muriseay.

It took me another year of erratic travels to reach Mesterline. As soon as I landed I fell in love with the place: it was a warm island of low hills, broad valleys, wide meandering rivers and yellow beaches. Flowers grew everywhere in a riot of effulgent colours. The buildings were constructed of white-painted brick and terracotta tiles and they clustered on hilltops or against the steep sides of the cliffs above the sea. It was a rainy island: midway through most afternoons a brisk storm would sweep in from the west, drenching the countryside and the towns, running noisy rivulets through the streets. The Mester people loved these intense showers and would stand out in the streets or the public squares, their faces upturned and their arms raised, the rain coursing sensually through their long hair and drenching their flimsy clothes. Afterwards, as the hot sun returned and the ruts in the muddy streets hardened again, normal life would resume. Everyone was happier after the day's shower and began to get ready for the languid evenings that they passed in the open-air bars and restaurants.

For the first time in my life (as I thought of it with my erratic memory), or for the first time in many years (as I suspected was the reality), I felt the urge to paint what I saw. I was dazzled by light, by colour, by the harmony of places and plants and people.

I spent the daylight hours wandering wherever I could, feasting my eyes on the brashly coloured flowers and fields, the glinting rivers, the deep shade of the trees, the blue and yellow glare of the sunlit shores, the golden skins of the Mester people. Images leapt through my mind, making me crave for some artistic outlet by which I could capture them.

That was how I began sketching, knowing I was not yet ready for paint or pigments.

By this time I was able to earn enough money to afford to live in a small rented apartment. I supported myself by working in the kitchen of one of the harbourside bars. I was eating well, sleeping regularly, coming to terms with the extra mental blankness with which the war had left me. I felt as if my four years under arms had merely been time lost, an ellipsis, another area of forgotten life. In Mesterline I began to sense a full life extending around me, an identity, a past regainable and a future that could be envisaged.

I bought paper and pencils, borrowed a tiny stool, began the habit of setting myself up in the shade of the harbour wall, quickly drawing a likeness of anyone who walked into sight. I soon discovered that the Mesters were natural exhibitionists – when they realized what I was doing most of them would laughingly pose for me, or offer to return when they had more time, or even suggest they could meet me privately so that I could draw them again and in more intimate detail. Most of these offers came from young women. Already I was finding Mester women irresistibly beautiful. The harmony between their loveliness and the drowsy contentment of the Mesterline life inspired vivid graphic images in my mind that I found endlessly alluring to try to draw. Life spread even more fully around me, happiness grew. I started dreaming in colour.

Then a troopship arrived in Mesterline Town, breaking its voyage southwards to the war, its decks crammed with young conscripts.

It did not dock in the harbour of the town but moored a distance offshore. Lighters came ashore bringing hard currency to buy food and other materials and to replenish water supplies. While the transactions went on, an escouade of black-caps prowled the streets, staring intently at all men of military age, their synaptic batons at the ready. At first paralysed with fear at the sight of them, I managed to hide from them in the attic room of the town's only brothel, dreading what would happen if they found me.

After they had gone and the troopship had departed, I walked around Mesterline Town in a state of dread and disquiet.

My litany of names had a meaning after all. It was not simply an incantation of imagined names with a ghostly reality. It constituted a memory of my actual experience. The islands were connected but not in the way I had been trusting – a code of my own past, which when deciphered would restore me to myself. It was more prosaic than that: it was the route the troopships took to the south.

Yet it remained an unconscious message. I had made it mine, I had recited it when no one else could know it.

I had been planning to stay indefinitely in Mesterline, but the unexpected arrival of the troopship soured everything. When I tried next to draw beneath the harbour wall I felt myself exposed and nervous. My hand would no longer respond to my inner eye. I wasted paper, broke pencils, lost friends. I had reverted to being a steffer.

On the day I left Mesterline the youngest of the whores came to the quay. She gave me a list of names, not of islands but of her friends who were working in other parts of the Dream Archipelago. As we sailed I committed the names to memory, then threw the scrap of paper in the sea.

Fifteen days later I was on Piqay, an island I liked but which I found too similar to Mesterline, too full of memories that I was transplanting from the shallow soil of my memory. I moved on from Piqay to Paneron, a long journey that passed several other islands and the Coast of Helvard's Passion, a stupendous reef of towering rock, shadowing the coast of the island interior that lay beyond.

I had by this time travelled so far that I was off the edge of the map I had purchased, so I had only my memory of the names to guide me. I waited eagerly for each island to appear.

Paneron at first repelled me: much of its landscape was formed from volcanic rock, black and jagged and unwelcoming, but on the western side there was an enormous area of fertile land choked with rainforest that spread back from the shore as far as I could see. The coast was fringed with palms. I decided to rest in Paneron Town for a while.

Ahead lay the Swirl, beyond that vast chain of reefs and skerries were the Aubracs, beyond even those was the island I still yearned to find: Muriseay, home of my most vivid imaginings, birthplace of Rascar Acizzone.

The place, the artist – these were the only realities I knew, the only experience I thought I could call my own.

Another year of travel. I was confounded by the thirty-five islands of the Aubrac Group: work and accommodation were difficult to find in these underpopulated islets and I lacked the funds simply to sail past or around them. I had to make my way slowly through the group, island by island, working for subsistence, sweltering under the tropical sun. Now that I was travelling again my interest in drawing returned. In some of the busier Aubrac ports I would again set up my easel, draw for hire, for centimes and sous.

On AntiAubracia, close to the heart of the group of islands, I bought some pigments, oils and brushes. The Aubracs were a place largely devoid of colour: the flat, uninteresting islands lay under bleaching sunlight, the sand and pale gravel of the inland plains drifted into the towns on the constant winds, the pallid eggshell blue of the shallow lagoons could be glimpsed with every turn of the head. The absence of bright hues was a challenge to see and paint in colour.

I saw no more troopships, although I was always on my guard for their passing or arrival. I was still following their route because when I asked the island people about the ships they knew at once what I meant and therefore what my background must be. But reliable information about the army was hard to glean. Sometimes I was told that the troopships had stopped travelling south; sometimes that they had switched to a different route; sometimes I was told they only passed in the night.

My fear of the black-caps kept me on the move.

Finally, I made a last sea-crossing and arrived one night on a coal-carrier in Muriseay Town. From the upper deck, as we moved slowly through the wide bay that led to the harbour mouth, I viewed the place with a feeling of anticipation. I could make a fresh start here – what had happened during the long-ago shore leave was insignificant. I leaned on the rail, watching the reflections of coloured lights from the town darting on the dark water. I could hear the roar of engines, the hubbub of voices, the traces of distorted music. Heat rolled around me, as once before it had rolled from the town.

There were delays in docking the ship and by the time I was ashore it was after midnight. Finding somewhere to sleep for the night was a priority. Because of recent hardships I was unable to pay to stay anywhere. I had faced the same problem many times in the past, slept rough more often than not, but I was nonetheless tired.

I headed through the clamouring traffic to the back streets, looking for brothels. I was assaulted by a range of sensations: breathless equatorial heat, tropical perfumes of flowers and incense, the endless racket of cars, motorbikes and pedicabs, the smell of spicy meat being cooked on smoking sidewalk stalls, the continuous flash and dazzle of neon advertising, the beat of pop music blaring out tinnily from radios on the food stalls and from every window and open doorway. I stood for a while on one of the street corners, laden down with my baggage and my painting equipment. I turned a full circle, relishing the exciting racket, then put down my baggage and, like the Mester people savouring the rains, I raised my arms in exaltation and lifted my face to the glancing night-time sky, orange-hued above me, reflecting the dancing lights of the city.

Exhilarated and refreshed I took up my load more willingly and went on with my search for brothels.

I came to one in a small building two blocks away from the main quay, attained by a darkened door in an alley at the side. I went in, moneyless, throwing myself on the charity of the working women, seeking sanctuary for the night from the only church I knew. The cathedral of my dreams.

Because of its history, but more because of its marina, shops and sunbathing beaches, Muriseay Town was a tourist attraction for wealthy visitors from all over the Dream Archipelago. In my first months on the island I discovered I could make a lucrative income from painting harbour scenes and mountain landscapes, then displaying them on a section of wall next to one of the large cafés in Paramoundour Avenue, the street where all the fashion houses and smart nightclubs were situated.

In the off-seasons, or when I simply grew tired of painting for money, I would stay in my tenth-floor studio above the city centre and dedicate myself to my attempts to develop the work pioneered by Acizzone. Now that I was in the town where Acizzone had produced his finest paintings I was able at last to research his life and work in full, to understand the techniques he had employed.

Tactilism was by this time many years out of vogue, a fortunate state of affairs as it allowed me to experiment without interference, comment or critical interest. Ultrasound microcircuitry was no longer in use, except in the market for children's novelties, so the pigments I needed were plentiful and inexpensive, although at first difficult to track down in the quantities I needed them.

I set to work, building up the layers of pigments on a series of gesso-primed boards. The technique was intricate and hazardous – I ruined many boards by a single slip of the palette knife, some of them close to the moment of completion. I had much to learn.

Accepting this I made regular visits to the closed-case section of the Muriseayan Town Museum, where several of Acizzone's originals were stored in archive. The female curator was at first amused that I should take an interest in such an obscure, unfashionable and reputedly obscene artist, but she soon grew used to my repeated visits, the long silent sessions I spent inside the locked sanctums when I was alone, pressing my hands, my face, my limbs, my torso, to Acizzone's garish pictures. I was submerged in a kind of frenzy of artistic absorption, almost literally soaking up Acizzone's breathtaking imagery.

The ultrasonics produced by the tactile pigments operated directly on the hypothalamus, promoting sudden changes in serotonin concentrations and levels. The instantaneous result of this was to generate the images experienced by the viewer – the less obvious consequence was to cause depression and long-term loss of memory. When I left the museum after my first adult exposure to Acizzone's work I was shattered by the experience. While the erotic images created by the paintings still haunted me, I was almost blind with pain, confusion and a sense of unspecified terror.

After my first visit, I returned unsteadily to my studio and slept for nearly two days. When I awoke I was chastened by what I had discovered about the paintings. Exposure to tactilist art had a traumatic effect on the viewer.

I felt a familiar sense of blankness behind me. Memory had failed. Somewhere in the recent past, when I was travelling through the islands, I had missed visiting some of them.

The litany was still there and I recited the names to myself. Amnesia is not specific: I knew the names but in some cases I had no memory of the islands. Had I been to Winho? To Demmer? Nelquay? No recollections of any of them, but they had been on my route.

For two or three weeks I returned to my tourist painting, partly to gain some cash but also for a respite. I needed to think about what I had learned. My memories of childhood had been all but eradicated by something. Now I had a firm idea that it was my immersion in Acizzone's art.

I continued to work and gradually I found my vision.

The physical technique was fairly straightforward to master. The difficulty, I discovered, was the psychological process, transferring my own passions, cravings, compulsions to the artwork. When I had that, I could paint successfully. One by one my painted boards accumulated in my studio, leaning against the wall at the back of the long room.

Sometimes, I would stand at the window of my studio and stare down across the bustling, careless city below, my own shocking images concealed in the pigments behind me. I felt as if I were preparing an arsenal of potent imagic weapons. I had become an art terrorist, unseen and unsuspected by the world at large, my paintings no doubt destined to be misunderstood in their way as Acizzone's masterpieces had been. The tactilist paintings were the definitive expression of my life.

While Acizzone, who in life was a libertine and roué, had portrayed scenes of great erotic power, my own images were derived from a different source: I had lived a life of emotional repression, repetition, aimless wandering. My work was necessarily a reaction against Acizzone.

I painted to stay sane, to preserve my memory. After that first exposure to Acizzone I knew that only by putting myself into my work could I recapture what I had lost. To view tactilist art led to forgetting, but to create it, I found now, led to remembering.

I drew inspiration from Acizzone. I lost part of myself. I painted and recovered.

My art was entirely therapeutic. Every painting clarified a fresh area of confusion or amnesia. Each dab of the palette knife, each touch of the brush, was another detail of my past defined and placed in context. The paintings absorbed my traumas.

When I drew back from them, all that could be seen were

bland areas of uniform colour, much the same as Acizzone's work. Stepping up close, working with the pigments, or pressing my flesh against the stippled layers of dried paint, I entered a psychological realm of great calm and reassurance.

What someone else would experience of my tactilist therapy I did not care to think. My work was imagic weaponry. The potential was concealed until the moment of detonation, like a landmine waiting for the press of a foot.

After the first year, when I was working to establish myself, I entered my most prolific phase. I became so productive that to make space for myself I arranged to move some of the more ambitious pieces to a vacant building I had come across near the waterfront. It was a former dancing club, long abandoned and empty, but physically intact.

Although there was an extensive basement, with a warren of corridors and small chambers, the main hall was an enormous open area, easily large enough to take any number of my paintings.

I kept a few of the smaller pieces in my studio, but the larger ones and those with the most potent and disturbing images of fracture and loss I stored in the town.

I stacked the biggest paintings in the main hall of the building, but some nervous dread of discovery made me conceal the smaller pieces in the basement. In that maze of corridors and rooms, ill-lit and haunted by the stale fragrances of past occupiers, I found a dozen different places to hide my pieces.

I was constantly rearranging my work. Sometimes I would spend a whole day and night, working without a break in the near darkness, obsessively shifting my artwork from one room to another.

I found that the warren of interconnecting corridors and rooms, cheaply built with thin partition walls and lit only at intervals with low-power electric bulbs, presented what seemed to be an almost endless combination of random paths and routes. I stood my paintings like sentinels, at odd and hidden positions in the maze, behind doorways, beyond corners in the passageways, irrationally blocking the darkest places.

I would then leave the building and normal life returned for a while. I would start new paintings, or, just as often, walk down to the streets with my easel and stool and begin to work up a supply of commercially attractive landscapes. I was always in need of cash.

So my life continued like that, month after month, under the broiling Muriseayan sun. I knew that I had at last found a kind of fulfilment. Even the tourist art was not all drudgery, because I learnt that working with representational paintings required a discipline of line, subject and brushwork that only increased the intensity of the tactile art I went to afterwards and which no one saw. In the streets of Muriseay Town I built a small reputation as a journeyman landscape artist.

Five years went by. Life was as good to me as it ever had been.

Five years was not long enough to ensure that life could always be good. One night the black-caps came for me.

I was, as always, alone. My life was solitary, my mood introspective. I had no friends other than whores. I lived for my art, working through its mysterious agenda, post-Acizzone, unique, perhaps ultimately futile.

I was in my storage depot, obsessively rearranging my boards again, placing and replacing the sentinels in the corridors. Earlier that day I had hired a carter to bring down my five most recent works and since the man left I had been slowly moving them into place, touching them, holding them, arranging them.

The black-caps entered the building without my being aware of them. I was absorbed in a painting I had completed the week before. I was holding it so that my fingers were wrapped around the back of the board but my palms were pressing lightly against the paint at the edges.

The painting dealt obliquely with an incident that had occurred while I was in the army in the south. Night had fallen while I was on patrol alone and I had had difficulty getting back to our lines. For an hour I wandered in the dark and cold, slowly freezing. In the end someone had found me and led me back to our trenches, but until then I had been in terror of death.

Post-Acizzone, I depicted the extreme fright I experienced: total darkness, a bitter wind, a chill that struck through to the bone, ground so broken that you could not walk without stumbling, a constant threat from unseen enemies, loneliness, silence enforced by panic, distant explosions.

The painting was a comfort to me.

I surfaced from my comfort to find four black-caps standing back from me, watching me. They were carrying their batons in holsters. Terror struck me, as if with a physical blow.

I made a sound, an inarticulate throat noise, involuntary, like a trapped animal. I wanted to speak to them, shout at them, but all I was capable of was a bestial sound. I drew breath, tried again. This time the noise I made was halting, as if fear had added a stammer to the moan.

Hearing this, registering my fright, the black-caps drew their batons. They moved casually, in no hurry to start. I backed away, brushing against my painting, causing it to fall.

The men had no faces I could see: their capped helmets covered their heads, placed a smoked visor across their eyes, had a raised lip to protect their mouth and jaw.

Four clicks as the synaptic batons were armed – they were raised to the strike position.

'You've been discharged, trooper!' one of the men said and contemptuously threw a scrap of paper in my direction. It fluttered at once, fell close to his boots. 'Discharge for a coward!'

I said ... but I could only breathe in, shuddering, and say nothing.

There was another way out of the building that only I could know, through the under-floor warren. One of the men was between me and the short flight of steps that led down. I feinted, moving towards the scrap of paper, as if to pick it up. Then I spun around, dashed, collided with the man's leg. He swung the baton viciously at me. I took an intense bolt of electricity that dropped me. I skidded across the floor.

My leg was paralysed. I scrambled to get up, rolled on my side, tried again.

Seeing I was immobilized, one of the black-caps moved across to the painting I had been absorbed in when they arrived. He leaned over it, prodded at its surface with the end of his baton.

I managed to raise myself on my good leg, half-crouching.

Where the end of his baton touched the tactilist pigment, a spout of fierce white flame suddenly appeared, with a sharp crackling sound. Smoke rose copiously as the flame died. The man made a sardonic laughing sound and did it again.

The others went over to see what he was doing. They too pressed the live ends of their batons against the board, producing spurts of bright flame and much more smoke. They guffawed.

One of them crouched, leaned forward to see what it was that was burning. He brushed his bare fingertips across an undamaged portion of the pigment.

My terror and trauma reached out to him through the paint. The ultrasonics bonded him to the board.

He became still, four of his fingers resting on the pigment. For a moment he stayed in position, looking almost reflective as he squatted there with his hand extended. Then he tipped slowly forward. He tried to balance himself with his other hand, but that too landed on the pigments. As he fell across the painting, his body started jerking in spasms. Both his hands were bonded to the board. His baton had rolled away. Smoke still poured from the smouldering scars.

His three companions moved across to find out what was wrong with him. They kept an eye on me as they did so. I was trying to lever myself upright, putting all my weight on the leg that still had feeling, letting the other dangle lightly against the floor. Sensation was returning quickly, but the pain was unspeakable.

I watched the three black-caps, dreading the menace they

exuded. It could only be a matter of time before they did to me whatever it was they had come to do. They were grappling with the man who had fallen, trying to pull him away from the pigments. My breath was making a light screeching noise as I struggled for balance. I thought I had known fear before, but there was nothing in my remembered experience that equalled this.

I managed a step. They ignored me. They were still trying to lift the man away from my painting. The smoke swirled from the damage they had caused with their batons.

One of them shouted at me to help them.

'What is this stuff? What's holding him against that board?'

The man started screaming as the smouldering pigments reached his hands, but still he could not release himself. His pain, my agonies, contorted his body.

'His dreams!' I cried boldly. 'He is captive of his own vile dreams!'

I made a second step, then a third. Each was easier than the one before, although the pain was terrible. I hobbled towards the shallow stairs by the stage, took the top one, then another, nearly overbalanced, took the third and fourth.

They saw me as I reached the door beneath the old stage. I scarcely dared to look back, but I saw them abandoning the man who had fallen across the pigments and hoist their batons to the strike position. With athletic strength they were moving quickly across the short distance towards me. I dived through the door, dragging my hurt leg.

Breath rasped in my throat. I made a sobbing sound. There was one door, a passage, a chamber and another door. I passed through all of them. Behind me the black-caps were shouting, ordering me to halt. Someone blundered against one of the thin partition walls. I heard the wood creaking as he thudded against it.

I hurried on. The curving passage where I stored some of my smaller paintings was next, then a series of three small cubicles, all with doors wide open. I had placed one of my paintings inside each of these cubicles, standing guard within.

I passed along the corridor, slamming closed the doors at each end. My leg was working almost normally again, but the pain continued. I was in another corridor with an alcove at the end, where I had stood a painting. I doubled back, pushed the door of one of the larger chambers and propped open the spring-loaded door with the edge of one of my boards. I passed through. Another corridor was beyond, wider than the others. Here were a dozen of my paintings, stacked against the wall. I hooked my good foot beneath them, causing them to clatter down at an angle and partly block the way. I passed them. The men were yelling at me again, threatening me, ordering me to stop.

I heard a crash behind me, and another. One of the men shouted a curse.

I went through into the next short corridor, where four more chambers opened out. Some of my most intense paintings were hidden in each of these. I pulled them so that they extended into the corridor at knee height. I balanced a tall one against them, so that any disturbance of it would make it fall.

There was another crash, followed by shouting. The voices now were only a short distance away from me, on the other side of the decrepit dividing wall. There was a heavy sound, as if someone had fallen. Then I heard swearing – a man screamed. One of his companions began shouting. The thin wall bulged towards me as he fell against it. I heard paintings fall around them, heard the crackle of sudden fire as synaptic batons made contact with the pigments.

I smelt smoke.

I was regaining my strength, although the naked fear of being caught by the black-caps still had a grip on me. I came into another corridor, one that was wider and better lit than the others and not enclosed by walls that reached to the ceiling. Smoke drifted here.

I halted at the end, trying to control my breath. The warren of corridors behind me was silent. I went out of the corridor into the large sub-floor area beyond. The silence followed and wisps of smoke swirled around me. I stood and listened, tense and frightened, paralysed by the terror of what would happen if even one of the men had managed to push past the paintings without touching any of them.

The silence remained. Sound, thought, movement, life, absorbed by the paintings of trauma and loss.

They had surrendered to my fears. Fire licked around them.

I could see none of the flames myself, but gradually the smoke was thickening. It heaped along the ceiling, a dark grey cloud, heavy with the vapours of scorched pigments.

I realized at last that I had to leave before I became trapped by the spreading fire. I went quickly across the sub-floor area, struggled with the old iron-handled doors, fell out into the darkness. I walked stiffly up the cobbled alley that ran behind the building, turned a corner, then another, walked into one of Muriseay's market streets where the hot night was filled with people, lights, music and the raucous, thrilling sound of traffic.

For the rest of the night I stumbled through the back streets and alleys of the town, trailing my fingertips along the rough texture of the stuccoed walls, obsessed with thoughts of the paintings that were being lost while the building burned. My agonies were being consumed but I was released from my past.

I went through the port area again in the hour before dawn. The paintings must have smouldered for a time before properly igniting the shabby wooden walls of the warren, but now the whole of my building was consumed with flames. The doorways and windows I had sealed up for privacy had become apertures once more, square portals into the inferno within, white and yellow fire roaring in the gales of sucked air. Black smoke belched out through vents and gaps in the roof. Fire crews were ineffectually jetting cascades of water against the crumbling brick walls. I watched their efforts as I stood on the quay, a small bag with my belongings by my side. In the east the sky was lightening. Vapour trails lay widely dispersed across the dawn sky, reflecting the light from the sun that still hid beneath the horizon, glowing pink.

By the time the fire crews had brought the flames under control I was aboard the first ferry of the day, heading for other islands. Their names chimed in my mind, urging me on.

ORIGINAL APPEARANCES

The Dream Archipelago was first published in French: *L'archipel du rêve*
  – Lattès, Paris, 1981.
The Dream Archipelago was first published in English by Earthlight,
  London, 1999. 'The Equatorial Moment' was added to that edition.
  'The Trace of Him' and 'The Discharge' have been added to the
  present edition.

Individual stories:

'The Equatorial Moment' was first published in *The Dream Archipelago*
  – Earthlight, London, 1999.
'The Negation' was first published in *Anticipations* (edited by
  Christopher Priest) – Faber, London, 1978.
'Whores' was first published in *New Dimensions* (edited by Robert
  Silverberg) – Harper & Row, New York, 1978.
'The Trace of Him' was first published in *Interzone*, 2008.
'The Miraculous Cairn' was first published in *New Terrors* (edited by
  Ramsey Campbell) – Pan, London, 1980.
'The Cremation' was first published in *Andromeda* (edited by Peter R.
  Weston) – Futura, London, 1978.
'The Watched' was first published in *The Magazine of Fantasy & Science
  Fiction*, 1978.
'The Discharge' was first published in French as 'Retour au foyer'
  in *Destination 3001* (edited by Robert Silverberg and Jacques
  Chambon) – Flammarion, Paris, 2000.